I thought perhaps I should apologize . . .

Eliza's glance returned to Nate, to the mat of wiry black hair apparent between the edges of his white shirt. The chisled contours of his chest were visible, contours of muscle thrown into relief by the gaslight.

"You don't have anything to apologize for," he said, leaning against the doorframe. A thought struck him. Had she come just to apologize . . . or was there another reason? His pulse quickened.

He reached for her hand, drew her into the room, and closed the door behind her. When she said nothing more, he cupped her face between his hands and slowly lowered his mouth to hers.

Eliza melted into his kiss. He was wonderfully strong, so sure. His arms fit around her so well. His mouth was soft at first but soon grew more demanding, until his lips were crushing hers, parting hers, his tongue reaching deep into her mouth. Never had she felt this kind of pleasure, this kind of sweet warm weakness . . .

Heart Song

BARBARA HARGIS

AVON BOOKS ⬡ NEW YORK

AVON BOOKS
A division of
The Hearst Corporation
105 Madison Avenue
New York, New York 10016

Copyright © 1990 by Barbara Cockrell
Inside cover author photograph by Ron Cockrell
Published by arrangement with the author
Library of Congress Catalog Card Number: 89-91930
ISBN: 0-380-75928-4

First Avon Books Printing: February 1990

AVON TRADEMARK REG. U.S. PAT. OFF. AND IN OTHER COUNTRIES, MARCA REGISTRADA, HECHO EN U.S.A.

Printed in the U.S.A.

RA 10 9 8 7 6 5 4 3 2 1

To my agent, Joyce A. Flaherty,
with warm appreciation
for her guidance and friendship

Chapter 1

San Francisco, 1893

With the little girl's hand in her own, the young woman stepped smartly down from the train and cut a brisk, unhesitating path through the porters and baggage wagons and debarking passengers clotting the station walkways. The air was dim with smoke and steam, the hiss of boilers nearly deafening. The girl winced at the noise, but the woman walked on, unnoticing, pulling the little girl behind her on the leash of their joined hands.

At each prim step the woman's black ribbon-laden hat shivered. Behind a swooping black veil were faintly visible wide brown eyes, a pert nose, and a pursed mouth set in a white face. It was not so much a pretty face as an arresting one. In her soot-dusted black traveling suit, the young woman appeared thin to a fault and held her spine straight as a broom handle, shoulders back, breasts thrust forward.

No onlooker could have guessed at the tempest in her thoughts at that moment.

While young and old men, elderly ladies, mothers and children all pressed forward to greet arriving friends and family, the young woman anxiously looked beyond their faces and followed the movements of porters and baggage wagons. Behind her the little girl craned her neck to gaze up at the monster black engine shimmering with heat and sweating steam. She was only half as tall as the wheels. With the effort of twisting to see as high as the smokestack, she tripped.

"Pick up your feet, Daisy," the young woman said, frowning, turning slightly toward the trailing child.

"I can't keep up with you, Aunt Lizzie," she replied, a hint of a tired whine in her voice. She appeared to be six or seven years old, still baby-plump, and her wide straw hat was crushed along the left brim. Shiny fine brown hair covered the shoulders of her gray cape like a veil; hazel eyes stared in mild curiosity at the surrounding activity. Her round cheeks glowed pink and hot from an ineffective attempt to scrub away the grime of the lengthy train trip.

Without missing a brisk step, the young woman angled past a laden baggage wagon and plucked a gold watch from her jacket pocket. She snapped it open and closed again. "It's after three o'clock already," she said, tucking the watch back into its slim pocket. "We still have to find a hotel, and I had hoped to speak with Mr. Truesdale this afternoon . . . here we are. Excuse me," she said to a porter, "these are our bags, the two on the bottom there. Please carry them out to the street. We'll need a cab."

The porter stood up straighter as she addressed him. It was a phenomenon that often occurred in her presence. She was not particularly tall, but her bearing and manner inevitably brought those around her to attention. The porter gazed at her with smiling frankness as he lifted his hands, palms up, in a shrug.

"Yes, señora. Which bags? You speak fast, and I do not wish to take the wrong bags for you."

"These." She stooped and patted the two in question. "Please hurry. I'll go ahead and find a cab."

"*Sí,*" he said, still smiling, but she had turned away from him.

In her mind Eliza Nolenberg still heard the beating of looms, the whirring of spindles. The sounds had followed her these past two weeks and melded into the clacking of train wheels on steel joints. Ever since she was twelve years old she had worked in the Geddes Mill, a cotton mill, in Pittsburgh, Pennsylvania. The sound of the loom was as familiar as her own voice; the wetness of the weaving room as constant as her weariness.

As they walked across the main floor of the train station, toward the brilliant sunlight slanting in at the far doors, propped open with scuffed wood wedges, the little girl tugged at her aunt's hand and asked in a loud whisper, "Do you want me to act mean and nasty now?" Her expression was innocent and curious as she awaited an answer.

"Not just yet, Daisy my dear. I'll tell you when."

Eliza tried not to be impatient with Daisy, but she was at once both eager and filled with dread over her coming interview with Mr. Nate Truesdale. Exhaustion from the trip was making it all the more difficult to keep from remembering the images that had haunted her so long ago—of this man she was to meet today intimately embracing her sister.

On that day, when she was eighteen, she had come home early from the mill and found her younger sister in the bedroom with a man. He was young and darkly handsome, with gleaming black curls. His blue eyes were a bright, glittering contrast to his skin. Estelle had been smiling, facing into her mirror as she unpinned a flower from her dress; the man was standing behind her, watching. Before Eliza could make a sound, he had turned Estelle around and pulled her into his arms. For a shocked moment, Eliza had been witness to a kiss the like of which she had never seen before. The man's passion and hunger had stirred something deep inside her. When she saw his hand slide over Estelle's waist and cup one breast, the flush of pleasure was so immediate it could have been her own breast he touched. In a flurry of confusion, Eliza had whirled and silently let herself out of the apartment. She knew she should have said or done something to stop them. After all, Estelle was her responsibility; it wasn't right to have left her alone with him. But Eliza had been struggling with emotions that were new and too chaotic for logical thought.

The passing of eight years had not entirely wiped the experience from her mind, and the nearer she came to the interview with this man, the more disturbing were the memories.

Could she confront him in an interview without thinking about that long-ago afternoon? Or without expressing her anger? And she *was* angry—angry at him for seducing Estelle and then abandoning her. Just like their father, who had departed the family fourteen years ago, never to be seen or heard from again.

In eight years would this Mr. Truesdale have changed very much? What was he like now? Abruptly she recalled his curly black hair and blue eyes, and her heart beat in strange excitement as she realized she would be facing him in less than an hour.

For the first time since alighting from the train, Eliza paused and smiled. "Oh, Daisy!" she exclaimed. "We're really here in San Francisco!" She hugged the girl and gazed into her eyes with mixed apprehension and excitement. "I'll complete my business with Mr. Truesdale this afternoon, if I can, and then we'll have three entire days to ourselves. We can see the city, Daisy! Climb the hills—they've got hills just like Pittsburgh"—she licked the pad of her thumb and wiped off a smudge on Daisy's chin—"and maybe see the ocean. Excited?"

Daisy nodded.

"Scared?"

Daisy shook her head.

"Good. Then neither am I."

She grasped Daisy's hand again. From the shadows of the station they emerged under the hard weight of the California sunshine.

In a string of deep-toned la-da-da-dums, Nate Truesdale sang aloud a passage from Dvořák's eighth symphony as he mounted the five stone steps of the building. Raised gilt lettering over the double doors designated it as the Truesdale & Watts Shipping Company, International. Behind him, the wide stretch of Market Street teemed with noise and activity. The rumble of carriage wheels and clap of horses' hooves on the new asphalt paving, the shouts of hawkers peddling papers, and the squeaking rattle of a passing cable car were almost loud enough to drown out his voice, which had the strength and resonance to fill an auditorium.

In the narrow lobby a young receptionist smiled shyly at him as he entered. Her reaction was a common one; he had long ago grown used to the quick blushes, dimpled grins, and provocative glances of the women he met, the universal responses of a woman to a handsome man.

Nate wore an immaculate black frock coat over a high-buttoned beige waistcoat and trousers, a starched wing collar, and a stylish spotted bow tie. In one hand he held a brushed bowler hat. "Mr. Truesdale?" she said. He closed the door behind him, and the street sounds faded into a sudden silence broken only by the thrum of typewriters from the upper floor. "Mr. Truesdale?" she repeated.

"Of course," he said, turning his attention to her. His face was lean, cheekbones highlighted from below by the dark smudge his beard made in his skin and from above by the almost unnatural metallic blueness of his eyes. He had a full mouth and ink-black hair, thick and curly. His skin had the bronze glow of his Mediterranean ancestors.

He crossed the worn blue Turkish carpet, his long legs swinging in an elegant, loose-limbed stride. Just as he passed the receptionist's desk on his way to the bare wood staircase, she exclaimed, "Excuse me, excuse me. There's a young woman to see you—no appointment. She went up to your office already. I hope you don't mind?"

"Not at all. Is Mr. Watts around? He's my partner—did you meet him yet? If you see him, tell him I want to talk to him. How was your first day?"

"It's been very busy, actually." She gestured at the disordered papers on her desk and smiled apologetically, blushing.

"Oh." He looked sympathetic. "Well, I wouldn't worry too much about it—it'll get worse in another week or two, and by Christmas you won't be able to see over the top of it all."

The receptionist smiled, her heavy mouth turning down at the corner. "They warned me about you."

He paused on the stairs, drumming his fingers on the polished oak rail, and looked over at her. "They? You mean my devoted staff?"

She nodded, self-conscious and watchful.

"What did they say?"

"That I shouldn't believe everything you say."
She smiled nervously and fingered the cameo brooch
at her throat.

"Interesting. Order up some tar and feathers for
me, would you? What name did she give?—the
woman in my office."

Distracted, the receptionist fumbled through the
papers on her desk. "I thought I wrote it . . . I'm
sure I've got it here somewhere . . . I'm very sorry,
Mr. Truesdale . . . and on my first day . . ."

"Don't worry about it. I'll just go ask her myself."

He continued up the stairs, his step light, humming a tune to himself. In these last few weeks his
anticipation had been building, and he wondered if
every new father felt this excitement. It made no
difference that his daughter wasn't a newborn;
whatever her age, she was *his*. He couldn't wait to
meet her.

A center walkway bordered by polished oak bal-
ustrades divided the second floor into two work ar-
eas. As Nate followed the aisle across the room, men
and women bent over desks or sifted through standing files on either side of him. Tall windows lined
the room, gleaming clean and transparent, revealing
partially wooded hills beyond and evening fog rolling in over the city.

The pressure of public opinion had finally resulted
in legislation that had cut the work week from seven
days to six, but the firm of Truesdale & Watts had
shortened the work schedule for its employees three
years earlier, in 1890.

Passing through a low gate at the far end of the
room, Nate paused but could see nothing through
the frosted glass in the door of his office. When he
entered, a young woman swung around from her
perusal of the photographs and framed memorabilia
on his wall. She was dressed entirely in black, her

small bonnet trembling under its weight of ribbons. The thin light from the windows was at her back, and behind the low black veil her eyes were no more than dark smears in a ghostlike face. He noted the stiffness of her posture, the way she twisted her fingers tightly together, the tautness in her breathing.

"Hello," he said, his voice dulled by surprise and caution. With a practiced flick of his hand, he sailed his bowler hat across the wide office. It hit the top of the hat stand and abruptly tumbled to the floor.

"You missed." Her words were clearly enunciated and evenly pitched, lacking humor. A schoolteacher, he decided.

"I'm Nate Truesdale. What can I do for you, Mrs. . . .?"

"Miss."

"Miss . . . ?"

She relaxed her fingers from their grip on each other and drew in a slow breath. "Nolenberg. Eliza Nolenberg."

"Miss Nolenberg," he said without inflection. Surprise stopped his thoughts—she was the woman who was supposed to be bringing his daughter, but they weren't due to arrive until next week. He used the excuse of collecting his hat and settling himself in the swivel oak chair behind the desk to gain time and calm the sudden jolting of his heart.

"Please sit down," he suggested, but she had already seated herself in the chair in front of his desk, lifted back her veil, and was rummaging in a small black carpet-sack on her lap.

Without the distortions of the veil, he could see her pale skin, her colorless, unsmiling mouth. He would have dismissed her as unattractive had his eyes not caught the lovely sweep of her thick eyelashes, which reminded him of the soft feathery bristles of an artist's fine sable brushes. She looked up then and turned fully upon him a pair of cool, earth-toned eyes. They were remarkable eyes, large as a fawn's, both guileless and challenging. His glance moved to the pale rosebud mouth, traced the upward curves of a heart-shaped face, and met again the staring dark eyes. It was a direct gaze, with the feverish shine of an age-old invitation that sent heat to his loins.

Eliza had forgotten how striking he was. Her heart pounded almost as rapidly as it had the day she had witnessed him with her sister. She looked at the generous mouth, the handsome glow of his skin, the big lean frame, and quite suddenly in her mind she saw him embracing Estelle and bending his head to kiss her. She caught her breath at the uncomfortable pleasure of that image.

He was studying her too closely, with those blue eyes she remembered too well. She sat up straighter in her chair and looked away from him.

The luxury of his office and his position as owner of one of the largest shipping companies on the West Coast added to her discomfort. His desk was massive, almost entirely clean of papers or clutter, and held a small, unlit, red-bellied oil lamp. Behind him were three large windows with green leather shades pulled down precisely to the halfway level. Overhead a three-globed gaslight hissed softly.

Eliza was distinctly aware of her travel-worn appearance and imagined that every neatly stitched mend in her heavy black dress and jacket were visible. She wished she had taken the time to change before coming here. In all her mental stagings of this interview she had never felt the disparity between them as acutely as she did now. She was a simple millworker, and he, according to what the secretary outside his office had said, was wealthy and a member of the exclusive San Francisco society.

"I didn't expect you for another week, Miss Nolenberg," he was saying in his deep, smoothly modulated voice. "Had I known you were—"

"I abhor water and traveling over water, so I exchanged the tickets you sent for train tickets instead. Daisy and I arrived . . ." She reached for her pocket watch and snapped it open and closed again in a single fluid motion. ". . . a little over an hour ago."

"She's here!" Nate exclaimed.

Eliza Nolenberg's eyes widened in surprise as she tilted slightly back from him. "At the hotel. Now, Mr. Truesdale, here are the papers. I'm sure my lawyer, Mr. McPherson, wrote to you about the details. He told me he had done so, thoroughly. So if you will just sign here, I can be—"

"In a bit of a hurry, are we, Miss Nolenberg?" He leaned far over his desk toward her and saw her bend an equitable distance back, until he was sure her spine was wedged into the frame of the chair. Annoyed that she needed so much space between them, he said, "This is not something I want to rush through."

"For Daisy's sake, it's very important," Eliza replied briskly.

"Have you told her I'm her father?"

"No, I have not. I thought it best that she not know."

"Why is that?"

Eliza's face stiffened with shock and affront. She blinked twice. "Daisy has already been deeply hurt by the death of her mother. To also discover and lose a father would be a terrible hardship for her."

Nate sighed and slouched back in his chair. "I was sorry to hear about Estelle. No, sincerely, I mean that."

Eliza's voice took on a keen edge. "I hardly think one day with my sister eight years ago would remain in the memory of a man like you long enough for you to remember her name the next morning, much less feel any grief now."

"The lawyer mentioned her name in his letter."

The ribbon-laden hat shivered anew with her indignation as she thrust the paper in front of him. "Exactly, Mr. Truesdale," she said in a voice so low that he almost didn't hear. "My sister and I raised Daisy together. Before her death, Estelle signed this document making me Daisy's guardian. But the lawyer, Mr. McPherson, discovered your name on the birth certificate and insisted on contacting you. So if you'll just sign on this line here"—one trembling white finger pointed to the document—"I can take over legal guardianship of Daisy, and there will be no further trouble for you in any way."

"Now there's the mistake in your logic. You're thinking this is trouble for me." He pushed the papers back at her, his eyes narrowing to metallic flashes. "You and Estelle both owe me the pleasure of meeting my own daughter now that—what? seven, eight?—years have gone by. Why do you think I sent two tickets? It was wrong of Estelle not to tell me about the child. Now, I want you and Daisy to be my guests for dinner tonight . . . at my home." He slid a sheet of paper from a drawer at his right elbow and jotted down his address.

Angered as much by the breathless fluttering in her chest as by his flippant control of the interview, Eliza snapped, "I should think Estelle paid you well enough that afternoon!"

Surprised, Nate glanced up, the paper held between his first and second fingers, and caught the glimmer of perspiration on her forehead. Perversely, he found himself enjoying her discomfiture. She was acting like a stiff-spined, prissy woman, keeping her distance as if he had a disease. What a tight prude.

"That's what you think of me—a seducer of innocent women? A man of low character and morals? Ruled by simple animal lust?" He smiled as she reached for a handkerchief in her black carpet-sack and dabbed at her damp brow. Her hand trembled. "Are you afraid, Miss Nolenberg?" he asked.

She reached for the paper he extended to her and stood up to leave. "You got my sister with child, then abandoned her. I know about men like you. For Daisy's sake, I ask simply that you be polite to her. There is no need for her to know the truth. I'll bring these," she added, plucking the papers from the desk and folding them back into her black case. "Will you sign them tonight, Mr. Truesdale?"

He ignored her question and pointed to the small paper clenched in her fist. "Be there at seven," he said tightly. His eyes followed the outward thrust of her breasts and the gathered fabric over her backside as she left.

What a waste, he thought.

Evening traffic filled Market Street. Hawkers shouted headlines, phaetons and carriages careened past, heavily loaded wagons creaked with weight. On the bottom step leading from the building to the street, Eliza stumbled slightly. Blindly she turned east, unaware of the new strength in the wind or of the chill rolling in with the fog. She clutched her hat.

She *was* afraid. She had not been prepared to find any resemblance, but when Nate Truesdale had entered his office that afternoon she had seen Daisy's surprised, uptilted eyebrows in his own. And in his anger she had seen Daisy's chin draw taut. He had Daisy's fingernails, the same sturdy wrists, the same small bulbous tip to his nose, the same bronze tinge in his skin. Eliza felt it as an affront, a direct attack, that he should look so much like Daisy. As if he laid claim to her by the very fact of his resemblance to her.

What if he did want to claim Daisy? What if he wouldn't sign the papers?

Eliza took Daisy's existence for granted now; that Nate Truesdale was responsible for bringing into being the one person Eliza cherished most in the world had never entered her mind. As soon as Mr. McPherson's papers were signed, she decided, trembling slightly with the cold and bitter flavor of fear, she and Daisy would leave. Gone was her earlier plan to spend a few days in San Francisco; Eliza wanted only to get away from Nate Truesdale and safely home. Home again to the same third-floor apartment she had lived in all her life.

Eliza entered their hotel room, a small corner room on the second floor of the Cosmopolitan Hotel. It was shabby but clean; she insisted on clean. Daisy was sitting on the floor and bouncing her doll in a pretend walk.

"Look, look, Aunt Lizzie, Angelique is going to a party! See, over there is her house, in the chair, high up like we live, and here is the party." Daisy sat back on her heels and tossed her fine, shiny hair over her shoulder with the back of one hand. "She got all wrinkled on the train."

"Were you all right while I was gone?" Eliza asked as she unpinned her hat and laid it on the shelf in the closet. "You didn't get frightened being by yourself?"

"No. But you were gone a long time. Do I have to go to school tomorrow?"

"How could that be, Daisy? Your school is a long way away." After hanging up her jacket, Eliza pinned back the sleeves of her black dress and lit the two gas jets in the wall, then sat on the edge of the mattress. Rusted bedsprings squeaked under her weight. "Come here, sweetheart. I want to talk to you."

Daisy walked on her knees toward Eliza. "Are there other little girls in San Francisco?"

"Many," Eliza said with a half-smile. "Oh, Daisy, your stockings are ripped again! Get up from the floor."

"Do the other little girls in San Francisco go to school?"

"I'm sure they do. Take your stockings off and I'll try to mend them as I talk."

"Angelique's dress is wrinkled."

Eliza held Daisy's arm to keep the girl from falling over while she peeled down her dusty black stockings. "We're to have dinner tonight with Mr. Truesdale. I don't have time to get Angelique ready."

"Can I take Angelique?"

"*May* I take Angelique. Yes, you may, but now this is very, very important. Daisy, I want your full attention. We have some things to practice before we leave. I want you to be *very* mean and nasty tonight."

Chapter 2

After the carriage left them at the address on California Street, Eliza and Daisy surveyed Nate Truesdale's home. It was a mansion. They had to lean back slightly to see it all, for it was built on a gently sloping hill. A full flight of brick steps ascended to the front lawn. Three stories high, the house was square and built of stone, with a broad column of bay windows rising vertically above a portico over the front door. On the second floor a wrought-iron balcony extended almost the full length of the house and scalloped out around the protruding windows. Skirting the flat, squared-off roof was another balcony, an ornate widow's walk.

The house was monstrously beautiful, and Eliza's grip on Daisy's hand tightened in apprehension.

As they climbed the steps from the street, Eliza and Daisy came in view of the short lawn, trimmed and green, flanked by rows of eucalyptus trees that rustled with the wind. A pungent acid smell assailed them and Daisy complained, "It stinks here."

"Very good, my dear. That was a wonderfully mean and nasty thing to say."

"It's true."

"I agree. But a proper young lady shouldn't say

it aloud, especially to the owner . . . so be sure to do so.''

"Why don't you like Mr. Truesdale?"

"It's . . . it's hard to explain.''

"Why?"

"Not now, Daisy.''

The foundation of the structure was buried behind juniper bushes, and two five-foot-high blooming bird of paradise plants flanked the granite columns of the entry portico.

Nate Truesdale himself answered the bell. He was still wearing the frock coat and beige waistcoat and trousers he had worn earlier in the office, but he had changed into a fresh starched collar. His features were softened by the light from the two gaslamps framing the door, and the elation in his expression was evident. His straight, white teeth flashed in a huge smile.

"Good evening, ladies.'' His gaze fixed on Daisy. "Please come in.''

As Eliza ushered Daisy ahead of her onto the white tiled floor of the foyer, she gave the girl a sharp prod in the back. Daisy responded: "It *stinks* here.''

Nate laughed, rich and deep-timbred. He shut the door behind them and squatted low to see Daisy eye-to-eye. "That's the eucalyptus you smell. It's a bit obnoxious at first, but you get used to it. I love it now. At the first whiff I always know I'm home again. Sometimes, when I'm away on a long trip, I actually get homesick for eucalyptus.''

As he spoke he studied Daisy's round face and straight brown hair, the crushed hat and plain gray cape. He lifted her hands in his own. "What a mighty pretty young lady you are, Daisy. I've been looking forward to meeting you. My name is Mr. Truesdale, but I want you to call me Nate.''

Daisy beamed shyly at this attention and stood tongue-tied with pleasure. Her bright hazel eyes watched his mouth.

"And who is this delightful guest?" Nate inquired, tapping the doll tucked under Daisy's arm. "We'll have to lay another place at the table."

"Oh, this is just my doll," Daisy confessed, suddenly very serious, turning Angelique to face him. "She doesn't really eat. She has a mouth. See? And teeth. They're not real. Oh, I mean, they *are* real, but she can't use them."

As Nate smiled and assured Daisy that they could at least put another chair at the table, Eliza stood immobilized by dismay. As if the cold fog from outside had tunneled into her bones, she felt a chill in her heart—and suddenly very alone. She moved forward instinctively and placed her hands on Daisy's shoulders, then turned her away from Nate. "Let's get your cape and hat off now, sweetheart."

Nate rose to his feet, still smiling. He helped them both with their wraps and said, "Why don't you go ahead into the parlor there. I'll be right back." He carried the garments down the hall to the right of an elegantly curving staircase that led to the second floor. The stairs were covered with runners of burgundy carpet with a gold fleur-de-lis pattern. The walls of the hall and foyer were of rich wood intricately carved with curlicues and vines and cherubs, and ornate beyond anything Eliza had ever seen. The foyer was lit by a brilliant gas chandelier, the lights of which were reflected back in a thousand glimmers from the carved and polished wood.

Eliza was momentarily overwhelmed by such elegance and wealth and felt at a distinct disadvantage. Fear made her lift her head higher.

When Nate Truesdale was out of sight, Eliza marched Daisy into a small front parlor to the right of the entry hall. They stood self-consciously on a new Oriental rug amid delicate furniture fashioned of rosewood and mahogany. Plush upholstering covered the seats in intricate swirls of mauve and champagne.

Eliza's mouth pinched into a moue of displeasure. "What happened to all the practicing we did in the hotel, young lady?"

"But he's nice, Aunt Lizzie." Daisy frowned back at Eliza, her expression rebellious. "I don't want to be mean and nasty."

"You'll do as I say. It's for your own good, Daisy."

"Why don't you like him?" Daisy protested in a whine. "He likes Angelique."

"Never mind that. You listen to me, Daisy."

By the time Nate returned, Eliza was seated on the edge of a grape-carved sofa and Daisy slouched sullenly in a matching chair across the room. Her simple brown muslin dress was crushed up around the back of her neck; her feet in high-laced black shoes swung listlessly above the floor. Surveying them both, Nate rubbed his hands together. "Would you care for a glass of wine, Miss Nolenberg? California's red wine is excellent. No?" He turned to Daisy. "I'll bet you'd like some lemonade." Abruptly he added, "What is your last name?"

Eliza spoke up. "Nolenberg, Mr. Truesdale. I'll have lemonade also, thank you."

To keep Nate Truesdale's attention off Daisy, when he returned with lemonade for them and red wine for himself, Eliza asked, "Do you live alone here, Mr. Truesdale?"

He settled himself in a chair beside Daisy's. "That's right. I don't need much in the way of servants—most of the house is shut up now—but there's a woman, Mrs. Herlihy, who generally takes care of me. Feeds me, keeps me clean, and"—he studied Eliza's pursed lips as he added—"relatively decent."

"Is she your mama?" Daisy asked, scooting back in the chair till she could sit up straight against the padded upholstery. The doll in her lap stared blankly into middle space.

"No, but I wish she were. You'll like her. Right now she's in the kitchen steaming up the place with a delicious-smelling soup for dinner. Sniff."

Daisy sniffed.

"Smell that?"

"No, what is it?"

"It's a surprise."

Smiling, Nate reached over and gently stroked the fine, straight brown hair falling over Daisy's shoulders. Seeing him touching Daisy in this way, Eliza felt a new pang of fear. Anxiously she broke in. "There's an interesting flavor in the lemonade. What is it?"

"Meyer lemons." He glanced at Eliza with cool eyes. "They're sweet. I have two lemon trees in back. And I grow figs, plums, apples, oranges, and blackberries." Smiling at Daisy again, he lifted one of her hands and folded the fingers into a fist. "Blackberries almost as big as that. I'll bet they're too big for you to eat. You've got a very small mouth."

Daisy promptly opened her mouth wide. Nate laughed in delight and tousled the hair on top of her head. "And look at those teeth! Blackberries'll be no problem for you. But we'll have to watch what we put close to that mouth or lose it forever." Experimentally he held out his forefinger and, enraptured with the game, Daisy snapped at it.

"Oh, ho! What strong teeth you have, Grandma!" Giggling, Daisy leaned forward, snapping at him, and Nate hefted her onto his lap. Eliza caught her breath.

"Does your aunt hold you on her lap?" Nate asked.

Daisy shook her head. "Aunt Lizzie says I'm too big now."

"And what do you think? Are you too big?"

Daisy lifted her shoulders in a shrug and smiled at him. "I'm seven and a half years old."

Eliza's heart swelled painfully. She said loudly to interrupt them. "Tell me about your business, Mr. Truesdale."

"It's shipping. Seven years old?" he asked, awed.

"No, seven and a *half*," Daisy corrected.

"Seven and a *half*," he repeated. "My, you are a regular young lady now. You must go to school too. What grade are you in?"

"Second. My teacher is Mrs. Riley. Do you know Mrs. Riley?"

"No, I haven't met her."

"Oh. She's really, really, really nice."

"I'm awful glad to hear that. I'd hate to think you had a mean teacher. Do you know what? There are lots of nice, nice, nice teachers here in San Francisco. Maybe you'd like to go to school here."

Eliza jumped to her feet, fear exploding into anger. "Really, Mr. Truesdale! I think you're forgetting yourself now!"

"Oh, no, Miss Nolenberg. I'm just finding myself." His mouth softened, and he added, "I'll go see how Mrs. Herlihy is getting along with dinner." He shifted Daisy easily back to her own chair and stood up. "Any more lemonade here? No? I'll be only a minute."

As the sound of his footsteps receded down the hall, Eliza exclaimed, "Daisy! What's gotten into you!"

Daisy pushed out her lower lip. "I like him."

"Oh, sweetheart, you don't understand!"

"But Aunt Lizzie . . ." Daisy whined, upset and beginning to cry. "He's not mean at all."

Eliza bent over Daisy and tucked the girl's hair back over her shoulder. "Please, Daisy, trust me," she said more kindly. "Sometimes people are not what they seem to be."

When Nate returned, the residue of tears on Daisy's cheeks did not escape his notice. "Dinner's ready," he said, and reached out to take her hand. Head down, doll clutched in her arms, Daisy ran to Eliza.

Nate looked at Eliza, surprised, accusing. She met his gaze in silent triumph, though the breathless fluttering in her chest intensified under his long stare.

In the dining room, a broad room papered with images of cool green ferns and finished with dark wood molding and wainscoting, Mrs. Herlihy was laying a fourth place at the table. She was short and, though trim of waist and hip, had an imposing bosom. Her hair was abundant, as white as her apron, and caught in a high chignon.

"Well, you must be Miss Nolenberg and that's the little lamb, Daisy," said Mrs. Herlihy, smiling. She finished laying the table and adjusted a heavy soup tureen that did not need adjusting. Also arranged on the table were a platter of baked halibut, two dishes whose contents were hidden beneath lids, and a basket of fresh-baked rolls whose warm, yeasty fragrance escaped the linen towel tucked around them.

When all appeared to her satisfaction, she clasped her hands under her bosom and said, "Everything's here, Mr. Truesdale. The dessert's ready in the kitchen when you need it. Leave the dishes and I'll clean 'em up first thing in the mornin'. And for you, little lamb,'' she added, coming around the table to Daisy and bending down with her hands on her knees, "there's a soup made of shrimp no bigger'n that little finger of yours." She patted Daisy's head as she straightened. "Good night and enjoy. See you in the mornin', Mr. Truesdale.''

"Thanks, everything looks wonderful," Nate answered, pulling out a chair for Eliza at the foot of the table. Mrs. Herlihy disappeared into the kitchen, and a moment later came the sound of the back door opening and closing.

Eliza remarked as she snapped open her napkin, "How very convenient for you if your housekeeper leaves every evening. Do you often entertain unmarried women?''

Nate did not look up as he lifted Daisy onto a fat pillow on her chair, his ample shoulders dwarfing the little girl. He said casually, "I wouldn't be concerned. You're not my type, Miss Nolenberg. There's a place right across the table for . . . What's your doll's name?''

Daisy whispered, "Angelique."

"Angelique? Well, Angelique can sit right there, and you can watch her across the table. How's that?''

Daisy shook her head.

"You want to keep her? That's all right."

Eliza's angry gaze followed him as he took his seat at the other end of the table, opposite her. "And Estelle *was* your type?''

Two flickering ivory candles framed his face as he glanced down the length of the table at her. His lean, stubble-darkened jaw swelled slightly with a clenched muscle. "How much of an education do you want Daisy to have?'' he asked with maddening politeness, grasping a silver soup ladle with one hand and pulling the tureen toward him with the other. "We could discuss the topic of my preferences in a female companion at length, or, Daisy, you could slide your bowl over here so I can put some soup in it for you."

Glancing silently between the two adults, Daisy passed him her bowl. Eliza sat stiff and subdued, only her dark, angry eyes giving any hint to her emotions.

"We really have nothing at all to discuss this evening," she said when Nate had finished serving soup for each of them. "I have the papers with me as promised, for you to sign . . . as promised."

"I'm not in the habit of discussing business over the dinner table. It kills the appetite." His unnaturally blue eyes narrowed as he surveyed her thin frame in the severe black gown. "When was the last time you and Daisy had a decent meal?"

"Train travel is not conducive to proper living," Eliza retorted, furious to find she was blushing under his scrutiny.

"Eat up," Nate told Daisy with a wink. "Mrs. Herlihy makes a grand shrimp soup, doesn't she? She makes lots of good things, but this is my favorite."

"My mama made soup," Daisy announced. "But she's dead."

"Yes, I know, sweetheart," Nate answered solemnly. "I'm sorry."

"And my cat is dead. He didn't wake up either. Are you dead when you're asleep?"

"No, my dear," Eliza answered, in a soft voice that caught once. She went on more firmly, "Sleep is something else entirely."

"But it's *like* sleeping," Daisy insisted.

"That's right," Nate said gently. "Like sleeping

and having wonderful dreams, the happiest dreams ever.''

"Please, Mr. Truesdale, I am trying to help her through this time," Eliza said. "Fantasies are not necessary. Daisy is handling it all very well."

"Fantasies," Nate repeated. "I take it you know the subject well. You've had firsthand experience with the Reaper? No, please," he insisted. "Tell me all about it. I don't want to miss this rare opportunity."

"I don't like your sense of humor, Mr. Truesdale."

"Would you care for some halibut?"

After dinner Nate stood up. Eliza watched him as unobtrusively as she could as he collected their dinner plates and carried them through a swinging door into the kitchen. He walked with easy, elegant strides, his muscled thighs stretching the fabric of his trousers as he moved. Memories of that long-ago afternoon crowded in her, and she saw again that dark and hauntingly powerful body holding Estelle. She remembered the sight of that hand touching Estelle's breast, and her heart beat thick and hard. She slid a handkerchief from her sleeve and dabbed it gently on her forehead, cheeks, and throat.

"Too hot for you, Miss Nolenberg?" He was carrying a chocolate cake on a platter that he set on the table. He added in that overly polite tone he had been using toward her all evening, "I can open some doors or windows, if you wish."

"No, thank you. I'm fine."

He glanced at Daisy slumped against her chair, the doll still clutched on her lap. "Like chocolate cake? Well, of course you do, that was an idiot's question. What normal, healthy child doesn't like chocolate cake? And now sit up, I'm going to let you have a fingerful of icing right off the top. Mind you, this is the only time I'm going to let you do such a thing."

"Just what do you mean by that statement?" Eliza demanded.

Daisy glanced aside to her aunt, then reached out quickly with one extended finger and scooped icing from the top of the cake, set conveniently near.

"Daisy!" Eliza exclaimed.

"I meant exactly what I said," Nate answered, and took up a knife to cut the cake.

"You're talking about the *future*, Mr. Truesdale. You've been talking about the future all evening. There will be no future *anything*. I have the papers with me."

"Of course you do." He slid a plate of cake toward Daisy and asked in a loud aside, "Does Aunt Lizzie like chocolate cake? I didn't think so. Miss Nolenberg, there will be time later to discuss the papers. We haven't finished dinner yet."

Eliza snapped her napkin onto the table. Daisy looked from one adult to the other and very quietly set down her fork. Eliza announced, "Frankly, Mr. Truesdale, I want this business settled now!"

"You're losing your temper, Miss Nolenberg. There's plenty of time this evening—"

But Eliza stood up abruptly, so abruptly that her chair lurched back and toppled over onto the rug with a resounding thump that sent a shiver through the floorboards. *Do you intend to sign the papers?*"

"No, I do not," he answered calmly. "Now, why don't you let Daisy finish her cake before we—"

"I don't want it!" Daisy exclaimed. As tears flooded her eyes, she edged off the chair, threw her doll to the floor, and ran from the room.

Nate stood with a plate of cake in one hand and stared coldly at Eliza. His lean jaw swelled hard as stone. She stood frozen at the end of the table, staring back at him, her eyes bright, her throat working. Without a word, she turned and followed Daisy.

In the small front parlor Daisy was curled on a corner of the sofa. She refused to look at Eliza.

"What's the matter, sweetheart?" Eliza said. "Are you tired? It's been a long day for you, hasn't it?"

Daisy turned away and pressed her face into the upholstery. "I don't want you to fight," she said, her voice muffled against the sofa.

"We're not fighting, Daisy. I'm sorry about all this, but I have to go back and talk to Mr. Truesdale. Why don't you lie down and rest here a while. I'll be back shortly." Eliza brushed Daisy's hair away from her face and kissed her upturned cheek.

In the dining room Nate was sitting sideways in Daisy's chair, bending forward to pick up Angelique. He studied the doll pensively and stroked her cold porcelain face with his fingertip. When Eliza entered the room, he glanced up in concern.

"How is she?"

Eliza turned her back on him and slid closed the dining room doors. They rolled together smoothly and silently. "She has a right to be upset, don't you think? You won't sign the papers and talk as if you're going to take her away from her home and family." Eliza faced him once more. "How can you even think of doing such a thing!"

"I thought you said she didn't know anything about it."

"She's not a fool. She doesn't know details, but she's sensitive enough to catch the undercurrents."

"What *under*currents?" Nate exclaimed. "We could have discussed this reasonably, but you turned on the theatrics!" He made a sharp gesture at the upturned chair.

"Daisy means everything in the world to me, Mr.

Truesdale. You must understand this! I've raised that child—I love her! And now you want to take her away from me?''

Her eyes were large and accusing, and he looked away, sighing. ''Look, Miss Nolenberg, I can appreciate all you're saying, but let me tell you—'' He glanced down at the doll in his hands. ''Let me tell you from my end.''

''Mr. Truesdale!'' Eliza exclaimed, but his voice rose to drown her out.

''When I first learned of Daisy's existence I was surprised and not a little distrustful. I thought: Are they going to come after me for money? What if this is all a put-on, a hoax from some woman wanting revenge? But when no mention of payment was forthcoming, I began to believe I really had a daughter. And contrary to your opinion, I do remember Estelle. Frankly, I'm more than a little surprised you come from the same family. Uh-uh, let me finish. The whole idea of a daughter intrigued me, and I found I liked it immensely. And then seeing Daisy tonight, being with her . . . it felt right. It felt *good*. The kind of good that makes you swell up inside.''

He paused and stared at the doll in his hands. ''She's my daughter.'' Looking up at Eliza again, Nate's eyes glinted in the light as he continued adamantly, ''I'm her father, and I have a lot to offer her. She can be well-educated, tour Europe, have anything she wants. I know Ned Greenway and Mrs. Salisbury, the leading figures in San Francisco society, so when the time comes, Daisy can make a proper young lady's debut.''

He stood up, and with the doll in his hand, strode toward Eliza, righted the chair she had knocked over, and thrust it toward her. ''It's time to discuss business, Miss Nolenberg,'' he said with cold formality. ''Have a seat.''

"You can't take her away from me," Eliza said, her voice quiet and furious.

"What a terrible impression you have of me. I'm not going to. Sit down, please."

Eliza sat, shoulders back, spine rigidly against the back of the chair. "Then why did you say you wouldn't sign the papers?"

With casual agility he propped himself on the edge of the table and observed mildly, "When you're angry there's some very becoming color in your cheeks. You know, it wouldn't harm you, and might even be good for Daisy, if you'd unbend a little. When was the last time you and Daisy laughed together or played together? Or are you intent upon turning her also into a prudish old maid?"

Eliza shot to her feet in indignation. "How *dare* you say such a thing!"

"Ah, callous me. It slipped out before I could stop it."

"You have no idea what it's like!" She averted her eyes from his cool stare and sat down again. "Mr. Truesdale, I practically raised Estelle as well, though I was only two years her senior. Our father deserted the family when I was eleven and after that my mother was useless as a mother. Useless as a person. I took over the chores and the care of my sister because I loved her. I loved her. I've worked in a mill ever since I was twelve to take care of Estelle . . . and Daisy. My mother is dead now, as is Estelle. Daisy is all I have."

"I'm sorry," Nate said gravely. He stood up from the table and returned to Daisy's chair. "I understand what a burden your life has been."

"No, that's not it, don't mistake me," she said, lifting her chin. "But you must see how much I need Daisy."

"Yes, I do. But I also know how much I need

Daisy. Wait, wait—hear me out, would you! I never intended to cut you off from Daisy. Daisy needs you, and I'm not the cruel, insensitive man you may think. I'm inviting you to stay here, live with Daisy. Be her governess, or companion, or whatever you want to call it. I'll pay you a salary as well."

"Live *here*? Beholden to you? Absolutely not!"

"Well, I'm not going to let *my* daughter live in a smoking hellhole like Pittsburgh, Miss Nolenberg. And I can tell what a fortune you're making working in a mill. From the looks of you two and the clothes you're wearing, I'd say it's pretty near poverty level. How soon before you're forced to put Daisy to work?"

"We're happy together!"

"So be happy together here. Where Daisy can get some fresh air and sunshine, and where neither of you has to work in a stinking mill. If you haven't noticed, I'm being very generous."

Eliza pressed herself forward over the table. "Do you think I'll allow Daisy to live here? With a man like you, exposed to heaven knows what kind of immoralities? You have *no* idea what raising a child entails! What's going to happen to Daisy when the novelty wears off for you, and you leave?"

"A bit judgmental, are we?" he exclaimed with a sharp smile. "It's not Daisy you're protecting now, Miss Nolenberg, but yourself at Daisy's age. It hurt you, didn't it, when your father left? And it still hurts. I'm nothing like him. We're two different people." Nate set the doll on the table in front of him and eyed Eliza calmly. "I think we're down to the end of it now. Daisy stays with me. It's up to you whether you stay or not."

"You're used to having your own way in everything, aren't you. But I'll fight you on this," she said, her voice heavy and low.

"I'll warn my lawyers. For Daisy's sake, I hope it doesn't come to this, but we'll go to court if need be," he answered. "And in that event"—he stabbed his finger at her and his eyes were bright with suppressed anger—"if you put my daughter through that, I'll see that you lose her entirely."

Chapter 3

Nate Truesdale usually ate breakfast in the dining room every morning at seven, after which he poured himself another cup of coffee, read the paper, and made notes on the day's business. But sometimes he strolled through the kitchen, grabbed an apple or muffin or piece of cold meat from the night before—whatever was available—and took himself out to sit on the back steps. Instead of reading the paper or jotting down notes, he watched the birds feast in the fruit trees and mused on life's frailties and disappointments.

He was known to say to his friends at the Bohemian Club: The key to living a free life lies in continually surprising oneself. Which is what he'd certainly done this time, he thought as he sat on the clammy stones of the back steps and bit into a hot sausage roll that steamed in the November morning air. Mrs. Herlihy had anticipated his mood this morning and prepared a portable breakfast—sausage baked in a pastry.

Upstairs two strangers were asleep in his house. When he had learned they were staying at the Cosmopolitan Hotel, he had refused to let Eliza take Daisy back there, knowing that, although at one time a respectable hotel, it was now more often used for prostitution. And she had flatly refused to leave Daisy alone in his house with him. All night he had tossed in bed, overcome with the reality of his situation. A daughter!

What mess had he gotten himself into? He didn't know the first thing about children, must less a girl. He didn't know how to braid hair or pull a loose baby tooth or . . . anything. He frowned. He pictured interminable birthday parties with giggling girls and indulgent mothers; Daisy throwing a tantrum for a new dress or a pony; a procession of pockfaced, sly-eyed boys coming through his house to see Daisy. He saw it all as violations of his home, his life, his position.

More upsetting still was the image of himself as a father. But what he pictured was not his own image but that of *his* father, patriarchal and elegant, staring with one surprised eye propped wide behind a monocle, the other eye squinted. He remembered the endless arguments. Nate had not wanted to be in any way connected to the Truesdale family business. He hadn't known what he wanted instead but was willing to try anything other than shipping. ''Associating with riffraff, is that what you want?'' old Arnold had bellowed on numerous occasions, disappointed that his only son spurned what he had worked so hard to build, driven by the hope that he would pass on the business to his heir.

As an immigrant from Italy, Arnie Turcini had arrived in the city of sin in the heyday of its crime and degeneracy—when young French girls sat half-naked behind window slats and called teasing invitations to the passersby on Pike Street; when gamblers and thieves emerged like bats at sundown; and men boasted of their fights and kills.

An overworked and obviously nearsighted immigration official had written Truesdale in place of Tur-

cini, and, delighted to be rid of the old world and
ready to embrace the new, Arnie Turcini had never
corrected it. The young wife he had brought with
him died of consumption within two years of their
arrival, and eventually he sent away for another
wife, the niece of his cousin in Baltimore, a quiet,
hardworking girl who agreed to come to California
and marry the young Italian who was beginning to
make his fortune in shipping.

With the Gold Rush had come a demand for fast
transportation to California, resulting in the devel-
opment of the clipper ships which could carry more
sail, more cargo, and outdistance rivals. Arnie
Truesdale invested more than he could afford in the
Sovereign of the Seas, a twenty-four-hundred-ton ship
built by Donald McKay in his East Boston yard. Engaged in the China trade, it was one of the dozens
of new clippers that crossed the Pacific in record time
to deliver passengers, cargo, and unrivaled profits
to San Francisco.

Truesdale reinvested, always teetering on the
brink of financial ruin should any of the ships he
helped finance lose in the race across the Pacific or
meet disaster along the way. But he had an unerring
sense of where to put his money, and he put it on
the new skippers of those ships. In dockside taverns
he met the men who commanded the clippers,
bought them drinks, listened to them, and chose the
most hard-driving and steadiest and put his money
on them. He never lost. When he went into business
for himself he opted for a newer, lighter ship, a
down easter, with a more elliptical stern and additional cargo space, requiring a smaller crew than the
now traditional clippers. The *Prince Liberty* was the
first ship for what would become the highly successful Truesdale Shipping Company.

Arnie Truesdale's new wife, Lucille May, remained quiet and hardworking as the family stature increased and they moved into a respectable home on Nob Hill. She gave no indication that she was aware that her husband was still wont to stroll down Pike Street where the French girls had sat. She knew of his infidelities, but because he kept that side of his life hidden, she said nothing, growing quieter and pouring her affections onto baby Nate.

As if in reaction to his nature, or to conceal it, Arnie Truesdale developed an impeccable public life and an austere persona. He dropped the name Arnie and used Arnold. He gave to charities, to expanding hospitals and churches; he hosted fundraisers for local government candidates who promised to clean up the city and wipe out the blot of crime and indecency. And he became revered as the most honest, upstanding, and generous benefactor of the city.

Young Nate, born late in his father's life, grew up confused. On the one hand his father was a great man who instilled awe and fear in his son, but he also aroused feelings of failure. Sometimes Nate woke at night to find his mother weeping at his bedside. As the years passed, she grew quieter and quieter during the day, but in these nocturnal visits she spoke volubly, frighteningly. She hugged her young son to her bosom and stroked his hair, begging him to be better than his father. Nate smelled the reassuring scent of her skin and felt the warm spot between her breasts, and as she wept and told him what a fine and remarkable son he was, Nate shivered with a strange, voluptuous fear. Whenever he asked her what was wrong with his father and why he shouldn't be like him, she would only weep harder and then fall silent and release him and disappear down the dark corridor.

Nate learned the truth when he was sixteen. He

and his friend Rossie Watts, whom he would later
take into business with him, decided to satisfy their
curiosity about the nature of women in one of the
city's hidden and better brothels on Stockton Street
off Market. They stood awkwardly in the plush parlor, hands jammed into pants pockets to disguise
bulges of anticipation. Their faces betrayed such naked hunger and heightened nervousness that the ladies eyed them with amusement and laughed among
themselves.

Nate remembered little of the beginning of that
visit, but he found himself being taken by the arm
and led upstairs into a room by a friendly woman
who seemed older than he had expected. She was
beautiful in his eyes—with soft red hair trailing over
her shoulders, quick eyes, a full rouged mouth open
in a laugh. He didn't think about her age; he saw
only the round hips and heavy breasts as she bared
them for him. He was worried that he might embarrass himself ahead of time and so didn't hear what
she said.

" 'Scuse me?" he mumbled politely, eyes fixed on
the bushy juncture of her legs as he fumbled with
suspenders and buttons.

She laughed and lay back on the bed and spread
her legs. "You're a Truesdale, aren't you?" she said
in a husky voice. "I recognized you right off as his
son. Are you as good as he is?" She was teasing
him, and Nate tried to smile.

The woman must have seen his father at a political
caucus or noticed his picture in the newspaper. Nate
knelt between her legs and knew a moment's shame.
"Obviously not, ma'am, or I wouldn't be here."

She laughed harder, showing lots of gum line and
crinkling her nose, and caught one of his hands
where it was moving of its own volition over her
breasts. She pushed his hand between her legs. "I

meant here," she said, rubbing herself around his hand. "I'll bet you're as good *here*."

He looked at her, bewildered, his brain slow as he considered this impediment. Then he knew what she meant. His father knew this woman, had been here, in this room, in this bed, *in this woman*.

"Oh, God, oh, God," he breathed, and stumbled away from her off the bed. He thought of his mother's tears, and his brain clicked from association to association, the connections and meanings hitting him with such force that his mouth fell open and he gulped air, struggling like a dying animal. He looked at the woman, propped on one elbow, her legs still splayed, her expression sympathetic yet alarmed.

"It's all right," she said. "I guess you didn't know. I thought that's why you came here, but I guess men aren't that close with each other."

He was shocked all over again by the idea of his father as a sexual being, by the idea of his father naked, erect, lusting, coupling.

Here.

With this woman.

And Nate wondered if his father had stared at her private parts through his monocle. He returned to the bed, angry.

"That's right," she said, relieved, smiling again and lying back on the sheet as he loomed over her. He desired her in anger and took her in a frantic effort at revenge for his father and mother and himself. "Not so rough!" she protested, wincing. "You got lots of time."

But he ignored her and watched as her body rocked mightily in rhythm with his thrusts.

Did his father remove his monocle in bed? Or did he squint harder on it so he could watch her bounce like this? Nate looked at her open mouth and rocking breasts, and he loved and hated her both at once. With a gasp he fell heavily over her and was still.

She pushed at him. "That's it, get up," and he rolled away. He stood up, and though his head was clear with anger, his movements were awkward. He left the room as quickly as he could.

After that, recognizing the hypocrisy, Nate lost all fear and awe of his father and was equally impatient with his mother. She did not understand why he was curt with her and so could not understand that he was angry with her for not facing up to and confronting her husband. The battles between father and son escalated until the day when Nate was nineteen. In the middle of a raging tirade against Nate's ungratefulness, his father suffered a heart attack and died in his bed the following morning.

Six months later his mother moved back to Baltimore. "I've never really felt comfortable here," she explained. "I never quite felt I belonged." And Nate understood. He stayed in San Francisco and took over his father's company because, for some reason he did not understand, he felt this was where he belonged.

After twelve years he still felt that this was where he belonged. He felt responsible for the company. Now, chewing deliberately on the sausage, he wondered what his father would have thought of the situation with Daisy.

Eliza stepped onto the top step beside him. He glanced up. She wore a black dress, buttoned to the neck and edged in black piping. No jewelry or expensive buttons or hint of a velvet trim broke the severity, yet the impression was handsome, direct, and drew his gaze to the lines of her body.

Nate knew she would feel firm to his touch—firm breasts and firm buttocks and firm thighs. Nothing like Marietta Sharpe, the woman he was currently

courting. Marietta was soft and full-fleshed, decid-
edly sensual, which was more to his taste. Yet the
imagined feel of Eliza's body under his hands struck
him with unexpected excitement.

Nate rubbed his left palm over the rough fabric
covering his upraised knee. He sighed as he said,
"Good morning, Miss Nolenberg," and flung the
last bite of the sausage pastry into the grass. Immediately three redwing blackbirds dove to the soft
white shape and tore at it, flapping their wings in a
fury. Watching, Nate thinned his mouth in faint bit-
terness.

If she had noticed him staring at her, she made
no mention of it. She began pleasantly, though
briskly. "Mr. Truesdale, I hope you've reconsidered
this situation and that we—"

"Oh, I have."

"You have?"

"Yes, and I still feel the same curious response—
I want Daisy here. Foolish perhaps, and you're right,
I probably don't know what I'm letting myself in
for, but I've never been one to cling blindly to the
safe and sane. What a terrible life that would be!"

Again he glanced up where Eliza stood barely
three feet from him on the narrow landing. Her hair
was slicked tightly off her face and confined in a
thick roll on her neck. He studied the delicate heart-
shaped face, the rosebud lips, the direct and deep
gaze of those fawnlike eyes. She was regarding him
again as she had several times yesterday—with that
fever-shine, almost as of intoxication, that made his
heart labor to beat. From his viewpoint she appeared as tall as a pagan monolith and like a shadow
in her black garments.

What a challenge she would be.

"Please help yourself to a sausage roll, Miss Nolenberg." He lifted the napkin containing two rolls

and caught himself picturing a worshiper extending an offering to a statue. The thought amused him.

"Thank you, no. I prefer dining properly at table."

"You would, wouldn't you." He chose one of the rolls and took a healthy bite.

"Mr. Truesdale," she said, her voice tense, "you seem to give no consideration to the fact that Daisy is . . . is *illegitimate*. You talk of proper society and a debut—as if such a thing were possible for someone in Daisy's position."

"That can be overcome."

"How?"

"If I get married and adopt her. Oh, there are sure to be some repercussions, mild ripples is all. But there are ways to manipulate society, Miss Nolenberg. Taken as a whole, people are remarkably unintelligent and malleable."

"That's a disgusting and immature attitude," she answered with distaste.

"Disgusting perhaps, but not immature. Do you know what maturity is? I'll tell you!" He pointed his forefinger at her for emphasis. "Maturity is when you realize you're a jackass . . . that you've always *been* a jackass, that you will always *be* a jackass, and you stop trying to prove to the world that you're *not* a jackass!"

Eliza watched him coldly, turned her eyes to his extended finger, and when he self-consciously dropped his hand to cup his knee, she said, "Words of wisdom from Professor Truesdale?"

He grinned. "I knew you'd be a quick student."

"If you think vulgarity is going to shock me—it's not. I heard it at home and then at the mill for years."

Nate looked away to keep her from seeing his surprise. He had expected his words would shock her and had looked forward to seeing that response. "Why would you think I was trying to shock you?"

"Weren't you?"

"I can think of plenty of other ways to amuse myself."

"Like adopting daughters?"

"Like adopting daughters," he agreed gaily.

"Why don't you consider Daisy for a change? She's a human being with a life of her own, rights of her own—"

"Tell me something," he interrupted, now wholly serious. "Why did you get in touch with me? I would never have known of Daisy's existence and probably never discovered it. Why did you take the risk?"

Eliza shifted her eyes away from his and gazed blankly at the small carriage house just off the left corner of the main house. "It wasn't my idea. It was Mr. McPherson's. He wanted to be sure every possible obstacle was out of the way. He didn't want there to be any . . . any . . . surprises in the future."

She said this last with a brief catch in her voice, and Nate felt moved in some way he could not define. He asked, "Who is this Mr. McPherson that he goes to such lengths unasked? He's more thorough than any lawyer I've ever met."

"He was planning to marry Estelle."

"Oh." Nate paused. "She never married then? I wondered about that."

"Mr. Truesdale," Eliza began again quietly, her forehead compressed in a frown, "Daisy doesn't belong here. You'd like to think she does, but it won't work. People here won't accept her. Don't try to fight your battles like this—with her life and happiness at stake."

Nate watched her face in silent contemplation. "You're ashamed of her." He uttered it as a statement, no question involved, no question in his mind. Abruptly he rose to his feet, dusting the palms of his hands together. "That really does settle it, Miss Nolenberg. There is nothing in the least shameful about my daughter."

Eliza's face flushed with anger, futile and inexpressible.

Nate had never liked the smell of the office, or the smell of the docks with their rotting fish and hemp and exhaust from the donkey engines. The Mission Street pier, one of dozens that reached like wooden tentacles into the bay, was where the Truesdale ships docked. It was located only a few blocks from the office, and this morning he walked there first. Though different in design, the down easters were still referred to as clippers. Two of the Truesdale clippers were docked at the moment, the *Sea Bear* and the *Russell Adams*.

Because sailors weren't paid while onshore, they were forced to quarter in boardinghouses run by crimps who loaned them food, clothing, and liquor. To ensure that they got their money back, the crimps found jobs for the seamen on upcoming voyages and were paid in advance by the shipmasters. No sailor could find work except through the crimping system. If they refused to cooperate with the crimps, they were often shanghaied.

Tucked around the waterfront were the sailors' boardinghouses, weathered gray two- and three-story structures whose wooden walls were gouged by knives and flying glass. The boardinghouses stank of urine, whiskey, mildew, and salt-rot. Bits of smashed whiskey bottles glittered in the morning sun as Nate strode over them. Glass cracked and crunched under his feet. He walked over soft clots of dirt on the wooden sidewalk, which had willowy green weeds sprouting up between the boards.

Caught among the weeds and lifting delicately in the faint morning breeze was a woman's silk scarf, golden and shimmering. Nate glanced at it in bemusement. He recognized it, though he couldn't remember from where. Who among the women he knew could have lost a scarf in this disreputable neighborhood?

As he walked the length of the pier, his steps hollow thuds on the planks, Nate watched the multitude of small Whitehall boats rowing salesmen back and forth on the sparkling blue water of the Bay. Every arriving deepwaterman was met by boardinghouse runners, shipsmiths, and the saloon representatives called chandlers, every one of whom was soliciting business. Behind him, rising along the steep hills, the pastel buildings of the city reflected the bright morning sun.

Nate finally located the skipper of the *Russell Adams*.

He fired him.

Nate's partner, Rossie Watts, entered his office minutes after Nate did. Short and compact, Rossie was a bundle of tightly controlled energy. His straight black hair was kept smoothed around a deceptively genial face; his eyes, almost black, were quick, seeing all, revealing nothing.

"Mornin'," he exclaimed. "I've been waiting for you." Rossie pulled out the extra chair and sat down, leaning against it with one arm looped over the back, rubbing his palm down his thigh. "Looks like you had a rough night. Who was she?" He laughed at Nate's stiff expression. "Real rough, huh? Tell me about it. All right, don't tell me about it. Why did you want to see me? What's on your mind?"

"The skipper of the *Russell Adams*, Mr. Washington," Nate said. "I fired him."

Rossie exclaimed in surprised anger, "Who the hell gave you the right to do that without talking to me first?"

"Two murdered sailors. Did you know about them?"

"Sure, I knew," he said. "What d'you think happens in this business? And where do you come from, calling it murder?" He leaned forward. "I sometimes wonder about you, Truesdale. I know my business, I know how to hold up my end. You handle the customers. You don't have any right messing in my affairs. And you had no right to fire one of my skippers without my say-so!"

Nate gauged the other man in silence, his nostrils flaring as he experienced the revulsion he always felt in Rossie's presence. "I don't condone murder. This is my father's company, his good name—*my* name—is at stake!"

"Where have you been? This is the way of the business we're in." Rossie made a clicking sound of sympathy and murmured soothingly, "Accidents happen."

"I have to put up with the crimps!" Nate exclaimed in frustration. "I have to pay blood money! But I don't have to sanction sadistic murder for the pleasure of any bucko-mate skipper!"

Rossie smiled calmly. "Slow down, you're upset, you've got a right to be upset. These things happen . . . and it's unfortunate. Put it behind you, Truesdale. Next time, if you're upset about something, come see me first, all right? I would have talked to Washington—"

"Would you have fired him?"

"No, he's too good a skipper. Two record runs in a row. One hundred forty percent profit on those runs."

Nate and Rossie had long ago ceased to be friends. Bound now by their mutual share in the company, they tolerated each other. Shortly after Nate had taken over the business he had suffered a setback when two ships ran aground in the Bay. Rossie had brought family money with him and lifted the company back into its top slot. But each passing year divided them further and further, and Nate regretted ever making Rossie his partner.

"What are you saying, Rossie—that that excuses him?" Nate said with disgust. "Look ahead, look at the big picture and where this company's going to fit in. Unions, Rossie. The Coast Seamen's Union already—"

"We don't have any part of the coast trade," Rossie interrupted. "Deepwaterman sailors are another breed, too rough and simple-minded for anything like unionizing."

"You're not seeing it," Nate insisted, his temper rising again. Why could he never stay calm in these discussions? "Look at the legislation to shorten the work week. We have to stay on top of it, Rossie. That's the future—unions, workers' rights, legislation for the workers."

"A passing phenomenon, that's all," Rossie said in irritation. "Jesus, but you're not cut out for this. You never were. Come on, you've never liked this company, you don't like it now. Why do you keep at it? You've wanted to buy me out—but how about I buy your share? Get yourself out of this headache. Christ, you've put in your time, you don't need this anymore."

Nate sank back in his chair, but his gaze remained level. "You don't have any idea what I need. Think about a price, Rossie. How much do you want for your half?''

Rossie was grinning at him, but before he could say anything more, a quick, hard knock on the door interrupted them. Marietta Sharpe swung open the door and entered, her long fresh mist-green gown swishing. Her blonde hair was tucked up under a small flower-decked hat set at a rakish angle; her tailored dress followed the full curves of her figure, with fabric looped up in back and sweeping jauntily. A matching tailored jacket, cinched in at the waist, had padded shoulders. Only her hands and face were revealed, her plump flesh pink and hinting at hidden lusciousness.

Her blue-violet eyes slanted up at the corners as she smiled at Nate and Rossie. ''Why, hello, Rossie,'' she said gaily, extending her hand, palm down, as he stood up. ''I hope I'm not interrupting anything serious.'' She laughed, revealing small rounded teeth in a sugar-pink mouth. ''Nate, dear,''—she reached over the desk to give his forearm a quick squeeze—''you'll have to forgive me. I had to hear about''—she dropped her voice to a whisper—''*yesterday*. But I can return later and let you two finish up whatever you've been discussing.'' Her voice was high and lilting, and complemented her candy-sweet face.

''No, we're finished,'' Rossie protested, grinning. ''I'm sure Nate would rather talk to you anyway. Sweeten him up, would you? You know how to do it, don't you, angel. What's this about yesterday?''

''Later, Rossie,'' Nate said, frowning and waving him away.

Rossie winked at Marietta, who blew him a kiss as he left the office.

''Tell me now. Don't leave me in suspense, Nate!''

Marietta's eyes slanted and sparkled. "How is she? Did you meet her? What's she like?"

Nate grinned as he walked around the desk toward her. He lifted her face with one finger beneath her chin and dropped a quick kiss on her pretty pink mouth. She tasted of cherries.

"Daisy's precious. I want you to meet her."

Eliza held up the letter and blew across the shiny black webbing of wet ink. It was addressed to Mr. McPherson and contained a concisely written account of her interview with Nate Truesdale and the results. She needed his advice on how to counteract Nate's intentions regarding Daisy. She laid the paper carefully in the center of the desk and read it through again, her chin propped in the palm of her hand.

The room Nate had offered her was on the second floor, next to Daisy's. It overlooked the rear garden, and she had a view of trees heavy with globed fruit, of patches of succulent yellow orchids, of lush red roses, white milky gardenias, and purple bougainvillea. With her window slightly open, the room had been filled with fragrance rich from the day's warmth, but now the last odor of the sun-sweetened fruit and flowers was dissipating in the late afternoon coolness.

The bedroom itself was no less lush. On the walls framed watercolor renderings of wildflowers were interspersed with dark oil paintings.

The bed was high, with polished oak head- and footboards carved with roses. The mattress was too soft, and Eliza had sunk into it with a feeling of being drowned in cotton.

She finished reading the letter again, sighed, and left it in the middle of the writing table as she stood and checked the time on the watch pinned to her bodice. Almost six. She had not seen or heard Daisy since she'd begun the letter over an hour ago. Outside her door she paused, listening.

Six doors opened onto a broad, rectangular landing. Four of the doors led to bedrooms, another opened onto stairs leading up to the third floor, and behind the double doors at the head of the staircase a drawing room spread dim and empty and echoing. "Used but once a year for the Thanksgiving Day dinner," Mrs. Herlihy had said earlier that morning. The curving stairs from the first floor were railed on three sides with white banisters, the landing extending all around it.

Eliza heard Daisy's voice from downstairs. She followed it to the kitchen and paused on the threshold.

Instead of chatting to Mrs. Herlihy, as Eliza had expected, Daisy was talking to Nate. She was standing on a chair, an enormous apron wrapped around her and tucked up so as not to get tangled in her feet. Nate stood at the stove, a faded red apron tied under his arms to protect his white shirt and gray pin-striped waistcoat and trousers. His shirtsleeves were rolled back over corded forearms dark with wiry black hair. The kitchen was overheated from the massive cast-iron stove and smelled of bay leaves and garlic.

"I wanted to see a buffalo, but we didn't, and there weren't any Indians except in one town and they didn't have feathers. It was all so big, so really, really big and flat," Daisy was saying. "And there weren't any trees. Why weren't there any trees?" Eliza knew she was describing the trip to California. She waited, unnoticed, in the doorway.

The light from the windows was failing, and Nate lifted an amber-bellied oil lamp onto a shelf beside the stove so he could see better. He bent over the pot he was stirring and sniffed. "That's prairie land. I think it's always been like that. I've never seen it myself. I always travel by ship. I have lots of ships and it doesn't cost anything for me."

Daisy leaned her weight on her hands on the worktable, which was cluttered with tomato seeds, used bowls, spoons, knives, and paper-thin onion peels. The light caught her hair as she looked into the steaming pot Nate was stirring. "Can I go on a ship too?"

"Sure. I'll take you on a ship. I'll take you around the world, if you want. Here, baby dear, taste this." He turned toward her with a spoon with something tomatoey in it. Catching sight of Eliza in the doorway, he halted. "Hello, Aunt Lizzie," he said with false brightness. "Supper's almost ready."

Daisy flung her long straight hair over her shoulder with an absent sweep of her hand. She was smiling. "We're making soup. And I'm helping. See my apron?"

"Where is Mrs. Herlihy?" Eliza inquired.

Nate let Daisy taste from the spoon. "She always leaves early on Thursdays. Gives me a chance to poison myself. How's that, hmmm? Are we good cooks?"

Daisy nodded. "Mmmm. It's good. You didn't really put poison in it, did you?"

"Never, precious. Never, never." He laughed at her in profound amusement and turned back to the steaming pot.

Appalled by his use of endearments, Eliza marched across the floor and lifted Daisy from the chair. "Go into the dining room and set the table." She had not meant to sound so sharp, so punitive.

Daisy's lower lip jutted obstinately. "But I'm cooking!" She looked to Nate for support. "Isn't that right, Nate? I'm a cook tonight?"

"He is Mr. Truesdale to you, my dear," Eliza said in astonishment. "And the cooking is finished—go set the table as I asked you to."

"He *told* me to call him Nate!"

Eliza bent down to Daisy's height. "I'm talking about your manners, young lady! You are to call people by their proper names. And I told you to set the table—don't argue back to me!"

"She's right," Nate said. "I did tell her to call me Nate."

Eliza straightened to face him, brows drawn tight, eyes bright with anger. "Daisy is my responsibility, and I think you're forgetting it!"

He shot her a grim stare, then quietly told Daisy, "Since the cooking is finished and the table's already set, why don't you go on outside and play for a while?"

Daisy started to pull off her apron with furious jerks, but Eliza exclaimed, "It's almost dark outside. I never allow her out at dark."

"This isn't Pittsburgh, Miss Nolenberg. She's entirely safe in my yard. If that's your concern."

Eliza trembled inside, furious. "Nevertheless, I insist she stay indoors at this hour." More calmly, she added, "Daisy, I need to talk to Mr. Truesdale for a minute. Would you mind going to your room for a bit? How about getting Angelique ready for dinner?"

Daisy glanced at Nate, who nodded. The exchange did not escape Eliza's notice, and when Daisy was out of the room, she spun on him. "What right do you have? What right? We may be temporarily forced to remain here, but I am still responsible for Daisy. Do not countermand what I am doing with her!"

"What right?" he repeated incredulously. "If you could have heard yourself just now—the way you ordered her around! If you're angry with me, then talk to me, but don't take all this out on *her!* Do you understand me, Miss Nolenberg?''

"I'm talking to you right now! And I'm telling you, we need to get some things straightened . . . *Where are you going?*'' Nate had turned his back on her and slapped open the swinging door into the dining room. Eliza followed on his heels. "How dare you walk out when you've just told me to talk to you when I'm . . . What is that?''

She backed into the kitchen, Nate following with a decanter in his hand. "Bourbon," he said with a harsh smile. "I need a drink if I'm going to listen to you.''

Eliza whirled away in silent fury.

"Want any?" he inquired, the decanter clinking against the lip of a glass as he poured a two-finger helping. "You need it more than I do. Ah, but you'd be a temperance lady.''

"I'll take it," she snapped angrily.

Nate looked at her in surprise but reached for another glass from a shelf above the deep sink. When he handed her the drink, his eyes were steady and impossibly blue, his expression beneath his curly black hair amused. Eliza accepted the glass with a faint tremor.

"Don't tell me," Nate said. "You were accustomed to it at home for years, and then at the mill.''

Eliza remained silent while she sipped, blinked, and turned away from him as she exhaled from the raw heat.

"You're full of surprises today. What'll it be next?''

She spun on him in blushing anger. "That's something you'll never know!" she exclaimed.

"I'm relieved to hear it.''

Her jaw dropped in surprise. He laughed and set

his glass down as he turned to the soup and reached for the spoon again.

"Mr. Truesdale, I've written to my lawyer. I'll do whatever I must in order to get Daisy legally away from here. And then your money and influence won't be able to touch her. Are you listening to me?"

"How can I help it? All right, let's establish some basic rules then." Nate stirred the soup once more, rapped the spoon against the edge of the pot, and set it down. "First thing—" he began, again reaching for his glass and leaning comfortably against the corner of the table beside the stove, one long leg bent in front of the other.

"No, Mr. Truesdale. You won in that you have Daisy under your roof now, so the rules are mine to make."

He inclined his head. "I'll listen, but I won't promise anything. Let's hear what's on your mind."

Eliza clenched the glass with both hands and stormed inwardly. Why did he have to be so attractive! She felt at a disadvantage and not at all firm enough as she said, "I want you to treat Daisy as you would a guest, not as a father usurping my authority. That's the first point."

"Before you continue, tell me something. Who primarily raised Daisy? You or Estelle?"

"Why should that be of any relevance?" she demanded.

"It's a big factor as far as I'm concerned."

"Estelle and I cared equally for Daisy. We shared the responsibility and had identical viewpoints on her upbringing."

"Now there I'll disagree with you," Nate said. "I've never known two sisters to be so different."

"How would you even remember Estelle?" Eliza pressed her hand to her breast, against the sudden jolt of her heart. Looking into Nate's steady blue eyes, she recalled those eyes as they had looked long ago, glazed with passion as he gazed at Estelle's reflection in the mirror.

"I remember Estelle," Nate answered. "Let's just leave it at that. And what I meant was that whoever raised her thus far has done a damn fine job of it. So I wanted to know if it was primarily you, because then I'll agree to give you that authority here."

"I'll take the credit," Eliza announced more firmly than she felt. "First point settled. Second point: I don't want you ever to see Daisy alone."

Nate laughed. "Don't be absurd! Do you have a third point?"

"I'm set against you, Mr. Truesdale. You won't get Daisy, I promise you. I'll have you exposed. I'll see your reputation destroyed—"

"I have an appointment already set up tomorrow with my lawyer." Nate's face hardened into unfriendliness. "Don't ever threaten me, Miss Nolenberg," he said softly. "Your position here is very, very uncertain."

Eliza forced her gaze to remain steady on his, though her pulse hit a frantic tempo. "It's past Daisy's suppertime," she managed to say in a level voice.

"Then go call her."

She had to escape. As she pushed open the door into the dining room, she felt his gaze digging into her back.

Chapter 4

Afternoon sunlight penetrated the cloud cover with scant, watery beams that lit the dusty boards of the shop. Tall, dim shelves bearing tins of ladies' pills, bottles of hair restorer, waving irons, jars of bust ointment and cold cream, and decanters of perfume rose up behind the woman. A display of decorative gold and silver hatpins stood amid stacks of glove boxes on the cluttered counter. Elsewhere were shelves of food items—candied fruits and biscuits in decorated tins, chocolates in flower shapes. The perfumed scent of the tiny shop offered veiled promises of beauty and luxury.

The plump, tightly corseted woman behind the counter shook her head. Her dark eyes—ugly eyes, Eliza thought—were shiny holes in a pink, fleshy face, and she said with hard emphasis, "I can't afford to pay for any help. Better look somewhere else."

"Where?" Eliza pressed. She was exhausted and trying to hold on to her patience. Her fingers gripped the edge of the counter. "Please, can't you help me at all? Tell me where I might find employment."

"How am I supposed to know?" the woman retorted, and with a quick, backhanded motion she waved Eliza away.

53

"Thank you," Eliza said with pointed emphasis. "Thank you so very much for your help." Wet wind rushed into the shop when Eliza opened the door to leave.

"Try Truesdale and Watts," the woman called after her. Eliza glanced back, and the woman shrugged. "A couple blocks over on Market. They're hiring what they call lady typewriters."

Truesdale & Watts.

Eliza pushed the door closed behind her and tightened her fingers on the strings of her purse as she faced the rain-spanked street. Not what she had in mind. Not if it was the last job on earth. Never.

She hunched up her shoulders to keep the back of her neck warm in her cape as she waited for a cable car to pass, the faint hum of the heavy moving cable beneath the street audible to her, then crossed the street with short, quick steps. So far this day she had been in more stores and businesses than she could count. Bakeries and food shops, general stores and banks, dress shops and hat shops and children's shops. No one needed another employee. Her skills were too limited.

The big, blond-bearded man behind the counter in the saloon she entered next said, "Look, miss, no women in here."

Eliza faced him calmly. "I've served drinks before. I can handle a tray, handle the customers, handle—"

"You weren't listening to me," he said, staring at her through red-veined eyes. He flipped a dirty wet cloth over his shoulder. "You wanta work upstairs?" he questioned in sarcasm, hooking his thumb toward the second floor. "Naw, I didn't think so. Otherwise, no women in here. You hear me?"

"Yes," Eliza said. She held his gaze a moment longer, compressed her lips, then took a step toward the door. The sour odor and dust of the place disgusted her; she was almost glad to be leaving.

"Look," the man said. He leaned a big, hairy arm on the bar and opened his mouth several times, as if he was trying to say something he found difficult to voice. "Look," he said on a sigh. "It's not that you're not pretty enough. I mean . . ." He jerked his shoulder in a brief shrug. "You're all right, y'understand. It's just rules. I mean . . . No women down here in the saloon. You understand."

Eliza nodded, tight-lipped against her tiredness.

"But look," he continued, halting her again on her way to the door. When she glanced at him, he leaned both elbows on the bar and pulled the rag from his shoulder. "If you'd care to, we could get together later. I mean . . . if you want." His reddened eyes squinted at her, and he slapped the towel again over his shoulder.

Eliza walked out of the saloon, spine straight, purse strings clutched tighter in her fist. What had possessed her to go into a saloon in the first place? She had long ago promised herself never to do that again. Her father's brother had owned a saloon in Pittsburgh and offered her a job when she was fourteen.

"Better hours for you, Lizzie," he had said. "And a good sight healthier. I'll pay you three dollars a week—I know you can use it at home, eh, what with your pa gone and your ma and Estelle to be fed."

But Uncle Bill drank at his own saloon and was a different man on the job. "Lizzie, Lizzie," he had wheedled. "Come here and give your uncle a kiss. That's a good girl. Yes, *yes*, what a good girl! I can help you earn more, honey. You need the money, huh? Come upstairs with me and you can make four dollars a week. How would that be, honey?"

She had been serving whiskey for two months and

squirming out of the way of the drunker customers, but now Uncle Bill was hugging her and kissing her with a wet, open mouth and squeezing her buttocks with his big hands. Terrified, she had pushed and hit him, but he wouldn't let her go. When she had lifted the lamp in one free hand and held it up in a threat, she had seen the surprise freeze on his face. Even now in memory she felt the terror, heard the sloshing of the coal oil, saw the wavering flame and the slow hardening of his face as he realized what she meant. Before he could stop her, young Eliza had thrown down the lamp. As the oil ignited in a rushing crescendo, he had flung her aside with a shouted curse. And Eliza had bolted, her strong thin legs pumping under her heavy skirt, her shoes pounding down the crowded dirt road toward home. The saloon had burned to the ground, and Uncle Bill had never bothered her again. After that she had returned to the mill.

The memories followed her as she walked rapidly away, careless of the tears squeezing from her eyes, and the surprised and embarrassed glances she received from the pedestrians passing her.

She had six dollars with her in California and even less tucked away at home. Not enough to get Daisy and run away. They had the return tickets to Pittsburgh, but Nate would follow. She needed money to hire a lawyer!

Nate strolled home in the gathering dusk, head down as he kicked wet clumps of leaves littering the sidewalk. He started to climb the steps leading up to his house but caught sight of Eliza approaching from the opposite direction. Her steps were slower than usual. Nate started to continue up the stairs, but with a sigh of exasperation, he stopped and waited for her. He knew he'd have to talk to her sooner or later this evening. Might as well get it over with. He stood on the third step, flipping back his frock coat to shove his hands in his trouser pockets.

She was almost to the stairs before she noticed him. She paused, brushed her cheeks with her fingers, and continued with a new stiffness in her posture.

"Good evening," she said as she passed him on the stairs.

"Out for an evening stroll?" he inquired politely, following her. Her slender black-stockinged ankles were revealed intermittently in silhouette beneath the heavy hem of her skirt as she climbed the steps. He was surprised by how small she was, how petite the curves of her hips were under the hem of the cape. When faced straight on she seemed formidable. If she'd ever give it half a chance . . . Such a waste, he thought.

"No," she answered briskly. "I was looking for a job."

"Ah, the ever-resourceful Miss Nolenberg. And did you have any luck? Which of our fair establishments did you take by storm?"

She halted on the stair and swung around in anger. Nate had not expected it and bumped into her as he took the next step. Caught off-guard, he grasped her arm to steady himself. He was one step below her, and they stared at each other eye-to-eye. In the glare of the gaslights he saw the golden glitter of her wet gaze.

"You've been crying," he said, astonished. "What happened? No luck, I take it." Beneath his fingers, her arm was small and trembling. So the statue was warm and made of living flesh after all, he thought. As he steered her up the last four steps to the short front lawn, she said nothing.

"Look, Miss Nolenberg, I said I could pay you a

salary if you wished. Be Daisy's companion. There's no need for you to be walking the streets like a . . ."

"Like a common laborer?" she supplied, pulling her arm from his grasp.

Nate frowned in confused apology. "I didn't mean—"

"No, maybe you didn't mean it, but it's the truth. And there's nothing disgraceful about honest work."

"I never suggested there was." Nate regarded her gravely, aware of her regained composure and impressed in spite of himself. "So did you find employment?"

"Not yet," she said, picking up her skirts as she walked toward the door. "It's just a matter of time. And I'll be able to prove in court my competency to care for Daisy.

"Oh, is that what it's all about. Will you be moving out then?"

"Not without Daisy," she answered in crisp tones.

He looked down on the small, ribbon-bedecked black hat and the just-visible curve of one cheek glowing warmly in the gaslight. "You don't stand a chance," he said bluntly. "You can't possibly match what I can offer her."

Eliza made no comment, and they entered the house in silence.

"I'd like to have a word with you," he said before she could escape. "About Daisy." Nate gestured toward the front parlor and after a slight hesitation, Eliza entered. She removed her damp cape and unpinned her hat. Nate hung them both on the polished oak rack in the corner.

"I had a talk with my lawyer today," he began. He strolled across the room, rubbing his palms together, and wished he didn't feel so uncomfortable.

Eliza sat perched on the edge of the sofa; a wisp of dark hair displaced by wet wind hung damp and listless along her throat. A white residue of tears lay smudged high on her cheekbone. The sight made it all the more difficult for him to say his piece. Her dark eyes followed him calmly as he paced back and forth and finally took a seat opposite her. "You do realize how much is in my favor?" he asked.

"Just tell me what your lawyer said."

"The judge will look at what would be the best situation for the child, in terms of financial stability, consistency of care, the quality of home life . . . that sort of thing."

"Of course." She nodded and waited.

"Don't you see, Miss Nolenberg? You couldn't win. I have more on my side, and rather than—"

"I have the papers proving that Daisy's mother wished me to be her guardian," Eliza interrupted calmly. "You can't match that, Mr. Truesdale."

"Granted, that's in your favor, but you're not the natural mother. That's a big point. The fact that I'm her natural father gives me a stronger position."

"But you don't have maternal abilities, no matter what other talents you may claim, and I'm sure the judge would take that into consideration. A child belongs with a mothering figure, wouldn't you agree?"

"All right," Nate conceded, rising to his feet and moving restlessly about the room. "Let's get everything out on the table. I'm willing to be as honest as I can. There is a woman I'm courting now who wants me to marry her. She'd be a perfect mothering figure for Daisy. I thought I should tell you this, you realize, just to let you know what you're up against with this insistence on dragging everything through a public court."

Eliza's face flushed hotly. "Very good, Mr. Truesdale. More points for you, but what about your behavior? Getting an innocent girl with child out of wedlock! There's a moral issue here you can't win."

"But I'm making what could be called recompense now, don't you see?" He leaned slightly forward in emphasis. "The moral issue is resolved. Payment made. Besides," he added, straightening, "the judge is a man, not a committee of church women."

"So he understands immoral behavior, is that it?"

"Look, Miss Nolenberg, I'm just trying to spare you. You're forgetting my position in this city—and you have no idea yet what the damned Truesdale name means here. But believe me, the newspapers will have a heyday with this story. The morbid public will love it, every last juicy detail. I don't want to have to go to court. I told my lawyer I'd do whatever I could to spare Daisy that kind of an ordeal and the publicity it'll create around her. I would think you'd be relieved that I'm willing to work it out without resorting to legal procedure."

Forced by the unreasoning logic of painful emotions, Eliza stood up, facing him, as she accused, "So you marry one immoral woman to keep the child of another immoral woman. Two wrongs making a right, is that it? Am I correct, Mr. Truesdale? You're making everything *right* now?"

Nate laughed in derision. "You do realize you've just condemned your own sister? That dear 'innocent girl' you mentioned earlier." He stuffed his hands in his pockets and added with grim cruelty, "I wondered how much you knew."

Eliza collapsed onto the sofa like a lifeless rag doll. Nate wanted to kick himself. After a long pause she said, "Yes, I knew. How could I not? But you were the first. You did it, you started it. And she was only seventeen."

"I wasn't the first," Nate corrected. "Did she tell you I was?"

Eliza stared blankly, as if she saw inwardly and not what was in front of her. "Yes," she said, and he caught the tone of defeat in her voice. "It was—" She released a long sigh of resignation. "It was as though she tried to win back our father in the form of every man she met."

And you, Miss Nolenberg, he thought angrily, reject him in the form of every man you meet.

She buried her face in her hands. Nate suddenly regretted mocking her. He wanted to touch the hard knot of hair and soften it, stroke the pale cheek, tease away the frowns, and make her smile. He realized he had never seen her smile. He wanted to do these things but remained standing, watching her. She stood up abruptly and faced him. The brisk self-command had returned.

She said coolly, "Daisy is entirely innocent, and I want to keep her that way. I'll fight you to the very end to keep Daisy away from you."

"And hurt her in the bargain, is that it?" Nate snapped. He was amazed at the change in her and furious with himself for feeling anything remotely like sympathy. "All right, this is your decision then? I'll tell my lawyer and we'll get a court date. You'd better find local representation. Your Mr. McPherson won't be any good to you long distance."

"Thank you," she said crisply. "I've already considered it."

Sunday afternoon Daisy was beside herself with excitement. "Hurry, Aunt Lizzie!" She squirmed while Eliza rebraided her hair. She wore a short black-and-red-plaid dress sashed at the waist, the blouse billowing over the sash, and black cotton stockings.

"Hold still, Daisy, or I won't be able to get the braid even this time either. What do you want, the white ribbon or a red one?" Eliza sat on the edge of her bed, her mouth tight with exasperation as she worked with the fine strands of Daisy's hair.

Daisy bobbed as she waited. "White. Can I wear a brooch too? Please?" She tried to turn to see Eliza.

"Face front, please. How can I get this finished if you keep turning your head like that?"

"But what if he leaves without me?"

"He won't." Eliza tied the white ribbon into a bow at the end of the braid. "There. Now you'd better get your shoes."

Daisy ran toward the door, but caught herself at the door frame and skidded in her stocking feet as she tried to turn around. "Can I wear a brooch? I want to look pretty for Miss Sharpe." She came running back to Eliza's dresser and pulled open the top drawer. "Please, Aunt Lizzie?" She lifted out an enameled brooch bearing a single full-petaled rose trimmed in silver. Eliza's only brooch.

"All right, come here and I'll pin it on you."

With the brooch at her throat, Daisy ran out the door and collided with Nate who was heading toward the stairs. He grabbed her arms and steadied her. "Hello there, miss, you're in a hurry today." He dropped to his knees to see her. "And you look so pretty and all grown-up." He tapped the brooch. "Meeting some lucky fellow?" he said, and winked.

Daisy giggled at him. "It's you!"

"Well, I'm a lucky fellow indeed! Two beautiful ladies to escort to the beach. You on my left and Miss Sharpe on my right."

"And Aunt Lizzie," Daisy added.

"Is she—?" Nate straightened as Eliza appeared

in the doorway. "Good afternoon, Aunt Lizzie," he said.

"I couldn't help overhearing you," she said, adding, "Run along and get your shoes, Daisy. Hurry now." When Daisy disappeared into her room, Eliza looked at Nate again. "I'll be joining you today."

"Making yourself right at home, I see. What if I haven't invited you?"

"Daisy is my responsibility, and I choose to accompany her wherever she goes."

"What are you afraid of, Miss Nolenberg? That I'll resort to crude animal behavior in front of Daisy?" He lifted his eyebrows in mock innocence.

"Should I worry about that?" she responded, raising her own eyebrows gently as she imitated his tone and expression to perfection.

He laughed appreciatively. "Certainly not for yourself, but Marietta's another story. Perhaps you should come along today and keep me in line. We're leaving in about fifteen minutes. Can you be ready?"

"Yes," Eliza snapped and retreated to her room, flinging the door closed behind her. She heard his muted laughter trail down the stairs.

Eliza and Daisy rode in the cramped rear seat of Nate's carriage, Daisy's doll Angelique on her lap; Nate and Marietta occupied the main seat. When he escorted Marietta from her grandmother's home—a magnificent structure of sparkling bay windows and balconies, the whitewashed exterior cooled by pale green leafy shadows—Eliza saw an exquisitely beautiful woman, vivacious and fresh in a pink-and-white-striped gown. Her blonde curls were arranged under a tiny feather-tipped hat. Marietta nodded, smiling at Daisy as Nate assisted her into the carriage.

"Marietta, this is Daisy," Nate said, grinning proudly.

Marietta touched Daisy under her chin with one white-gloved finger. "How sweet you are, child. Why, you're cute as a button, aren't you. And this must be Miss Nolenberg." Marietta unobtrusively studied the prim black gown. "But you're in mourning now, aren't you, dear? I'm so terribly sorry."

The open carriage swept into the street. They crisscrossed the city, keeping to the lower hills. Nate drove the horse at a fast clip, and the wind rushing past her ears prevented Eliza from overhearing what Nate and Marietta were laughing about. Marietta was a good deal younger than Nate, and also, Eliza thought with some discomfort, much younger than she was.

She watched Marietta lean toward Nate, noticed the way her pink mouth spoke into his ear and he attentively dipped his head toward her to catch lost syllables. Beside Marietta's trim shoulders in the pink-and-white puffed sleeves, Nate's shoulders were broad and thick under his charcoal-gray coat. Once Nate bent to speak into Marietta's ear and when she laughed at what he had said, he kissed the small pink earlobe peeking under a blonde curl. Eliza looked away, distressed and unhappy.

The rear seat bounced gently behind the wheels, and Daisy tugged at Eliza's arm. "She's so pretty," Daisy exclaimed, her eyes shining. "I want to be pretty when I grow up."

Eliza put her arm around Daisy. "But you will be, my dear," she said, and smiled at Daisy's rapt attention. "You'll be even prettier."

"Really and truly?"

Eliza nodded.

Daisy giggled behind her hand and tugged to get Eliza to lean down to her. "He really likes her, doesn't he," she said with a little girl's fascination with romance.

Eliza tried to maintain her smile. Oh, but Daisy was so innocent! And with no idea what was being planned around her. "It looks like it," she managed to say.

The carriage rounded a broad turn, and the ocean came into view over the tops of the Monterey cypress trees that sloped down the hillside to their right. Eliza's heart beat faster at her first view of the Pacific Ocean stretching smooth and silvery toward the horizon. She wanted to open her arms and embrace it all.

Appearing no bigger than a toy boat, a distant clipper under full sail moved slowly across the water. Ahead, at the bottom of the hill, the great white facade of the Cliff House restaurant rose six floors high from its perch on an outcropping of rocks. The black roof with its many pinnacles and central tower gave it a somber appearance. The road curved to the left in front of the Cliff House and angled down to skirt the ocean.

With the sun unencumbered by clouds and the usual sleek and chilled Pacific wind reduced to a soft breeze, the beach beneath the brooding Cliff House was warm and dotted with people. Nate brought the horses to a halt amid other carriages alongside the road and secured the reins to an iron railing bordering the beach. Eliza heard the distant barking of seals and the splashing slap of waves against the rocks.

"What a delightful day, Nate!" Marietta exclaimed as he helped her down. "I believe you made it this way just for me."

"Of course. You didn't have any doubts, did you?"

As Nate assisted Eliza down, she was aware of the warm, dry feel of his fingers holding hers. She didn't look at him as she stepped onto the gritty sand. He grasped Daisy and swung her high over the side of the carriage, and she screamed, high-pitched and loud. "I'm flying!" After lifting out an old coffee-brown wool blanket, he led them across the beach.

Marietta opened a pink beaded parasol and held it high in one hand, the other grasping Nate's arm for support as her feet sank in the sand. Trailing behind, watching, Eliza had never felt more drab. Beyond ensuring that her hair was tidy, and that her dresses were clean and mended, she had never considered her appearance. She glanced down at the black skirt, at the faint wrinkles that she could never quite iron out. How long had it been since she had worn a light color or a bit of lace? And she had a necklace strung with pearls and dropping to a heart-shaped pendant that had belonged to her mother. Something she had treasured but never worn.

Over the odor of seaweed and saltwater, she caught the faint essence of Marietta's perfume. The scent brought confusing, exciting, mysterious memories of Estelle . . .

She remembered Estelle twirling as she flaunted a new gown; Estelle laughing as she lifted white arms to stroke her hair and draw attention to it; Estelle unpinning a yellow blossom from her bodice as she smiled enticingly at Nate's dark reflection in the mirror.

Nate spread the blanket over the sand and held Marietta's hand to help her take a seat. He looked at Eliza, his blue eyes narrowing against the sunlight, and held her gaze for a long moment. Long enough for Eliza to feel the blush that broke like a wave under her skin.

"There's plenty of room for you to sit here, Miss Nolenberg," he suggested, holding out his hand to her. "It's perfectly safe. I'll be taking Daisy down to the water."

She put her hand in his as she said with brisk

sarcasm, "Of course, in that case," and allowed him to help her sit on the warm blanket beside Marietta.

He laughed as he took off his coat and folded it for Marietta to hold. "You're getting brave, Miss Nolenberg."

Daisy hopped toward Eliza and leaned against her shoulder for support as she tugged at the lacings of her shoe. "Help me get them off." She bent down, brushing Eliza's cheek with her braid, and pushed off her stockings. She dropped the shoes and stockings in Eliza's lap on top of Angelique, and then Daisy and Nate were running toward the water, hand in hand. Nate's pants legs were rolled up to just below his knees, and he had folded back the sleeves of his white shirt.

"California must seem like a paradise after Pittsburgh," Marietta commented, shading her eyes with the parasol as she watched Nate and Daisy wade into the first waves.

"Not really," Eliza said. "Just brighter."

"I'd never want to live there. I can't imagine anyone preferring any place to California."

Eliza looked at Marietta's delicate, perfect profile in the pink shade of the parasol and considered the fact that this woman might become Daisy's stepmother. She was furious at the thought. "I understand you and Mr. Truesdale might be married," she remarked. "Is that true?"

Marietta's blue-violet glance turned cool. "I don't think it's your place to question me about it, Miss Nolenberg."

"Has he told you about Daisy?" Eliza persisted, ignoring the sting of Marietta's remark.

"Yes, he has. She's not of our social set, but in time everything will work out."

A squeal from Daisy caught their attention, and they watched as Nate swung her up just in time to avoid being hit by a large wave. She clung to his neck, her wet bare feet dangling against his thigh.

Marietta watched them. "He adores her." She smiled to herself. "You know, Miss Nolenberg, you really should consider allowing us to hire you as Daisy's governess. It would be an ideal situation for you."

"Because it's part of your world?"

"Don't be absurd, Miss Nolenberg, you haven't the proper family. Daisy at least has Mr. Truesdale. Otherwise . . . But you have excellent qualifications, Miss Nolenberg. You're experienced with children, and I understand from Mr. Truesdale that you'd also make an excellent housekeeper."

"He said that?" Eliza snapped in a brittle voice.

"He wouldn't have offered you the position in his household if he didn't trust your abilities. I could arrange for you a respectable situation in any one of a dozen homes. So there, you see, everything will work out well. There's nothing at all for you to be so concerned about."

"Don't you worry about our being alone in the house at night?" Eliza couldn't help saying. "Mrs. Herlihy leaves every afternoon, you do know."

"Now don't belittle yourself, Miss Nolenberg. I'm sure you can manage the household superbly in Mrs. Herlihy's absence."

Marietta's attention remained fixed on Nate and Daisy.

The fact that she completely missed Eliza's insinuation, and for the simple reason that she obviously did not consider Eliza a threat, hurt more than any snideness or direct cruelty.

Eliza stood up, brushing sand from her skirt, and without a word to Marietta, sauntered down to the water's edge. She paused briefly to remove her shoes and give the blush of anger in her cheeks a

chance to cool in the breeze, then waded carefully
into the glistening foam. The icy sting of water made
her gasp. But anything was preferable to being near
Marietta. To distract herself from the hurt of the
woman's thoughtless remarks, she lifted her skirts
as high as she decently dared and waded in deeper.
Delighted, Daisy splashed toward her. They held
hands and walked in the edge of sliding water and
sand.

Nate kicked idly at the surf as he watched Eliza
and Daisy together. There was something about the
sight of the two of them that puzzled and pleased
him. Eliza had bunched up her skirts in one hand to
keep them above the water line, and he caught tantalizing glimpses of her slender calves and ankles in
their black stockings. He was aware of an innate and
provocative femininity about her that she couldn't
entirely disguise. It revealed itself in her eyes and in
the delicate, graceful way she moved and gestured.
She was a mystery, and he was intrigued.

An unexpectedly large wave churned toward
them, and he saw Eliza leap nimbly out of its way,
pulling Daisy with her. They were laughing, and
though the sound of the waves around him prevented his hearing their voices, the sudden and open
merriment on Eliza's face caught him by surprise.
She was beautiful.

Marietta accompanied them back to the house for
dinner. As soon as they returned from the beach,
Eliza took Daisy upstairs to change her wet dress.
With the distant sound of Marietta's gay, teasing
laughter floating up into Daisy's bedroom, Eliza
paused in front of the mirror over Daisy's dresser.
She gazed at the round dark eyes staring back at
her, the pale face and pinched mouth. She looked
grim, even to herself. The plain black gown looked

grim. Turning her head slightly, she studied the tight knot of hair behind her neck. She frowned.

Daisy watched as Eliza unpinned her hair and shook out the heavy roll with her fingers. It fell to her waist, as dark and shiny as the polished mahogany dresser she was leaning against. Daisy pushed a chair to the dresser and climbed onto it to stand beside Eliza.

"You have such pretty hair, Aunt Lizzie," she said. With plump fingers she stroked the thick waves. "I've never seen your hair down. Why don't you ever wear it down? Mama did."

Eliza stared at her reflection with a pensive gaze as she plucked at the dark cascade framing her face and shoulders. Her eyes shifted, and she met Daisy's curious, enraptured expression in the mirror. "Yes, I know she did," she said softly. "And she was very pretty, wasn't she? Prettier even than Miss Sharpe."

Daisy leaned her arm around Eliza's back. "Don't cry, Aunt Lizzie. You look like you're going to cry again."

Eliza shook her head and looked around. "Where is your hairbrush, Daisy?" She found it on the floor by the bed. Together they brushed out the heavy mass of hair until the waves flowed glossy as satin.

"Wear it down tonight. Please?" Daisy begged. She observed Eliza quizzically and stroked one braid. "Put it in a ribbon like Mama did. You can use one of mine." And she jumped down from the chair to search out a ribbon from a lower drawer.

Eliza smiled. "Well, let's just see."

Daisy handed her a wide yellow ribbon which Eliza looped around her hair and tied into a bow at her neck. "What else, Daisy? What else should I do? You watched your mother—how did she make it wave around her face?"

Daisy shrugged. "She used pins, I think."

With Daisy's help and after several unsuccessful tries that made them both laugh until they were weak, Eliza stood before the mirror with her hair in neat waves lifting above her forehead and sweeping in a generous dip over her ears. She turned her head from side to side to catch the effect from different angles. Eliza and Daisy's eyes met in the mirror. They both smiled.

Daisy hooked her arm over Eliza's shoulder and leaned her head against her arm as she sighed. "You look so pretty, Aunt Lizzie. Do it like that all the time."

"Oh, I don't know, Daisy. It's a bit too frivolous, I think."

"No, it's not. You're going to wear it like that tonight, aren't you?"

Eliza frowned uncertainly and studied her reflection. She looked so different . . . younger. Somehow softer. And yes, prettier. "I don't know, Daisy."

What are you afraid of, Miss Nolenberg?

"I just don't know," she repeated, pensive.

Eliza turned impulsively to Daisy and hugged her. "Oh, all right! Yes, I will wear it like this for tonight. After that, why, we'll just have to see."

Chapter 5

Nate sat beside Marietta on the parlor sofa, watching the vivacious expressions playing on her face as she talked about the Hobarts and the party they were to give for the season. He smiled in spite of himself as he pictured having her for his wife. She was lovely, enchanting. And she was lively and laughed often and easily, which cheered his sometimes bitter heart.

"It really was rather annoying that you invited her along, Nate." Marietta had switched subjects; she did that with surprising regularity.

"Who?"

"Miss Nolenberg." She laughed and her eyes sparkled deep violet. "Weren't you listening to me? I swear, you get more absentminded all the time. She works in a mill! I know you have to be polite because of the little girl, but to invite her along with us—why, she's not our kind. I found it insulting to have to associate with her. Don't do that to me again."

Nate chuckled and patted her hand. "While you were talking about the Hobarts, I *was* absentminded. But do you want to know what I was thinking? I was imagining being married to you."

"Oh, Nate." Marietta smiled and reached up to

73

bring his face down to her. She kissed his cheek gently, at the crescent curve of his smile. "Is this a proposal?"

Nate sighed and cupped her hand between his palms. "I know it's what you want, sweetheart, but—"

"But you're not ready? I'll wait. Look at me, dear." She turned his face toward her again with a cool finger on his jaw. "You're the man I want, the man I love. I have no reason to go elsewhere, and I can wait."

Nate put his arm around her and with her delicate chin held in his hand, kissed her sweetly pink candy mouth. The tingling in his chest descended to his lap. He touched her lips with his tongue, but before he could kiss her as thoroughly as he wanted, she squirmed and twisted her face away from his.

"Not here, Nate. My goodness, you do get ardent quickly." She touched her hair, her bodice, smoothed the lace trim on her sleeve. "Someone could walk in on us."

Exasperated, Nate lifted his arm from around her and stood up. "I think I'll get a drink. Want anything?"

Marietta declined, and Nate left the room. As he passed the foot of the stairs, a sound from the second floor caught his attention and he paused, looking upward at the sun-streaked light above the stairs. Laughter. It was no more than a dim resonance in his ears, but there just the same. And it wasn't just Daisy, though he could detect her childish giggling. That other sound, as high and clear as a girl's, must be Eliza. He listened, enchanted with the heartfelt gaiety so freely expressed in the rising tones of that laughter. Not knowing why he should feel such uplifting relief, he smiled as at last he turned away.

In the kitchen Mrs. Herlihy's cheeks were flushed

from the heat of the great stove. Perspiration beaded her forehead and wilted the wisps of white hair in front of her ears. One streamer of hair that had escaped the broad bun atop her head hung over her collar.

"Smells delicious," Nate said as he strolled through the sky-blue room and reached into the cupboard for a glass.

Mrs. Herlihy raised the hem of her apron and dried her perspiring face. "Daisy asked for it special this mornin'. Shrimp soup again. That daughter of yours is an angel, Mr. Truesdale."

Nate grinned as he pulled open the icebox door and squatted to chip ice off the block.

Mrs. Herlihy watched him. "So's Eliza," she added.

"What d'you mean?" he said, glancing over his arm at her.

"She's a good woman. Just be careful not to play any games with her."

"Games?" He shattered a corner of the ice into tiny splinters that fell into his waiting glass.

"Mr. Truesdale, I'm real fond of you, you know. And in the years I've been here, I've seen you with any number of lady friends—none of 'em I ever worried about. But now Eliza . . . You'd only be breaking her heart if you played up to her like you do with the others."

Nate latched the door of the icebox and tossed the pick onto the counter. "You think I'm going to start flirting with her?"

"You're under the same roof together."

"I don't think there's anything for you to worry about. Besides, Miss Nolenberg is entirely capable of taking care of herself."

"Is that what you really think?" She shook her head, a small grin on her face as she emptied a bowlful of tiny pink peeled shrimp into the pot on the stove. "And what about you? Are you entirely capable of taking care of that soft heart of yours?"

Nate laughed as he poured bourbon over the ice chips. He thoroughly enjoyed his housekeeper's bluntness and was glad he didn't have the kind of stiff servants Marietta employed. "My heart is already taken by a lovely lady who makes the grandest shrimp soup."

She chuckled and wiped her hands down the front of her apron before catching his arm and pushing him toward the door. "Oh, *you*. Now go on before I really tell you a thing or two!"

"I'm leaving." Nate winked at her as he pushed open the swinging door and walked out through the dining room.

At the stairs he paused, but the upper floor was silent. In the parlor Marietta was still sitting as he had left her.

He could do worse.

Such as marry Tess Brody.

He had seen Tess off and on during the four years before he'd met Marietta, and he had never been with a more cynical woman. It must have been the novelty, he decided. She stood almost as tall as he and observed the world through cold eyes that were perpetually half-closed. Passionate and determined, she had been the one to pursue him into bed. Not that he'd minded. He'd enjoyed it tremendously. But her cynical remarks about people, events, and life in general had begun to wear on him. In addition, he had grown aware of an undercurrent of violent emotions in her that made him apprehensive. He had been disentangling himself from Tess's animal aura when he'd met Marietta. Her lightness, her laughter, her pure sweetness had captivated him immediately.

He strolled toward her and had just resumed his seat beside her when he heard Daisy's rapid steps descending the stairs. She ran into the parlor, braid flying behind her, halted a moment awkwardly as she stared at Marietta, then when Nate motioned to her, she flung herself toward him. She settled beside him with much side-to-side wiggling.

"What are you grinning about, you little scamp?" he teased, rubbing her silky braid between his fingers. "You look like the cat that swallowed the canary."

"What?" She looked up quizzically. "Did you have a canary? Did a cat really eat it?"

Nate laughed, and Marietta reached over to squeeze Daisy's hand as she said, "No, dear, he's just joking. It's an old expression and means you look as if you have a great big secret."

"Oh." Daisy tucked her head into her shoulder and smiled again at Nate. "I do have a secret, but I'm not going to tell."

Nate scooped her into the crook of his arm and glanced up at the sound of Eliza's step approaching the parlor. She entered with her head up, proud as always, arms at her side, back straight—but the brisk greeting he was about to utter died on his lips. His heart struck a double beat in surprise.

Her hair was down, tied in back with a shiny yellow ribbon, and it waved luxuriously around her face, accenting the heart shape of her face, softening her large fawn eyes. Around her neck hung a pearl necklace and golden pendant. Its luminous glow softened the stark black gown and the planes of her face.

Good God, he thought with warm pleasure, she really is lovely. She didn't look anything like a statue. She looked vulnerable, young. He thought of that happy, clear laughter and smiled.

At the sight of them all sitting silently on the sofa looking at her, she halted, much as Daisy had done. Nate caught the almost imperceptible break in her composure and the faint leap of pink in her face. But she swung around and seated herself in the chair across from the sofa, and when she looked up again, her firm self-command was back in place. But the pink remained becomingly bright in her cheeks. He saw her hands folded one atop the other on her lap, the tapered fingers slim and soft despite the years of work. She tucked slender ankles beneath the folds of the black gown.

Her eyes met his, defiant.

And Nate realized he was staring. He averted his eyes and glanced down at Daisy. She was watching him brightly, expectantly. "Is that your secret?" he asked with a broad smile.

"We fixed her hair real pretty, didn't we? Don't you think Aunt Lizzie is pretty?"

Before Nate could answer, Eliza burst out, "Daisy! Why don't you . . . go see how long dinner will be." She spoke breathlessly and finished in a rush, and Nate realized she was painfully embarrassed. The thought touched his heart.

"Oh, I think Aunt Lizzie is more than pretty," he said to Daisy. "I think she's downright beautiful."

Daisy laughed happily, and her eyes shone as she ran from the room. Eliza's face turned a deep pink color. Marietta put her hand over his where it rested on his knee. He patted it absently as he said, "Really, Miss Nolenberg, I like your hair like that. It reminds me of—"

He halted, but she supplied his missing word: "Estelle."

"Yes, I suppose that's what it is," he agreed reluctantly.

"Nothing else about me should remind you of

her," she added defensively. "I'm not like her in the least."

"Of course not." Why was she protesting so vehemently? "I'd never mistake the two of you. Why, the very thought never entered my mind."

He saw the brightness of anger in her gaze, and it was obvious to him that what she protested so strongly was exactly what she wanted. To be just a little more like Estelle? Desired and desirable? He grinned to himself as he contemplated the challenge of wooing the unwooable.

"That's an interesting necklace, Miss Nolenberg," Marietta said, grasping Nate's hand between hers.

Eliza reached up, self-conscious, and fingered the pearls. "It was my mother's. I've never worn it before."

"Oh?" Marietta's eyebrows lifted. "Is there a special reason now?"

"We have a guest for dinner."

"Do you usually dine with the family?"

Leave her alone, Marietta, thought Nate. But Eliza's composure was faultless.

"Always," Eliza answered. "But now, if you'll excuse me, I think I'll see if Mrs. Herlihy needs any help."

As Eliza left the room, Nate looked at the thick glossy dark hair caught into the yellow bow. It formed a waterfall of soft waves down her back. He realized he wanted to pull open the bow, enjoy all that rich, abundant hair.

"I don't know what's going on here, Nate," Marietta said, "but do you really intend that Miss Nolenberg sit at the table with us?"

"The circumstances are unusual," he started to explain, but she interrupted coldly.

"Too unusual! Do you expect me to put up with it?"

"Come on, sweetheart," he said, irritated. "Daisy is at stake here. Be patient."

Marietta sighed and squeezed his fingers reassuringly. "To tell you the truth, Nate, after you get custody of Daisy, I think Miss Nolenberg ought to leave. No, wait, dear—I know you think she'd make a good companion and governess for the child, but after having such privileges in this house, Miss Nolenberg will have ideas beyond her place. She won't fit in easily, don't you understand? She's not of our set, but she'll imagine that she is."

Nate shifted to face her, one arm stretching along the carved back of the sofa. "Our set," he repeated, and thumbed the raised image of a leaf in the wood behind Marietta's head. "Aren't you forgetting where I come from? My father was an immigrant from Italy."

Marietta winced slightly. "Now, Nate, that was a long time ago. Besides, your father was an exceptional man. His name is on hospital plaques and library memorials and schools. Almost every week I hear or see something about Arnold Truesdale and the fine contributions he made."

Such a fine man! The old hypocrite! Nate thought. "But what if Miss Nolenberg is an exceptional woman that no one knows about yet?" he asked.

"Are you defending her to me?" Marietta's eyes darkened to violet.

"No, sweetheart." He leaned over and kissed one upraised eyebrow. "Just trying to understand some things. I hear them in the dining room now. Shall we go into dinner?"

"Just a minute." Marietta smiled up at him, her eyes slanting. She ran her fingers through the short black curls on his head and drew him to her. She pressed her mouth to his and kissed him as deeply as he desired, then stroked his chest and slipped her fingers between his thighs.

When Nate drew back from her, he commented with a wry twist of his mouth, "Well, I can't walk in there now. Give me a minute to get back to normal."

Marietta smiled with what he vaguely suspected was triumph.

In the following days, Eliza wore her hair in the new waves and plump rolls, always with a ribbon, though, instead of loose down her back. She looped the tail of hair in shining whorls behind her head.

Nate made an effort to be friendlier, but she clung to her aloof briskness. The sound of the clear, girlish laughter he had overheard from the foot of the stairs haunted him. He found himself waiting, listening, almost stalking her in the hope of discovering her in a carefree moment or of hearing a giggle.

He came home early one afternoon on a day when the sun was huge in an unusually clear sky, intending to spend a few hours working in the yard—one of the few occupations that engaged him thoroughly, mind, body, and soul. But when he entered the front door he found Daisy sitting on the stairs, crying huge tears that fell one after another in rapid succession down her cheeks. Though he had witnessed tearful scenes several times in his life, he had never seen such a display.

He bent his long legs and sat on the bottom step next to her. "Where's the crocodile?" he asked.

Daisy hiccupped through her tears. "What crocodile?" she said in a dull voice that jerked convulsively.

"These are called crocodile tears," Nate said, and touched her wet cheek with his finger. "So where did you hide the crocodile? Is he in this hand?'' He tried to lift her hand for a playful search, but she clenched her fist and yanked it from him.

''I don't care about crocodiles!'' she answered, shoulders twitching with her hiccups. ''I just wanta go home! I wanta go h-h-home! There's no one here to play with. I wanta see Marjorie and Katie at school, and Mrs. Riley, and have all my old toys, and my—my mama!'' She cried more loudly and jerked away from him when he tried to put his arm around her. ''No!'' she exclaimed, mouth open and wet with abundant tears. ''*I want my mama!*''

''Daisy,'' he said sadly, and tried to pull her toward him again. But she pushed him away, screaming ''No!'' and hugged the wall as she cried.

''Where's Aunt Lizzie?'' he asked, uncertain how to deal with the situation.

''She—she—she went out.''

''Where?''

''To find a job. And Mrs. Herlihy is washing clothes with someone in the backyard.''

That would be Sylvia Hatcher, he knew, who appeared regularly to help with laundry and cleaning.

''I'm here, Daisy. Why don't you and I go take a walk?''

''No-o-o! I don't wanta take a walk!'' The hiccups grew stronger. ''I wanta go home!''

''You miss your friends,'' he said soothingly. He tried to put a smile in his voice. ''That's called being homesick, and it happens to everybody—even me.''

''I don't care!'' she exclaimed, and cried all the harder in that extravagant expression of grief that comes so easily to children.

Nate stretched out his legs along the hall floor and rubbed his palms on his trousers as he watched her. He felt horribly inadequate. He couldn't decide what to do in the situation, so he just sat beside her in silent commiseration. It would have seemed too heartless to walk away, but she had resisted his every effort to hold or comfort her. She'd have to quit sooner or later. But this waiting was distinctly uncomfortable.

At last she grew calm. She gulped air as the sobs grew more hushed. He stroked her hair, and this time she threw her arms around his neck and pushed her wet face against the front of his shirt. "I want my mama," she whined. Nate lifted her across his legs and hugged her to his chest.

"Oh, baby dear," he said softly, "I know you miss her."

She looked up at him. Her face was wet and shiny, and her small body jerked spastically with the aftereffects of such violent sobbing. He picked the hair out of her face where it was stuck with the tears.

"I have an idea," he said. She looked at him skeptically. "Would you like to find some little girls to play with?"

"I don't know," she said without interest, and leaned against his chest again, curling her legs around his knees.

"There's a school just a couple of blocks away, and I think it would be a good idea for you to go there." He lifted the hair from the curve of her neck and smoothed it down her back. "Don't want you to forget your lessons. And there are lots of little girls."

Daisy shrugged and uttered a quivering sigh. "I guess so," she said again in a dispirited tone.

Nate coaxed her head up. Solemnly he wiped her cheeks with the flat of his thumbs. "I love your smile, baby dear," he said. "Will you show me your smile?"

Daisy smiled halfheartedly.

"Ah," he said, grinning broadly in triumph, and put his hand to his heart. "What a dream smile.

You're going to break my heart with such beautiful smiles.''

She smiled again, more brightly this time, and tucked her head against his shoulder. "Do you really like me?" she asked.

"Oh, I like you so much you'll never guess!" he answered.

"I like you," she said. "You're handsome. I'm going to faint!" And she threw herself against his arm, shutting her eyes in imitation of a feminine swoon that dissolved into giggles.

"What a heartbreaker you're going to be," Nate said, shaking his head in confused wonder.

"Is that good?" she asked, sitting up straight again.

Nate drew back in surprise. "Well, I don't know. That depends."

"On what?"

"Well, on—well, on lots of things." How do you describe such a thing to a seven-year-old? he wondered. He tried to find a way to rescue himself. "Why don't you come outside with me and help trim the roses, eh?"

"All right," she said brightly, and hopped off his lap.

What a bundle of surprises she was!

The woman was a witch. It was the first image to appear in Eliza's mind as the door of the narrow, three-storied house opened and she faced a tiny, wizened figure no taller than her shoulder. Quick eyes the color and depth of a summer sky gazed up from a face so matted with wrinkles that the woman looked as if someone had wadded up her skin as if it were a piece of paper and then tried to smooth it out again.

"May I help you?" The voice from that tiny frame

emerged as husky and deep as a dockside dray-
man's. "You're here to fetch back a gown?"

"No, I'm not. Are you Mrs. Penchelli?"

"Yes." The bent witch figure stepped back as she
added, "Won't you come in," and Eliza entered a
dim foyer redolent with the lingering perfumes of
many women.

"My name is Eliza Nolenberg," Eliza began, eyes
drawn to stacks of boxes and tissue-wrapped clothes
hanging on a rod in what appeared to be a dining
room to the left of the foyer. "I received your name
from the owner of the cloak shop just down the
street. I understand you might be looking for a
seamstress, and I've come to ask about employment."

Mrs. Penchelli nodded and with slow, deliberate
steps, began to ascend the stairs to the side of the
long hall leading off the foyer. "Come upstairs and
we can talk."

Eliza followed the woman into a long room on the
second floor. It appeared to have been two bedrooms at one time, but the intervening wall had been
removed to create a workroom. Though it was early
afternoon and the sun was bright outside, the room
was dark except for the artificial light provided by
four flickering gas jets in the wall and two oil lamps,
each set in the center of a long worktable. A thin,
gray-haired woman stood at the farthest table, piec-
ing together sections of iridescent turquoise-blue
satin.

"Some fabrics fade rapidly in sunlight," Mrs.
Penchelli explained in her deep voice. "It's in the
dye. So we shutter the windows and use the lamps.
I've grown accustomed to it." With thin, remarkably
agile fingers, she pointed to the woman on the other
side of the room. "My daughter. But come over
here."

Eliza passed rolled fabrics standing on end in double rows against the wall; a dresser topped by small boxes containing scissors, papers of pins, an assortment of gingham-covered wrist pincushions; and two padded forms of the human female body standing on wire frames. She took a seat on the stool indicated, while Mrs. Penchelli lowered herself to the other, facing her.

"Tell me about your experience," the woman began.

Eliza had never been a professional seamstress; she had only the clothing she'd sewn for herself and her family to her credit. She described her situation to Mrs. Penchelli, who nodded.

"We'll see," she said. "Now stand up and remove your cape, please."

Eliza did so, and the woman studied the prim black gown, making Eliza turn so she could see it from every angle. She picked at the seams. "Did you do the mending? A good hand you have there. I'll try you with a man's shirt. The pay's not so high as for an evening gown, but if you prove yourself, I'll give you as much work as you want."

As she said this, Mrs. Penchelli moved slowly around a desk facing from the wall behind her and stooped to lift a box the size of a hatbox from the floor. She deposited this on the desk and lifted the lid.

"I conduct business in my own way; it works well. Here's the fabric—this paper holds the specifications and instructions from the customer. See that you follow them exactly. Buttons, thread, needles, pins—in short, everything you'll need to complete the shirt—are included here. Except for when using certain more sensitive fabrics, all my seamstresses work at their homes. Use only threads and trimmings you receive here. There are certain standards I insist upon. If you need more, please come to me for them. Return the garment when you're finished, but no later than noon two days from now."

"And the pay?" Eliza asked.

"You'll be paid by the piece. This shirt will be a dollar twenty, a gown such as my daughter is working on will be as much as fifteen dollars in some cases."

Eliza nodded. "And how much work can I expect? This is important to me, Mrs. Penchelli—I need the money."

Summer-blue eyes peered shrewdly at Eliza. "I assign work to those who are eager for it. If there's nothing for you on one day, return the next day and the next. You come to me. And one more thing: return every bit of unused thread and binding, every needle and pin, whatever's been given to you for each piece. I know what's given and how much is required to complete each garment. Do not use my materials for other projects."

"I understand, Mrs. Penchelli," Eliza said, holding her hand to her heart to still the wild beating that threatened to burst her chest. So she had at last found employment, and such that would pay her according to the swiftness and perfection of her work—instead of wages that never rose, or did so at too slow a pace to be of much use to her in her situation with Mr. Truesdale. Now she could hire a lawyer.

Mrs. Penchelli lowered herself to the chair behind the desk and pulled two ledgers toward her. In the first she copied Eliza's name and address. In the second went Eliza's current sewing project.

"You'll do fine, Eliza." The bent woman smiled for the first time. "Remember, I employ more than twenty women, all highly accomplished. If you're not here, someone else will get the work."

Eliza thanked Mrs. Penchelli, and with the box in her arms, hurried back to the mansion on Nob Hill. She rushed through the front door but saw no one and received no answer when she called to Daisy. Unalarmed and eager to start, Eliza carried the box to her room, pinned back her sleeves, and set to work.

Three hours later, as the light failed toward dusk, Eliza put the sewing aside and stood to relieve the cramped muscles in her back and neck. She had been so preoccupied she had not given thought to where Daisy might be. Sure that the girl was with Mrs. Herlihy, Eliza was not concerned. She went down to the kitchen, entering by the hall door just as Mrs. Herlihy was taking her hat and coat from the hooks inside the pantry door.

"There you are, Eliza," Mrs. Herlihy exclaimed. "I was just about to look for you. Would you mind finishin' up the supper for me? I just got a message that my husband, my Bob, has been feelin' poorly today and is askin' for me, and I want to leave early."

"I wouldn't mind at all, Mrs. Herlihy. I hope it's nothing serious."

"He has bad days now and again," she said, straightening the collar of her coat. "Just need to brown the potatoes—they're washed and peeled and settin' in that bowl—and keep the roast cookin' slow in the oven for a mite longer. Greens are simmerin' over there." Mrs. Herlihy settled her hat on her head and shoved a long pin through the crown. "There's a dear," she exclaimed, pressing a kiss to Eliza's cheek. "I should be back tomorrow. We'll need the wages if Bob has to have more of his medicine."

Eliza followed her to the back door and stood on the landing as Mrs. Herlihy spoke to Nate who had harnessed her horse—Old Johnny, she called him—

to the wagon she used for transportation. A minute later the housekeeper was slapping the reins on the horse's rump and guiding him down the sloping graveled drive that led to the side street.

Daisy appeared out of the evening's gloom and hopped up the steps toward Eliza. Her face was smudged with dirt, her hands left muddy stains on the white railing, and her dress was matted with leaves and mud.

"Mr. Truesdale let me work in the garden with him! He says I'm a good gardener. I'm a good cook, I'm a good gardener. And he's going to take me to school tomorrow!"

"School?" Eliza's attention was caught between Daisy's appearance and the sight of Nate strolling toward the stairs. He had just locked the side door of the carriage house where he had replaced a shovel. He wore muddied work pants, boots, and a muslin shirt, collarless, the sleeves rolled back over his sturdy forearms. With the black earth caked on him, he looked vital and virile, like a god of nature.

"School?" she repeated, distracted by too many things at once and not knowing where to focus her attention first.

Nate mounted the stairs and paused beside her, glancing sideways with a grin as he bent to unlace and remove his boots before entering the house. He carried the fecund scent of wet black soil, and he had never seemed so strong, so entirely masculine. "Don't you agree she shouldn't neglect her lessons in the meantime?" he said. "Come along, Daisy, I'll help you get cleaned up for dinner."

Eliza followed them into the house. "I will see to Daisy." With hands on Daisy's shoulders, Eliza steered her down the short hall off the kitchen and into the large bathroom with its floor-to-shoulder wood molding and faded yellow ceiling. As she lit the lamp in its brass wall sconce, Eliza exclaimed, "What were you doing? You look as if you were rolling around in the mud!" Without waiting for an answer, she went back to the kitchen and returned with a bucketful of water kept hot in the side of the stove. She poured it into the tub and added cold water from the big iron tap as Daisy stripped off her dress and stockings.

Smooth and plump in her little-girl nakedness, Daisy stepped into the tub, protesting happily, "All good gardeners get muddy, Aunt Lizzie. That's what Nate—Mr. Truesdale—says. He says it's good, the mud. It gives life to all the plants."

Eliza decided not to get into another argument with Daisy. "Wash yourself well. I'll be back with clean clothes for you. And hurry. I still have to finish cooking supper."

In the kitchen Nate stood at the sink in his wool socks and soaped his forearms, digging the mud off his skin with his thumbs. Eliza paused with Daisy's dirty garments in her arms.

"Mr. Truesdale, I don't appreciate this." She held out the clothes. "And you have no authority to decide about Daisy's schooling."

He glanced aside at her with mild indifference, then back at his hands. "Where were you this afternoon?" he inquired. He lifted his dripping arms and stepped in front of her as he peered over her shoulder toward the bathroom. "Is the door there closed?"

"Of course it's closed," Eliza exclaimed. "I wouldn't leave Daisy undressed with the door open. And you here."

Nate's eyes widened, and he leaned down to within inches of her face as his voice exploded in a loud whisper. "I don't want her to *overhear* me.

What other little thoughts are in that perverted mind of yours?''

/ Eliza jerked back, but before she could find a retort, he said, "I came home today to find that poor little girl crying like the world had come to an end." He plunged his dripping brown arms into the water again. "I invited her to help me outside, because it seems, Aunt Lizzie, you were off on some selfish pursuit. Helping me out there cheered her right up, and she and I together decided she should go to school. She needs to be around other little girls as friends, to have school lessons to occupy her so that she doesn't get too far behind the others in their studies while we're carrying on here about her future."

"It was not a selfish pursuit!" Eliza said, choosing to address the issue that struck the most guilt in her. "I had to find employment—for Daisy's sake. And I did."

"Look." He flung the water from his hands and yanked a towel off the rack beside the sink. "Let's get something clear. Let's just both of us acknowledge that we have Daisy's welfare at heart. Let's work together as long as we have to be together. Otherwise, that little girl in there is going to get hurt in the crossfire."

"Then don't accuse me of selfish pursuits when I'm trying to do what I must for her!"

"All right, a valid point. I said that in anger over your insinuations. But since we're stuck together for the duration, we have to establish some sort of truce. You have to believe that I have Daisy's best interests at heart, and not continually accuse *me* at every turn."

Eliza looked away from the honesty of his gaze. He was right. And more than that, he had been kind and thoughtful in all things concerning Daisy. She struggled in her heart to admit this to herself. In so many ways he had been more than considerate.

Eliza nodded. "You have been . . . decent," she said. "A truce it is, then. But only a temporary one, until I can take Daisy home again." She looked up at him in defiance, the hint of tears in her eyes. Her voice was strong but quavered slightly as she said, "And I will be taking her home again."

Nate made no response, only looked at her with a frown.

When Eliza started out of the kitchen, she glanced toward the bathroom and found the door open a few inches, Daisy's hurt-filled, confused eyes peering at her. When she realized she had been discovered, Daisy shut the door.

Chapter 6

Shifting his top hat from hand to hand, Nate pulled an overcoat over his tuxedo as he descended the long curving stairs. Though the afternoon had been warm, the Pacific wind and fog had sent the evening temperatures plunging twenty degrees. In the larger parlor behind the formal front room, the fire he had lit before going upstairs to get dressed for the evening burned low and warm.

Daisy lay on her stomach on the floor in front of the hearth, her legs bent at the knees, ankles crossed and weaving back and forth in the air. She was looking at pictures in a book. Eliza sat in a chair drawn closer to the fire. Her head was bent over another of the sewing projects she worked so diligently on these days. He could not quite tell yet what this one was going to be.

Eliza's cheeks were flushed in the firelight, and a tiny frown puckered her eyebrows. She alternately pursed her lips and bit on the lower one as she concentrated. What was she thinking of besides the stitches? Tonight she wore a pink satin ribbon in her hair—an incongruous touch of gaiety, but not at all unwelcome. He delighted in it.

Nate watched from beyond the doorway. Of late, Eliza and Daisy had taken to spending evenings here with him instead of locking themselves away in their rooms upstairs. Though there was usually little in the way of conversation between them, the silences were companionable. He watched them enviously. He wished he hadn't let Marietta talk him into attending Ned Greenway's cotillion tonight.

Daisy rolled onto her back and saw him. She jumped up and ran toward him; a few strands of her hair had slipped from her braid.

"Are you going out?" she asked.

"To a big party," he said. "I promised Miss Sharpe."

"But you were going to help me with my lessons tonight," Daisy protested. "You promised me you'd help." She slid her moist warm hand into his and tried to lead him into the room.

Good grief, he'd forgotten all about it. "Listen, Daisy," he started to say, but she was poking one finger into the hard veins on the back of his hand.

"Why do your hands do that? That's the way old people's hands look." She was engrossed in mashing the veins with her fingertip and watching them swell and rise again.

"I guess that's what I am then, an old man."

"I guess," she agreed.

He tried to shake loose his hand from her grasp. "Look, Daisy, I'm sorry about your lessons. Really, I feel bad about this, but I have to go out tonight."

Daisy clung to his hand, now gripping it with both of hers. "No, you promised to help me." She regarded him with a coaxing smile.

"Now look, I said I'm sorry. I just can't stay, and I'm a bit late already . . ." Nate put the top hat on his head and used his free hand to try to extricate himself. "I know you'll do just fine with your work. You're a smart young lady. And Aunt Lizzie is here." But Daisy hung on, pouting.

He glanced at Eliza, who was watching them. His eyes pleaded for help, but she only lifted her eyebrows in a gentle refusal. Nate scowled at her. He was already in a bad humor from having let Marietta talk him into this cotillion, and from the news he had learned today that Rossie Watts had rehired Joseph Washington, the skipper Nate had fired several weeks earlier. That news alone was enough to set him off.

His voice rose angrily as he set Daisy away from him. "I'll be home tomorrow night, I swear to you, and I can help you then."

Her lower lip jutted forth, and she appeared to be on the verge of tears. "Look," he said, "I just can't help you tonight! Try to understand—"

"No!" Daisy screamed the word at him and pushed past him when he tried to hold her back. "You promised!" she shouted as she ran across the hall toward the stairs. "You're not my friend! I hate you!"

"Daisy!" Nate exclaimed as he followed, his face heating with impatience. "I said I'm sorry! I'll help you tomorrow night—word of honor!"

"I don't want to see you again! Ever!" she yelled down from the top of the stairs, and ran into her room, the slam of the door breaking off the sound of her crying.

Nate marched back to the parlor door. Eliza remained seated beside the fire as if nothing had happened. "Aren't you going to do something?" he snapped.

"No," she answered calmly as she unraveled red threads dangling from her needle. "This is between the two of you."

Nate swung his arm in front of his chest and pointed to the stairs. "But she's upset. She's crying!"

"And why is that?"

Damn Eliza for that calm self-sufficiency of hers, Nate thought. "You know damned good and well why. Don't you care?"

Eliza lifted her head and looked at him at last. "Don't you?"

"Well, of course, I do!"

"Daisy will be fine. It's a disappointment, that's all. She'll get over it." Eliza went back to her sewing. "Why don't you go on? If you're late, Miss Sharpe will be disappointed."

"Ah!" He yanked at the lapels of his overcoat. "So it's a question of who to disappoint, is it? My daughter or the woman I might marry. And you're thinking I'm rejecting Daisy. I can see it in your eyes, Miss Nolenberg. You think the 'novelty' has worn off as you predicted, and now I'm rejecting Daisy—well, that's not it!"

"Mr. Truesdale, you're getting very worked up over nothing significant."

"Daisy is very significant to me! And you just sit there ignoring her crying up there!"

Eliza threw the sewing to the floor and stood up, advancing on him. "If you get custody of Daisy and I'm not here, what are you going to do then? If you think these kinds of little scenes with her are never going to happen, then you're dreaming rainbows! If you want to be her father, then take the responsibility. Don't ask me to patch it all up!"

She stood adamantly close in front of him, the firelight catching her hair, her eyes hard and hot, her rosebud lips puckered in defiance.

Excitement incited by anger hit his brain and flared in his loins. The quarrel was abruptly absent from his mind, though the residue of emotion still burned in him. He stared at her . . . and sensed the change almost at once. As if something palpable leaped between them.

Without thinking, he caught her face between his hands and kissed that provocative mouth. And although, in all his imagining of such a moment, he hadn't planned it to be so, the kiss was hard and bruised him as much as it must her. But he didn't let up. He couldn't let up.

To Eliza his kiss was a revelation. Though she had received attentions from some of the men at the mill, no other kiss had ever been so potent or caused such a stirring deep inside her. How had it happened? How could one kiss be so different? How could one man's kiss seem so right compared to the others? His arms dropped and closed around her, and she was pulled against him. She swayed into him, enraptured with the sensations, forgetting all other thoughts. Until the one question—"Why?"—rose in her mind.

Nate held her tightly, his manhood stretching and tingling against her warmth. She was exciting in his arms. Her body, so astonishingly delicate, molded to his with ease and eagerness. He marveled at the sweetness of her response, her avid answering mouth, the heat of her breasts crushed to his chest. He held her all the closer.

Before Nate knew what was happening, Eliza reared back and slapped him hard across the cheek.

He dropped his arms and stared at her in angry surprise, his face burning. He heard her shallow breathing, whether from passion or outrage or both, he didn't know.

"Hadn't you better leave?" she said.

Damn right! he thought. "What's the matter, Miss Nolenberg—did you forget your anger for a minute?" He lifted his eyebrows in a faint, mocking question.

Eliza caught her breath in renewed outrage. "You thought I'd allow you to . . . grab me like that?"

"My mistake. I was under the impression you enjoyed it, but obviously that's not the case."

She could find nothing to say. It was true that in his arms she'd known pleasure that swelled in her breasts and left a sweet ache in her middle. She could still feel the heat of his mouth on her lips.

At her silence, Nate said more softly, "I'm sorry if I upset you. I didn't mean to kiss you, though I admit I've wanted to for some time. Even though you try to hide it, you're actually an attractive—"

"You're going to be late," she reminded him, her heart beating swiftly in strange, sweet excitement at his words. She had to look away from the warm light of his eyes; he was too handsome by far.

"Right," he snapped, and she knew he was angry again.

Nate readjusted his top hat as he strode to the front door. Outside, the chill Pacific wind hit him. He skimmed rapidly down the brick stairs and whistled for a cab.

Eliza listened to his departure, her fingertips sliding over her still-tingling lips. Why had he kissed her? Why had she allowed it? And beyond that, why had she so enjoyed it? He had abandoned her sister; he could just as easily love and abandon her.

And he was going to marry Marietta Sharpe. He would take everything from her—even Daisy—and leave her nothing!

Plump, genial Ned Greenway was shaking his hand. "Nate, it's been too long. You used to join us all the time. I could always count on you to help keep all our little debutantes dancing out their slippers. Where have you been lately?"

"I must have danced out my own shoes."

Ned laughed. "Hope you have a new pair now. Can I count on you to help me keep some of the girls happy tonight? Good man." He slapped Nate's shoulder and leaned close to his ear to say, "A few of the plainer ones are getting ignored by the fellows, poor girls. But what do you think? I tried to pair that one over there in the peach gown with a fellow for her first turn around the floor, and she refused to dance with him. Said he was a married man and she didn't want to waste her time. Trouble with her is she wasn't spanked often enough as a child."

Ned shook Nate's hand once again before moving away to speak to someone else. Ned Greenway's cotillions, known as Greenways, were more popular with the young men than Mrs. Salisbury's fortnightlies for the simple reason that Ned served champagne with the supper. Nate helped himself to a glass now as he looked over the young men and women crowded into the Native Sons' Hall. Crystal gaslights along the walls gave a honey-tinged aura to the room, and the couples circling in a waltz appeared to be moving through pale liquid.

No one's home was large enough to accommodate such gatherings, and hotels weren't private enough, so Ned used this place and Mrs. Salisbury held her fortnightlies in Lunt's Hall, a dancing academy on Polk Street. Both Native Sons' Hall and Lunt's Hall were shabby, but no one minded.

Nate glanced around. He was glad the imprint of a hand on his face had subsided. What a fool he had been! What had made him kiss Eliza like that? He took a quick swallow of champagne.

That kiss had been something else again. He could almost feel her slender body bending so easily into his embrace . . .

He heard a deep feminine laugh, infectious in its

heartiness, and turned to look, knowing Tess Brody was nearby. Her auburn head was clearly visible above the others. Tess was built like a goddess and was utterly ruthless. She glanced up and noticed him at the same instant. Again he heard her loud laughter, and she was shaking her head as she extricated herself from the group around her. She came toward him, looking stunning in her gilt-trimmed ivory gown. A matching golden silk scarf shimmered around her neck. He frowned slightly at the sight of it.

"Nate, you old rascal, what brought you out tonight?"

"Hello, Tess." He grinned and lifted her proffered hand to kiss it. "Aren't you getting too old for these things?"

"Not at all. I'm old only compared to the juvenile company you've been keeping lately. Incidentally, I'll be joining you again next week at your house."

"What for?"

"Your Thanksgiving dinner. I'm being escorted around now by Rossie, didn't you know? He's invited me."

With all the to-do over Daisy, Nate had forgotten about the Thanksgiving tradition. He and Rossie hosted a dinner for employees who had no other family to join for the holiday. Because he had the bigger house, Nate held the dinner, and Rossie paid a larger share for the food and drink.

"Is Rossie here tonight too?" Nate asked.

"Nope, playing cards somewhere, which I doubt he'd want spread about."

"Very considerate of you to mention it then."

"I thought you hated him."

"When did you and Rossie start keeping company?"

Tess smirked. "Don't tell me—are you jealous?"

"Not a bit. You two are perfect for each other. I can't think of anyone who deserves your dangerous little clutches more than Rossie." Nate glanced again at her scarf and, as memory returned to him, his mouth tightened. He'd seen that scarf caught in the weeds in front of one of the crimp's boarding-houses. So Tess was making forays down to the waterfront. The thought should have surprised him, but it didn't. He'd long ago grown wary of her love of danger and animal appetites, and doubted if there was anything she wouldn't do to satisfy them. "I could say your standards have fallen, but then again, you don't have any, do you?"

Tess laughed. "You're the one to talk, boy. Where's that universally pampered child you spend so much time with these days?"

"Marietta's upstairs leaving her coat."

"Now that was really robbing the cradle. She's at least ten years younger than you are. Maybe more?" The heavy-lidded tawny eyes looked long and hard at him. "You let me know if you get tired of nursery games."

Nate gave her upper arm a quick, unobtrusive squeeze as he nodded amiably to an acquaintance passing on the periphery of the dance floor. "Not a chance. Besides, we're just friends, Tess," he said, low. "Remember?"

She gave a halfhearted laugh that ended in a sigh. "You bastard," she said tightly.

"Ah, sweetheart, you're stooping to name-calling." He smiled a greeting as someone else he recognized raised a hand to say hello from a distance. "We did enough of that before. No need to resort to burning insults now. Put a smile on your face. People are beginning to notice us."

She gave her usual cynical half-smile. "Friends

should be able to tell each other the truth always. And I think you're a jackass.''

Nate laughed with such abrupt amusement that he almost spilled his champagne. ''I agree with you there, Tess.'' He switched the glass to his other hand and shook a drop from the side of his finger. ''I'm a jackass, and I'll be the first to admit it. You'll have to do worse than that.''

''Oh, I will, Nate. Uh-oh, hang onto your trousers, here's the child now.''

Marietta threaded her way toward them. Her fashionably bustle-less gown was sewn with vertical strips of rose and white silk and left a portion of her white shoulders bare. She and Tess offered each other their cheeks in a chilling parody of an embrace.

Marietta smiled too brightly. ''Why, Tess dear, you look lovely tonight.''

''The same to you, you sweet little thing you.'' Tess turned her back on them and walked away into the crowd.

''Oh, Nate, she makes me so angry! Why, I could just scream! What was she saying to you? Probably making herself a nuisance as usual.''

''As usual. Here, dance this next waltz with me; Ned's coming this way, and he's going to want me to dance with some horse-faced debutante who can't tell one foot from another.''

Marietta laughed, feigning shock, and put her hand on Nate's arm as he steered them past a tray, where he deposited his glass, then into the crowd of dancers. ''Besides,'' he said, smiling down at her as they moved effortlessly in time to the music, ''I should be able to claim your first dance, shouldn't I?''

''And the seat beside mine at supper?'' Marietta crinkled her eyes in a teasing smile.

"Don't you dare offer it to anyone else."

"Now, Nate, you're acting like a husband . . . or a fiancé at least, claiming such privileges."

Marietta was trying to tease him, but instead of provoking a smile or a protest, she reminded him of Eliza. Why in hell should he think of her now? She did nothing but accuse him or reprimand him or ignore him in that aloof way she had. Bigger fool, he, kissing her like that!

"Nate, what are you so angry about?"

"Huh?" He almost missed a step. "What makes you think I'm angry?"

"The back of your jaw always swells a little when you're angry, and it was doing it just now." Marietta tried a brisk smile. "If you can't appreciate a joke, then maybe I should seek out a more entertaining supper partner."

"I'm sorry. Just thinking about some things that upset me earlier."

"Tess?"

"No . . . uh . . . Daisy and I had a bit of a misunderstanding."

"Nate, do you remember—it was here at a Greenway just last year that we met." Marietta smiled wistfully and looked up into his eyes. "Do you remember that night? You were the most handsome man I'd ever seen, and I begged Ned to arrange a dance between us."

"I remember," Nate said, grinning. "I didn't want to stop dancing with you that night. You were the first debutante who didn't mash my shoes once during an entire dance." He caught sight of John Ryckman, his lawyer, standing near the dance floor.

"Ryckman's here," he exclaimed. "Listen, I'm going to steer us over to the side there. I've been trying to get in touch with that scoundrel for two weeks. Just want to talk to him for a minute."

Marietta pouted briefly. "All right. But sometime tonight I want an entire dance with you all to myself."

Nate and Marietta stopped in front of the lawyer, and the two men shook hands.

"Where've you been?" Nate asked. "I've been trying to get in touch with you, but all your office would say is that you were out of town."

John Ryckman was a thin, nervous, precise young man. "Now, Nate," he said, "there's no need for you to worry. I was in Sacramento for a couple of weeks, but I've got everything under control as far as your case goes. We have a court date set for February seventh."

"February! Good God, why so long a wait?"

"It's the Christmas season," Ryckman explained quickly. "Backs up every year. I did what I could, but so many of the judges leave town—there's nothing anybody can do."

Marietta grimaced. "Oh, Nate, we'll have to put up with that Miss Nolenberg till February."

He regarded her with an inscrutable expression. "That's right," he said, feeling not at all put out anymore. "Well, thanks, John. Don't worry about it. Happy Thanksgiving."

Eliza counted her money again. She had thirty-eight dollars and fifty-five cents. But more precious than that was the promise from Mr. McPherson, expressed in his return letter to her. She held it up before the lamp on her writing table as she reread:

I feel as if this entire situation is my fault. I was intending to send you money, but instead I will come out there myself to handle your case. You and Daisy were very nearly my own family, and I cannot abandon you at this point. Delay the court date as I cannot arrive until mid-January. If you have employment by this time, as you said you wished, so much the better. I will gather sworn affidavits to attest to your character and naturally exceptional talents for raising Daisy. Your employer, Mr. Jenkins, has already signed a statement to the effect that he is holding your job and will raise your weekly pay to nine dollars on your return. Remain in good cheer, dear Eliza. All will be well! You are in an excellent position, and we should have no trouble gaining custody of our dear Daisy.

In addition to that cheering news, Mr. McPherson had also sent three twenty-dollar bills to see them through the weeks until their return. All total, Eliza now had almost one hundred dollars. She had never in her life held so much money at one time.

Enough to contemplate making herself a new gown for the annual Thanksgiving Day festivities.

Mrs. Herlihy had talked of nothing else for the last week. Sylvia Hatcher, the local girl she hired for extra help, was already bumping around in the second-floor drawing room every day as she swept down cobwebs, polished chairs, and washed the crystal globes of the gaslamps.

If she had to dip into Mr. McPherson's money, Eliza thought, she would pay him back when they had all returned home. But there was a roll of beautiful teal-blue silk in Mrs. Penchelli's workroom . . .

Much relieved to be near success after the previous weeks of despair, Eliza was smiling as she entered the dining room the following morning. She carried the plate of eggs and graham rolls to which she had helped herself in the kitchen.

"Good morning, Mr. Truesdale," she said lightly,

sweeping out her heavy black skirt as she took a seat at the far end of the table.

Nate's coffee cup hit the saucer.

Eliza glanced up at the sound. He was studying her over a corner of the newspaper clutched in one hand, an absentminded frown on his face. His empty breakfast plate was shoved aside to make room for the paper and coffee cup. He was dressed for work in a starched white shirt and a wool suit of tiny beige and black checks. Morning sunlight whitened the linen tablecloth between them.

"You're smiling," he commented. He lowered the paper further to glance at her plate. "Not only that, but you have an appetite. I'm almost afraid to ask what the occasion might be."

They had ignored each other for the two days since the night of his kiss. Eliza had kept Daisy upstairs in the evenings, despite the girl's protests, and the dining table had been the scene of silent suppers. Silent except for Daisy's chatter—about her new friends, her new teacher, and the games of Old Diggelly Bones she played in the schoolyard.

Eliza was still smiling in triumph as she said, "I'd like to have the court date set for no sooner than mid-January, Mr. Truesdale. Not that I want to remain here such a length of time, but it's what my lawyer wishes."

"Ah, you have a lawyer. That's what the good humor is all about." A muscle tensed in his lean jaw. "How does the seventh of February suit you?"

"You've already had a date and didn't bother to tell me or make sure I agreed?"

The newspaper snapped as he closed it, folded it, and smacked it down beside his coffee cup. "How could I? I'm not about to discuss it in front of Daisy, and you've been a damned disappearing sphinx these last couple of days."

With an effort, Eliza kept her gaze on his alarmingly beautiful blue stare. She wanted to make some remark about him taking liberties that night, but she could not bring herself to refer to the kiss aloud. It was so much easier to pretend it hadn't happened, to hide emotion behind their usual antagonism. "Since neither of us wishes to subject Daisy to a court battle, perhaps you'd like to reconsider," she suggested.

"You want me to back down because you have a lawyer? Not likely, Miss Nolenberg. Who is he? I might know him."

"I doubt it. It's Mr. McPherson from Pittsburgh, and he's traveling out here to conduct the case for me. Here, you might want to read this yourself. It may help you change your mind." Eliza took the letter from the pocket in her skirt and walked the length of the table to set the pages on Nate's newspaper. She returned to her seat.

Nate scanned the letter from Mr. McPherson as Eliza ate a buttered graham roll and watched his face.

He looked up with a faint scowl. "You think I'm going to be scared by this? I don't give up that easily. And I still don't believe you have as strong a case as I do—though this is certainly a sight better for you. Let's see, how did you put it?—more points for you."

"Yes, I think you're scared by it," Eliza said. "So why don't we just forget this whole thing. Daisy wants to go home. She keeps asking me why we're staying here. It's getting harder to keep the truth from her."

"Then why don't we tell her the truth? Why don't we tell her who I am?"

"What! That you weren't married to her mother?

I thought you didn't want to hurt her, Mr. Truesdale."

"She's too young to know the difference and . . . all—"he waved his hand in an airy gesture as he searched for words—"all the implications."

"But what about the new friends she has, and her teacher . . . and those new friends telling their parents? It won't take long before she's laughed at, Mr. Truesdale, and ignored by the—"

"*All right!*" Nate exploded. He stood up, grabbed his newspaper, and slapped it against his palm. "I get your point!"

"My letter, please," Eliza murmured.

Nate dropped it on the tablecloth beside her hand. He walked toward the door but paused, hesitated, and returned. "Look, Miss Nolenberg," he said grimly, "I apologize for kissing you."

Eliza blushed and looked away. "Thank you, Mr. Truesdale, but it won't make me change my mind about Daisy."

"Is that what you think I meant? Is that why you think I kissed you in the first place?"

She glanced aside at him and saw he was regarding her with a curious expression, a blend of anger and mystification. He whacked his palm with the newspaper once more. "God almighty!" he exclaimed furiously. "And where is Daisy? She'll be late for school."

"She's getting her book satchel and cape," Eliza started to say, but Nate had left the room. She heard the hard click of his heels on the tiles of the hall, then his shout:

"Daisy! We have to leave!"

Shortly, Daisy's steps sounded muffled and rapid on the staircase, and the front door opened and closed. From the dining room window, Eliza watched them walk hand-in-hand in the pale green sunlight as they crossed the lawn and descended the brick steps.

Eliza stood at the window for a long time.

When she talked to Mrs. Penchelli that morning, the woman was agreeable. "Certainly, Eliza, you can purchase any materials you like." The tiny wrinkled woman smiled as she held a length of fabric up to Eliza's chin. "The blue silk is a good choice for you. I don't know how you're planning to design it, but try it a little off the shoulder. From what I've seen, you've got the clearest skin, Eliza. Show it while you've got it, eh? And let me see the gown when it's finished. If you're any good, I could use you on a few new things."

Daisy was as delighted as Eliza over the fabric. "It's so pretty, Aunt Lizzie!" she exclaimed that afternoon after school as she rubbed the folds of material between her palms. "It's so soft." Daisy climbed onto the bed to sit beside Eliza. She rubbed her hand over the front of Eliza's stiff black gown, as if to reassure herself. "You won't be the same."

"Oh, yes, I will." Eliza laughed and put her arm around the small warm body that fit so well in her arms, that had always fit so well in her arms.

I think Aunt Lizzie's more than pretty. I think she's downright beautiful.

Eliza recalled Nate's words as she studied her reflection in the mirror. "Why are you so excited?" she asked herself out loud.

Hypnotically bright eyes stared back at her. The woman in the mirror wore a teal-blue silk gown with low-set balloon sleeves and a low square neckline. Stiff, pointed silver lace fanned out around the neckline. The soft silk was smoothed back over her hips to hang in long folds behind her.

The dress emphasized her figure as she had never seen it before.

She felt and looked all woman.

She had swept her hair off her neck, looped it in swirls around a loose knot at the crown of her head, and cut a fringe at her temples and across her forehead. Daisy had showed her how to wet the short strands and twirl them until they dried. They now hung in wispy curls that softened her expression. The woman looking back at her from the mirror sparkled with silver lace and expectant eyes and a radiant smile.

She held out her arms, admiring the new ivory, full-length gloves with their many tiny pearl buttons. She had also purchased for the occasion ivory satin shoes and ivory stockings to match. Lifting her skirt, she pirouetted before the mirror.

Distant voices reached Eliza's ears, and she hurried to the door to listen. People were arriving already! The first group was ascending the stairs to the drawing room. She opened her door a crack and peered out. Three women and two men were being escorted upstairs by the man who had been hired as servant for the evening. Sylvia Hatcher and two other girls were on hand to assist Mrs. Herlihy, who was also a guest tonight. Because this gathering was in honor of his employees, Nate had invited Mrs. Herlihy and her husband.

The gas jets in the hall had been lit, and their light blended with the crystal brightness flowing onto the stairs from the open drawing room doors. The glow illuminated the women in their modestly elegant gowns, their wide skirts flaring around their feet, bodices heavy with lace and ornamental buttons. The men wore black long-tailed coats and trousers. One carried a lit cigar; its pungent odor wafted into Eliza's room.

Nervously tense, as if she waited center stage behind a curtain that was about to go up, Eliza shut the door and went back to the mirror. She studied her reflection with pride.

Prudish old maid, he had said! What are you afraid of? he had said! Not his type!

Though light-headed with eagerness, Eliza frowned severely at her reflection. Nate Truesdale wanted to take Daisy away from her, yet here she was dressing like this, looking like this, all for him!

. . . *downright beautiful.*

"I just want to show him," she said to the mirror. "That's all. Show him. And Marietta." She smoothed the lace, touched her hips, leaned into her reflection again with an earnest appeal: "That's what it is, only that. Nothing more."

Chapter 7

Nate scanned the rapidly filling room and noticed Rossie—short, grinning, and strutting like a banty rooster. Through narrowed eyes Nate idly watched him circulate among the crowd and stop to laugh with one or another of the employees. That new ginger-haired receptionist, Maggie something-or-other, was politely trying to avoid him. What good sense she had. But Rossie wasn't going to be put off. Poor Maggie was being subjected to a lengthy conversation, which was sure to be full of sexual innuendo. Nate contemplated intervening to rescue her and save the company a bright and capable employee, but Maggie put her hand to her forehead in what looked like a pantomime of having had too much champagne, smiled an apology, and left the room. Smart woman.

Nate hoped she wouldn't give notice. But it wouldn't be the first time they'd lost a good office person—male or female—because of Rossie. Nate helped himself to a glass of champagne and drank half of it in one gulp.

"Wonderful party, Mr. Truesdale. I wanted my wife to meet you."

The couple had approached behind Nate, and he turned in surprise. One of the accountants. Bearded and overweight. What was his name again? Bill Ruggle, that was it. The two men shook hands, and Nate smiled at the woman. "Mrs. Ruggle, it's a pleasure." She was equally overweight as her husband and had a mustache. Good match.

After they moved on, others drifted toward Nate where he stood near the center of the room. He smiled graciously. "So glad you could come. So glad. Wonderful night for a party, yes. So glad you could come." The faces were familiar, and he remembered most of the names.

He shook hands until his fingers hurt, smiled until his cheek muscles were numb. Where had all these people come from? In the beginning, because he and Rossie had no family to share Thanksgiving with, they had invited other "orphans" from the company to eat dinner with them. Every year more and more people attended, and Nate realized the Truesdale & Watts Thanksgiving Day dinner was rapidly becoming an event of the season. The working classes playing society for an evening. Marietta hated it, but she attended with him.

With a fresh glass of champagne in hand, Nate escaped and stood by the glass doors leading on to the balcony over the portico. Although the doors were closed, he could feel a slight chill from the panes. It felt good. The green-and-gold brocade drapes had been tied back, but he could smell the mustiness in them. The blond wood floor had been polished so thoroughly that it reflected back each gleam of light. The room was a relentless glare in his eyes, and the air was growing dense with the scents of various colognes, fumes from the gas flames, tobacco smoke, the pungency of formal black coats and trousers packed too long in cedar chests. The noise of so many voices talking at once was a dull roar in his ears.

Two hired musicians in the wide alcove of bay windows overlooking the front lawn played a piano and violin. Couples were already dancing a lively pas de quatre in the center of the room. Good for them. He hoped they all enjoyed themselves but didn't stay till dawn, as so often happened at the society parties he and Marietta attended.

He was just sipping his iced champagne when he saw Eliza enter through the double doors across the room. He choked as he swallowed.

My God, what had she done to herself? He coughed hard and stared at her.

She was beautiful! A vision. And what a smile! What it did for her. She was radiant. The difference in her was more than he could take in all at once.

Her hair was brushed upwards into a soft, curling knot, its dark sheen begging to be stroked. Her delicate heart-shaped face glowed with pink softness. Her eyes were large, velvet-brown, and vibrant. And her shoulders. Look at those shoulders! White and sloping, they were made for kisses. Beneath the long points of silver lace that framed the low neckline of her dress, he saw the curve of her waist and hips sheathed in tight silk. Dear God, what a tiny waist! He wanted to touch the curves, remembered the feel of her surprisingly delicate body bending, willowy and easy, in his arms. His glance abruptly dropped, and he watched the just-perceptible thrust of her thighs beneath the gown as she walked. He pictured them firm and white, imagined stroking them, imagined them feeling warm and as slick as satin.

She turned her head and saw him. She smiled again—with even more radiance. Nate realized he was grinning hugely, like a damned schoolboy.

What an enigma she was! It was exhilarating!

Before Nate could make a move toward her, Rossie was suddenly at her side. He was smiling, saying something. She turned quickly to him, and he took her hand politely. The bastard! And Eliza was smiling at him! Angrily, Nate started toward them, but was halted by a hand on his chest.

Marietta was watching his face curiously. "Nate, you're always so angry lately. What is the matter with you? And your collar is damp, dear. Did you know?"

He pulled her hand from the front of his shirt, too aware of the storm in his chest. "It's hot in here."

"Let's go outside on the balcony."

"No!" He shot a frustrated glance at Eliza and Rossie. They were still talking.

"There's no need to speak so sharply to me."

"Huh? No, of course not. Sorry. It's just that I have to stay around. My party and all." He took a long drink of champagne without tasting it. His attention jumped from Marietta to Eliza and Rossie. She was still smiling at him!

Marietta reached up to push his hair back at his temple. "I know, poor dear. And you're so hot, your hair is a little damp too."

Did she always touch him and pick at him like this? He had never noticed before but was irritated by it now. Rossie was inviting Eliza to dance; he was gesturing to the moving couples as he touched Eliza's arm. Couldn't she tell what a snake he was? But she was still smiling. Nate started to invite Marietta to dance also, planning to get onto the dance floor where he could cut in and—

Cut in? Abandon Marietta on the dance floor? What was he thinking?

But Eliza was refusing to dance. Smart girl. Good girl. He saw Mrs. Herlihy intervene and lead Eliza toward the side wall near the entrance where her husband was sitting in one of the salon chairs. She was introducing Eliza to her husband. Bless her heart! Nate let out a long sigh and relaxed.

He danced with Marietta.

Afterward, she moved off into the crowd, teeth set, smile firm. Nate watched her stiff back disappear into the throng. She hated these gatherings— this was her second Thanksgiving dinner with him—but would charm the common folk, by God, if it was the last thing she did, like a not-so-benevolent missionary among the lepers. Perversely, he enjoyed the idea of thrusting her among the ordinary people. Maybe she'd learn something from stepping outside of the closed society set in which she'd been raised.

Straightening his shoulders, he started toward Eliza, who was standing with a trio of the office women, but he was cut off by a cigar-waving man— Harve Dunlocke, who ran the warehouse.

"Always enjoy these evenings, Mr. Truesdale. Wouldn't miss 'em. You remember my wife?"

"Of course. Delighted." He took the blushing young woman's icy hand. "So glad you could come." Eliza disappeared from his sight. Where had she gone?

He danced with Mrs. Dunlocke. He danced with the mustached Mrs. Ruggle. He danced with the wives of several other employees. Even smart Maggie Receptionist who, he found out, liked her job and had no intention of quitting.

As he steered different partners around the floor, his eyes scanned for Eliza. What a surprise she was! Fascinating. He watched as she spoke to a variety of people, mostly men. Damn it. But she never danced. He saw her several times from the back and had a chance to watch her provocative, delicate hips with that eye-catching poof of silk fabric pleated in the back.

He thanked Maggie Receptionist for the dance and headed through the glaring room toward Eliza, who was smiling and chatting with the overweight Bill Ruggle. Nate pinched his tie back into shape at his throat and touched the stiff starched edges of his wing collar to be sure they hadn't wilted. He would ask her for a dance.

But someone closed in on him.

"A fine party, Mr. Truesdale. You're real decent to do this, and we surely do appreciate it."

He shook hands. "Yes, it's a good party this year, isn't it? So glad you could come."

Nate moved on with a nod of apology before the conversation could continue.

"Mr. Truesdale, there you are! Wonderful evening. Have you met my better half?"

Get out of my way! "Don't think I've had the pleasure. How do you do?"

He shook hands and muttered pleasantries and tried not to sweat. He lost sight of Eliza again. Marietta claimed him for another dance, apparently needing a reprieve from her duties as hostess.

At last he escaped to the chilled windows again, pushed the balcony doors open slightly to cool the room, and downed another glass of iced champagne. His glance moved restlessly over the crowd. Where was she? Every time he'd planned to talk to Eliza someone had interrupted him. His temper was rising. He couldn't see her anywhere.

Where are you, Satin Thighs?

His searching glance encountered Tess moving toward him. Her tawny eyes were bright, her smile purely predatory.

Oh, hell.

"You can't fool me, Nate. I know what that smile of yours means." She was on the scent of blood. "Is there a woman in particular, or are you just in the mood?''

"This is a snarl, not a smile," he bit back. "And now it's permanent where you're concerned."

Making no pretense at conversation, he searched the crowd again.

The air in the drawing room was stale and warm. Eliza made her way among the clusters of people and reached one of the many scattered trays, covered with a white linen cloth and champagne bottles and miniature orchids, as fragile as soft soap. She had never been to such a luxurious party. Everyone was so refined, so sophisticated. She hoped no one could tell how inept she felt.

How different Nate's world was from hers. It was all magic, a bright, shimmering dream. She was in love with the night. In love with the taste of champagne. In love with the fragrance of ivory orchids.

She had glanced at Nate as often as she dared. Black coat and trousers, starched white shirt, impeccably stiff white collar and white silk tie, and white satin waistcoat. She had watched his elegant loose strides as he walked and danced. Watched his face with its olive-bronze skin. The short crisp curls of his hair gleamed blue-black as he moved through the glittering light. He looked so handsome!

And those eyes. When she had first entered and seen him, he had been staring at her. The intensity of that impossibly blue gaze had excited her. And she had felt self-conscious about her gown, as if his eyes were spotlights on her. The butterflies in her stomach had started then and grew more urgent every time she saw him looking at her.

He watched her with glowing alertness, his attention as intoxicating as champagne.

Several times he had started toward her, and Eliza's stomach had leaped in nervous excitement. What would he say? What should she say?

But someone else had always claimed his attention before he got near her, and she had tried to hide her disappointment. She refused to approach him herself.

With a glass of champagne in hand, Eliza turned to face the room again, momentarily at a loss as to where to go or what to do next. Over the rim of her glass she caught sight of Nate with a tall, stunning woman. He was ignoring the woman as he looked around the room. Abruptly his glance jumped to meet hers, as if he had sensed her attention on him. Without a word to the woman, who was speaking to him, Nate left her side and approached Eliza.

He was smiling. Such a warm smile that Eliza quivered inside. She set down her champagne glass, afraid she might spill it.

"Miss Nolenberg?" He said it as if he wasn't sure of her identity. "That's a beautiful gown. Did you make it? I haven't seen you working on anything like that lately."

He was standing so close that she had to tip her head back to look into his eyes. "Yes, I did."

He laughed, a deep, rich sound. "Kept it as a surprise, eh? Well, it's a terrific one. Almost killed me."

"What?"

"Swallowed champagne down my windpipe when I saw you walk in. Couldn't you hear me choking?"

Eliza tried not to laugh but couldn't help herself, and the laughter broke free in loud peals. She felt so wonderful tonight!

Nate touched her arm lightly, and she felt it as if a little burst of energy had passed into her. She tingled. "Dance with me?" he said.

He was smiling so warmly that she was momentarily lost. Then she realized what he had said. "Oh, no," she exclaimed.

"It's all right." He held her arm, coaxing her toward the dancing couples.

She pulled back. "No, please. Thank you, though."

"I insist. Just one dance."

"No, Mr. Truesdale, really. I'm very sorry."

"Why not?"

"Mr. Truesdale," she said, trying to sound firm, "thank you for the invitation, but I'd prefer not—"

"Give me one good reason why you can't dance even one dance with me."

Eliza drew herself up firmly, alarmed and embarrassed. "Because I don't know how. So you see, it would only be a miserable ordeal for both of us."

He was silent for a moment, then laughed and gave her arm a quick, reassuring squeeze. "Well, this is certainly interesting. You can't dance at all? You've never danced before?"

"You may find it amusing, but I had to work to feed my family, and when would I have danced, anyway? I'm not at all ashamed of it."

"Good. You shouldn't be." Nate smiled and put his hand on the small of her back to steer her toward the dancing couples. "But this is your opportunity to learn. I'll teach you."

Eliza reeled back against his hand. "Don't be silly!"

"Come along."

"I have no intention of embarrassing myself in front of all these people."

"You won't. I'm a good dancer, and you have an easy, natural grace—you'll follow beautifully."

Eliza looked up in quizzical protest. "What makes you so sure of that?"

"I held you once, and I know." His gaze was so

direct that Eliza felt a pang of excitement as she remembered their kiss. "You'll be able to follow me," he assured her.

Eliza was trapped by that direct look. "Yes," she murmured. "All right."

He touched her elbow and led her into the dancing crowd. "This is called a waltz, and the timing is most important," he said as he reached for her right hand. "You'll need to hold your train up. See how the other women do it? That's right. Beautiful gown, by the way. Did I tell you?"

Eliza nodded. Acutely aware of him, she trembled with excitement. On the side of his jaw, just above the level of her eyes, was a pearly, crescent-shaped scar. She'd never noticed it before.

"You're too tense. Try to relax against my arm, Eliza. I'll lead you, don't worry, and you'll feel the directions through my hand on your back."

"Miss Nolenberg," she corrected, catching her breath as she felt him reach around her.

"Miss Nolenberg," he repeated stiffly. "All right, all right."

She looked up at him. "I think we shouldn't forget ourselves, Mr. Truesdale."

"Do you want to learn to dance or not? No, don't answer that. Count with me: one, two, three. One, two, three. It's not hard."

"I hate it when people say something isn't hard. It always turns out to be hard."

"Just pay attention to my hand."

How could she not?

At first he led her slowly through the steps, ignoring the tempo of the music. Eliza tried to follow, aware of the varying pressure of his palm, the pressure of his foot against the side of hers as he coaxed her steps. She looked down at his feet to see where he was going.

"Enough of that. You've got the idea now. Look up here."

She did so, gazing into his smile, seeing the windows and then the blinding chandeliers slide past behind his head.

"You're relaxing now. Good," he said. "Feel the movements, feel the timing?"

Eliza smiled. As if growing fluent in a new language, she recognized the commands from his fingers and the heel of his palm. He increased the tempo of their steps, bringing them into synchronization with the music, and Eliza marveled as the circling movements and music blended. It was beautiful! It was free! Air rushed over her face. She closed her eyes, and she was floating among ivory orchids, suspended by his arm.

He was so excitingly near! She felt the faint brush of his knee against her leg. It reminded her of the kiss, of being pulled against him. She longed for such a kiss again. His arm was around her, holding her . . . If he just drew her closer . . .

Nate tightened his arm, and Eliza blinked open her eyes. She stumbled against his foot. "Oh, Mr. Truesdale," she exclaimed, mortified, as she came to a dead stop on the dance floor. "I'm so sorry. Oh, I just knew it couldn't work."

"Nonsense! Do you know how long you were dancing before you missed a step? I thought you'd be good at it, and I was right."

She smiled vaguely, still embarrassed. "Oh, the music is finished. Thank you so much, Mr. Truesdale. It was very kind of you to teach me."

Nate caught her arm. He didn't want her to get away again. It had taken too long to find her, and he was ecstatic. "Not so fast. You still need to practice, Miss Nolenberg. And as long as you have the time and a willing teacher . . . ?"

Eliza looked up at him, clearly uncertain, but she didn't try to leave again. She was acting so different tonight! She glanced around, watching couples move past. Her lips were wet—had she just licked them? It drove him crazy, wanting to kiss that succulent mouth, find that small wet tongue.

Don't think about it, he told himself.

"Did you enjoy dancing?" he asked as he drew her back into his arm for the next round.

"Yes, very much. I felt so . . . free."

"You'd like to be free?" Look at that sweet white shoulder! It was near enough to kiss.

"We each have responsibilities we can't ignore, Mr. Truesdale."

"Oh, how right. Why don't you try closing your eyes again? Be free for even a little while."

She did so, and Nate looked down at the dark lashes on her flushed peach-pink cheeks. He led them around and around, aware of her movements, feeling her waist curving in his arm. She bent her whole body with the music, releasing herself, drifting. He couldn't help watching her, languid and responsive like this within his arm, just inches away. The dark shadow between her breasts plunged out of sight beneath the silver lace . . .

Don't think about it.

But her silk-sheathed waist was slender and supple in his hand. He could close his hands around it. Imagine! No, don't imagine it. He stroked her back through the warm smooth silk.

He murmured near her ear, "What else haven't you learned, dear Miss Nolenberg?"

"Too many things." Her voice was a soft sigh, and he felt her faint, warm breath against his throat. She opened her eyes, deep brown eyes that dominated her face.

Exquisite. Her eyes opened and closed slowly. She

looked up at him. Her velvet gaze was sleepy . . . glazed with dreams and passion. Nate's chest felt tight. He couldn't concentrate on the music.

Focus on the music. Only the music.

Her fingers tightened in his hand.

"You're so lovely, Eliza," he murmured. Concentrate! Find the music. One, two, three. One, two . . .

Her rosebud mouth opened slightly. All succulent and wet and . . . Oh, this was too much! He flushed all the way to his toes and missed a step. He wanted to go down on his knees before her. He stopped abruptly, pulling her against him, and kissed her. She gave one quick, involuntary start, but he caught her head to hold her. She was so delicious, her mouth so warm, so moist.

Enough! Enough! Remember where you are!

Nate straightened and glanced around. Everyone was still dancing. He received a few cold stares, a few grins. But being on the edge of danger thrilled him. He swept Eliza back into the waltz. Could they escape somewhere?

Eliza felt dazed, light headed, disoriented. He'd kissed her! How could she dance now? Excitement had plunged through her, and she wished he would kiss her again. She stared at the black lapel of his jacket against his white shirt. He glanced down, and she met his eyes. His face was set, almost stern.

"How do you feel?" he asked.

How did one describe the indescribable? "What do you mean?" she murmured.

"Angry? Happy? Shocked? No, of course you'd be shocked. I think I shocked myself too. You know what I mean—are you ready to slap my face again?"

"No."

"Good. So how do you feel?"

Eliza said nothing. She couldn't admit to feeling

as if she was in heaven, so hopeful . . . She focused on the timing and the steps and stared past his shoulder at the blur of gowns and black-coated backs.

She could tell he was looking at her.

"Slip away with me somewhere," he murmured in her ear. "After this dance."

Eliza imagined kissing him again. The jolt of eager delight made her heart pound. His fingers squeezed hers encouragingly. She hadn't planned on this, though she had wanted it. She had only thought to prove herself to him, but now . . . Oh, what was happening? What should she do?

Suddenly she was angry, furious with both of them. What about Marietta?

Marietta!

"How could you!" she exclaimed in a loud whisper. "And with Miss Sharpe here!"

He said nothing for an instant, his face almost frozen, then he frowned and she saw his mouth form the word *damn*. Aloud he said, "I'm sorry. I forgot myself."

"You most certainly did," she said, indignant . . . and terribly disappointed.

"Miss Nolenberg, I want you to know I've never done that before . . . kissing a woman in the middle of a dance."

"Well, now you can chalk up that experience!"

She saw the back of his jaw swell with a clenched muscle. In a harsh whisper he said, "I thought you said you didn't want to slap my face this time."

"Maybe I should have."

"You've already done a pretty damn good imitation."

"Who do you think I am that you can just grab me like—"

"Come down off your high horse, Miss Nolen-berg!"

"That's quite *enough*, Mr. Truesdale!"

Eliza pulled away and turned her back on him, then eased her way past the other dancers. Nate followed, his face a mask. He veered off toward the champagne table.

Eliza left the drawing room and walked quickly to the end of the long hall to her bedroom. She closed the door and sank against it, her back on the cool wood as she stared into the darkness. Her heart echoed into the silence.

Why did she want so much to cry? She had wanted to prove herself to him, show him she wasn't such an old prude as he'd said. She put her hand to her mouth against the first choked sob as she realized just how desperately she'd wanted to show him she could be as much a woman as Marietta or Estelle.

Oh, Estelle, she thought, you laughed at me for being plain.

The sob broke into a quiet laugh. She had certainly shown him! Never kissed a woman in the middle of a dance! And the way he'd looked at her all that time from a distance. Said she was lovely . . . She had shown him, proved it to him, and had fairly lit up all the way to her toes when he'd kissed her.

Then why did she feel so terrible and wonderful and happy and bitter all at once?

She pushed away from the door and turned around, touching the outer corners of her eyes, wiping her trembling mouth with her fingers. Daisy. She had to remember what was really important and focus on that alone.

In the hall she glanced toward the drawing room. After the warm darkness of her room, the brightness was blinding, the noise of music and voices and laughter rushing loud and sudden to her ears. The hot aroma of the food being laid out in the dining room wafted up the stairs.

Before returning to the party, she checked on Daisy. The little girl was asleep, her lamp still burning on the bedside table. A fat catalog opened to pictures of dolls was sliding off her lap.

Nate took his champagne onto the balcony. How many glasses did this make? He was feeling the effects. He set the crystal on the railing and looked out over the lawn, brilliant with scallops of light from the windows upstairs and down, the grass disappearing into fuzzy blackened edges. He saw the street far below, glistening with moisture, heard the clacking of carriage wheels in the next block. Beneath his hands, the iron rail stung with cold.

That woman, *that woman.* What was she doing to him? First she was a pompous prude, making him angrier than he'd ever been with any woman. He'd even felt sorry for her! He'd wanted to make her smile, loved it when she unbent at last. Then she came in looking like a damned goddess . . . mouth glowing . . . body moving . . .

What was she trying to do to him? No other woman had ever affected him like Eliza did.

He gripped the iron railing and scowled into the night, turning when he heard a gritty footstep behind him. Rossie was crossing the granite stone balcony, eyes gleaming, huge smile beaming. Nate straightened and ran a hand down the front of his shirt.

"What's the problem, Rossie? If you've lost Tess, you ought to check the bedrooms."

Rossie laughed negligently and leaned the small of his back against the railing. He crossed his arms.

"No. Was thinking about your houseguest—Eliza. Marietta told me she's living here. Pretty nice arrangement. And you're a father—belated congratulations."

Damn Marietta, she knew he needed that kept quiet! Had she ever been trustworthy? "All right, what the hell do you want?"

"Come on, Nate, cool down. I'll keep it under my hat."

"Huh!"

"Just tell me about Eliza. Who is she? Where does she come from?"

"Why do you want to know?"

Rossie grinned at him. "Come on, Nate! We've been partners for a long time."

"So what's your point?"

"If you're running a little something on the side with Eliza, I'll keep my hands off. But if not . . ."

Nate stared at him, incredulous.

Rossie chuckled. "I'm interested. She'd different, and . . . I can't put my finger on it. Tell me, are you sleeping with her? What's she like? Does she squirm and moan, or is she loud—"

"*That's enough!*" Nate slapped his palm on the railing. He was beside himself. "You just shut your mouth right now! I don't want to hear you even say her name!"

Rossie straightened, his pit-black eyes narrowing. "Hey, what's the matter with you? You think you're so much better?"

Nate jabbed his finger into Rossie's chest, forcing the man back a step. "You're damned right! I'm not a walking *gutter*. You get a little edge off talking, huh? Do you know how many employees have left the company because of you?" Nate jerked forward, accidentally knocking his champagne off the railing. The glass shattered on the balcony.

Bits of glass cracked under his feet as Rossie backed up, his thin face hardening. "Get your hand off me—that's not smart, you know. You're not too smart, Truesdale."

"That's right, my brain's not in my trousers, like yours!"

Eliza closed Daisy's door and walked quietly back down the hall toward the drawing room. When she entered, she felt the hush at once. The music was still playing, couples were still dancing, people were still milling about in groups. But an almost palpable tension crackled in the large room. People were staring hard toward the open balcony doors.

And then she heard the voices.

Unmistakably Nate and another man. Arguing. She couldn't see them, and much of what they were saying was indecipherable, but parts stood out clearly.

The other voice: ". . . balls for it, but it would give me pleasure to . . ."

Nate shouting: ". . . kill you with my bare hands!"

Eliza held her breath, shocked. It sounded as if an actual physical fight might erupt. Didn't Nate know how loud they were, how easily overheard? She was embarrassed and alarmed for him.

The tall, stunningly beautiful woman whom Nate had ignored earlier that evening was pushing her way through the crowd. More people had moved closer to the doors, and she was making slow progress. Eliza heard her voice rising as she exclaimed, "Excuse me, let me pass! Let me pass!"

Finally she disappeared onto the balcony. Abruptly there was silence. Even the two musicians had stopped playing. An electric and deadly hush fell over the room. Then Nate's voice erupted again:

"Get the hell out of my house, you slimy little bastard! Both of you, out!"

Rossie Watts appeared. His face was blood-red,
contorted. As if his rage rushed before him like a
solid force, a path opened up for him through the
crowd, and he strode blindly through the room toward the double doors. Following behind him was
the woman. She was a good half a head taller than
Rossie, her expression harsh and ugly.

When they disappeared, a crescendoing noise of
many voices exclaiming all at once rose to fill the air.
Eliza squeezed past the people clotting together in
amazement. She felt drawn to Nate in some way she
couldn't explain or understand. But he entered the
room before she could reach the doors. She halted.

He stopped and looked over the paralyzed and
abruptly silent crowd. She was close enough to see
the dark flush on his skin, his half-closed eyes.
When he spoke, his voice was scratchy, hoarse. "I
apologize—" He cleared his throat and continued
more loudly. "I apologize for the disruption. Everything's under control now, so please . . . continue
to enjoy yourselves." He strode toward the double
doors, pausing only momentarily to speak to Marietta and lead her into the hall with him.

Eliza was sure the evening had been ruined, that
Mrs. Herlihy's dinner would be ignored. But the
music began again. The guests circulated in excited
discussion as they speculated on the argument between the two company owners. They were shaken
and keyed up and feverish with interest.

When Nate returned minutes later, he was smiling again, though his eyes held a hard glint of anger. Marietta remained beside him, aloof and also
bright-eyed with fury. Eliza wondered if they had
quarreled. Had it been about her?

The dancing resumed.

Chapter 8

Eliza's heart dropped in dismay when she entered the dining room the next morning. Marietta was eating breakfast with Nate and Daisy. Had she spent the night? How galling it was, the ease with which Nate could kiss her, Eliza, and want her to slip away with him . . . and then return to Marietta! It was what she had expected of him all along, but still, the proof of his womanizing left her dazed and . . . yes, hurt.

All night she had danced with him in her dreams, kissed him again and again. In those slow and shadowed images of passion she had felt cherished. In her simple mind, she now accused herself silently, she had imagined possibilities where none existed. How could they? She was a virtually uneducated millworker from Pittsburgh; he a wealthy member of San Francisco society. They were worlds apart, separated by social boundaries that could never be crossed.

"Good morning," Nate said with a half-smile as he scanned her stiff black dress. "We've got enough leftovers to drown in. I hope you're hungry."

"Not particularly," Eliza answered. She nodded briefly to Marietta, who returned the gesture in cool silence. This morning she wore a fresh day dress of

rose silk with gigot sleeves and an immaculate white
yoke that narrowed over her breasts as it descended
to her waist. So she had brought a change of attire
with her last night, Eliza thought. Nate must have
known she would be staying—must have invited
her. And yet he had kissed her, Eliza, and asked to
meet her alone. What gall! What did he think of
her?—that she was common? As easy as Estelle?

Eliza took the chair beside Daisy. The little girl
was engrossed in a book which she shoved over the
tablecloth toward Eliza. "Look, Miss Sharpe brought
a book for me. *Alice's Adventures in Wonderland.*"

After pouring herself a cup of coffee from the silver pot, Eliza glanced at the book—fine brown leather
binding with raised gilt lettering; thick pages, perfectly inked; exquisite and detailed illustration
plates. She smelled the pulp of the pages, the pungency of the ink and leather. It was an expensive
gift. A pretty bribe, she thought angrily.

Marietta murmured quietly to Nate, too low for
Eliza to distinguish the words. Love whispers, she
imagined. She caught herself trying to both listen
and shut out the sounds at the same time.

Daisy chattered about the new book. The crisp
linen tablecloth gleamed almost incandescent in the
gray-white light from the windows. Eliza looked in
Nate's direction. He was staring outside, studying
the sky and the low fog. The light made a slash
across his eyes. When he glanced unexpectedly
down the table and met her gaze, Eliza felt a rapid,
breathless fluttering in her chest. He was studying
her closely, and she had the impression he was
searching for something. So heightened were her
senses that it seemed to her that her thoughts and
dreams of him must be visible, and he could see just
by looking at her how attracted she was to him.

Marietta touched him, and his attention jumped

back to her. Eliza wanted to melt into the warm shadows clinging to the edges of the room, away from the incandescent spotlight of the table where she could see and be seen.

Daisy was speaking to her. The little mouth moved and smiled, and Eliza saw she was indicating the book. Automatically, Eliza looked where Daisy was pointing. Automatically, she nodded. Automatically, her glance returned to Nate.

He was grinning at Marietta. Then he pushed back his chair and stood up to help her rise. They left the room. Eliza's heart plunged, then she heard them leaving the house. Had she expected they would disappear upstairs together? Relief gave way to fresh fury. Why should she even *care* what he did? Marietta had already spent the night!

Eliza was angry enough to leave the room without even realizing Daisy was still talking to her.

That night Nate read aloud to Daisy from *Alice's Adventures in Wonderland*, and Eliza was forced by her own rule of never leaving them alone together to sit in the large parlor with them. Much more comfortable than the formal front parlor, this room was furnished with heavier, older, well-used pieces. Eliza sat in the corner of a walnut sofa upholstered in soft, faded rose damask; Nate held Daisy on his lap in an armchair covered in the same faded fabric. The scattered tables and single small chest reflected the copper firelight. The tall glass doors of the bookcase mirrored the flickering yellow firelight. Nate had lit a small oil lamp, and Daisy's smooth ivory forehead tucked under his dark chin caught Eliza's eye more and more often. Though Nate had shaved that morning, his beard had since grown out enough to catch tiny blue points of light—and she imagined the scrape of those sharp hairs on her fingers if she were to stroke his cheek.

She tried to keep her mind on the blouse she was sewing for Mrs. Penchelli, but she couldn't close out his deep, mesmerizing voice as he read. The sewing slid forgotten to her lap as she listened.

As the tale unfolded, she could feel little Alice's frustrations and frights and curiosity, and she rested her cheek on the plush scrolled arm of the sofa and stared into the leaping flames of the hearth.

When Nate stopped reading, she lifted her head in surprise. Daisy was asleep, sprawled across his lap, breathing deeply and evenly. Her cheek lay against his chest, one pink plump arm curled in her lap, the other flung across his arm; her legs flopped open on either side of his knee. Nate chuckled as he closed the book and set it aside.

"She's been asleep for a while," he said quietly, "but you were having such a good time listening, I didn't have the heart to stop. But she's getting heavy."

Eliza glanced at the watch pinned to her bodice. "It's after ten. No wonder she's asleep."

Smiling, he looked down again at the little body slumped across his lap. Her navy-blue sailor dress lay rumpled, the white collar crushed against his shiny brown waistcoat. "Oh, I think she's comfortable enough to sleep through the night. No harm done." He resettled her into his arms as he stood up. Daisy murmured in her sleep and blinked rapidly, then drifted down once again in slumber.

Eliza moved toward Nate, arms held out. "Here, I'll take her."

"Would you just go on upstairs and open the door for me? I've got her. I'm not going to drop her."

In Daisy's room he laid her on the turned-back sheet. "Here, roll over, precious—let's get you ready for bed."

"Mr. Truesdale, I can take care of this," Eliza protested. "Thank you for bringing her upstairs."

Daisy mumbled and looked up, her gaze vague and unfocused in sleep. In response to the prodding, she turned so Nate could unfasten the buttons at her back. Eliza sat on the edge of the bed beside her and tried to intervene, her fingers racing his over the buttons.

Despite Eliza's protests and attempts to stop him, Nate didn't pause as he helped remove Daisy's dress, lifting it over her head. Her arms dropped back down, heavy with slumber. She closed her eyes, swaying in her sleeveless white shift, and slumped onto her pillow.

"Aren't you forgetting what you pointed out so recently?" Nate inquired. "What would I do if you weren't here?"

"I'll always be near her," Eliza snapped. "So you can leave now." But Nate started unlacing the little girl's tall black shoes. "Please, Mr. Truesdale, let's not have an argument right here."

"I'm not arguing, Miss Nolenberg. You are."

Daisy's voice was sleepy, almost a sigh as she pleaded, "Don't fight."

Nate glanced to Eliza and lifted his eyebrows significantly.

"Fetch me her nightgown then," Eliza whispered. "You'll find it in the second drawer."

As he straightened and went to the dresser, Eliza removed Daisy's shoes and stockings and set them on the floor beside the bed. Once the sleeping girl was finally attired in her plain cotton nightdress and the covers were tucked up to her ear, Eliza picked up the lamp she had brought from the parlor and followed Nate into the hall.

He paused outside the door and watched her. A question seemed to form in his eyes. She looked from his eyes to his mouth, the dazzling hard mouth that had so excited her.

"Good night, Mr. Truesdale," she said quickly, and started toward her door.

"Don't you want to hear any more of the book?"

"Thank you, no."

"Wait a minute, Miss Nolenberg. I'd like to talk." Without hesitation he followed her into her room.

She swung around in shock. "Please get out! How dare you?"

"I'd like to talk," he said simply, ignoring her agitation. "Do you want to talk here or downstairs?"

Nate watched color suffuse her cheeks. What lovely curves she had in her face. Her skin was luminous. He wanted to touch those cheeks, kiss that pursed mouth until it blossomed open as it had last night. He tried to think of something to say. "Do you want another apology?" he asked. "I seem to have to do that quite often."

"It's not necessary."

"Glad to hear it," he said. Her back was stiff, shoulders back. White shoulders beneath that stiff black dress. Beautiful white shoulders sloping in regal lines. It was hard not to think about those shoulders, or the tight little rear he'd imagined all night.

Last night he had dreamed of a statue of a nude woman—a Greek statue he had once admired in a museum in New York. White marble, so cool, so smooth to the touch. In the dream he had kissed the pale lips, and they had warmed to flesh under his touch. He had pressed his mouth to the sloping white shoulders and then to the stone breasts, and blood had flushed through the marble wherever he touched, transforming the stone to woman, living, warm, human. Enthralled, in a fever, he had pressed his mouth to the resisting stone at the apex of the closed thighs. His arms had gone around the statue, and the thighs had moved within his arms, opening to his mouth, opening to accept his touch, his kisses. And there, instead of the white marble, was an exquisite woman—flushed pink and moist. The sight and taste of that newly warmed flesh had aroused him to unutterable heights.

"Did you apologize to Miss Sharpe last night?" she asked, her eyebrows lifting so quickly that they might have been yanked up by strings.

"Why? She owed *me* an apology. She'd been spreading the news that Daisy was my daughter—and illegitimate."

"Yes, but what about the fact that you're in love with her and planning to marry her, yet on the dance floor—"

"Who said anything about love? I never said I was in love with her."

Her eyes widened. "How despicable!"

"No," he said coolly, "I'm neither engaged to her nor have I ever told her I was in love with her." He didn't add that he was growing more sure that he would never marry Marietta. Her snobbishness and the fact that he couldn't trust her with anything confidential bothered him more and more. "I've never been in love with any woman, unfortunately, and it troubles me a bit. Some I like more than others . . . Have you ever been in love?"

The lamp wavered in her hand. He saw that she was trembling. How curious!

"This is irrelevant, Mr. Truesdale, and you're still in my room."

"All right, I'm leaving," he said, frowning, shoving his hands into his trouser pockets. "I just want to add that you looked lovely last night, and I enjoyed teaching you to dance. Did you enjoy it?"

"Yes, I told you so," she said angrily, and set the

lamp behind her on the dresser top. "Now please, good night."

Good night, Eliza of the hidden passion, he thought. He was smiling to himself as he left the room and returned downstairs.

As Nate's open-topped carriage rolled through the streets, Eliza admired everything she saw: patches of lush green grass, succulent pale ice plant that pushed in streamers over the ground, whitewashed clapboard houses, stands of pine and Monterey cypress trees, the last of the season's delicate waxy camellia blossoms, and orange geraniums so abundant that the plants looked like bushes.

The dark morning fog had burned off, as Nate had assured her it would, and the sun blazed above them.

Eliza rode in the front seat beside Nate, Mrs. Herlihy and Daisy in the tiny cramped rear seat located over the high back wheels.

"You want to see something of California while you're here, don't you?" Nate had said this morning. Eliza had protested because of the sewing she had to do for Mrs. Penchelli.

"Forget that," he said. "I'll hire you to sew a half-dozen new shirts—and pay twice whatever she'd give you." He knew about Mrs. Penchelli; Marietta regularly ordered clothing from her. "Just get ready. Blue skies await."

And Eliza had been tempted beyond her ability to resist. She had hummed to herself as she settled the black hat on her hair and shoved a single hatpin across the crown. Two pins were needed for such a heavy hat, but she couldn't find her other one and she gave up, unconcerned, still humming as she left the room.

He drove past miles of piers, pointing out to them

the river steamers, lumber schooners, coasting
schooners, steam schooners, whaling barks, coal
ships, sternwheelers, and square riggers, a Southern
Pacific ferry and Key Route ferry.

When Daisy wanted to ride on a boat, he said,
"Another time, baby dear."

He guided the carriage down Market to Kearney
Street and stopped in front of Lotta's Fountain.
"This is where you wanted to go?" he asked Mrs.
Herlihy as he climbed down to help her out.

"This is it," she said. "Why don't you come along
too, Daisy, lamb? You can shop with me, and I'll
buy you a nice cherry ice."

Realizing she would be alone with Nate, Eliza
turned quickly to protest, but Daisy squinted at her
in the sunlight and begged, "Please, Aunt Lizzie?
May I, may I, please?"

Mrs. Herlihy stood in the street, her long burlap
shopping bag folded in her arms. "I'd enjoy her
company, Eliza. And I'll take good care of her, don't
you fret."

Nate fished for coins in his pocket and handed
them over to Mrs. Herlihy. "Here. The cherry ice is
on me." With a grin to Daisy as he lifted her out of
the carriage, he added, "And there's enough for a
ride home on a cable car. How would you like that,
hmmm?"

"Oh, no," Eliza exclaimed.

"It's perfectly safe," Nate said.

Mrs. Herlihy agreed with him: "Not a thing for
you to fret yourself about."

It struck Eliza then that this turn of events had
been planned ahead of time. She would be alone
with him. She didn't know whether to be excited or
angry, but she didn't protest again.

After Nate climbed back up beside her and they
started away, she turned in her seat to wave to

Daisy. The little girl put her hand in Mrs. Herlihy's and skipped to keep up with the woman's brisk steps as they joined the stream of pedestrians.

"Where are we going now?" Eliza asked. "To the ocean?"

"You've already seen that, haven't you? No, the ocean side might still be fogged in. It's a shame the Midwinter Exposition isn't open yet; that won't be till January. I was thinking of getting out of the city altogether. There's beautiful country further south."

Eliza sat silent, watching as Nate pointed out buildings to her. They rattled up hills so steep that Eliza was sure they would roll back down at any minute, then continued over cobbled streets and hard rutted dirt roads, past narrow three-storied wooden houses, some in need of fresh paint, all crowded side-by-side in neat rows. The Mission District, he said. "Marietta will travel through it under protest," he remarked, "but Chinatown is definitely off her map. What she knows of this city would fit on the head of a pin, I swear. She's been all the way to Europe but never through her own city."

Eliza kept silent; she wished he wouldn't talk of Marietta.

Clear now of the city congestion, they were surrounded by leafless oak and dogwood trees. Rain-lush grass and milkweed grew dense alongside the road. The sunlight was the whitest Eliza had ever seen. With the wide dirt road empty ahead, Nate slapped the reins and the chestnut mare stretched its legs. Past the limits of safe speed, he urged the horse faster. The roadside grass and weeds melted into a rushing blur.

Faster yet they went. Bits of dirt flung up from the hooves stung Eliza's face, and still he urged the animal to greater speed.

Eliza clung to the deep padded side railing of the

seat with one hand. The other flattened the crown of her hat to hold it in place. They were traveling so fast! Flying up over small rises, plunging down the other side. The wind thundered against her ears. She sat bolt upright and gripped the side of the seat with all her strength. Her eyes were wide in the wind. *She loved it!*

All the world was rushing toward her at an exhilarating speed! With a heart-stopping explosion of freedom. Her hat strained against her efforts to hold it. Nate's expression was serious, his eyes narrowed in concentration. His fingers were tight on the leather reins, and he'd braced one foot against the black leather front edge of the carriage. He glanced at her, his eyes bright. "Take off your hat!" he shouted above the rush of the wind.

Eliza pulled out the long pin, but before she could catch it, the black hat was snatched away by the wind. She uttered a cry of dismay and turned to see it drop into the dust far behind them. Nate started to pull back on the reins to slow the mare, but she put her hand on his arm.

"No!" she cried, and gave in to a burst of wild laughter. "Don't stop. It was only a hat, and I hated it anyway."

"Sure?" Nate laughed with her and slapped the reins again. "I hated it too!"

It was hard to talk when the laughter felt so good. Peals and peals, releasing, unable to stop. "Do you always go this fast?"

"Like it?"

"Yes!" She pushed streams of hair from her eyes. "Where are we going?"

"I don't know. I never think about destinations, but I love beginnings. Curtains going up, chapter one, page one. Mysteries awaiting. What about you?" He laughed loudly as he looked at her, his eyes lit by some inner combustion. "Where do you want to go?"

"Anywhere!"

"Anywhere it is then!"

They stood beside a small, spring-fed lake. Crystal Springs, he called it. Slivers of sunlight rippled silvery blue on the surface of the water; a line of giant green-forested hills rolled into the hazy distance in both directions. She smelled the pines, the weeds and water, the pure essence of limitless mountain air. "The Coastal Range," he explained when she asked about the long hills. "An earthquake fault runs right down the center here, under the water. I was just reading about it."

"We're standing on an earthquake fault?" Eliza exclaimed, stunned. She imagined the giant seam under the water parting, the lake dropping into it, the two of them disappearing into it. "Shouldn't we back up to a safer distance?"

"Like where—St. Louis? I don't think you realize how big the fault is. No, never mind, we're safe."

Nate had brought the coffee-brown wool blanket, and they spread it on the tall weeds of the sun-heated hillside. The winter air in the shade was cool, but with the hard, undiluted California sunshine on them they were warm enough to leave aside coat and cape. Nate's shirt was blindingly white in the sun.

They talked idly, Nate commenting on early history, the missions, the Indians. Relaxed, Eliza listened with genuine interest. She sat with her ankles tucked against her hip; Nate stretched out on his side, head propped on his elbow. He asked her about her education. "When you talk, I sometimes get the impression you've had extensive schooling, but I can't imagine when you had time for it."

She watched a flock of birds swoop low and skim over the water. "A retired teacher lived just below us," she explained, thinking it seemed so easy to talk to Nate today. "An elderly man, so refined. Estelle and I used to run downstairs for visits with him, and he served us tea and cookies, just as if we were fine ladies come calling. And there we were, probably just as giggly as Daisy, though we imagined ourselves to be grown up. At first he just read to us as we ate, or talked to us of different things. Queens, dinosaurs, talking jungle birds—" She plucked a stalk of tall grass and twisted it around her fingers. "Fun things."

"That's it? He must have fit quite a lot of learning into those tea parties."

"Oh, no, the real learning came later. You see, he woke early every morning. Couldn't sleep at his age, he said. I had to work during the day, so I used to go down to see him at about three or four every morning. Everyone else was sleeping, so they didn't miss me. I studied with him until I had to start to the mill. He had all these old books, you see . . ."

Nate gave a long sigh. "You must have wanted it pretty badly."

"I suppose so."

She leaned back with one hand against the scratchy hot threads of the blanket and looked down at Nate's black curls, glittering in the sunlight. He covered her hand with his, a soft touch that thrilled her. She considered drawing back her hand but couldn't bring herself to do so. Right now the world and her responsibilities seemed far away. The reckless speed of their ride, the bursting sensation of flight, escape, freedom, had snapped the threads to that other world. She felt as if she existed quite apart from the demands and problems of her life.

And the man beside her, the man touching her

hand, was Nate Truesdale. Her awareness of this moment grew so pleasurably acute that it was almost more than she could bear.

"Tell me about you," she said. "What has your life been like?"

He stroked her fingers. "I was a spoiled brat—an only child."

"No, I can't believe you were a spoiled brat." She grinned at his upturned teasing expression and waved the stalk of grass at him. "If you had been, you'd have a hundred servants now and gardeners so you wouldn't have to dig in the mud yourself."

He chuckled softly and swatted away a gnat. "All right, then. Cancel the spoiled brat. How 'bout a born cynic?"

"Hmmm. Let me think about that one."

"Not too long, or you'll worry me."

She laughed. "No—you're not a born cynic."

"What a relief!"

She asked about his parents, and he laced his fingers with hers. "My father died about twelve years ago, and my mother lives in Baltimore. She moved there right after my father's death and has never been back to California since then. I visit her every few years."

"What's she like?"

"You're pretty inquisitive today, aren't you?" He rolled onto his back, easing the strain in his arm, and watched her face as he put his hand on the warm black fabric of her back. "She's vague. A chronic martyr. Nothing I do ever makes her happy. Sometimes I'd like to see her get angry—you know, from-the-gut mad. Stand up for herself. Like you do."

"Me? But I'm such a coward."

"That's right. And I believe in the man in the moon and Santa Claus too."

Eliza uttered a small laugh and brushed the grass from her lap.

"You're such a surprise sometimes," he said softly.

Eliza felt the slow stroking of his palm on her back and closed her eyes, enjoying it. It was too good to resist. How easy it was to forget all else when he was near. Maybe it was because she wanted so much to forget.

His arm scooped her toward him, and she leaned over his face, looking down into the brilliant blue eyes, narrowed against the sun, that held hers deeply. Black silky lashes. Faint sheen of perspiration on his brow. He stroked the wind-loosened streaks of hair from her face. He held her cheeks between his hands and tried to draw her down to him, but she resisted. "Eliza!" he whispered.

She longed to kiss him. The sun was hot on her back, the cries of birds over the water fading. The wind trying to catch her hair felt like a caress. She lowered her head and shut her eyes as her lips met his.

His arms closed around her, and with a warm shock she felt his chest against hers. A long, slow exhalation of breath brushed her cheek as he turned his mouth on hers. She felt his excitement in the tightness of his arms around her. She reveled in the sensations, returning his kisses, savoring the moments. When he shifted beneath her, she started to sit up, but he rolled her under him so quickly and easily that she lost her breath. The strength of him! A thrill went through her. He leaned above her, blocking the sun from her face, his eyes glittering as he lowered his head to hers.

At the first thrust of his tongue into her mouth, her heart thudded upwards in joy. Gone was the

brief tenderness; as his tongue probed the wet re-
cesses he became reckless and relentless.

The cries of the birds vanished; the wind brushing
across the ground was gone from her awareness.
Such delight—the weight of his body over hers, the
smooth fabric of his shirt, his hard chest. Beneath
her lay the hot blanket and winter earth. As his hand
squeezed her waist and slid higher to cup the side
of her breast, she stretched her arms around his
back, grasping him ever more tightly in excitement.

"That's right," he said, breathless, "hold me."

She had long ago ceased remembering him with
Estelle. It was only Nate with her, as she had imagined these last weeks. His weight partially rested on
his knee between her thighs, pinning her legs within
the fabric of her skirt and underskirt. His mouth was
demanding; tongue slick and hard, his hand tight
around her breast. With every touch and kiss, the
deep pleasure in the heart of her accelerated. His
sex, rigid and trapped against the top of her thigh,
inflamed her.

He leaned back on one elbow and began unbut-
toning her dress. Eliza squinted against the sun and
the brightness of his white shirt. His face was dark,
flushed. Eager though she was, she grasped his
hand to stop him. But his fingers were sure. The
black gown opened past the level of her breasts, and
her plain mended cotton camisole lay exposed to his
gaze.

"You don't wear a corset?" His voice was deeper
than usual.

Eliza was ashamed. A fashionable woman would
have worn one. Estelle—beautiful, desirable Estelle—had worn corsets with tiny lace edging and
slender white satin ribbons. Eliza slid her arm from
around his shoulder and tried to hide the much-
mended undergarment. Her other hand still gripped

the top of his, holding it tight against his efforts to
further unbutton the dress.

"Don't be embarrassed." There was a quick flash
of teeth as he grinned before he turned serious
again: "No, never that. All right?" His hand
dragged hers with it as he reached into the opening
of her dress and caressed one firm, upthrusting
breast through the camisole. He muttered something that sounded to her like "delicious." His fingertips tightened on her nipple. The deep thrill of
pleasure brought a surprised groan from her.

"No, don't," she protested. She pulled at his
hand, tried to pry it from her breast.

"Be with me completely, Eliza," he whispered.
He held her wrists down on the blanket on either
side of her head, out of his way, as his mouth covered her rigid nipple through the camisole. She
loved it! She wanted it!

But he had never loved any woman, had never
returned to Estelle. Soon Marietta would sit at the
breakfast table every morning in her fresh rose silk
day dress. Now was the time to think of that. Not
later, when it might be too late. Eliza squirmed under his mouth, uttering, "No, no, no," in a too-
weak voice. She tried to pull her hands from under
his.

Nate lifted his head. "Did I hurt you?"

She flung her head from side to side, wanting both
to laugh and cry at the same time.

He released her hands to slip open the top buttons
of her camisole. A soft brushing of his hand over
her bare breast brought such astonishing pleasure,
she recoiled. She felt the shock of his mouth on her
breast. Eliza pushed against him, desperate.

But he leaned his long body over hers, pinning
her, his breath coming in short bursts. "Eliza, you're
beautiful—don't worry, relax—be with me." He

stroked her cheek, his eyes shining, beautiful and urgent.

Eyes to lose herself in. His heart pounded in tempo over hers, as rapid and enthralling as music.

"I'll make it so good for you," he whispered.

The anticipation of pleasure crested in her, threatened to shut off her brain. Frantic, she pushed all the harder against him, until, with a loud groan, he rolled abruptly away from her. Then she was on her feet and running through the thick grass, crushing the supple stalks beneath her.

Chapter 9

Eliza stared through the sun-lit display window. Dark red hats with silky black feathers. Post-boy hats of soft shiny beaver. White boat-shaped hats with delicate blue birds' wings. Wide-brimmed hats and little bonnets with large bows. Such a lot to choose from! She sighed, and her breath left a misty oval of steam on the glass.

Behind her, pedestrians streamed past, and she watched their reflection in the windowpane. More and more she was aware of the young women in San Francisco and the colorful, decorated gowns they wore; the abundance of lace, ornamental buttons, and full gigot sleeves; the new styles of hair, tight curls over the forehead, sparkling combs. She heard the light voices, the variety of feminine tones, from liquid to husky. Forced into early maturity by the circumstances of her life, Eliza craved the negligence of fashion and carefree laughter.

She bought a new hat, a jaunty boater that made her feel young. Then she bought a lacy corset that made her feel wicked. It was more fun than she'd ever imagined. From Mrs. Penchelli she purchased fabric for two new gowns. With the Christmas season approaching, there was more than enough work available these days from the elderly seamstress, and

Eliza suffered guilt not at all as she spent that hard-won money.

After all, she had work now. And a lawyer.

But as she approached Nate Truesdale's granite-stone house, rising high above California Street and shaded from the sun by the whispering eucalyptus trees, her buoyant mood evaporated.

In direct proportion to her attraction to Nate, Eliza tried to avoid him. She was absolutely certain he would forget her as easily as he had forgotten Estelle, that he would wed Marietta as planned. He would probably also win custody of Daisy. She stood to lose too much; she couldn't afford to lose her heart to Nate as well. She already felt more for him than she was willing to admit. The loss of Daisy would be hard enough to bear . . .

That Nate now avoided her almost as much as she avoided him did not escape her notice. He spent his evenings with friends from the Bohemian Club. Chance meetings in the house brought a flush to both of them. Meals were strained. Tempers frequently hit the bursting point.

One afternoon Daisy had been sitting at the dining room table, painting pictures, when Nate arrived from the office. Newspapers had been spread open to protect the table, and Daisy had lined up her completed paintings for Nate to see. When she caught sight of him in the foyer beyond the dining room doors, she slid off her chair and ran to him, holding a brush that was wet with purple paint.

"Nate, come see what I did!" she exclaimed, catching his hand and trying to pull him into the next room.

"All right, all right." He extracted his hand from her grasp and removed his frock coat, tossing it over his forearm as he followed her. "Nice," he said, looking over the stiff, brightly colored pieces of thick paper. His heart wasn't in it; he was preoccupied and on edge over the strain in his relationship with Eliza, though he tried to pretend enthusiasm. "Why, baby dear, you're quite an artist."

"Do you really like them?" she asked.

"Of course. You're very talented."

Daisy bounced delightedly on her toes, then twirled around, the paintbrush held out as if she were a conductor of a symphony orchestra. It swept the air in a wide arc and slapped against the sleeve of Nate's shirt, leaving a splattered streak of purple on the white fabric and tiny droplets dotting the front of his dove-gray waistcoat.

His patience snapped, and he plucked the brush from her hand. "Look what you did! You don't deserve to have paints if you can't be responsible with them."

"But, Nate—" Daisy started to whine.

"Put everything away right now. No arguments!"

The door leading to the kitchen swung open, and Eliza stood on the threshold glaring at Nate. "What's going on in here?"

"Who gave her permission to use paints?" Nate exclaimed, a sharp scowl on his face. "Was it you? Well, look what happened." He indicated the vivid purple stains on his clothing.

"I'm sure it was an accident, and there's no cause for—"

"You know best, obviously," he said in an icy voice. "Excuse me, I have to change my shirt now."

Nate had marched out of the room, leaving Eliza staring furiously after him, and Daisy wide-eyed with dismay.

At dinner another evening, Daisy had proudly told him that Eliza was making herself a pretty new dress with yellow lace. Nate had glanced down at the table at Eliza and remarked. "Is that right? Are you certain you should wear something feminine, instead of a piece of armor?'' and Eliza had furiously pushed back her chair and left the table.

Daisy had looked at Nate with hurt disbelief, and he had frowned as he muttered, ''I'm sorry, baby dear. Go on and eat your dinner.''

But Daisy had started to cry. ''I can't,'' she said, and slipped from the room with her head down, leaving him feeling unendurably alone.

With Eliza and Nate on edge, Daisy threw tantrums with understandable regularity. After a particularly loud outburst one evening, when Daisy shouted that she hated creamed peas and wouldn't eat them, Eliza exclaimed, ''You're an ungrateful child, and I don't want to listen to you any longer! Leave the table!'' Daisy knocked her dinner plate to the floor and bolted in tears from the dining room.

Ashamed and upset, Eliza gathered the china fragments. Nate scraped creamed peas off the rug with a spoon.

''You are the most remarkably aggravating woman I have ever had the bad luck to run across,'' he muttered. He stood up, flicking the spoonful of peas into an empty bowl on the table. ''And I have to put up with you in *my house!*''

Eliza dumped a half-eaten roll and a stack of clinking china pieces on the tablecloth. ''Whose fault is that? It was your choice. You insisted on her being here, and it was selfish and inconsiderate . . . You started all this, right from the very beginning. With *Estelle.* And you can end it anytime you want. Just say the word and we'll be gone.''

''I'm sure as hell not going to let you have her now, when I hear you speak to her the way you did. My God, you should have heard yourself.''

''What about the way you carried on when she

got paint on your shirt. Oh, that was really unforgivable.''

''She shouldn't have been dancing around with a
paintbrush in her hand in the first place! But, *excuse
me*, you wouldn't understand. You wear those old
black rags—no harm done if paint splats all over
them.''

''I refuse to listen to this. It's your house, your
daughter, you can clean up the mess.'' She flung
down the dirty fork she'd just retrieved from under
the table. It bounced on the rug and clattered against
the baseboard.

''That hit a nerve, didn't it,'' he shouted down at
her. ''Old black rags. Well, it's the truth. Keep all
males at a distance, huh, Miss Nolenberg? We're all
such despicable creatures. Not a single redeeming
quality in the whole goddamned male population!''
His eyes shone with suppressed emotion. ''When
are you going to start acting like a woman? But
heaven help anyone who ever discovers you *are* one!
Slap his face good and proper, that crude bastard!''

Eliza's angry expression abruptly disappeared in
shock. ''I can't believe—'' she gasped, and tears
welled in her eyes. She couldn't stop the flow; huge
drops spilled onto her cheeks, hot and excruciating.
She snatched up her skirt and fled, missing the
flicker of pain in his eyes.

Nate drank his glass of bourbon, neat, and sat
alone in the gloomy parlor. The hand clutching the
glass dangled over the scrolled arm of the sofa as he
stared at the rug. The pad of footsteps on the floor
over his head had ceased long ago. It was late, but
he was too weary and pained to stir himself. He felt
welded to the sofa.

He remembered that Eliza Nolenberg had never
complained of her portion in life. She'd studied with

an old man in a shabby, dusty room at three in the morning because that was the only way she could get an education. He remembered the tenement building as he had seen it the day he met Estelle. It had been decaying even then. The rooms were tiny and noisy; buildings crowded so closely on each side that the windows must have been forever dim. He recalled the scratch of rats in the halls, the smoking stink of the mills, and the soot-laden air that hung over the city and sifted dirt into every corner.

Estelle had hated it desperately. In his mind he saw her again—the fair, young face framed by shining dark hair; the imploring eyes; and the single, yellow blossom pinned over her breast. She was one of the lost ones. He'd seen them all over, women who believed so little in themselves that they traded the only thing they thought they had in hopes of gaining something better. It wasn't money that Estelle had wanted. "Take me with you," she'd pleaded.

He had arrived in Pittsburgh only that morning, eager to secure a shipping contract with a glass manufacturer who wanted to transport some of his products to the West Coast. Representatives from both railroad and shipping companies were vying for the contract. Because his appointment with the factory owner wasn't scheduled until the following morning, Nate spent his first day in the city strolling the streets.

It was late in the afternoon when he met Estelle. She smiled at him as they neared each other on the crowded sidewalk, and flirtatiously twitched a provocative petticoat. Despite her prettiness, Nate was preoccupied with thoughts of the next day's interview and would have continued on his way with only a brief tip of his hat, but she bumped him as he walked past. It was no accident, that brush

against his arm that sent her armful of packages
tumbling to the ground. As he helped her retrieve
them, she placed her hand on his arm and gave him
a long look from beneath silken brows. Her mouth
curved into the age-old, inviting smile of a knowing
woman. And he felt that grinding surge of blood in
him, a remorseless passion.

He had known even then that he shouldn't go
with her. Maybe it was the desperately adoring look
in her eyes or the proper cut of her gown and jacket,
but he knew she was no prostitute. He could have
stopped everything, but he didn't. Afterward, when
he refused to take her back to California with him
and she burst into tears, he felt ashamed of himself.
If he had wanted a woman, he should have found a
prostitute whom he could pay and be done with.
Instead, he'd gone with a young woman who had
ended up hurt and crying pitifully when he left. He
could still see the sweet, vibrant shimmer of the yellow blossom she'd worn on her bodice, and it
seemed a sad symbol of her. The mere memory of
her flower always brought back his feelings of guilt.

He swung his arm up and took another swallow
of the bourbon, wincing at the scratch of it in his
throat. The fire snapped and cast a soft glimmer of
light into the gloom. In that decaying tenement
where he'd gone with Estelle, where the bricks were
so rotten they looked like dirt, the sheets at least had
been clean. The floors had been worn down to pale
wood, but they were clean too. Instead of the dank,
smoky dust he'd smelled in the foyer and greasy
halls, the apartment had held the scent of soap and
the dissipating aroma of freshly baked bread. He had
looked around with curious interest. Now he knew
it had been Eliza who had cleaned and cared for the
home. She was the true blossom blooming in the
decay.

He felt miserable for making Eliza cry, and he cursed himself for being a damned bastard. The day they had gone to the lake and Eliza had run away, he had sat on the blanket, aroused, frustrated. His male pride toppling, he had glared at the water and felt like a hideous monster. It had been easy to blame her and coldly ignore her when she finally came walking back.

How it had hurt to see her cry tonight, and to know he'd brought on the tears. He couldn't really blame her for anything—not for his actions, not for those of that miserable father who'd left her, not for the pitiful mother who'd drifted out of contact with the world. She had never given up, the way Estelle had done. Eliza had risen to the challenges life had thrust upon her, working to keep her mother and Estelle fed and cared for—when she had been only a child herself. Goddamned stinking mills, paying scant pennies for child labor.

Nate glanced around the room, remembering the succession of women who had participated briefly in his life. He had admired none of them the way he admired Eliza. He was disgusted with Marietta, who refused even to associate with her. What an unforgivable snob Marietta was! She wouldn't have had the strength and determination to go to work to support her family the way Eliza had done. Marietta didn't have the goodness of heart to do such a thing.

He smiled to himself, remembering the past weeks with Eliza. How she'd laughed that day in the carriage! How sweet the sound had been. How beautiful she'd been in her surprise evening gown, and how precious she'd looked, dancing with her eyes closed. A blossom.

Recalling the cruel things he'd said to her and the sight of the tears, he felt ashamed again—as if she were a real flower struggling to bloom and in his

selfishness he'd crushed it, stepped on it and ground
it into the powdery bricks. All he'd been doing was
trying to seduce her, without any real regard for her
feelings. Well, it would all change now, he decided.
He wouldn't try to force his attentions on her. She
was more deserving of respect and consideration
than any woman he'd ever met. He would be a gentleman with her, he vowed determinedly. His decision pleased him, and he swallowed the last of the
bourbon.

Eliza reared up out of sleep. Her ears rang with
the after-echoes of the sound she'd heard while still
asleep. A noise like no other—a quick roaring *crack*,
as deafening as the most immediate thunder. Her
body still recorded the movement, not felt so much
as remembered. The lift and drop. So sudden. So
heart-stopping. She looked around the room, lit by
the whitest moonlight. The painting on the wall of
the little girl standing before the obscure black gloom
of a forest seemed for a moment to leap at her, until
she realized it was faintly shivering and hanging off-
kilter. What on earth . . . ?

There was a loud sob. "Aunt Lizzie!"

Dear God, was Daisy hurt?

Eliza, her hands shaking badly, managed to light
the lamp on her bedside table. *"Aunt Lizzie!"* She
ran to Daisy's room, not bothering with a robe or
slippers. When she flung open the door, her lamp
illuminated Daisy sitting bolt upright in bed, her
terror-filled face bleached of color.

"There's a monster outside," she cried, hardly
able to speak. "It tried to pick up the house. It wants
to take us away."

Before Eliza could reassure her, a hard rapid step
hit the floor behind her and she whirled, about to
scream. Nate emerged from the deep shadows of

the hall. He had come upstairs from the parlor without a light, knowing his way through the house even
in its darkest moments.

"I heard Daisy. Is she all right? Nothing fell on
her, did it?" His eyes were bloodshot, shining faintly
with intoxication. He pushed past Eliza in the doorway and sat down on the bed to put his arm around
the girl, who was shaking with fright.

"Nate, it was a monster," Daisy cried, staring up
at him, tears threatening. Wetness clumped together
the short dark lashes. "There's a monster outside,
and he tried to pick up the house."

"No, no, no," Nate said gently. He pushed the
hair from her eyes. "There's no monster—it was just
a little tremor in the earth. It happens here sometimes. It makes a big noise, and it gives a little shake,
and then it's gone."

Eliza approached holding the lamp, her eyes wide.
"You mean it was an earthquake?"

"That's it. You've been initiated. And there was
nothing to it, really, was there?" He talked to her
as if he was still comforting Daisy. "It happens two
or three times a year, sometimes so slight that you
miss it completely. The only thing you have to be
careful of is that nothing falls on you from a shelf.
But here, Daisy—see? We never keep anything over
the beds that could fall." He reached above her head
as he pointed to the bare green wall. "This used to
be my room when I was your age, and nothing has
ever hung on that wall that I can remember."

He dropped his hand back to his knee. His gray
pin-striped waistcoat hung open over his shirt.
Without a collar and with his sleeves rolled back on
his arms, he looked as near to unkempt as Eliza had
ever seen him, except for the evening when he came
in muddy from the garden. The stubble of his beard

was dark on his face. His mouth was somewhat slack with drink; she smelled bourbon.

He smiled reassuringly at Daisy. "Do you feel better now?"

"Sort of. But don't go yet."

"Not on your life. Do you know what my mother used to do when I was scared at night? She'd sing to me. Want me to sing to you?"

Eliza shifted the lamp to the other hand to see him better. "Have you been drinking heavily, Mr. Truesdale?"

He looked up and narrowed his eyes at her. "Yes, I have. Is that Miss Nolenberg speaking? I know the difference, you know. There's Eliza and then there's Miss Nolenberg." With a sigh he reached out and took her hand. "Put that light down and come sit here with us."

She started to protest and draw back, but he tightened his fingers around hers. "It's all right. Actually, I'm trying to apologize for the way I spoke to you tonight. It never fails, does it, that I owe you apologies?"

Eliza felt a soft, warm lift of her heart. "I said some pretty nasty things too."

"Are you apologizing?"

"I suppose I am."

"Thank you. Now sit down and please put that light away."

"You shouldn't have been drinking so much."

"Miss Nolenberg can leave the room, but I like Eliza and I want her to stay."

Eliza put the lamp on the table by the bed and sat beside Daisy, turning her face away so that Nate wouldn't see the tears in her eyes. How he touched her heart sometimes.

Nate began to sing. It was a little song about a frog courting a lady mouse. He'd heard it often from

the Negro minstrels who held forth with their ban-
jos at the Bush Street Theater. He smiled at Daisy
as he sang.

Long before he'd finished the entire song, Daisy
was giggling and joining in on the chorus. Even Eliza
sang along, her laughter melding with Daisy's. He
loved the sound of it, loved looking at her. Her hair
shone soft around her shoulders, shimmering in the
fuzzy light. She was an angel. Eve.

Daisy became so excited she hopped off the bed
and pranced around the room on her bare pink feet,
and sang for him something the girls at school had
taught her.

When she had finished, she jumped onto the bed
between Eliza and Nate, bouncing them. "Now it's
your turn, Aunt Lizzie!" When Eliza protested that
she didn't know any songs, Daisy said, "It's time to
learn. It's Christmas! This is the season of song.
That's what Mrs. Rodriguez says at school."

"No, no, dear, I think it's the season for sleep.
It's the middle of the night."

Nate stood up to make room for Daisy on the bed.
He slouched against the door frame and watched
Eliza tuck her under the covers. He could tell he
wasn't drunk, but he was tight enough to get a too-
easy rush as Eliza bent over the bed and he saw her
rear stretch the white flannel nightgown. He focused on the shape, so blatantly feminine and so
near his hand. She was too luscious for words.

"I want to give you a kiss too, Nate," Daisy said,
breaking his concentration.

He felt a little catch in his heart as he leaned over
her, and she clasped her soft arms around his neck.
How could anything be sweeter than these moments
with the three of them? Blessed be the earthquake.
Daisy planted a smacking kiss on his cheek, and he
kissed hers. "Oooh, you've got needles on your

face," she said. Embarrassed, he reached up and scraped his palm across his cheek. What must he look like to Eliza?

In the hall, Eliza nodded to him and turned toward her door. He was in agony, wanting her to say something, trying desperately to think of something to say to her.

She paused and looked at him again. In the glow of the lamp she carried she looked like a vision, ethereal and luminous against the darkness, her white flannel nightgown a gentle silhouette. Masses of hair tumbled around her shoulders, curling over her arms. As if suddenly aware that she wasn't wearing a robe, she lifted one arm across her chest. Instead of shielding her, it pressed the fabric into the valley between her breasts, and emphasized how firm and high they were. Goddamn it, he wouldn't flirt with her; he'd promised himself he wouldn't do that again. He'd leave her alone. But wasn't she a vision!

"Mr. Truesdale . . ." she began.

"Nate."

She smiled, her small teeth gleaming white in the light. "Nate," she said. Her beguiling fawnlike eyes were suddenly direct and warm, then downcast in shyness.

"What did you want to say?" he prompted.

"I suppose I mean . . . I'm sorry about the things I said earlier . . . and thank you for helping with Daisy. It was very kind of you."

"My pleasure," he responded, aware that he was beaming like a praised schoolboy, yet he was not embarrassed.

"And you have a very nice singing voice. I enjoyed it." An unbelievably beautiful smile appeared on that lovely mouth of hers. She opened the door and stepped inside before closing it again.

He found himself grinning at the closed door. Goddamned fool, he told himself.

Mrs. Penchelli approved of Eliza's design and craftsmanship on the evening gown she had made. "I have a rush order here," the old woman said in her deep voice. "My best customer. So please give it your best, eh? Come here. The materials are on my desk. Miss Sharpe and I have gone over—"

"You mean Marietta Sharpe?" Eliza asked in surprise.

"You know her?" At Eliza's nod, Mrs. Penchelli sighed. "A sweet-looking young thing, she is, but difficult to work with. Anyway—"she thrust up her hands in resignation—"we finally came to an agreement concerning this gown. She needs it in a week— for the Hobarts' Christmas ball. I'm sorry to give you so little time, but I know you can do it, Eliza."

It was the most difficult project Eliza had ever undertaken. Not because of the intricacy of detail or the huge amount of fabric required, but because Marietta would wear it for Nate. Across this section of the gown his hand would rest as he danced with her—and she remembered the magic of the evening when she herself had waltzed with him. The bodice here would catch his eye, not because of the gown so much as the woman in it. Would Nate embrace Marietta in this gown? Would his hands stroke the satin? Unfasten these tiny hidden hooks? Slide this ribbon-laced strap from her shoulder? Jealous, Eliza imagined every possible scenario that might take place.

As she worked in the evenings, she was in such a poor humor that both Nate and Daisy tried to keep out of her way. Nate sat on the floor with Daisy and scowled through endless games of jackstraws. Everything he said to Eliza provoked a hot retort or icy snub. It seemed as if the sweet camaraderie they had shared the night of the earthquake had been only a dream. And Daisy, attuned to the emotions around her, grew too quiet. It was the first time Nate wished Eliza would start spending more of her time upstairs in her room.

Only one night of that week did she not have the cherry satin heaped in her lap and spread around her on the sofa. That was the evening Marietta joined them in the large, comfortable parlor. She had brought a big package for Daisy and sat beside the ecstatic girl as Daisy opened it and with a delighted gasp pulled from the white tissue paper a doll. Marietta smiled at Daisy's reaction. "When I saw it, I thought it looked so like you that I had to have it for you."

"Oh," Daisy breathed. Her small fingers touched the smooth porcelain cheeks painted rose, stroked the thick strands of human hair so shiny in their brunette waves. Reverently, Daisy smoothed the lawn dress with its pink and white stripes and wide pink velvet sash.

Nate bent down on one knee as he, too, admired the doll. "She does look like you, baby dear," he said, smiling. "But not as pretty—almost, but not quite." He rocked back, catching his balance by bracing his hand against the floor as Daisy leaned forward and hugged him around the neck.

"Do I get a hug too?" Marietta asked. Daisy promptly threw her arms around Marietta and, self-conscious and surprisingly ill at ease, the woman patted Daisy's back. "What are you planning to name her?"

"I think . . ." Daisy sat up straight on the edge of the faded pink damask couch, her hazel eyes bright, one finger under her chin as she looked from Nate to Marietta to the doll. "Marietta," she announced.

"Why, that's very sweet of you, child," Marietta exclaimed. "Did you hear, Nate?"

"That's nice," he said as he returned to stand by the mantel. Daisy sat back against the sofa and held the doll on her legs to admire her.

Eliza, seated in the chair across the room, could hardly remain still while Marietta and Daisy hugged and exclaimed together over the gift. She felt so alone, as if Nate had already married Marietta and won custody of Daisy. This is how they would look together, the three of them, when she had returned alone to Pittsburgh.

"Come here, Daisy, may I see her?" she said. When Daisy brought her new doll near, Eliza lifted the girl to her lap. How could she ever bear to lose her?

And to Marietta! Didn't Nate have any better taste? But wouldn't it still feel terrible no matter whom he brought in as stepmother for Daisy?

Marietta rose and went to stand beside Nate at the mantel, her skirts and petticoats swishing gently, silk on silk. She wore a dark red gown with white ermine trim on the high wired collar. She put her hand on his arm, and whispered something to him. "Oh, of course," he said. "I'll be right back. Miss Nolenberg—a glass of wine?"

She shook her head, and he left the room. Daisy kissed the doll's cheek.

Marietta's blue-violet eyes narrowed as she produced a cool smile. "Are you not in mourning now, Miss Nolenberg?" she asked, and Eliza touched the lace that lifted like a soft scalloped cloud from the neckline of her new yellow gown. Tonight was the first time she had worn it. The sewing for Mrs. Penchelli had occupied so much of her time she hadn't been able to complete it until now.

Nate had smiled when he saw it. "Perfect," he'd said. And she'd been pleased.

Marietta continued before Eliza could respond. "You do realize, do you not, that your situation in this household is highly irregular, Miss Nolenberg? Someone of your position is not usually accorded the freedom to spend evenings with the family."

"What is your point, Miss Sharpe?" Eliza asked with forced politeness, though she seethed with anger.

"I'm merely giving you a reminder. Don't expect that your future experiences in Mr. Truesdale's household will be as they are at present."

"I expect nothing of the kind," Eliza retorted.

"Very sensible of you, Miss Nolenberg. I'm glad to hear that you know your place."

Eliza was speechless and trembled with fury. Marietta turned a smile upon Daisy. "How would you like to go out with me tomorrow? It will be just you, me, and Mr. Truesdale, and we'll have a wonderful time together."

"I'm afraid that's not possible," Eliza interrupted. "Daisy is still under my care. I decide her activities and accompany her wherever she goes."

Nate walked back into the parlor at that moment, and Marietta turned a shocked glanced to him. "Is this true?" she demanded. "Does Miss Nolenberg make all decisions about the child and never allow Daisy to go anywhere without her?"

Frowning, Nate handed her the glass of red wine he'd brought. This whole situation was getting stickier by the day, he thought. Though Marietta's treatment of Eliza irritated him, he likewise didn't agree with Eliza's overly protective attitude toward Daisy. He refused to have to take sides and merely shrugged noncommittally.

Marietta shot a glare at Eliza. "Miss Nolenberg,"

she said cooly, "in future, things will be very different around here, let me assure you."

"Oh, yes. Daisy and I will be in Pittsburgh," Eliza stood up, barely controlling her anger. Clutching Daisy's hand, she said, "Let's get you ready for bed now."

"But it's early, Aunt Lizzie," Daisy argued. "Why do I have to go to bed? I wanta stay here."

"I'll read to you in bed tonight, my dear. Now come along."

Daisy agreed, but before she left the room, she found her manners, smiled shyly at Marietta, and said, "Thank you for my doll." Eliza ushered her quickly from the room before Daisy would think to give that woman another hug.

When they were past the doorway, she heard Nate's voice. Apparently aggravated, he spoke too loudly. "Why did you have to say that to her? Look, sweetheart, things are difficult enough without you adding fuel to the fire."

Eliza fumed. Difficult, was she! Marietta irked *her!*

She was still upset the next morning when Nate commented in irritation, "What's wrong with me taking Daisy out with Marietta? I walk that little girl to school every day, and it doesn't bother you that you're not along."

"Daisy is my responsibi—"

Nate cut her off as he brushed past on the upstairs landing. "Oh, yes, I've heard all this before. But it's going to change." Eyes hard, he looked back up. "Do you understand me, Miss Nolenberg?"

"Don't you ever talk to me in that tone!"

"This is my house! That—"he mouthed the words in a harsh whisper so that Daisy wouldn't overhear—"*is my daughter*, and I think it's time you recognized it!"

Eliza leaned over the wooden railing. "Your

house? I still have our tickets back to Pittsburgh. We can be out of here tonight, Mr. Truesdale."

The door opened behind Eliza, and she turned in guilty surprise. "You're fighting," Daisy accused sullenly. Her lower lip pushed out, and she looked as if she had been crying. Her book satchel dangled from one hand. A big red bow anchored her shiny, straight hair in its single braid; she wore her navy-blue sailor dress and high-laced black shoes with black stockings. She looked at Eliza, then Nate. "Why are you always fighting?"

A brittle smile on his face, Nate said, "No, no, precious. Just a little disagreement. Are you ready for school? Let's go then." After Daisy clumped past him on her way down the stairs, he turned and glanced back up at Eliza, who was still glaring at him over the railing. In a tight whisper, he said, *"You try that and I'll have the police after you."* Then, in a normal tone for Daisy's benefit, he added casually, "Last night after you left the room, Marietta made a good point. I have certain rights in this situation which you don't see fit to acknowledge. I've decided to exercise those rights, so I'm letting you know now that Marietta and I will be picking up Daisy after school today to take her out. We'll see you this evening, Aunt Lizzie."

A violent outburst strangled in Eliza's mouth. Daisy watched her vigilantly from the bottom of the stairs. Eliza couldn't bring herself to say anything further with Daisy's hurt and accusing gaze on her. She whirled away.

So Marietta had made a good point, had she? And she'd probably be smug and victorious, satisfied that Nate had finally put Eliza in her place. Remembering Marietta's cutting remark from the previous night—*I'm glad to hear that you know your place*—Eliza shook with rage.

That day, the day she was to return Marietta's completed gown to Mrs. Penchelli, Eliza deliberately and with relish slit virtually every other one of her neat little stitches.

Let the gown fall off Marietta in rags!

Chapter 10

❧

Daisy was standing in the foyer when Nate descended the stairs. She wore a new pink velvet robe and matching slippers, and looked as delicate as one of her porcelain dolls. A drop of water glistened at one corner of her upper lip. Her fists were propped on nonexistent hips, her face puckered into a frown of disapproval—a perfect miniature of Mrs. Herlihy when the boy from the market was late. She said with mock severity, "What is that hat doing on your head?"

Grinning, Nate hunkered down to see her eye-to-eye. "I think it's just sitting there. What do you think?"

"I think you're going to another big party."

"Is that right?" He scooped her into his arms and stood up, lifting her to his shoulder. "Yes, I am, so how 'bout a big kiss good-bye?"

Her shining hazel eyes smiled back into his. "Can I wear your hat?"

"I don't know. Why don't you try it on first and see if it fits."

She grasped the brim in both hands, took it from his head, and set it on hers. The shiny black top hat dropped over her face, revealing only a laughing mouth and chin. He chuckled, bouncing her in his arm, and she clutched his shoulder to hold on, streams of giggles pouring from her like liquid sweetness. She left the hat on and clowned, waggling her head so the hat rocked back and forth. Nate laughed with her, delighted beyond measure to see her happy again, after the sadness and tears and scenes, all reflections of the tension between him and Eliza. His hearty chuckles bounced her against his chest.

And suddenly he wasn't laughing anymore.

An ache filled his chest and he wanted to tell her who he was, wanted to hear that light voice call him father. Nothing else had ever seemed so important, nor so necessary.

He lifted the hat from her face. "Give me a hug, precious," he said, and felt the slight tremor in his voice. "Give me the biggest hug you've got."

Eliza sat propped up in bed, two fluffy pillows behind her back, a dressing robe belted over her nightgown in readiness. It was already midnight. The book on her lap couldn't hold her attention for more than a paragraph at a time. What was happening at the Hobarts' ball? Had Marietta discovered the fragile seams and worn a different gown instead? Eliza was both apprehensive and eager. It was such a silly trick to have pulled. Childish and despicable, really. Still . . . She wished she could be there to see. Every clatter of a carriage in the street sent her heart clamoring. The wait for Nate's return was impossibly long. She sighed and lifted the book again as she shifted further down in the bed. Its softness was such a luxury to her now. Someday when she and Daisy were back home—she experienced a tiny prick of regret at the thought—she would save up enough money for such a bed.

Thirty minutes later she heard Nate slam the front

door with a resounding *thunk*, and his footsteps pounded up the stairs. He was taking the stairs two at a time. Something must have happened at the party. Rapid strides sounded along the corridor . . . to her door—

He burst into her room without knocking. His face was set in such anger he was almost livid, nostrils flaring. She stuffed a scrap of red satin ribbon into her book as a marker and shoved it aside.

"What in the hell are you trying to do?" he shouted.

"What are you talking about?" There was no need to admit to anything, she thought, staring at him with a rigid expression—after all, he had just barged into her room—but her mouth trembled with suppressed eagerness. Whatever had happened to Marietta's dress must have been terrible!

One long finger flashed out and jabbed the air. "You know damned good and well what I'm talking about! You made that gown!"

She tried to keep an excited smile off her face. "Which gown?"

"Marietta's gown for the Hobarts' ball. You knew it was hers, didn't you." His face flamed in anger, and a pulse leaped on his temple. "That was the lowest thing you could have done, sewing it so that it fell apart. I would never have believed you could stoop so low!"

Eliza caught her breath. "You didn't tell her I made it, did you?"

"Of course not!" he exclaimed. "I didn't want to be responsible for your death! But you've put me in the middle, and I *don't like it!*" He paced back and forth. "That was the meanest, lowest—"

"What happened? Tell me!"

He stopped. "Can't you imagine?"

"No, tell me, tell me."

"Her gown fell apart!"

Eliza pinched her mouth with her fingers, trying not to so much as smile. "Oh, my," she said quietly, and attempted a shocked expression. Her lips trembled uncontrollably.

Nate regarded her in shock. "You're enjoying this! Aren't you ashamed in the least? The poor woman's dress was coming open—"

Eliza covered her mouth with her hand.

"—right there at the biggest social event of the year! You don't know what that party meant to her. And there she was . . ." Nate paced again.

"Oh, please. Tell me," Eliza said in a whisper, not able to trust her voice.

Nate's lower lip compressed in anger, until his mouth was a tight line. He marched to the bedside and pointed his finger at her as he said in a too-low voice, "I want you to picture the humiliation of this incident, Miss Nolenberg. Soften up that bitter heart of yours." Nate waved his fingers at his right shoulder. "First of all, the bow on the strap slid off. It just flopped there. And while I was trying to help her fix it, the whole damned strap came undone!"

Eliza bent her head to her knees to hide her face. Her shoulders twitched.

"She almost lost the whole damned top of it right then!"

It was much better than Eliza had ever imagined! All at once she couldn't stop herself; she muffled her laughter against the covers.

"You're really enjoying this, aren't you?" he said in amazement.

Eliza lifted her head, carefully controlling herself. "Oh, this is terrible," she said in a weak voice. "What did her face look like?"

"What in the hell do you think her face looked like? She was mortified! I've never seen anybody turn so red." He bent over her as he declared, "It was the worst moment of her life! She almost didn't make it out of the room!"

"There's more?" It was too good to be true! Eliza was fairly choking.

"What d'you think? You made the dress!" Nate straightened. "She stepped on the hem when she was trying to leave the room, and the entire skirt split at the waist. Can you picture it? I was grabbing handfuls of skirt to keep her from losing it entirely!"

Eliza fell back against the pillows, clutched her middle, and burst out laughing.

"It wasn't funny in the least!" he shouted. "Do you know how many panels of fabric were in that skirt? Yes, of course you do—and the more I grabbed, the more they split apart. This is not funny!" He stood looking at her, but she was beyond remorse. Tears rolled down her cheeks. "It wasn't funny," he repeated, as if in defeat. "At least . . ." He watched her hanging onto her sides. ". . . it wasn't funny then."

He tried not to smile. "Please, Eliza," he pleaded, "this is very serious!" But his mouth twitched. "Oh, hell, you should have seen it. It was really something." A chuckle escaped him.

Eliza was gasping. "More, more! Tell me more!"

He pinched up the knees of his trousers and sat down on the edge of the mattress. "I never want to go through anything like it again. Please. Promise me." He gave a swift chuckle. "You should have seen it—a couple of ladies rushed toward us, to help out, and Marietta was hanging onto the top of the gown." He patted his chest to indicate that she was trying to hold it over her breasts. "And I was clutching all these pieces of satin. She was running, and I was trying to keep up. I kept sliding on all this material dragging along behind her. Do you have any idea how slippery satin is when you're stepping on it?''

Eliza had never laughed so hard. Her sides ached, but still she couldn't stop.

Nate laughed with her, shaking his head. ''Oh, what a night! She was trying to hang onto everything and push people out of her way at the same time. She wouldn't let anyone help. She started slapping *my* hands out of the way. Did she think I was trying to take the dress *apart*? Hell, if it weren't for me—''

But Eliza was rolling back and forth on the pillows, gasping. ''Stop, stop! I can't stand it!''

''And the things she screamed. I never knew she had such a vocabulary. You know, she always seemed so—well, I don't mean innocent exactly. Just kind of sweet, too sheltered maybe. And then the shock of what she was yelling . . .'' Nate threw back his head, roaring. ''I almost dropped everything. And we were trailing ribbons . . . bits of material . . . A whole frantic procession of people was trying to help out.''

''No, no, no—no more!'' Eliza couldn't catch her breath.

''Serves you right,'' he exclaimed, shaking his head at her. ''You think I'm going to let you make any shirts for me now? Not on you life! I could be in the middle of a crucial negotiation with a customer . . . and my shirt would start sliding out of my coat sleeves. I could be bowing to some sweet young lady and suddenly popping a hairy chest in her face! Oh, and forget *entirely* any notion of sewing trousers. I'll take the air another way, thank you very much.''

Eliza wrapped her arms around her middle, hugging herself as she pleaded with him to stop.

He chuckled, watching. ''You've got a mean

streak in you, lady. It wasn't funny being there, you know. And you probably should apologize, but if I were you I wouldn't get too close to Marietta for a while."

It was several more minutes before Eliza sobered sufficiently to sit up straight and wipe her eyes on the sleeve of her robe. "You're right," she said in a weak, uneven voice. "It really wasn't nice."

"That's an understatement! Why did you do it?"

Eliza glanced away. "I just—" She shrugged and looked at his hand on the bedspread, at the long fingers with fine black hairs. "She'd just been so . . . mean . . . sometimes. She was smug and insisted that I know my place, as if I was some kind of servant here."

"So she said a few things that weren't exactly polite. There must be some other reason. I mean, what you did was really—"

"Yes, it was really awful, I know," Eliza interrupted crisply. She tightened the edges of the robe around her throat, aware of his presence now as she had not been before. He was sitting on her bed, watching her with those heart-melting eyes. He leaned his weight on one hand. He was, she noticed, actually propped over her legs. She tried to maintain her composure, but her stomach was falling away as she realized how much she wanted to keep him there, in her room, in her bed. Her glance slid to his mouth.

"Eliza?" he said slowly, thoughtfully, and her eyes jumped guiltily back to his. "Were you . . ." His eyebrows lifted as he watched her, ". . . jealous?"

Her face heated with an uncomfortable flush.

Nate watched the pink bloom rise higher under her skin. Her face fairly glowed . . . such a lovely face! He'd been so preoccupied earlier, he hadn't

even considered the fact that they were in her bedroom. Alone. On her bed together. The whole con-
cept and its attendant possibilities now burst
through his mind.

Over the shoulders of a faded green-flowered robe
her hair curled, tangled from her wild hilarity. In the
wavering light of the bedside lamp the curls looked
glossy, with a sheen like polished mahogany, rich
and abundant. He wanted to touch the curls, feel
the soft thickness with his fingers. Those exquisite
eyes were trained down at the bedcovers, then
slanted off to the side, refusing to meet his gaze.
Why was she so shy now? Was she thinking what
he was thinking?

He realized he wanted her to be jealous. ''Are
you . . . ?'' he pressed gently.

''What a silly notion,'' she murmured, trying to
pass it off with a short laugh and a negligent wave
of her hand. Slender fingers, tapering, airy, graceful. He would kiss each delicate finger, one at a time.

''No, it's not,'' he said.

Beside his hips she shifted her legs slightly, and
he couldn't help thinking of feminine thighs, warm,
firm. He put his hand on the covers over her knees,
and she jerked slightly but did not pull away.

He felt his face heating. ''Eliza, silly or not, it's
rather a . . . uh . . .'' He gave a soft laugh, and her
eyes finally connected with his. ''It's a notion I
rather . . . like.'' His eyebrows lifted slightly in a
question.

Her gaze melted, infinitely inviting. She *was*
thinking what he was thinking, he realized. Beneath
the robe her breasts kept pushing out with her
breathing. He couldn't tear his eyes from the firm
thrusting. When her breathing grew deeper, so
much more pronounced, the sound drifted to him
like a lover's call. As the blood rushed through him,

he moved his hand up the blanket, stroking her thighs, unable to stop. Her eyes locked on his, glazing with passion, drawing him.

Eliza watched him lean toward her, felt his hand slide through her hair to cup the back of her head. Her lips trembled as his mouth drew nearer. He kissed her with more passion than she'd expected, crushing her mouth, wiping away all thought but the single affirmative *Yes!* She lifted her arms around his back, her breath catching at the sudden exciting contact of his chest, as hard as iron against hers. Shocks of passion streaked through her from his kiss. When he drew back slightly, she moaned in protest. But he touched her cheek gently with his fingers, looking down into her eyes. What breathtakingly soft, sparkling eyes he had. He pressed little kisses on her lips. And then, as his mouth hardened and moved over hers in another deep, reaching kiss, she was aware of a difference. There was no recklessness here, but tenderness, too. The sweet warmth of it took her breath away. Her heart beat hard against his chest.

Nate felt the answering passion in those blossoming rose-petal lips, so warm and moist. He felt her relaxing, melting under his caresses, under the hand that had found its way to her breast. Her pleasure almost made him lose control, and he wanted to snatch that robe and nightgown out of his way *at once*—he who prided himself on lengthy lovemaking sessions.

Abruptly his heart was pounding too strangely. Like an animal sensing danger, he felt the hair on the back of his neck rise. He pulled away from her. She opened her eyes slowly, so dreamy and hazy with passion. And she murmured a small protest and tried to draw him back to her. He clutched his fingers in her hair, looked down into those beckoning eyes. Beneath his hand her breast was warm, molded into the cup of his palm. The tiny rigid nipple was like the head of a match burning into his skin. Under his side as he leaned over her were those thighs and lush center.

She was such an angel. He wanted her with him always.

A warning erupted in his brain. This woman was not like the others he'd known. She would change him forever. He sensed it and pulled away from her, frowning as he tried to sort out his feelings. What was happening to him? Was he getting emotionally involved? He had a vague sense of losing control of his life and knew he had to get away.

But he didn't want to leave. Eliza was beautiful, exciting, and too tempting to resist. He'd never desired any other woman as strongly as he wanted Eliza, but making love with her was suddenly a disturbing thought. Was he falling in love with her?

Abruptly, he was on his feet. "Eliza, I'm . . . I have to leave." He strode to the door.

She sat up. "Nate? What's wrong?"

He glanced back, and she looked more desirable than ever before. That deliciously feminine body beseeched him. What kind of fool was he to be leaving? But there was something deeper going on between them. It was a situation he wasn't at all sure he could handle.

With a muttered curse, he wrenched open the door and escaped into the hall.

"I don't care what your reasons were, there is no explanation adequate enough to explain this kind of childish perversity!" Mrs. Penchelli's summer-blue eyes were irate. She lifted bits of cherry satin from her desk, pieces disconnected, unrecognizable as a gown. "Miss Sharpe was one of my best customers.

Notice I use the past tense. Do you imagine she's going to trust me again after an incident like this? Do you imagine she's going to recommend me?''

The woman slammed down the cherry satin pieces on the desktop. "It'll never happen again, Mrs. Penchelli," Eliza promised. "I'm sorry and I'll apologize to Miss Sharpe. I'll explain to her—"

"How can I trust you again, Eliza? How can I know when I give you a project for someone who irritated you—and wind up with this kind of disaster? I can't use you anymore. That's it.''

"Please, I need the work, Mrs. Penchelli. It will never happen again, you have my word on it.'' Eliza leaned toward the woman, desperate. "I'm a good seamstress, you've said it yourself.''

"You're good, Eliza," Mrs. Penchelli flatly answered, "but not so good that I can't do without you.''

Eliza left the house and walked slowly along the street. She no longer had employment. How long would it take to find another job? How was she to get by in the next weeks, after Mr. McPherson's money was gone? She couldn't go to Nate and ask for a loan. Though he supported Daisy entirely now, she had been proud of the fact that she needed nothing from him for herself. In her mind she heard the beating of the looms at the mill back in Pittsburgh. At least she had the promise of that job to help her case with Daisy. But she didn't want to think about it—neither the mill nor the probable loss of Daisy. Nate was right, she didn't stand a chance of winning custody. But she couldn't give up without trying her hardest. She just couldn't.

Her heart beat faster, as it did whenever she thought of Nate. What had happened that night? Her disappointment had been keen when he'd departed her room so abruptly. And in these last two days, he'd been preoccupied and disinclined to engage in conversation. He'd taken his breakfast out on the back steps both mornings, though the air was sharp with cold in those early hours. So cold that when she'd glanced through the window, she'd seen his breath escaping in cotton-puff clouds.

So heightened was her awareness that the mere sight of him in those odd moments when they encountered each other in the house made her heart beat faster. The situation couldn't continue!

What was she to do now?

That afternoon Nate pushed aside the papers on his desk. The contract demands from the MDK Paper Company in Oregon were going to take more concentration than he had at the moment. On the stacked bills of lading were the opera tickets he'd ordered for the evening of December twenty-sixth, four days away. He shoved them aside and glanced through the bills of lading. Despite the new law that had gone into effect last July, Rossie was still adding statements saying the company was not liable for damage to shipments. Nate had memorized that clause, he'd gone over it so often with Rossie, who kept insisting it was worthless. In effect the law held carrier companies responsible for all damage to merchandise that they were transporting, and made it illegal to insert the kinds of disclaimers that Rossie insisted on including in their contracts. The ruling was simple and consistent with good business practice, regardless of the law, but Rossie chose to ignore it.

Nate sat back in his chair, propping his elbows on the polished oak arms, and swiveled around until he could look out the row of windows behind him.

The green leather shades were lowered halfway, and he stared out at a gray day. Low fog obliterated the sky. Below on Market Street the usual stream of carriages and wagons moved briskly past. A few black umbrellas fanned open.

Nate made his mind purposefully blank for a time. Usually he structured his life so that when he was in the office nothing else existed but the work at hand. When he was elsewhere, he wiped work from his mind entirely. He gave the company its due, to the best of his abilities, but after that he owed it nothing. But it was difficult to concentrate these days.

A carriage halted on the street directly below him. He rolled the chair nearer to the window to see. Marietta was alighting from the carriage. He scowled with impatience. She'd better not take too long.

A minute later she knocked, and he called out to her to come in. When he saw her blue-violet eyes glittering in anger, he cursed under his breath. She was the last person he wanted to see now. Marietta closed the door with a hard snap and walked forward to lean toward him over the desktop.

"Nate, you'll never guess—I was at Mrs. Penchelli's this morning, and do you know who made that gown? Miss Nolenberg!"

She whirled and began to pace, and in that time Nate mentally listed the names of the other three paper companies he did business with. He would ask Peg Walters to find the files for him. He wanted to compare contracts. What clauses—?

"I'm not surprised it was her. I always knew she was a low sort. Nothing is beneath her." Marietta uttered a sharp sound and flung up her hands. "Obviously *nothing* is beneath her! But I talked to Mrs. Penchelli this morning and let her know precisely how I feel. I told her she'd not have *my* business again if she didn't fire Miss Nolenberg immediately. I'm almost of a mind to go elsewhere anyway. Then again, Miss Nolenberg might be hired by another seamstress and I wouldn't know it. Oh, the humiliation—I'll never be able to live it down!''

She paced again, growing more incensed. "Firing her is not enough. I want you to talk to her, Nate. She mustn't get away with this! The mortification—"

"I'm not going to get involved," he said, still leaning back in his chair, detached.

"What?" She spun on him, planted her hands on the desktop, and speared him with a sharp, incredulous stare. "You know what she did to me! How she humiliated me!"

"Don't try to put me in the middle, Marietta. I wash my hands of the whole thing.''

"But you're letting her stay at your house—'' Another thought occurred to her, and she glared furiously. "Did you know she was making that gown?"

"She was sewing a gown," he explained, spreading wide his hands. "I didn't know it was yours until I saw you in it.''

"Did you talk to her about it afterward? You *knew* she'd done that to me!" Marietta was so irate that her blonde curls quivered under the velvet brim of her mauve hat.

Nate frowned. "I'm not going to discuss the matter. You know, some of the things you said to her over the last weeks weren't exactly polite.''

"She's nothing more than *hired help*, Nate. I want her out of your house. She doesn't belong there . . . and after what she did to me, there's no reason for you to be so cordial to her.''

He exhaled in brief exasperation. "Daisy needs her," he said, fighting back his anger.

"What about me? What about what she did to me? Aren't I more important? After such a spiteful, malicious trick like that!"

"Look," he snapped, "Miss Nolenberg's having a difficult enough time now, what with Daisy—"

"What's going on in that house, Nate?" She narrowed her eyes into hard slits. "What's going on between the two of you?"

"I'm not going to discuss it, Marietta," he warned.

"Oh! I should have seen it coming when she started fixing her hair and wearing new gowns! I should have guessed, but I didn't realize you'd go so low, behind my back, with *hired help!* But why should that surprise me—after all, Daisy is proof you'd stoop to sluts in the street! Blood will win out over breeding, won't it? And those two are sisters— just alike!"

He stood up slowly. With grim fury he said, "Be careful what you say. About me, and about that woman, who is a guest in my house."

"Are you actually defending her to me?"

"After hearing the false accusations you're making, I think she needs someone to stand up for her."

"I don't believe you're saying this to me," Marietta exclaimed. "You're taking her side. Well, I won't stand for it! You get her out of your house or we're finished. Do you hear me?"

"No one dictates to me," Nate said through clenched teeth. "The door is behind you. If you're leaving, make it quick. I have work to do."

Marietta was taken aback. "Are you asking me to go? Why, you insufferable beast! Do you think you can get away with treating me like this? Well, you just go on back to your little millworker. I hope you two will be very happy raising your soot-faced brats. I have better things to do."

"In that case, don't waste any more of your time or mine." Striding to the door, Nate yanked it open for her.

Marietta stood completely still, her face redden-
ing. Then she marched briskly to the door, hissing
as she passed him, "We're finished! I wouldn't
take you back even if you came to me on your
knees."

"Don't wait around for it," he answered, following her out of the office. Marietta stormed down the
aisle between the wooden railings, but Nate didn't
watch her.

To the short, bespectacled woman at the nearby
desk, he said calmly, "Peg, get me the files for the
Coast, Albrecht, and Mission Bay paper companies."

Eliza walked the streets for the rest of the afternoon. Although a light sprinkle of rain fell intermittently, she didn't care. Climbing the street into the
Nob Hill area, she saw a crowd milling outside of a
home. She had to pass the people on her way to
Nate's house, and she approached with mild curiosity. Carriages drew up one by one at the door, and
Eliza paused at the outskirts of the spectators to
watch the elegant, bejeweled women and black-
suited men alight.

Beside Eliza an older woman clucked her tongue.
"Ain't they pretty?" she said with a sigh. "I swear,
them society ladies are the most bee-u-tiful ladies
in the world. God knew where to give the looks,
didn't He though?"

Thinking of Marietta Sharpe, Eliza couldn't share
the woman's reverence. "What's happening here
today?" she asked.

The old woman tore her gaze from the sparkling
gowns and winked at Eliza. "A wedding reception," she said in a confidential tone, as if sharing
some wonderful news. "The daughter of the house
just got married. And you should've been here to
see *him*. That groom was as handsome as they

get.'' With a sudden excited poke at Eliza's ribs, she indicated another arriving black carriage. ''Lookee in there. I ain't never seen a grander tiara than that one yonder.''

Eliza glanced around at the other ordinary people crowding the lawn and street. They were all envious, thrilling to this glimpse into a privileged world.

Thinking of Nate, Eliza felt a stab of hurt and dismay. He was a member of this elite class. Why did she keep forgetting how wide the chasm was between them? Did she think he could ever be seriously interested in her, a factory worker?

Deeply upset, Eliza started to move past the house, but the old woman stopped her. ''Ain't you gonna stay around? Sometimes they toss money. Once I even got a slice of wedding cake. The lady offered some to them who were still around when they was all done with their partying. Stick around, dearie. You never know.''

But Eliza shook her head. She couldn't help picturing Nate flinging her money or offering a last crumb of wedding cake when he finally married one of those women she had seen today. The image was like a slap in the face, and she hurried away from the crowd.

When she returned to Nate's house it was near dusk. She climbed the brick steps and entered the house, left her cape and hat on the oak rack in the front parlor instead of taking them upstairs, and went into the kitchen. Mrs. Herlihy had already gone, and Eliza remembered that it was Thursday, the day the housekeeper left early. In the gloom, Daisy sat on a stool beside the worktable.

''I'm hungry, Aunt Lizzie,'' she complained. ''Nate isn't coming in . . .''

''Where is he? Out back?''

''Mmm-hmm. He's working. But I don't think he

wants help," she added as Eliza pulled open the
back door to go out.

She could see Nate squatting as he lit a kerosene
lantern set on the ground beside the gaping black
door of the carriage house.

"Nate," she said, crossing the wet grass toward
him. "Can we talk?"

"Anytime we want."

He wore work pants of faded brown cotton, a
plain shirt without a collar, and heavy boots. His
clothing was damp from the earlier light rain. Bending, he grabbed a pair of work gloves, the lantern,
and reached for a small shovel leaning against the
carriage house. As he started crossing the yard, he
said, "Was there something in particular you wanted
to discuss?"

Eliza followed. This was going to be more difficult
than she'd imagined. "I was fired today . . . because
of Miss Sharpe's gown," she began.

He set the lantern down beside a broad row of
rose bushes and leaned his forearm on the handle
of the shovel as he looked at her. "I know. I heard
about it from Marietta. I'm sorry, Eliza. Really."

"I probably should apologize to her. In fact, I
know I should."

"No," he said, shaking his head firmly and laying
down the shovel. "Don't do that. Just leave it alone.
She doesn't deserve it anyway." He pulled on the
work gloves and squatted beside the rose beds,
where wispy green weeds were sprouting lush from
winter rain.

Eliza stepped nearer, careful not to cross the light
and throw shadow on his work. He yanked handfuls of weeds and dropped them into a pile behind
him. "When you next see her," she said, "or if it
comes up in conversation, would you let her know?"

"I won't be seeing her again. We've terminated our . . . relationship."

Eliza suppressed a tug of elation. "I'm sorry."

Nate gave a vicious yank on a thick clump of weeds. "Why don't we be honest? I'm not sorry and you're not either. You never liked her, so don't pretend you did."

She watched him work, the elation dissipating under the weight of reality. "She might have made a fine stepmother for Daisy, I don't mean to say she wouldn't, but I would probably dislike any woman who tried to take my place in Daisy's life. So if you want honesty," she added, drawing a deep breath, "that's it." So what if Marietta was no longer in his life, she thought. Another woman just like her would soon take her place.

Nate glanced up at Eliza in surprise. He saw the agitation in her face, the fingers clutching her new blue-and-white-striped dress. Rising, he stripped off one glove and reached for her arm.

"Your being fired doesn't have to change anything," he said quietly. "I told you you're welcome to stay with Daisy. You can be here as long as you want."

His very touch sent a flush of pleasurable warmth through her, and Eliza pulled away from his grasp. The attraction she felt for him was growing too strong; the night when he had returned from the Hobarts' ball, she had almost made love with him, she remembered guiltily. "I'll find work somewhere else," she insisted. "What I wanted to ask you about is if you know of any places where I might find employment."

"How about right here? I'll pay you to be Daisy's governess."

Surprised and still smarting from the image of Nate flinging money to her in the crowd gawking at his wedding reception, Eliza stared at him. Their relationship had changed considerably since he had first proposed this idea, and he'd already made several attempts to seduce her. What could he be thinking of to suggest such a thing now? Did he hope to keep her near so he might eventually be successful and have a convenient mistress? It was insulting! "Absolutely not," she protested vehemently. "How can you even think I'd stay here with you on an indefinite basis, and be paid for it?"

Nate's voice grew louder in annoyance. "What's unreasonable about it? I want the best governess for my daughter, and who's better for the position than you?"

"I don't care if you *are* Daisy's father—it's not her welfare you're so concerned about but your own, and—"

"What are you getting upset about? Can't you see that it's the perfect solution for you, as well? You want work, and I can provide it."

He tried to make it sound so innocent, she thought, fuming. Did he expect that after her response to him the night of the Hobarts' ball, she would willingly compromise herself and become a kept woman? "I'm not staying in your house," she announced.

Nate scowled in frustration. "Why are you so opposed all of a sudden? You want to be near Daisy."

Furious, Eliza gripped her skirts. "I shouldn't have been here as long as I have, and especially not after what's happened. But now I'm leaving. I intend to find another place for Daisy and me to live."

"You are not taking my daughter!" Nate exclaimed. "I don't know what kind of problem you have, you're not going to take Daisy away from me."

"We'll just see about that," she retorted. "After the

hearing in February, she'll be going back to Pittsburgh with me. In the meantime, I refuse to be insulted any further by you." Snatching up the hem of her gown, she spun around and returned to the house.

When she had disappeared inside, Nate yanked on his work glove again, grabbed the shovel, and drove it deep into the earth. He exhaled a sharp breath through clenched teeth. What in the hell was wrong with her now? No woman had ever been such a maddening enigma, yet at the same time so utterly desirable.

Eliza brushed past Daisy in the kitchen doorway and went to the icebox to find something to prepare for their supper. The little girl was white-faced and anxious.

"Aunt Lizzie," she started to say, but Eliza was too upset to pay attention. She unwrapped a chicken, flung the paper aside, then disappeared into the pantry to fetch onions and potatoes, which she dumped onto the worktable. In silence Daisy watched Eliza angrily slam drawers and whack a knife through the vegetables. At last the girl slipped out of the kitchen. Eliza never noticed her absence.

Not until supper was ready did she realize Daisy was no longer in the room. Calling for her, Eliza searched the first-floor rooms, then headed up the stairs. But Daisy's bedroom was empty. Irritated, wondering where she could have gone, Eliza was about to leave when she noticed a paper on the bed. She snatched it up and scanned it, her frown turning to shock as the meaning of the words registered.

Nate was still outside, working by the stark illumination of the lantern, when Eliza ran out onto the porch.

"Nate!" she cried. "She's gone! Daisy's run away!"

Chapter 11

Nate started toward her at a run, shedding gloves as he went. He hit the top of the stairs beside Eliza, and she shoved toward him a piece of paper speckled with black ink. Her face was white, strained.

"What is it, what is it?"

"From Daisy. Read it."

He pushed past her into the kitchen, taking the paper to the amber-bellied oil lamp she'd lit on the worktable. Scowling, he stared at the paper, twisted it, turned it, and finally thrust it back to Eliza.

"Goddamn it, read it to me! I can't make out these chicken scratches! When is she going to learn to spell?"

Her voice breaking, Eliza read aloud as Nate looked over her shoulder. " 'When you fight I feel too sad.' This right here is a picture of her crying. 'So I will leave and find a new home.' Oh, Nate, she's run away!"

"You're sure she's already gone?"

"I couldn't find her in the house. But I haven't checked everywhere."

"She can't have gotten far. There hasn't been enough time." He started toward the hall. "I'll find her, don't worry."

Outside, he ignored the rising wind that bit through his damp shirt. Looking in both directions, he descended the brick steps and paused on the street. "Daisy!" he shouted, turning in one direction, then another. He cupped his hands around his mouth and called again. No answer. He started at a slow run down the street, eyes skimming the surrounding bushes and lawns.

Find a new home. What would she do—knock on doors? He scanned the fronts of houses as he passed them. He imagined Daisy walking down the street—what had she been wearing? A pale dress with a fat sash and big collar. He hoped she'd had the sense to wear her coat.

Passing his house again, he searched in the opposite direction. Never had he felt so frantic with worry. Repeatedly he called her name. Passersby stared at him, but he ignored them. Considering the way he looked—dressed in old muddy pants, heavy boots, and an unstarched shirt, and running wild-eyed and hollering around the exclusive neighborhood of Nob Hill—the police would probably be summoned.

Good! he thought. Get the police here. That's the next step.

She couldn't have gotten far. But in which direction had she gone?

He imagined Daisy walking down the street. Imagined a black enclosed carriage slowing beside her. Imagined a man reaching out and snatching her into the interior, the coach picking up speed as it rolled away. Forever away. Gone from him more thoroughly than he could ever bear.

As he continued his desperate search, he began to realize just how much Daisy meant to him. No matter how many tantrums she threw or how many shirts she ruined with paint, she was more dear to him than he'd ever believed possible. He'd put up with anything and be more patient if only he could find her again.

A rustling in the bushes caught his ear. "Daisy?" He approached, reached out to the wet shiny branches. "Baby dear?" He tried to push his way into the dripping, tangled mass of vegetation. Spitting erupted. A dark shape with gleaming yellow eyes streaked past him.

A cat! A goddamned *cat*.

Eliza combed the first and second floors, calling out to Daisy as she went from room to room. Nothing but silence greeted her. She tried to hold back her tears. How could she have been so heartless as to ignore Daisy when the little girl wanted to talk to her in the kitchen? She was ashamed of herself and guilt-ridden for the many arguments she'd had with Nate. She'd never realized how terrible the situation must have been for Daisy.

Holding up the lamp she'd brought from the kitchen for her search, Eliza climbed the stairs to the musty and unused third floor. For the most part, the rooms were empty except for bed frames, unmarked cartons stacked high, and furniture shoved every which way for storage. Though she checked every possible hiding place, Daisy was nowhere to be found.

Eliza's pulse raced with mounting fear as she retraced her steps to the first floor. After a quick tour of the front yard, she descended the damp brick steps to watch for Nate. Maybe he had been able to find Daisy.

Eliza was standing vigilantly at the foot of the brick stairs when Nate retraced his steps to the house. "She hasn't come back?" he called when he saw her.

"You didn't find her?"

Eliza was crying quietly. He put his arm around her as they returned to the house together. "Look, she's all right, we're going to find her. We just haven't looked in the right place yet." He clenched his fist so tightly that he felt the veins go taut as wire. "I've got to get my coat; I'm going to go for the police."

"I feel so awful, Nate! I didn't know how hard the situation had become for her—I've been so selfish . . ." She leaned into him, her face pressed against his shirt.

"Oh, no, now look, Eliza, none of that. Hear me? If anybody's been selfish, it's me. Stop blaming yourself; you haven't done anything. I'm going straight to the police . . . they'll be able to do a better job of searching." He had to keep talking. "The more eyes the better. So why don't you go fix yourself a cup of tea or something. God, I need a drink! Help yourself to the bourbon if you want it—no, that's right, you don't—"

They had entered the foyer, immaculate with its white tile floor, and a sound caught Nate's attention—a tiny whisper of something soft scraping the wallpaper on the stairway. He glanced up, his eyes stabbing into the shadows above the stairs.

"Daisy?" he breathed. "Daisy, is that you?"

He took the stairs two and three at a time, watching the small, pale shape gain definition as he approached. Daisy sat on the top step, hugging the wall. Her head was down, her shiny brown hair falling around her face. Nate swept her up in his arms. Eliza was immediately behind him, reaching out to touch and embrace her. Nate's heart was hammering loudly in mixed fear and relief.

"Daisy!" he exclaimed. "Where have you been?

Have you been here the whole time? We've been so worried about you, precious!"

Daisy put her arms around his neck and lay her head on his shoulder. "I didn't have anywhere else to go," she whispered. She watched Eliza's face. "I heard you upstairs when I came back, but I hid again."

Eliza stroked her back, smiling through her tears. "Oh, my dear, we love you. We don't want you to leave."

Nate heard Eliza's words *We love you.* So simple, yet so stunning and true. "That's right," he said. "We love you."

Daisy lifted her head. "Are you really my papa?"

Nate studied her in surprise. A small frown appeared between his eyes. "Did you overhear us talking in the garden?" When Daisy nodded, he asked, "And is that why you ran away?" It upset him to think that the news that he was her father might have prompted her to run away. He would have kept his identity a secret from her forever if it hurt her.

"You're always fighting," Daisy said, wiping the back of her hand over one eye. "I don't want you to. I don't like it."

"I'm sorry, precious," Nate said, tenderly brushing her hair from her face. "I promise not to argue with Aunt Lizzie anymore. Will you promise not to run away again?"

Daisy nodded, fixing him with a quizzical stare. "Are you really my papa then?"

"That's right." Nate watched her expression closely. "How do you feel about that?"

Daisy considered it. "My friend Marjorie's papa spanks her sometimes. Are you going to spank me?"

Nate stared at her incredulously. Was that what she expected from a father? "Not on your life."

"Will you give me rides on your back?" Daisy asked, smiling shyly.

"Whenever you want," he promised, feeling a hard tug at his heart.

She squeezed his neck in a happy hug, and Nate returned the embrace, both relieved at her acceptance of him and overwhelmed by emotions of love he'd never known before.

Eliza watched in concern. What would happen now? Daisy knew about her father and was obviously pleased. A link had been formed, and she felt as if everything was moving too swiftly out of her control. How could she keep Daisy and herself from being hurt?

Nate and Daisy helped her reheat their supper and set the dining room table. Delighted with the attention and the lack of malice between the two adults, Daisy clowned ceaselessly during the meal. Eliza found it hard not to respond to Daisy's antics. It had been so long since she'd seen such animation in the little girl, she couldn't help but be moved by it. She propped her chin in her hand and smiled as she watched the newly discovered father and daughter. Daisy was so happy, and Nate was beaming. He winked at Daisy, affectionately touched her hair, and hugged her when she pressed happy, smacking kisses all over his face. Eliza's heart swelled with warmth, and she knew that she cared deeply for them both. Tears of deep joy pricked her eyes. Seeing Nate's obvious love for Daisy started a soft glow of passion in her. It was like being a family, she thought. Was this how a wife felt when she watched her husband, the father of her child, in tender moments together? Did a wife love a husband all the more because of the love they shared for their children?

But her enjoyment was abruptly smothered in the realization that the three of them could never be a *real* family. Nate would never marry her. It was absurd even to imagine such a thing. Who was she but a simple millworker, while he was a member of the upper class, part of society. Not only were there social distinctions to keep them apart, but Nate didn't love her.

Eliza looked down at her plate and pushed the last of her potato to the edge as she tried not to cry. Face the facts, she commanded herself. She had always been practical, capable, and not given to foolish imaginings. Now was not the time to be weak and sentimental.

She folded her napkin and laid it aside. "Daisy, it's getting late, and I'm sure it's past time for you to get ready for bed."

Daisy looked up, pouting. "Not yet. Please, please, Aunt Lizzie, can't I stay up?"

"Tomorrow you have school, and it must be at least nine o'clock already," Eliza said firmly.

Nate stood up. "Come along, Daisy. I'll give you a ride, just as I promised."

As he helped Daisy stand on her chair to climb onto his back, Nate wondered about Eliza. What had caused the change in her? During dinner she had been almost radiant, and her nearness had made him ache with desire. He tried to push aside thoughts of making love with her, but images of her tortured him as he carried Daisy upstairs.

Eliza followed, and together they tucked Daisy into bed. He admired the curve of her hips as she leaned down to kiss Daisy's cheek, and had to hold himself in check so he wouldn't touch her.

Eliza slowly paced the length of her room, her fingers knotting together as she thought about Nate.

As much as her head might tell her to keep as far
from him as possible, her heart was clamoring for
his presence. She remembered his caresses, the feeling of his lips on hers, and she longed to go to him.
But fear of the consequences kept her away. She had
never believed she would make love with any man
who wasn't her husband, much less put herself in a
position in which she could be emotionally hurt by
a man so far out of her class. Yet here she was,
thinking the unthinkable.

The tenderness and affection Nate had shown
Daisy had made her aware of him in an entirely new
way, and she was sure she had misjudged him earlier. Maybe he really had been concerned for her
welfare and had offered his home to her out of kind-
ness, and not just because he thought she might be
a handy mistress. Hadn't he left her bedroom the
night she had been ready to make love with him?
That act proved his good intentions.

Besides, Nate wasn't like those people she had
seen today. He kept no valet, or a host of servants
to do his bidding. He worked in the garden himself.
Social distinctions would have no meaning to him.
He wouldn't spurn her because of her background.

Eliza stood still in her room, wavering in the agony of indecision. She recalled the feel of his mouth
on her breast, and felt a pang of desire. The passion
that had begun to burn in her as she watched Nate
and Daisy at the dinner table still smoldered,
spreading, ready to burst into flame. Confused and
torn, Eliza approached her door and halted with her
hand on the knob. Maybe she should just apologize
for her heated words earlier in the evening, then
return immediately to her room. It would ease her
conscience . . . if not the hunger in her body. She
groaned aloud in her turmoil. What should she do?
Though all logic shouted warnings, Eliza felt irresist-

ibly drawn to Nate. Each successive thought of him increased her longing and muted her ability to reason. Like iron to a magnet, she felt pulled toward him. As she swung open her door, her cheeks felt hot and her heart was pounding.

After securing the house for the night, Nate went to his room. He lit one of the gas jets in the wall beside the bed and was smiling to himself as he sat down in the bent-wood rocker to unlace his boots and kick them aside. He stood up and emptied some coins from his pants pocket onto the dresser top, then unbuttoned his shirt and yanked the tails free of his trousers. A soft knock on the door halted him as he started to remove his shirt. He shrugged it back over his shoulders as he went to the door.

Eliza stood in the hallway, her blue-and-white-striped dress vivid against the dark corridor behind her. She smiled apologetically. Her glance slid back and forth between his eyes and his exposed chest as she said, "I thought perhaps I . . . should apologize for the . . . for some of the things I said today."

She had never seen his room before, and her first impression was of lush green vines. A profusion of dark stems and fragile leaves in the wallpaper surrounded the room, reaching from floor to ceiling. The window was draped with filmy white curtains so long that they trailed on the floor. The bed was wide, covered with a thin white spread, with tall head- and footboards of dark wood carved with roses. On the floor was a thick green carpet like a layer of moss.

Her glance returned to Nate, to the mat of wiry black hair visible between the edges of his white shirt. The chiseled contours of his chest were visible, contours of muscle thrown into relief by the gaslight. Crisp black hair curled lightly, descending, disappearing under the waistband of his trousers. Bronzed olive skin gleamed. He was so attractive. She wanted to put out her hand, feel the tickle of hair, the solidity of his chest. But the eyes watching her were amused, warming the blush in her cheeks.

"You don't have anything to apologize for," he said, leaning against the door frame.

Nate gazed at the top of her head as she nodded. Her hair was thick and loose, as if with the removal of a single pin, the mass of it would burst in dark luxury over her shoulders. What would her hair look like against those smooth white, sloping shoulders? He reached out unconsciously and stroked a fingertip over the silky curl beside her ear. Great brown eyes looked up into his, so warm, so inviting . . . A thought struck him. What was she here for? Had she come just to apologize . . . or was there another reason? His pulse quickened.

He reached for her hand, drew her into the room, and closed the door behind her. For an infinitely fragile moment they stood in silence, looking at each other. When he touched her hair and let his hands slide down her arms, she swayed toward him.

"Nate . . ." She started to say, almost as if she were confused.

"Hmmm?" He sighed, then waited, holding himself in check, unsure of her. Had she really come to his room for a reason other than to apologize? Gazing into her eyes, he felt again the warning uneasiness, although desire for her surged in him. When she said nothing more, he cupped her face between his hands and slowly lowered his mouth to hers.

Eliza melted into his kiss. His mouth was soft at first but soon grew more demanding, until his lips were crushing hers, parting hers, his tongue reaching deep into her mouth. Her heart pounded. This was why she had been drawn to his room; this was what she had wanted. As he pulled her into his arms, eagerly she pressed herself to his chest, to the crisp black hair. He was so wonderfully strong, so sure, and his arms fit around her so well. Never had she felt this kind of pleasure, this kind of sweet warm weakness.

His hand was at her waist, thumb and fingers cupping the curve. He lifted his head and grinned at her.

"You're wearing a corset, aren't you?" he said.

She smiled. "Do you like it?"

"I like you either way," he answered. Thoughts of what she would look like in the undergarment quenched the last of his reservations about making love with her. His voice dropped lower as he added, "But now you'll have to let me see you in it."

Eliza caught her breath as she felt his hands under her chin, unfastening her gown, moving lower. The slight brush of his fingers over her breasts was exquisitely tormenting. As his hands descended, her stomach fluttered. When he pushed the dress from her shoulders and let it fall around her legs, she watched his face. His eyes glinted brightly with an inner light as he looked down at her, and the sight sent a shock of pleasure through her.

He untied her petticoat and let that also drop to a whispering heap around her. His fingers traced the edgings of lace on her corset, the tiny thread of baby-blue satin ribbon over the top curve of her breasts. And she stood still, her breathing growing rapid. Her heart pounded under his palm as he cupped both breasts through the corset.

"Take the rest of it off," he whispered.

He was smiling faintly, eyes bright and narrowed. Eliza looked at the face she so loved to look at, his skin glowing in the soft light, his beautiful shining eyes destroying any thought in her of refusing. She was mesmerized, her heart thudding hard with excitement.

He tilted his eyebrows up as if to say, Go on, I'm waiting.

Eliza kicked out of her shoes and reached down, tearing her gaze from his as she unhooked her stockings and rolled them down her legs. She unlaced the corset, dropped it; unbuttoned her camisole, let it slip off her shoulders to land with a sigh on the floor; bent and pushed off her drawers, toed them aside. Only then did she look at him again, and his intent gaze took her breath away. She blushed self-consciously and put an arm across her breasts, a hand over her pubic hair.

"Oh, no, no," he whispered, and lifted her hands away. "Don't be embarrassed, Eliza—never."

He took the pins from her hair and tossed them onto the bedside table. Plucking out the roll of hair, he shook the strands till they fell loose around her. "This is beautiful," he murmured, stroking her hair, her shoulders. "I never even pictured it this wonderful."

His warm hands slid to her waist and hips and then cupped the undersides of her breasts. Wherever he touched her, her skin grew sensitive, tingling.

"I can't resist touching you," he whispered. "Everything about you was made soft and perfect for love."

Eliza put her hand on his chest, feeling the crisp hair. A thrill of excitement streaked through her when his thumbs brushed her nipples. "I want to see you," she said in an unsteady voice. "Please." Her fingers slid to his shoulders, and she reveled in the hardness beneath his skin.

She watched him peel off his shirt and walk to the polished wardrobe, his movements surprisingly lithe and graceful for so big a man. When he pushed off his trousers and socks, she turned and studied the bed. Trembling, she sat down on the edge, then scooted back until she was sitting in the center of the thin white spread, her legs tucked against her hip. She wished he would hurry before she got too nervous . . .

When he closed the doors and approached the bed, she kept her eyes on his face, though she was acutely aware of his erect state. He had an easy, comfortable attitude about his own nakedness. It was somehow soothing. His shoulders were wide, his chest broad, with curves of muscles gleaming in the soft light. She admired the dark glow of his skin. Her attention was drawn like a magnet by his pronounced erection, so surprisingly beautiful. Her breath caught, tugged. She watched his faint smile, the soft, compelling shine of his eyes, and her heart beat harder with desire. He put one knee on the bed and reached for her ankles, drawing her legs out. His hands were warm, gentle, his touch electric.

Nate felt the small, slender ankles in his hands, looked at her waiting in the middle of his bed. Dark abundant hair tumbled in lovely confusion over her shoulders, separating around her arms and breasts. Dusky-rose aureoles crowned firm high white breasts, teasing him. Bewitchingly delicate was that slender body, yet with pronounced and stunning curves of waist and hips. He longed for her. She looked back at him with exquisite eyes glittering softly in age-old invitation.

He was afraid he wouldn't make it past the temptation of her thighs. Passion pulsed harder through him. Her ankles in his hands . . . slide them apart . . .

Nate forced himself to move past the white thighs and that tantalizing crown of dark hair that drew

him. Relinquishing himself to the dream, he kissed
sloping shoulders, beautiful high breasts, and teased
the tight little nipples that so teased him. He heard
with enjoyment her unconscious moans, felt with
triumph her excited quivers. The statue that was
pure woman curved her round, sweet-scented arms
around him. Cool fingers moved over his back and
hips, irresistibly tantalizing. He struggled not to lose
control. Every caress of her thigh against his erection almost sent him over the edge. But he held himself in check, watched passion intoxicate her and
shine back at him from eyes filled with . . . love.

Love. He hesitated imperceptibly, a dim warning
sounding in his brain. Was he falling in love with
her? The prickling of danger was abruptly wiped out
as her fingers slid to his erection. At the excitement
of her touch, he caught his breath, then let it out in
a groan.

Eliza arched against his hands, trembling with
waves of accelerating passion. She clasped him to
her, entwined her legs with his, wanting to feel the
heated contact with him along every inch of her
body. He shifted out of her embrace and pressed a
soft kiss to the curve of her hip. She tried to reach
for him and bring him back into her arms, but when
she felt the touch of his fingers between her legs,
delight shot through her.

His mouth was hot yet tender on the insides of
her thighs, and she was breathing hard in expecta-
tion as she twisted to make contact with that mouth.
When it came, she exclaimed aloud with the stunning pleasure.

Nate tried to wait, but he was hardly able to control himself, to keep from lifting up and driving hard
into that slick velvet woman-flesh. She arched and
reached for him, trying to bring him to her.

At last, when Eliza thought she couldn't bear the

pleasure another minute, he shifted position. She lost herself in the urgent melting eyes above her as she felt the pressure of him, hard and insistent between her legs. A momentary stinging burn, so full did she feel, and then she was glad beyond anything else she'd ever known in her life. Her mouth opened, she gasped with the elation of him going deeper in her. She locked eyes with his, so bright, and yet breathtakingly tender as he gazed down at her. Eliza cherished the moment, tried to hold fast to it.

But then he swept away all thought entirely.

She could do nothing but cling to him, mindless with rising ecstacy. Though she tried to hold each moment, they slid from her as rapidly as each breath, to be replaced by ever more urgently ecstatic moments, until she was sure she could not physically contain the pleasure.

She wanted to stretch out each minute to savor every sensation, but her body moved of its own volition, her hips twisting, grinding with the endless lifting passion.

"Eliza—" Nate exclaimed in a deep groan. "You're exciting me too much . . . you'll make me lose control." He wanted to slow down and make sure she experienced the climax. But even as he tried to still himself, she moaned and writhed beneath him, and he couldn't stop.

Eliza was caught in an irresistible tide. When she climbed nearer the crest she heard as if from afar her own panting cries of urgency. She peaked with spasm after spasm, clasping him in her, writhing, driven onward by his every movement, until she thought it would never end and she would drown in the exquisite suffering of such pleasure.

She was drained and limp, melting into the bed, the shudders subsiding, when Nate bent over her and clasped her to him with one arm, arching her body sharply against him. He uttered a loud groan, thrusting deep, his body stiffening in her arms. His excitement ignited another splintering crash of pleasure in her. And then she relaxed, utterly spent, into the last weakening throbs.

They lay together for a long time. Nate rolled her to her side, still joined to him, arms and legs and bodies entwined. Gradually the music of heartbeats and breathing calmed and grew still in the room. When he finally rolled and stretched out on his back, she felt the warm slipperiness between her thighs. "Oh, lady." He sighed and pulled her closer in the curve of his arm. "That's got to be heaven." Eliza agreed as she lay her head on his chest, the black hair tickling her cheek.

They never slipped under the covers that night. They rested, slid lightly asleep. But each shifting of a soft leg or hip against his brought Nate awake and Eliza was roused by the heat of his mouth on her shoulder or breast, by the touch of his fingers between her legs. The flickering gaslight paled as dawn stretched tentatively across the horizon, but they never noticed . . .

Nate woke with a start. White sunshine blinded him and he squinted, raising a hand to shield his eyes. What time was it? He tried to focus on the face of the clock on the dresser, the wood-encased ornate clock with gilt curlicues. Almost eight-thirty. He was late.

What the hell. He felt too good to care.

He remembered the MDK Paper Company and George Matinga coming to see him this morning about the contract. He sat up abruptly. Beside him Eliza lay curled on her side, her hair tangled in sultry waves over her back and across the bedspread. Her skin was still faintly flushed with well-being.

Where her thighs curved together he saw the white pearl streaks, and passion moved in him again. But there was no time. Damn it. He swung his legs over the side of the bed and stood up, wondering if he had time to get her a flower from the garden.

Eliza stirred when he patted her thigh and shook her gently. "Wake up, beautiful," he said. "We're late. I have an appointment, have to leave. Can you take Daisy to school?" She opened her eyes. It was an effort to do so, so pleasurably tired did she feel.

Nate was sitting on the edge of the bed beside her, fully dressed in a crisp black frock coat open over a black silk waistcoat. He wore a starched, immaculate white wing collar and a beige-and-white dotted tie, a four-in-hand. He was smiling at her, his teeth white against the glowing dark skin, his eyes deep and sparkling as he watched her. He lifted a strand of her hair and slowly twined it around one rising nipple. She held her breath at the teasing, quickening pleasure. He grinned. Feeling suddenly self-conscious with the sober sunlight and his fully dressed state, she reached behind her for a handful of the thin spread and flung it over herself.

"Oh, don't deprive me," he said with a chuckle. Then he sighed and added quietly, "I have to leave. Will you get Daisy to school?"

She nodded, watched him stand up. She saw the crisp, razor-edged crease in his beige trousers and a flash of sunlight on a polished black shoe. Then he was gone, and she lay curled in a cocoon of white sheets.

Why did night and wonderful dreams always have to end? she wondered.

Her eyes closed and she relived their lovemaking in her memory. Then she rolled over and flung off the sheets, arms stretched out, staring at the ceiling.

She must wake Daisy.

Eliza sat up and slid from the bed. The spread was stiff in spots with pinkish streaks that might have been blood. Later she might be embarrassed about it; for now she stretched her arms high above her and felt sleek and utterly content. She walked around the bed and found her clothing folded and laid over a small ladder-backed chair beside Nate's wardrobe. She had left all the garments in a heap on the floor last night, but this morning he must have picked them up and put them in order over the chair while she slept.

She approached the chair but halted, her heart swelling. A pink rose still sparkling with dew lay on the folds of her blue-and-white-striped dress.

Later, Eliza could never quite tell when the doubts started.

She smelled the coolly crisp fragrance of the rose, laid it aside on the bed as she donned only the dress and scooped up the undergarments to carry them back to her room. She experienced faint pricklings of worry over the fact that she had made love with a man outside of marriage, but her concern was easily extinguished in the lingering contentment. At the washstand in her room she bathed quickly. There would be time later for a full bath, and she relished the idea of having one. To stretch out in the luxury of a hot bath, add drops of perfume into the water— she'd have to buy some—was so wickedly delightful an idea. The pink rose she set on her washstand in a water glass. She'd even take it with her and look at it while she luxuriated in hot scented water. She'd pamper herself outrageously. She couldn't wait!

Daisy was already dressed and on her hands and knees hunting under the bed when Eliza entered her room. The little girl slid her shoe out and looked up.

"I think I'm late," she said worriedly. She sat down on the floor to pull on her shoe.

Eliza smiled. "How would you like to skip school today and go on an adventure with me?"

"What's an adventure?" Daisy pushed her tangled hair over her shoulder as she struggled with the laces.

Eliza sat on the edge of the bed. "Well, first we could go shopping and then maybe . . . maybe ride on a cable car down a big hill and lean out the side. Have you seen the way the boys hang way out in the wind when they're riding? We could do that too."

Daisy considered the suggestion in silence. "But Mrs. Rodriguez was going to give out the awards for reading today, and I think I'm going to get one." She added in exasperation, "My shoelace is all knotted! Fix it for me, Aunt Lizzie."

"Well, Mrs. Rodriguez will save your award for you, my dear." She took the shoe Daisy thrust into her lap and picked at the tiny knot. "You don't have to worry about that. So how about a special day just for the two of us?"

"No, I don't wanta miss school. Did you know I have a friend Katie here too? She's a different Katie, not the same as at home." Daisy hopped to her feet and watched Eliza for a minute. Then she asked pensively, "Is Nate really my papa?"

Eliza gave her a one-armed hug. "Yes, precious," she exclaimed, adopting the endearment he sometimes used for Daisy. "And you're a very lucky little girl."

"But, Aunt Lizzie, does that mean we aren't going home again? Are we going to stay here?"

Eliza frowned slightly and gave another tug with her fingernails at the knot, which finally loosened.

"How would you like that? Would you like to stay here?"

Daisy leaned into Eliza's arm. "I don't know. I like Mrs. Rodriguez, but do you think Mrs. Riley is worried about me? I haven't been at school for so long. And Katie—the Katie at home—probably misses me." She accepted the shoe that Eliza handed back to her and sat on the bed to pull it on. Abruptly she burst into tears and kicked the shoe to the floor.

"Daisy!" Eliza put her arm around the girl. "What's the matter? Are you missing Katie at home?"

"I don't know!" she wailed. "I wanta go home, but I don't wanta leave. And I don't know if I want a papa!"

"Oh, my dear, oh, sweetheart." Eliza tried not to smile. "There's a lot happening to you now, isn't there? It's going to take a while to get used to so many new things." She reached down for the shoe and put it on Daisy's foot. As she laced it up she said, "You and I need a day all to ourselves, just to have fun. And how about if we keep it a secret that you have a papa now. It'll be a special secret, just between us. Hmmm?"

Eliza had reassured Daisy, but not herself. So many new things *were* happening. She left Daisy to get her hair brushed while she went downstairs to see about breakfast. In the lower hall she could hear Mrs. Herlihy moving furniture in the large parlor as she cleaned. Sylvia Hatcher was here today. Through the kitchen window Eliza could see the thin young girl, faded blue kerchief bound around her hair, heavy brown coat buttoned up to her chin against the chill, as she beat rugs on a line behind the carriage house. Crisp bright sunshine warmed the air and lit up the clouds of dust from the rugs, but the wind off the Pacific carried a chill.

Eliza sipped sweetened coffee kept hot on the stove and stared out the window. She herself had a faded blue kerchief she sometimes wore at the mill to keep her hair from falling accidentally into a moving piece of equipment. Could she go back to the mill now if she had to, after spending these weeks in Nate's home?

Daisy ran into the kitchen, hair brushed into a filmy cloud that looked ready to crackle if anyone touched it. "I don't want any oatmeal," she exclaimed when she saw the bowl Eliza handed to her.

"Hush, it'll stick to your ribs," Eliza said. "And eat it here—Mrs. Herlihy has already cleaned the dining room."

Daisy sulked, but set the bowl on the worktable, found a spoon in a drawer, and climbed onto the high stool to eat. "Can't I have some raisins on it?" she asked with a pout, patting the mound of oatmeal with the back of her spoon.

"My, you're getting to be a spoiled young lady, aren't you? When did you get used to raisins?"

They were both getting spoiled—raisins, perfumed baths, corsets. But she went to the pantry anyway. It smelled of dry wood and flour. It was well stocked, with so much more food and in greater variety than anything they'd known at home. She searched among the shelves and brought out the small wooden box that held the raisins. When she emerged she looked across the bright kitchen, so light and airy, the white tiles trimmed with sky-blue molding. Daisy watched her from the worktable.

In that moment Eliza saw Estelle in the little girl. Saw again Estelle sitting in their windowless kitchen back in Pittsburgh, surrounded by exposed bare wood studs they'd used as shelves. Estelle's dark eyes had burned in her white face, her hands stroking and stroking, in a hypnotic rhythm, her tightly swollen belly. *I won't ever leave, will I, Eliza?* she'd said. Eliza had not then understood her sister's desperate desire to escape their home, the only world they'd known.

She saw again Nate's dark reflection behind Estelle's smiling face in the mirror. He had made love to Estelle once and never returned. Would he abandon her, Eliza, as well? Was there anything at all that made her special, different from Estelle?

Eliza's stomach clenched. She gave the raisins to Daisy, stroked the little girl's hair briefly, smoothing the flyaway strands. "I'll be upstairs, sweetheart. When you're finished, come up and we'll get ready to leave. We'll have such fun, won't we?"

At the top of the stairs Eliza stared at the double doors leading to the drawing room. She pushed them open and stepped over the threshold. A dust ball rolled away in the stir of air. Dimly yellowish-gray with the drapes closed, the room seemed strangely hushed, as if someone was holding his breath. There was a mustiness in the air; she heard the empty echo of her footsteps. The piano in the broad alcove of bay windows was a ghostly mound under a sheet. Salon chairs were pushed helter-skelter along one wall.

How glitteringly bright the room had been the night of the Thanksgiving Day party. She remembered it shimmering like crystal, with fragile ivory orchids, their fragrance hanging on the air. Nate had looked so elegant in evening dress and white silk tie, his hair gleaming blue-black under the light.

It was a different world entirely from the one she'd always known.

How had she ever imagined she would fit in?

Eliza left the drawing room and entered her own room.

She lifted the pink rose out of its glass, stretching

out on her bed and smelled the flower and examined the petals with minute care. The first rose she'd ever received from a man. She pursed her lips, then let out a quivering sigh.

She didn't belong here.

What was she doing imagining she could spend a lifetime with Nate? He had loved Estelle for only a night. Loved? He had said it himself—he had never really loved any woman. Why had Eliza gone to his room last night?

She had given in to impossible, romantic notions of love and family. Just because he had deep and honorable feelings for Daisy didn't mean he had the same kind of response to her, Eliza. With a stab of shame she remembered that she had virtually thrown herself at him, going to his room as she had done. Nate hadn't sought her out; he'd only responded as he would to any woman who offered herself to him. There was nothing special or meaningful about what had happened between them. She should have listened to the practical voice of reason, instead of foolish imaginings.

But why the rose? Twirling the flower stem between her fingers, she realized it could have no significance whatsoever—a simple thanks. Suddenly it seemed like a coin tossed to her. Or was the rose an apology? He knew how far beneath him she was socially. She was virtually on the level of a servant. Hadn't Marietta been making that plain enough all these weeks? But Eliza had been too proud to recognize and admit her place. Now Nate had felt the need to leave some token in apology; he couldn't marry her. One had to be born into society; the walls weren't breached by pride, money . . . or the simple, romantic longings of an uneducated millworker. Oh, the shame of it all!

Eliza dropped the rose back into the water glass

and wiped the back of her wrist over her suddenly wet eyes. How soon would it be before Nate looked again among the women who belonged with his world and chose one to fill Marietta's place? He would never understand that it would be impossible for her, Eliza, to remain here then. He thought it so easy that she act as companion or caretaker of Daisy. He wanted to *hire* her for the job.

The bouncing of the bed jolted her out of her thoughts, and she looked around to see Daisy flopped on her stomach, half on, half off the bed. Her small pink mouth grinned. "So when do we leave?"

Eliza smiled absently and reached out to tap Daisy's nose. Now Daisy knew that Nate was her father. It probably wouldn't take her long to grow devoted to him. She was like that, was Daisy. Too much was happening now too fast! And the potential for heartbreak was growing so strong. For both her and Daisy, because eventually they'd have to be separated, wouldn't they? And she, Eliza, would have to be separated from Nate. Too much heartbreak . . . and so much worse now . . . after . . . If only they had never come to San Francisco!

In a listless voice she told Daisy, "Run get your cape." When Daisy bounced back off the bed again, Eliza stood up. From her dresser drawer she removed two dollars and opened her purse to put the money into it.

The tickets were there still. Train tickets back to Pittsburgh, where she and Daisy belonged.

Train tickets home.

Chapter 12

George Matinga was a tall, spare man with wings of gray hair sweeping back from a humorless face. He was difficult to deal with. Nate sat behind his desk, sunlight warm on his back, as they discussed each point of the contract. If Nate wasn't careful, Matinga would get away with a hell of a deal.

This was not the time to be feeling so relaxed and warm.

Not the time to be thinking of a beautiful drowsy woman in his bed . . .

In desperation, Nate swung around and pulled down the shades to block out the sun. The sudden coolness at his back helped sharpen his concentration, and he turned back to a debate of protective packaging for the freight.

Matinga wasn't satisfied until almost one o'clock in the afternoon. After he departed, Nate headed out of his office. He dropped a pile of pages for the contract on Peg Walters' desk. "Two copies, Peg?" he said, stretching his arms behind his head to work out the ache between his shoulder blades. "Simon Legree will be back in the morning to sign them. I'll need them as soon as I come in tomorrow."

Peg Walters lifted her spectacles onto her forehead

as she rifled through the pages. She dropped her eyeglasses back on her nose and looked at Nate rubbing one aching shoulder blade. "You're the Simon Legree. This'll take all afternoon."

"You're sweet, Peg. Have I ever told you that? I'll see you later. I'm going to get some lunch."

He walked jauntily down the street, stretching his legs, enjoying the sting of the wind on his face. Near the Bohemian Club on Pine Street was Manning's Oyster Grotto, a restaurant popular with society people. Passing workmen unpacking their dinner pails, Nate entered Manning's and paused to look around the plush dining room redolent with the smells of cigar smoke, frying butter, and boiled shrimp. Ceiling-high palms filled the corners of the room, walls of dark wood were hung with paintings, tables gleamed white with linen tablecloths.

Every one of the tables was full, groups of men at some, individuals lingering over newspapers and cigars at others. The first-floor dining room was for men only. Due to the emergence of women into the working world, the women's rights movement, the suffragettes demanding attention, many saloons and restaurants offered male-only rooms, providing their patrons with a male retreat, a private club atmosphere, where they could relax in the comfortable camaraderie of members of their own sex.

Nate headed up the stairs. Here was another dining room for women and couples, smaller than the room downstairs, lighter, airier, lacking the cigar fumes. He was shown to an empty table and given a menu and complimentary bowl of tiny boiled shrimp. Famished, he peeled and ate several shrimp, but he was frowning thoughtfully. Now that the distraction of doing business with George Matinga was out of the way, his mind returned to memories of Eliza and the night he had just shared with her. He'd made love with countless women and never suffered the compunctions he did with Eliza. For a brief few moments he acknowledged that he might, indeed, be in love with her, and that thought brought ideas of proposing marriage to her. But wedding any woman was an alien notion; he'd never wanted to get married. He resolutely pushed away any consideration of such a drastic step.

Leaning back in his chair, he snapped open his menu.

A figure approached the table. "Good afternoon," said a familiar feminine voice.

"Is it?" Nate snapped, glaring at Tess Brody, who smiled lazily at him, eyes languid. She set down a plate of half-eaten king crab legs and a teacup and took the chair beside him.

"What is this, Tess?" he exclaimed in annoyance. "Are you trying to share my table? I was planning to eat alone."

She planted her elbows on the table and sipped her tea. The cocked brim of her emerald-green hat cast a slanting shadow over half her face. She watched Nate scan the menu and said, "I heard you've graduated from the nursery."

"What, did Marietta call on you?" he said, slapping the menu onto the table. "Did she tell you to come pester me?"

"I'll act as if I didn't hear that."

"You shouldn't!" He signaled to the waiter and ordered the grilled red snapper with potatoes, broccoli, and coffee.

When the man bowed slightly and left them, Tess eyed Nate for a minute in silence. He detected predatory watchfulness, though he avoided looking at her. "I thought we were friends," she finally said.

"Well, now, how could I have forgotten that?"

He reached for another shrimp. "You're not hoping I'll pay for your lunch, are you?"

"Look, we can at least be civil." Her eyes narrowed. "I'm willing to forgive you for that outburst at your Thanksgiving Day party."

He noticed that she pressed her breasts over the table. He refused to look. "When were we ever civil?"

She ignored him as she finished her cup of tea and motioned for the waiter. "Any Moravian slivovitz here?" she asked, and the waiter nodded with a surprised smile and moved away.

Nate's eyebrows lifted. "I'm not paying for that."

She made no response and Nate looked around the room, shifting in his chair to avoid the soft foot that curled around his calf. It was the first time he ever truly appreciated the idea of a male-only dining room. Tess took up her glass when the waiter set it beside her on the table and slid the check unobtrusively onto the tablecloth.

"Is it true about you and Marietta?" she asked, tilting her head slightly so the hat threw no shadow over her. Her eyes watched his with animal cunning.

"Don't get any ideas, Tess," he warned.

"I always have ideas. You know that better than any man."

"What happened to Rossie? You trying to get rid of him?"

"Want me to?"

Exasperated, he glanced around the room. "Just what are you after?"

She smiled with a look that chilled him. There was something about her that made him increasingly uneasy. Tess was too unpredictable, and he caught hints of icy depths in her.

"I want the best," she fairly purred, and cocked one eyebrow at him.

"Did you hope to find it down at the crimps' boardinghouses?" he couldn't resist asking. "I saw a scarf you left behind."

For an instant he caught a savage glitter in her eyes, an almost imperceptible tightening of her lips against her teeth, but she altered her expression quickly to one of shocked innocence. "I didn't know you could be so cruel."

He considered his feelings for Eliza and the nagging idea of proposing to her. "There's a lot that's surprising about both of us," he remarked.

Tess pursed her lips slightly. "Let me see," she began slowly, tapping her fingertip idly on the tablecloth, "there was a woman at your Thanksgiving Day party . . . Oh, yes, I saw you, Nate. Quite an entertaining dancer you can be—"

"It won't work, sweetheart. Now finish up your brandy and take your check with you. I want to enjoy my lunch."

"You have a lot of nerve," she said with quiet poison.

He grinned suddenly, harshly. "But you used to love it."

"I expected at least some civility from you."

"Why?"

A familiar figure strolled past the table then, and catching sight of the man, Nate stood up eagerly. "Mr. Matinga," he said.

"Why, Mr. Truesdale. I didn't expect to run into you again so soon." The tall man held out his hand, a surprised smile on his face. The two men shook hands.

"I had no idea you were without lunch plans or I would have invited you," Nate commented, the lie coming easily since at the moment George Matinga's company was infinitely preferable to being alone with Tess. "Won't you join me?"

Matinga glanced at Tess, who smiled back as she sipped her brandy. "But you have such delightful company. I wouldn't dream of intruding."

"No, no, it's fine. Miss Brody was just leaving." Nate shot Tess a hard, dark stare. "Weren't you?"

For an instant Tess' eyes narrowed to slits, then she flashed a familiar cynical half-smile as she put down her glass and lifted her purse from her lap. She rose, nodded to George Matinga, and said to Nate, "It was lovely, darling, thank you."

Only after she was gone did Nate find her lunch check still on the table.

He scowled to himself a half hour later as he tossed several green bills on the tablecloth to pay not only for his lunch and Tess' but also for George Matinga's.

He felt oddly sordid after the encounter with Tess. How had he ever enjoyed her company? And after the previous evening with Daisy, and especially the night with Eliza—he felt a jolt of masculine pride and passion at the thought—everything else paled.

He remembered Daisy's hugs and kisses and the soft explosion of love he'd felt. Even more powerfully, images of the night with Eliza flitted across his mind, and he felt renewed stirrings of passion. It surprised him how thoroughly Daisy and Eliza had filled his heart. He couldn't imagine what his life had been like before they had come to San Francisco, but he was sure it had been barren, a meaningless void.

Outside Manning's, Nate flagged a passing cab. Business would have to wait a bit longer; he couldn't resist the memories of the previous night, and desire for Eliza burned hard and bright in his loins.

* * *

Eliza had been watching the rectangle of sunlight slide over the floor. It had started at the edge of the first row of benches, lit the dusty shoes of the man sitting asleep on the floor with his head against the wall, and was now two inches from the corner of the ticket counter. White sunlight such as she had never seen back home. She remembered it blindingly white on Nate's shirt as he sat on the hillside at Crystal Springs. She sighed suddenly in deep longing, then focused her thoughts elsewhere.

She and Daisy had packed swiftly, trying not to forget anything important. The only thing she knew she was missing was one of her two black gowns. She hadn't been able to find it.

The rows of benches in the broad train station were almost filled. Beyond the glass windows in the doors leading to the trains, Eliza watched people walk idly past, occasionally heard a squeak of wheels of a laden baggage wagon.

Beside her, Daisy was asleep, her head in Eliza's lap. At first impatient with the long wait, Daisy had finally given in to boredom and fallen asleep. Eliza was glad of it. Daisy had cried—she'd not wanted to leave—and it had wrenched Eliza's heart to know how hurt Daisy would be by the departure. Would she be happier if she stayed alone while Eliza returned to Pittsburgh? Eliza had been agonizing over the possibility all afternoon. Perhaps that was the best course. But Daisy, as much as Eliza, was caught between the two worlds. Adjustments would have to be made either way. But wouldn't Nate's world be a better place for her, after all? And Nate did love Daisy.

Eliza sighed sharply and blinked against the sting of tears.

They would spend Christmas on the train. She had already wrapped her gifts for Daisy and tucked them in her bag, which now sat on a cart waiting to be loaded onto the two-twenty train. She had made a tiny wardrobe for Daisy's doll Angelique from remnants Mrs. Penchelli had given her. Even a little teal-blue silk party dress. Now Eliza wished she hadn't made that outfit. It aroused too many painful memories of Nate's Thanksgiving Day party.

Her gifts to Nate and Mrs. Herlihy she had left on the dresser in her room. For Nate she had carefully hemmed a discreet charcoal and black fleur-de-lis silk tie, which, now that she thought about it, was probably a useless gift, considering that he most likely had dozens of ties and could easily afford hundreds more. Mrs. Herlihy, though, would appreciate the big red scarf.

The loud breathing of the man asleep on the floor was interrupted by a trio of well-dressed businessmen entering the station. As they approached the ticket counter, one said, "Have we missed the two-twenty to Sacramento?"

"No, sir, it should be pulling in any minute. Late out of Fresno," the ticket seller said briskly.

"Three round-trip tickets then," said the man.

A distant whistle blew shrilly.

The ticket man grinned. "You just made it. There's your train now."

Several waiting passengers stood up and made their way toward the doors that were now being propped open with scuffed wood wedges. Beyond the doors the hissing of steam from other waiting trains could be heard.

The squeal of steel wheels and hissing of a boiler grew deafening as the approaching train entered the station and braked to a slow stop. The smell of hot metal and oil filled the air.

Daisy shifted her legs, accidentally poked a gentleman sitting beside her, and woke up with a start.

"This is our train," Eliza said in a tremulous voice. She wiped quickly at the corners of her eyes so Daisy wouldn't see her tears and be upset or worried. Rising, she took up her carpet-sack and reached for Daisy's hand. "It's time to go," she said with forced cheerfulness.

Mrs. Herlihy had just paid the launderer at the front door when Nate climbed the brick steps. The delivery boy returned to his wagon, drawn up before the door, and whistled to the horse to start him down the steep flagged drive to the street. Mrs. Herlihy saw Nate and waited, her arms full of packages bearing his cleaned and starched shirts, collars, and cuffs.

"Are you going to work in the yard today?" she asked. He never came home during the day for any other reason.

"No. Is Eliza here?" He held the door for her.

"I don't think so. At least I haven't seen her. Then again, I haven't been upstairs since I cleaned, and she was here then."

Nate took the brown paper-wrapped packages from her. "Here, I'll take these up—I'm going to look for her."

He climbed the stairs, dropped the packages on his bed, and called out, "Eliza?" as he approached her door. He knocked, but there was no answer. Pushing open the door, Nate stepped inside. The room looked different, but at first he couldn't figure out why. Then he noticed two small, white paper-wrapped boxes on the dresser and looked at them curiously.

An envelope was attached to each box, one addressed to him, the other to Mrs. Herlihy. He took the envelope with his name on it, opened it, and slid out a tiny lace-edged Christmas card signed with Eliza's name. Was this a Christmas present from her?

Vaguely uneasy, he glanced around again, and then it hit him. There was no hairbrush on the dresser, no hairpins or sewing pins and pincushions, no sign of occupancy. Nate yanked open the top dresser drawer. Empty. The next drawer and the next—empty! He went to the wardrobe and flung open the doors. *Empty!*

He felt cold all over as he entered Daisy's room. There was no doll on the bed, no shift or hair ribbons or dusty black stocking left on the floor, not even the catalog she'd confiscated to cut pictures from. He pulled drawers completely free of the dresser, tossing them on the floor, pulled open the wardrobe and let the door crash back against the wall, and was greeted with only the scent of cedar.

Gone!

He wanted to smash his fist into the wall.

His feet barely touched the stairs as he ran back down to the first floor. Mrs. Herlihy was in the kitchen washing a pot when he burst into the room.

"They're gone! Do you know anything about it?" Even to his own ears his voice had murder in it. He took a deep breath, held up his hands palms forward in apology. "They're not here, and they've taken all their things. Do you have any idea what happened? Is there a note? Isn't there even a goddamned note? She left without writing even a single *god*damned *lousy note!*"

Mrs. Herlihy had set the pot back in the sink and was drying her hands on her apron as she regarded Nate in agitation. "Oh, no! Are you sure they're not just out someplace?"

"Their clothes are gone! Everything is gone! It's as if they were never here!" His voice broke off suddenly. "Oh, hell." He paced the floor.

"I can't imagine Eliza would just up and leave like this without reason," Mrs. Herlihy exclaimed.

Distracted, Nate muttered, "She had reason. We had a fight, and Daisy ran away. Well, we thought she'd run away. But she was here all the time. She'd overheard us talking and found out I'm her father. I mean, everything came out last night."

Mrs. Herlihy frowned thoughtfully and leaned back against the edge of the sink. "That's probably why she's gone."

Nate stuffed his hands in his pockets. "Why?"

"You can't see it, I suppose. Never mind."

"*Never mind?*" He spun around, muttering "Hell!" and started out of the kitchen. "I'm going to the train station. She still had those damned tickets. Maybe they haven't left yet. And"—he stopped and glanced back over his shoulder—"if they show up, keep them here! She owes me an explanation."

Nate leaped from the cab and shoved a bill at the driver. Inside the train station he thrust his way past milling people, scanned the benches for Eliza and Daisy, and disregarded the line at the ticket counter as he leaned toward the clerk. "Someone bound for Pennsylvania—what train would they have taken?"

The young ticket seller glanced up from counting change for an elderly man, who looked perturbed by the disruption. "That would be the Sacramento train. One left at nine-ten this morning, another this afternoon. Only two a day."

"When this afternoon?"

The clerk turned around to look at the clock on the wall behind him. "Should be just leaving. Track Three."

Nate pushed his way through the crowd at the doors, ran down the walkway, scanned the signs above him for track three.

He found it empty.

The caboose was just clearing the station, a trail of black smoke dissipating in the sunlight, the clack of wheels on steel fading. Nate stood on the edge of the platform. His black frock coat blew open in a gust of air as he watched the dark curve of train disappear from sight.

It seemed to him as if a huge portion of himself had been ripped away. The pain of their departure seared through him, and in a daze he walked slowly back toward the waiting room. Behind the first shock of pain rose fury so overwhelming that he paused and slammed his fist into the wall beside the door. Oblivious to the ache in his knuckles and the appalled glances cast by nearby people, he stalked into the station and approached the ticket counter.

Eliza lifted Daisy onto her lap to watch out the window as the sun-bright pastel buildings and homes slid by, as the hills rose and fell in slow rhythm beyond the window. "But we didn't get to say good-bye, Aunt Lizzie," Daisy whined. "Will they worry about us?"

"No, my precious, not really," Eliza answered, her heart breaking.

The buildings gave way to winter-thick vegetation, leafless dogwood and oak trees, blue-green pines, lush grass, ice-plant, milkweed as tall as fences. Hills verdant from winter rains blocked the last view of the city.

Mrs. Herlihy inspected Nate's bleeding knuckles. "What on earth did you do?"

"I punched a wall in the train station," he answered, expressionless, propping himself on the stool beside the kitchen worktable.

She filled a bowl with water from the tank in the

stove. "What about taking a ferry over to Oakland and catching the train there?" She brought the water and soap to the table.

"I asked about that. The train they're on doesn't stop until Sacramento. It's only the nine-ten train that stops in Oakland and Santa Rosa and all the— Careful! That hurts."

Mrs. Herlihy looked up from dabbing soap on his hand. "What are you going to do?"

"Well, there's no way I can catch up to them now." He scowled, remembering that George Matinga would be returning to the office tomorrow to sign the contract. Beyond that, he had several other appointments lined up in the coming month with prospective and existing customers. There was no way he could drop everything at work and take off after Daisy and Eliza when the trip to Pittsburgh and back would take several weeks. He needed a few days to cancel appointments and make arrangements. "I'll be catching a train east the day after Christmas," he informed her. "I don't know for sure when I'll be back."

"So you are going after them."

"Of course! She's got my daughter! Do you think I'm just going to sit here and say, 'Well, that's that'?"

Mrs. Herlihy didn't reply as she dried his hand and wrapped it carefully in a strip of clean cloth. "Is it just Daisy you're going after?" she asked.

Nate studied his bound hand, exhaled sharply, and stood up from the stool. "No," he said bluntly. He glanced around the kitchen then disappeared through the swinging doors into the dining room, returning with a crystal decanter of bourbon.

"I want you to be honest with me," he said as he poured a generous three-finger helping of the amber liquid into a glass. "You're a woman—maybe you can help me understand. Why would Eliza leave so suddenly and without saying anything?''

Mrs. Herlihy emptied the bowl of rust-tinged water into the sink and pursed her lips thoughtfully. ''She might be in love with you,'' she suggested.

''I thought of that.'' He lifted the glass and lowered it again without taking a drink. ''It's not an answer. It doesn't explain anything—in fact, that would give her more reason to stay, not leave.''

''Not necessarily. At least not to Eliza.''

Nate stared out the kitchen window. ''Tomorrow's Christmas Eve,'' he said perversely. ''They'll spend Christmas on a goddamned train.'' He took a hard swallow of the bourbon and turned around again. ''Why would love not necessarily be a reason for Eliza to stay?''

Mrs. Herlihy sighed and bent to unlatch the icebox door. She pulled out a package of meat wrapped in brown butcher paper. ''Think about this: she's a millworker and you're out of her class.''

''What the hell are you saying? That she wants to throw away her life in a goddamned stinking mill, working for practically nothing? Oh, put that away,'' he said in disgust. ''I don't want anything to eat tonight.''

''You have to eat.''

''I'll go out.''

Mrs. Herlihy shrugged and returned the package. ''Want me to stay for a while longer tonight? I could.''

''No, no, I'll probably head over to the club later. Don't try to sidetrack me—why would she prefer the mill to what she has here?''

''*What* does she have here?'' Mrs. Herlihy said sharply. ''Now, excuse me, I may be overstepping my place, but I've got to speak my piece. There's no future for Eliza here, and she's smart enough to rec-

ognize it. The two of you are from different social
classes. If the truth be known, I don't blame her one
whit for going." Mrs. Herlihy thought of the pinkish smears she'd found that morning on his sheets
and sighed to herself. It was obvious to her what
had occurred. "If she felt insulted in any way, Eliza
would believe she had no choice but to leave. She's
a decent sort, Mr. Truesdale."

Nate's eyes narrowed as he realized what she was
hinting at, and the stab of guilt he felt surprised him.
Without saying another word, he grabbed up the
decanter of bourbon and left the kitchen.

Mrs. Herlihy turned back to the sink in frustration. He had become like a son to her, despite their
positions as employer and servant, and she recognized in Eliza the kind of woman who'd make him
a fine wife, which was not true of any of the other
lady friends she'd seen him with. But the social barriers were too high, and she'd known of situations
before where a young man had fallen in love with a
woman only to reject her later when he discovered
that she lived in an unacceptable section of the city.
Though she knew Mr. Truesdale didn't have social
prejudices like so many others of his class, the pres-
sures of society were still not easy to overcome.

She thought of Eliza's abrupt departure with sadness. The young woman must have felt terribly hurt
to have left so quickly and without saying good-bye,
and Mrs. Herlihy's heart ached for her.

Nate carried the bourbon decanter upstairs to his
room. The feeling of guilt over Eliza's leaving
haunted him. Never mind that she had come to his
room; he hadn't behaved as a gentleman. He'd seduced a virgin and then blithely departed for work
without any indication that he would take responsibility for his actions and marry her. Proposing
would have been the honorable thing to do. Instead,

he'd treated her like a prostitute. He realized he'd been too long with women like Tess and Marietta. To Tess, lovemaking was entirely casual; to Marietta, it was calculated. But Eliza was altogether different—a decent woman.

He set the decanter and his glass on the bedside table and stretched out wearily on the bed, folding his hands behind his head as he stared at the ceiling. Thoughts of Eliza flitted through his mind. He remembered the night they had spent together, the excitement of having her in his arms, and fresh desire for her thudded through him. He wanted her desperately, and the proper thing to do would be to propose to her when he next saw her, despite the fact that the idea of marriage still frightened him. Unable to forget the unhappiness in his parents' marriage, he shied from tying himself up in any permanent arrangement.

Besides, he thought with sudden anguish, how did he know Eliza would want to be married to him? She might refuse even to speak to him again. With an inner groan he reached for the glass of bourbon and rose to pace the room.

Moonless, the night was like a solid mass beyond the train windows. With Daisy asleep beside her, her head in Eliza's lap, Eliza absently cupped the small face with her palm as she stared out the window. She rested her head against the glass and looked into the reflection of the train car overlaid on the black night beyond the window. Earlier the porter had come through and turned down the lamps placed high on the walls. Now they emitted only a soft light, leaving the car in muted shadow. A minute ago she had glanced around, seen a faint light on the surface of an eye here and there, the ghostly glow of faces, hands, exposed shirts and collars.

Now as she watched the eerie reflections that made the lamps seem to hang in space beyond the window, she considered the situation with more soberness than she had earlier. In selfishness she had taken Daisy with her, but she knew Nate could offer the girl a better life: a luxurious home, sturdy Mrs. Herlihy, the love of a father. A lot more than she, Eliza, could offer. What would Daisy face in Pittsburgh? Someday she would no doubt be working in the mill. Would she be as desperate to leave as her mother had been? Would she remember Nate, the weeks she'd spent in San Francisco, and hate Eliza for denying her a home and a father?

The glass window was still icy although they'd already left the Sierras behind them. Climbing, shifting ever higher in the switchbacks through the snowy mountains, Eliza and Daisy had watched together through the window. They'd eaten sandwiches Eliza had purchased from the dining car for their dinner. After passing Winnemucca, Nevada, Daisy had fallen asleep.

Eliza closed her eyes, her head resting in the cushioned corner of the seat back and window frame. The swinging rhythm of the train and the clacketing of the wheels were soothing, creating a lullaby for her restless mind and heart.

Nate reeled into the office the next morning. His head felt like a hot-air balloon, stretched to painful proportions, swaying out of control on his neck. His stomach was queasy. His eyeballs were gouged marbles, grinding in his head. Though he'd washed before getting dressed, he still felt sweaty. As he dressed, he'd had to hang onto the wardrobe door while the room wheeled around him.

He paused at Peg Walters' desk and held onto it. "The contracts?" he said. The effort to think and talk rocked the balloon in his head and made him feel dizzy again. Last night he had thought the bourbon in his head felt better than the pain in his heart, but this morning he wasn't so sure.

As Peg pushed the papers into his shaky hand, she had the gall to laugh. He squinted cautiously at her blurred face.

With a broad smile she said, "If you feel as bad as you look—"

"How important is this job to you?" he said through gritted teeth . . . and had to hold his breath against the queasy turmoil in his stomach

She laughed again, the sound grating against his every nerve. He let go of her desk and walked carefully into his office. The first thing he did was pull down each heavy green shade. He had to hang onto the window sashes so he didn't lurch against the panes.

Wrapped in blessed darkness, he slumped in his chair and put his face in his hands.

He could remember going to the Bohemian Club last night and sitting at a table with brothers Henry and Richard Carlisle. They had protested the quantity of his drinking, but had laughed at his bitter jokes. He could remember climbing brick steps, fumbling to open a door. But the emptiness in the house had sobered him too much. He knew he had walked through each room. Once, the silence and privacy and freedom had been important to him. After his father's death and his mother's departure, he had dismissed each servant—the maids, the gardener, the butler, even his own valet. He'd hired a decorator and ordered almost every room redone. He'd hired Mrs. Herlihy from an agency, had liked her from the first minute in the interview when she hadn't picked at crumbs on the kitchen worktable as had so many others. If there was one thing he didn't want, it was a judgmental perfectionist nit-picking around him daily.

But last night the emptiness and solitude had been too much for him. After touring each silent room, he had retreated to the large parlor with the decanter of bourbon in his hand and sat in a chair, remembering the soft weight of Daisy on his lap and Eliza resting her head on the arm of the sofa as she listened to that idiot tale of singing mock turtles and rabbits in waistcoats.

He had woken up in the chair the next morning.

Mrs. Herlihy could deal with the bourbon he'd spilled on the carpet. Tomorrow was Christmas Day, and he had to pull himself together and arrange work at the office so he could catch the train to Pittsburgh on the morning after the holiday.

Eventually he would get Daisy and Eliza back. Whether it took weeks, or months, eventually he would get them back.

Chapter 13

Eliza woke to the pale gray-and-pink light of dawn illuminating the sky and flat landscape. She looked out the window at what appeared to be endless stretches of snow-covered ground, but then she realized she was looking across miles and miles of salt flats. The other passengers were still asleep, and there was time yet before they pulled into Salt Lake City.

When Daisy awoke, Eliza lifted her onto her lap so that she could look outside too. Daisy complained that her neck hurt. "I was supposed to get an award for reading," she added, beginning to cry. "Now I won't ever get it, and Mrs. Rodriguez doesn't know where I am."

Eliza rubbed Daisy's neck to ease the kink and asked thoughtfully, "Daisy, if you could be anywhere at all, where would you like to be right now?"

"I don't know," the girl said, and lay her head on Eliza's shoulder.

"Let me ask you something," Eliza persisted. "Where would you like to live if you had a choice? In our apartment in Pittsburgh, with Katie at school and Marjorie and Mrs. Riley? Or at Nate's house with the other Katie at school and Mrs. Herlihy and Mrs. Rodriguez?"

Daisy sat up and picked at the top button of Eliza's cape. She frowned. "Could we have shrimp soup and raisins at home? I'm hungry."

"No, that's only at Nate's house."

"Would Nate come see us?"

"Maybe. But it wouldn't be very often at all. It's a long way." She tried to keep her voice steady over the rising lump in her throat.

"Could we go visit Nate and Mrs. Herlihy?" Daisy asked.

"*You* could . . . maybe. Would you like to live with Nate and Mrs. Herlihy?" Eliza watched Daisy closely as she added, "If I stayed in Pittsburgh and you came to visit me sometimes?" Tears stung her eyes as she thought of losing the girl.

Daisy sighed and frowned. "I want you to stay with Nate and Mrs. Herlihy too. When can we eat, Aunt Lizzie?"

"Soon. Soon," Eliza said. She smoothed Daisy's hair off her neck. "I can't stay at Nate's house, but you could. Would you like that? And have shrimp soup and rides on Nate's back and play with Katie?" Eliza's heart twisted. "Would you like that?"

"Yes, but I want you to stay too." Daisy turned around and climbed off Eliza's lap. "I have to go to the bathroom, Aunt Lizzie. I know where it is. Can I go all by myself?"

"All right." Eliza forced herself to smile. "But hurry back so we can go get some breakfast."

As soon as Daisy was out of sight, Eliza let the tears fall. The time had come to put away her own selfish wishes and take Daisy back to Nate. Though the thought of losing Daisy was almost unbearable, she knew he could offer her a far better life. It wasn't right to deprive Daisy of such opportunities. Blindly, as the tears trailed slowly down her cheeks, Eliza groped in her carpet-sack for a handkerchief.

They had time for only a hasty meal before the buildings of Salt Lake City rose up in the distance against a backdrop of hills. Eliza and Daisy were back in their seats in time to watch the streets and houses and stopped carriages at crossings slide past.

When the train had finally come to a stop at the station, they climbed off and worked their way, hand-in-hand, along the crowded walkway until they reached the baggage car. The broad doors had been slid back and luggage tagged for Salt Lake City was being removed to a waiting wagon.

Eliza spotted their bags on a shelf at the back of the car. "We'll be getting off here," she said to the porter. "We need our bags. They're in the back there."

"You're not going all the way through then?" the porter asked as he headed to the back of the car. "Which ones?"

He brought out the bags Eliza requested and lowered them to another porter on the walkway who said, "We'll take them to the station for you, ma'am."

"Actually, I'm not staying here either, so I'll take them now."

The porter shrugged and handed over the two worn valises.

Daisy, wide-eyed and content after her breakfast, skipped beside Eliza as they entered the station.

Eliza cashed in the balance of their tickets and purchased two return tickets. They sat down to wait, Eliza smiling bravely, as their bags were stacked onto another wagon and set aside to be loaded onto the eleven o'clock train heading west to California.

Someone was knocking on the front door. Nate lifted his head from the pillow and squinted toward the ornate clock on his dresser. It was seven-ten on

Christmas morning and someone had the *nerve* to come to the door and pull twice on the bell. He rolled onto his stomach and jammed the pillow over his head. Whoever it was could just go away and leave him alone.

The bell rang again.

He wanted to ignore it, but a thought struck him, and he pushed aside the pillow, raising himself on one elbow. Who would want to disturb someone so early—and on Christmas morning? Whatever it was about, it wasn't anything ordinary. He tossed off the sheet and stood up, pushing a half-packed suitcase out of his way as he reached into the wardrobe for a shirt and pair of trousers.

The bell rang again as he descended the stairs. "I'm coming!" he exclaimed.

He finished tucking the shirttails into the waist of his trousers and pulled open the door. For a minute he stared incredulously.

Eliza, wearing her boater hat and the simple black cape over a familiar blue-and-white striped gown, gazed back at him with tired brown eyes, hopeful and hesitant. She had never looked more beautiful to him. His heart hit a string of double beats in surprise and happiness. Daisy was beaming. In her new blue sailor coat she looked as pretty as one of her dolls.

Speechless with sudden, overwhelming emotion, Nate bent and held out his arms to Daisy. She hopped up the steps and flung her arms around his neck. "Nate! Did you miss us? We went on a train, but we didn't go all the way home. We turned around and came back. Are you happy to see us?"

He stood up with her in his arms. His voice was hoarse as he tried to talk over the thick lump in his throat. "Am I happy to see you? Why, you little scamp, I'm so happy, you'll never guess."

As Daisy hugged him and pressed delighted kisses to his cheek, Nate looked at Eliza, who waited on the threshold. He smiled and felt his heart lift, then he held out his hand. When she took it and stepped into the foyer, he said softly, "Merry Christmas," and pulled her into the curve of his free arm. "You came back," he whispered.

Seeing the shine of wetness in his eyes, Eliza realized how moved he was by their return, and she was overcome by an ache of mixed longing and happiness. She felt the light scratch of his beard against her face as he kissed her, but then, almost as if he was embarrassed by his own emotions, he released her, set Daisy down, and turned briskly to the business of getting their suitcases into the house.

As she watched him ascend the stairs with their bags, Eliza couldn't help smiling with the pleasure of being near him again. Every fiber of her being felt vibrant and glowing with excitement. Then her spirits dropped. Nothing had changed. She was still a millworker, on the level of a servant; Nate was still a member of an elite and self-contained society. As much as she might like to wish otherwise, there were boundaries between them that weren't easily breached.

With heavy steps she followed Nate and Daisy up the stairs, unpinning her boater hat as she went. As the other two entered Daisy's room, she continued to her own chamber. Wearily, she slipped off her cape and dropped it onto the bed, then walked to the window. Pushing aside the soft lace drapes, she gazed down on the last bright blooms of the season in Nate's garden. The door closed behind her, and she turned to see Nate crossing the room toward her.

"I know we left rather—" She never finished her sentence. He snatched her up against him and kissed her roughly and greedily. Her thoughts fled as quickly as her breath. In his crushing embrace, her determined practicality evaporated, and she clung to him, weak with sudden and overwhelming need. His hungry kisses forced her head back against his arm. She felt the slow, warm ache of passion in her breasts and abdomen and thighs, wherever she was pressed against his hard frame. He had missed her! He had wanted her back! He felt the same way about her as she did for him! Eagerly she held him, her desire matching his, climbing with it.

Abruptly, the pressure of his mouth eased, though he still held her tightly. "I should be furious with you," he muttered. She looked up into his eyes, narrowed and glittering. "You left without a word, without any explanation. Did you think I wouldn't care?" His voice deepened, and she felt the vibrations of it in his chest as he demanded, "Or were you trying to hurt me by leaving and taking Daisy? Damn you."

Before Eliza could answer, he bent his mouth to hers again. Caught in a web of shared passion, she returned his kisses, feeling his anger melt, replaced by an ardor that was powerful yet tender. How could she have even thought of returning to Pittsburgh? How could she have abandoned the pleasure she knew in his arms?

"Why did you leave me?" he whispered, his breath warm against her cheek as he lowered his head to kiss her earlobe and the side of her throat.

Her voice trembled audibly as she murmured, "I can't remember now," and at that moment it was the truth. His kisses dissolved all barriers between them. Her earlier doubts seemed as insubstantial as wisps of smoke.

"Do you know what that did to me?" he muttered

hoarsely. "Do you know how losing you and Daisy made me feel?"

A moan of delight slipped from her as his hand stroked over one breast, then suddenly the bedroom door swung open. Nate and Eliza jerked apart in surprise. Daisy stood in the threshold, grinning in quizzical astonishment.

"What were you doing?" she asked.

Striding toward her, Nate lifted the little girl to his shoulder. "I'll bet you're hungry for some breakfast," he suggested, trying to distract her, his voice still deep with passion. "Let's go see what we can find."

Embarrassed by what Daisy had seen, Eliza followed them down to the kitchen, but her legs felt curiously weak and her breathing unsteady. She tried to be cheerfully busy, as if nothing at all had happened. While they ate stacks of steaming hotcakes smothered in warm maple syrup, Daisy chatted about the train ride. Then she asked, "Nate, are you going on a trip too? You have suitcases in your room."

Nate glanced down the table to Eliza, and he couldn't quite keep the annoyance out of his voice as he answered, "Well, precious, I was planning to leave tomorrow on a train to go find you. You and Aunt Lizzie departed in a big hurry, didn't you? You didn't even say a word about it . . . not even goodbye." With anger and desire warring within him, his eyes took on a caustic glint, and to Eliza he said coldly, "Not a very *polite* thing to do, was it?"

Daisy broke in with a peevish exclamation. "Are you going to fight? You promised you wouldn't."

"No, we're not fighting," Nate assured her, abruptly ashamed, though his smile was too forced to be genuine. For Daisy's sake he had to remember to watch his temper. But though he held his tongue, he couldn't halt his growing resentment. What had Eliza been doing by taking Daisy and then turning around and coming back? Was she trying to stir him up and make him jealous? Marietta or Tess would have pulled a trick like that on him. He'd never expected such manipulative behavior from Eliza.

Under his long cool stares, Eliza felt her face redden. In his arms earlier she had been sure of his feelings for her, but now she scolded herself. He had not said a word of apology or indicated that his intentions toward her were honorable. And it was her own fault, she told herself furiously. She'd gone to his room that night like any easy woman, and because of it, to his mind, he could just grab her and kiss her any time. Well, it would be different from now on, she fumed. Come morning she'd be back on the train to Pittsburgh, just as she had planned.

After the meal Nate followed her into the kitchen. He had a few questions and was determined to get answers. No woman would get away with manipulating him, he thought.

Eliza was preparing to wash dishes, and he reached around her to shut off the water. But before he could say anything, she pointed to his injured hand on the spigot. "What happened?" she asked in surprise and concern.

He glanced down at the scabbed knuckles and scowled at her as he said with sharp sarcasm, "It seems that a few days ago I reached the station only slightly too late to catch a certain train. Impatient jackass that I am, I took out my frustration on a wall."

"Are you blaming me?" she exclaimed.

"You offered not even a single word of explanation, do you realize that? You just up and took my daughter without any regard for how her loss might hurt me." Nate's mouth tightened. "What were you trying to do?"

Eliza marched to the worktable and angrily stacked the used breakfast plates. "You think I owe you an explanation? You think I've greatly wronged you?"

"I offered you every consideration," he said with barely controlled anger. "You had the use of my home instead of having to stay in that decrepit hotel. You ate at my table. And if you hadn't been so proud, you wouldn't have had to work either! Then, after all that, you absconded with my daughter, and I had to make arrangements to set aside my work for at least a month in order to go after her. After all that, I don't even get an apology?"

Dumping the plates into the sink with a loud clatter of crockery, she spun on him. "Don't you dare insinuate that I owe you anything at all! You got everything you wanted, so don't try to tell—"

"I've been more than generous with you!" he exclaimed. "And if you weren't so pompous and prickly you'd see it."

"Generous?" she repeated with fury. "Was what happened between us another charitable gesture on your part? Well, excuse me, but I'm not going to fall all over myself with gratitude."

Nate straightened perceptibly in surprise. "You know damn good and well that you can't entirely blame me for what happened that night."

"It was what you wanted all along, wasn't it!"

"Who went to whose room?" he pointed out. "You're pretty quick to cast stones."

Eliza felt her cheeks grow hot. "I've heard enough of this! You don't have any decency."

Nate scowled in angry embarrassment, remembering his earlier conviction that he should have behaved more honorably . . . at least afterward. "How do you know I might not have done the right thing? You took off and didn't give me a chance to say anything!''

Before Eliza could answer him, Daisy ran into the kitchen, breathless and distressed.

''Nate, you don't have a Christmas tree! Why don't you have a tree?''

He shot Eliza a hard glance. *Because you left!* he wanted to say. *Because you took her with you!* Eliza turned her back on him and began restacking the dishes with noisy vehemence.

Daisy looked between the two adults. ''You weren't fighting, were you?'' she accused petulantly.

''Of course not,'' Nate answered. ''Why don't you and I go out back and see what we can find in the way of a Christmas tree?''

''Do you grow them in your garden?'' she asked brightly.

''No, not Christmas-tree-types, but we can make do with something else, can't we?'' He took her hand, ignoring her pout, and they went into the backyard together.

Daisy began to cheer up when he gathered branches of cypress and bound them together into a big green bouquet almost three feet high. ''How's that?'' he asked her.

She shook her head, crinkling her nose at him in a grin. ''That's the worst Christmas tree I've ever seen.''

''You're right,'' he agreed with a rueful smile. ''Here, you take it into the parlor and find the best spot for it.''

Nate trailed her into the house. When Daisy ran ahead to the parlor, he looked around for Eliza and found her in the dining room, sweeping crumbs off the tablecloth.

He knew he had to say something, had to patch things up between them somehow. What could he say? He cleared his throat. "Eliza, I'm sorry about what happened," he began. She ignored him and continued to work. "We've had a misunderstanding, but we can work it out."

"I don't think so," she answered briskly, stepping past him to return to the kitchen.

Nate grasped her elbow and turned her to face him in the doorway. Eliza set her lips in anger. "It's Christmas, and for the sake of that child in the other room," he said, frowning darkly, "at least let's call a truce."

Eliza dropped her gaze but said nothing as she pulled free of him. His nearness made her heart ache. She longed to tear down the barriers between them, longed for the freedom to love him as she so desired. But mere longing never changed facts. She'd known that too well all her life. There was no future for her here, and the sooner she left, the better.

Nate watched her slip past him into the kitchen. He wanted to pull her into his arms, and kiss and pleasure her until she begged for him and promised to stay. But she'd probably reject him all the more strongly afterward. Hadn't she run away after the first time? What could he do? Scowling in frustration, he headed toward the parlor. He needed time. He needed to court her. The idea pleased him, and he stroked his chin thoughtfully as he considered it. Feeling the prick of stubble on his face, he swore softly to himself. Hell, he needed a shave, and there he'd been grabbing her one minute, shouting at her the next, and all the while looking like a homeless tramp.

Daisy was crossing the foyer when he stepped from the dining room. "I found the perfect spot," she said, "on the table in the parlor and—"

"Can you wait, precious?" he asked. "I'll be down as soon as I can." He gave her a wink and took the stairs two at a time, feeling buoyant and optimistic. As he strode the length of the hall to his room, he whistled to himself, eager to begin wooing and winning the only woman in his life who had ever become vitally important to him.

When he returned to the parlor to find Daisy, he had shaved twice and was dressed in dove-gray flannel trousers and frock coat, with a black waistcoat and starched shirt. He'd fastened his cuffs with pearl and gold pins, and a pearl stickpin anchored his black silk tie.

Daisy had cleared off an end table beside the damask rose couch, and he hunted through the lower cupboards in the bookcase until he found a vase. He planted their cypress-bough Christmas tree in it and set it on the table.

"There," he said, and Daisy stood back with him, clasping her hands behind her in imitation of him. The lamps hadn't been lit and only pale streaks of daylight slanted between the heavy burgundy drapes. He thought he could still detect the stench of bourbon. It made his stomach slightly queasy, and he vowed he would never drink bourbon again.

"But Nate," Daisy said, "there aren't any decorations. It's not a Christmas tree without decorations."

"Right you are. Come along."

He led the way to the third floor, down a shadowed corridor, past empty servant's rooms, and entered a door at the end of the hall. The room contained a bare yellowed mattress, a dusty dresser and chair, and piles of boxes set haphazardly along the wall, over the floor, and on the mattress. Unused, the rooms up here were cleaned only twice a year. As Nate sat down on the mattress to glance through one of the boxes, Daisy wandered around the room and went to the window to peer out.

"Whose rooms are these?" she asked.

"The servants used to live here . . . back when I was your age," he answered absently as he shoved aside one box and flipped open another.

"So they don't belong to anyone?" she asked in wonder.

"They belong to me."

"It's like a playhouse," she said finally. "An apartment for dolls." She pantomimed putting a doll to bed and covering it up.

"Well, now, that's an idea," Nate said, watching her. "You don't have a playroom, do you?"

"What's a playroom? Is that like a playhouse, where you pretend?"

"Come here." He lifted her onto his lap. "How would you like to have one of these rooms all for yourself, to play in? Or have the whole floor? You could have toys here, and make-believe apartments, if you want. I'll give you all of it. I'll hire a maid to help Mrs. Herlihy keep it clean and dusted all the time. Just for you."

Daisy crinkled her nose at him in a dubious grin. "Really?"

"Absolutely." Nate kissed her forehead and set her on her feet. "Now, let's find those decorations. That pathetic tree downstairs needs all the help it can get."

Eliza laughed when she saw the decorated tree. Nate and Daisy had come into the kitchen where she was stuffing a chicken for their Christmas dinner— Nate had canceled his order for the traditional goose—and they took her hands to lead her to the parlor. Daisy made her close her eyes for this surprise. The tree was nothing more than a clump of branches in a green vase, with small red and white satin ribbons tied here and there, tiny blown-glass angels perched among them. But to her eyes it was the most beautiful of all Christmas trees. Two silver candelabras on the mantel and a bright fire in the hearth gave the room a golden aura that Eliza thought was splendid.

She looked to Nate, who was watching her expectantly. His eyes shone in the firelight, and Eliza wanted to look at him forever.

"What do you think, Aunt Lizzie?" Daisy asked, bouncing on her toes.

"It's . . . perfect," she said.

From the mantel Nate brought two slim crystal glasses of ruby-colored wine. "For the occasion," he said, handing one to Eliza. They lifted their glasses, and the lip of his clinked lightly against hers. "Merry Christmas, Eliza," he said softly. "I can't think of any other way I'd prefer to spend this day than with you." He wanted to toast to many more Christmases to come, but decided to take his courtship of her one step at a time.

Eliza smiled, though her lips trembled slightly with emotion. He could so easily touch her heart, yet was probably unaware of his profound effect on her. "Merry Christmas, Nate," she answered.

They drank the toast, and then Daisy tugged at her skirt. "Here, Aunt Lizzie—mistletoe," she exclaimed, giggling, and handed Eliza a piece of green cypress.

"Mistletoe?" Eliza laughed. "My dear, this isn't—"

"But that's what Nate told me to say," Daisy protested.

Laughing, Nate shushed her with a finger over her mouth. "Not fair. You weren't supposed to tell her that."

Eliza's pulse quickened. What harm could there be in an innocent holiday kiss under feigned mistletoe? She could still feel the warm glow from his ear-

lier kisses, and she knew she wanted to kiss him
again. "Oh, I've made a mistake," she said as if in
surprise. "It *is* mistletoe." Impulsively, she held it
over her head, her heart beating rapidly.

Nate winked at Daisy and suggested she go into
the kitchen and pour herself some lemonade. When
the girl had disappeared, he cupped Eliza's face in
his hands. "Just keep that damned thing up there
for a while," he said, smiling at her.

When his mouth touched hers, she trembled with
the sweetness of his lips and the soft stirring of desire. Though at first he was light and affectionate, as
befitted a kiss under the mistletoe, something deeper
and almost electric passed between them, and his
mouth abruptly slanted hard across hers. Eliza's
pulse raced. Her hand trembled, and she dropped
the mistletoe to stretch her arms around his neck.
All else was erased from her mind, and her awareness was filled with the delight of his mouth, his
hard frame, and his arms pulling her tightly to him.
Her heart pounded at the thrust of his tongue into
her mouth, and passion plunged through her. She
longed to feel his hands on her, yearned to reexper-
ience the elation of him deep inside her. When she
answered his tongue with her own, she heard his
groan of excitement.

Daisy pushed her way between them, and they
broke apart with effort. "I can't find the lemonade,"
Daisy said, grasping Nate's hand. "Come help me."

As Nate was drawn away, Eliza stood still, trans-
fixed with the aching glow of arousal.

During dinner she had difficulty keeping her eyes
off him. They sat together, the three of them, in
comfortable fellowship at one end of the table. Daisy
chatted happily about Nate's promise of a playroom
upstairs. His eyes strayed again and again to Eliza's
face. He smiled, and she knew she had seen that

smile in her dreams. When Daisy laid out plans for her dolls and a doll apartment, he put his hand over Eliza's where it rested on the tablecloth. The touch sent a quiver of pleasure through her.

They unwrapped their Christmas presents in the large parlor. Nate gave Daisy a porcelain tea set, a wicker doll carriage, books to read, a new paint set, and a train set with tracks that they could lay out. Daisy was ecstatic with everything and sat on the floor amid shiny red paper and fat red ribbons.

"But so much, Nate," Eliza protested. "You're going to turn her head."

He stood in front of the low-burning fire in the hearth as he watched Daisy play. "I've got to make up for lost time."

Nate opened his package from Eliza and promptly removed his tie to replace it with the new one. She had to admit, he looked distinguished in it.

He grinned at her as he felt the knot of the tie. "This isn't going to unravel and drop into a bowl of soup sometime, is it?"

"Of course not!" Eliza laughed, but she was embarrassed at this reference to Marietta's gown.

"Well, if it's safe to wear . . . Thank you, it's a fine gift, and I'll be proud to wear it."

Eliza was overwhelmed by his gift to her—three new gowns. Two day dresses—one of yellow silk, the other cranberry taffeta—and an evening gown in pale ice-green satin. All were as fashionable as she'd ever seen. "Oh, Nate." Sighing in bliss, she sat on the faded rose damask couch and touched the folds of the gowns strewn around her. "This is too much. They must have cost you—"

"Please," he said in mock annoyance. "Forget about the money for a change, all right? It was no hardship at all. But do you know what? I went to Mrs. Penchelli to have these done. Oh, I love the irony—she fired you as a seamstress and all the while she was sewing gowns for you as a customer."

"You didn't! Did she know they were for me?"

"I had to tell her so she didn't turn around and give them to you to make. But I had her word she wouldn't mention it to you. It must have been something when she had to bring herself to fire you like that. Marietta wouldn't let up about that damned dress, and I don't think the poor woman had any choice in the matter." Nate chuckled, watching Eliza. "Do you like them?"

"Very much. I'm so surprised . . . I don't know what to say. I can't begin to thank you enough."

"Oh, I think you can find a way," he said with a suggestive grin.

Eliza blushed and laughed, feeling a sudden tug at her heart. "Yes," she said simply, ignoring that part of her mind that warned her how much harder it would be to leave a second time if she let herself make love to him again. "Yes." But then she had another thought. "How did you know my measurements?"

"I borrowed one of your old gowns and gave it to Mrs. Penchelli. I hope everything fits."

"*That's* where it went! *You.*" But she was smiling.

Because she was tired from the trip and the excitement of the day, Daisy retired early to bed that evening. The first time she complained that the engine of her toy train wasn't turning as it should, Eliza packed her off upstairs. Still dreaming of hot scented water, and feeling tired herself after two nights on a train, Eliza slipped away for a bath while Nate read Daisy to sleep from one of the new books.

The hot water was ready as Eliza looked through the drawers of the tall dresser in the bathroom to find towels, lots of big towels. In the bottom drawer she discovered three bottles of perfume. Delighted, she lifted them out. Probably left behind by women in Nate's life over the years, she thought, then sniffed each and chose one that smelled of gardenias. So exotic! She washed her hair and lounged in the almost burningly hot water, brushing at islands of soapy foam floating on the surface.

After Daisy was asleep, Nate went in search of Eliza. He couldn't forget the thrill of her response to his kiss under the makeshift mistletoe.

He located her by the sound of a splash of water in the bathroom and the light essence of gardenia filtering from under the closed door. But having found her, he paused in uncertainty. What did **he** mean to do? Just walk in on her? He shoved his hands in his pockets, leaned one shoulder against the door frame, and considered the situation.

He knew he should walk away, and leave her to finish her bath and retire for the night undisturbed, but he was rooted to the spot, held there by remembrances of the pleasure they had shared and by the intoxicating image of what lay just behind the closed portal. Agitated, he paced in front of the door. Leave, he told himself. But he didn't; the sudden dripping splashes of water and the sound of a soft footstep told him she had left the bath. He pictured her, and felt the hard pounding of blood in his veins. Scowling, he ordered himself to turn around and leave immediately . . . but his hand was already on the doorknob.

She stood in the center of the room, reaching for a towel folded over the top of the old walnut dresser. In the soft light her skin was like pink cream; her breasts, stomach, and thighs glistened with water drops. Her brunette hair was sleek with water. She was more beautiful than ever. The dark wet triangle of hair at the apex of her slender legs drew his attention. In the eternity of that moment, he realized he was holding his breath.

Eliza gasped in surprise and yanked open the towel to cover herself. She stared, waiting, but he neither entered nor left the room. At the sight of the growing heat in his eyes, she felt a blush of mixed embarrassment and excitement fill her face.

Then he crossed the space separating them and reached for the towel. "Nate!" she exclaimed, but he shook his head and lifted the towel to press water from her hair. His presence, and the cool touch of his hands on her flushed cheeks and throat, were irresistible. As he patted her dry, she shivered with the pleasure of each soft touch, each exquisite ministration. Clear drops of water gathered at the ends of her hair and slid down her skin, and he licked a drop from the tip of one sensitized breast. The contact brought a shock of delight.

When she was dry and her hair had been rubbed to a soft damp cloud around her shoulders, Nate gathered her to him. He pressed a kiss to her throat, breathing the scent of gardenias on her. "I missed you," he muttered. "Why did you leave, Eliza? Why did you do that to me?"

His hand was on her breast, his cool fingers a torment on her skin, still warm from the bath. "I had to go," she whispered, catching her breath in surprise when he lowered his head and his mouth closed around her nipple, drawing on it until it was tight and throbbing with pleasure.

He couldn't stop his slowly rising anger. Had she been manipulating him with that trick of leaving? It was what Tess might have done. All this time, he had thought Eliza was different. But she wasn't. Disillusionment burned in him.

"You never had to leave," he said at last, his voice sharp. "I offered you everything you needed." He stared down at her, waiting for her answer, his face tight. When she remained silent, he caught her head between his hands, turning her face up to his as he kissed her. The hungry slant of his mouth stirred heat deep in her body, and she moaned with the fiery shock of excitement when his tongue thrust sharply past her lips. Desire intoxicated her. She wound her arms around his neck, feeling the crisply starched collar and the soft flannel frock coat over his hard shoulders.

"You like this well enough," he said tightly, in angry frustration, letting his hands drift down the delicate curve of her back and curl around her warm buttocks. His touch was rewarded with a perceptible tremor. He pulled her pelvis firmly against him, holding her soft form against his erection. Through the fabric of his trousers he felt the heat of her body bathing him, and desire for her surged devastatingly in him.

"What was it you didn't like?" he questioned harshly. "What was it you had to play tricks with me to get?"

Clinging to him, Eliza never realized he had shifted them both until she felt the abrupt reality of the wall against her back.

"Nate . . ." she protested weakly, lost in passion and confusion. "What are you doing?" She still felt the throbbing pressure of him against her pelvis, but he was holding her against the wall, his hands stroking her waist and hips, then moving up to her breasts. She shivered with the exquisite torment of his touch.

He saw his own hands dark against the feminine whiteness of her skin, felt the luscious warm hollows and curves of flesh soft against his palms, and the contrast excited him. Her small nipples rose in miniature erections. Watching the transformation, and the pink flush of passion that surfaced on her breasts, he was hit by simultaneous jolts of lust and fury. Ambivalent feelings warred within him. He should just walk away and forget her. After all, what special hold did she have over him that he couldn't just brush her out of his life as easily as he'd done with Marietta?

"I did nothing but dream of you all that time you were gone," he said in a hushed, ragged voice. "I couldn't forget the feel of you in my arms or the excitement of being inside you, of making love to you."

His hand slid to her thighs, between them, and Eliza's pulse leaped. Excitement pounded through her veins, and she moaned softly, closing her eyes, breathing shallowly through her mouth. His fingers and the pressure of his clothed body against hers sharpened her arousal until she was trembling and dazed.

"I was thinking of you," she whispered, opening her eyes and staring up into his bright, penetrating gaze. "On the train, I dreamed of you. I didn't want to leave. But I had to." She slid her fingers over his shoulders and into the short, black curls. Eliza tried to bring his mouth down to hers again, but his thoughts were elsewhere. With single-minded intensity born of the ache of frustration, he explored the slippery sweetness of her and felt her response through the excited tremors in that lushly feminine form. He was suffocating with desire. He had wanted her all day, had thought of little else. Briefly he stepped back from her, scalding heat breaking out on his skin as he tugged at his clothes. He ripped off the frock coat and tossed it behind him on the floor, then rapidly unfastened the buttons on his trousers.

When he resolutely reached down and raised one

of her legs, holding it under the knee, Eliza gasped, startled by the sensual anticipation that crested in her. His eyes were blue glints between narrowed lashes as he said in a harsh whisper, ''Put your arms around me and hold tight.'' She did so and in the next moment felt the ravaging probe of him. A little cry of astonishment and ecstacy escaped her as he determinedly plunged deep, impaling her against the wall.

Nate gasped heavily and leaned into the wall, holding still, momentarily relaxing in the warm rapture of her body. ''Oh, Eliza,'' he breathed. ''I . . .'' He paused, stroking her cheek and the damp curls against her shoulder. Against his chest, she emitted a weak sigh and tightened her arms around his neck. He had wanted to tell her he loved her, but would she believe him if he said it now? He couldn't resist the soft incitement of her body, and with a low groan of appreciation he withdrew slightly and pressed in again.

With the tantalizing friction of the soft fabric of his waistcoat against her breasts and the delicious, heated movements, Eliza arched toward him in abandon. He released her legs and reached behind her, grasping her buttocks and lifted her to her toes.

Eliza was drowning in desire, straining closer to Nate in mounting urgency. Her breathing was shallow, her body drawn taut. She met his thrusts with increasing fervency. Moment by moment, she rose higher, tauter.

''I won't let you get away from me again,'' he muttered, his voice deep, thick. ''You'll have to stay.'' He was shaken by the wild fierceness of their lovemaking. More than the rapture of the long night they had spent together before she'd left, this experience was obliterating every other. How had he ever thought he could live without her?

Eliza heard his words dimly, but the meaning was stark and clear. She wanted to answer him, but blind need gripped her, forced her on, and she was too near the crest to think of anything else. Then, shuddering, twisting her hips sharply, she peaked with seemingly endless spasms, so exquisite that had he not been holding her she would have collapsed. Her convulsions erased his last desperate effort at control. Eliza was still moaning with ecstacy when Nate pinned her tightly against the wall in the throes of his own excruciating release.

After a long, quiet, still moment of diminishing intensity, he slowly withdrew from her. She clung to him, too sweetly languid to stand alone.

"Eliza," he muttered, his breathing ragged, the words difficult to form. He lifted her chin until she looked at him, and gently he brushed the wispy, damp curls off her face. "I'm sorry. I hadn't planned to do this. I wanted to tell you . . . I love you."

Eliza's heart swelled, and she laughed weakly with the joy of this moment. All would be well. She had nothing to worry about.

"Do you love me?" he pressed, alarmed by her soft laugh. What did she find so amusing?

"Yes, yes, I do," she answered, smiling.

"Then why did you leave? I've considered so many different possibilities—"

But Eliza held her silence. How could she phrase her reasons without sounding as if she was either blatantly proposing to him . . . or begging him to propose to her? At last she answered with a portion of the truth. "I didn't realize you returned my feelings."

He uttered a short half-laugh and, kissing her temple, murmured, "Now you know, and I won't let you ever have the reason or the opportunity to forget it."

Happier than she'd ever been, Eliza went with him to his room. Exhausted from spending two nights on the train, she fell asleep almost immediately. Nate lay curled behind her, awake long after her breathing reached the smooth, deep rhythm of sleep. He felt the warmth of her skin against his, smelled the fragrance of gardenias in her hair, and sighed in satisfaction, thinking of a garden.

He wanted her here with him every night.

Chapter 14

When Nate awoke, Eliza was watching him pensively. She leaned her weight on one elbow and held the sheet over her breasts. A cloud of dark hair waved over one shoulder and lay in coils on the pillow. Her eyes were fathomless. He had a premonition of disaster.

"What is it?" he murmured, blinking in the pale morning light.

There were purplish shadows beneath her eyes. He reached out and touched her face, let his hand drift down her arm. It was so soft, so round and pink against the white sheet. She'd gained weight since first coming to him. From a prim scarecrow dressed in black, who had sat across the dining room table from him that first evening in early November, she had filled out and loosened her tight self-control. He felt the tingling of renewed desire.

Eliza shifted and sat up against the carved roses in the dark wood headboard, stretching the sheet over her. He pulled at it, but she kept a firm hold on the edge. "No, Nate," she said.

"Eliza?" he murmured, a sigh, a longing.

"It's just that I can't stay."

Eliza glanced around her. How clear and devastating logic seemed this morning, she thought. What kind of foolishness had she given in to last night that she could have imagined all would be well simply because he had professed his love? He had said not one word about making their relationship a proper and honorable one, and she had faced life on practical terms for too long to cling to hopeless romanticism. Now that she had made love with him yet again, and had even admitted her love for him, the situation was moving too swiftly toward a point of no return. She had to get away before she abandoned all decency entirely.

Nate watched her lift her arm, graceful and curved, and push her fingers through her masses of hair, a provocatively feminine gesture. "But there's time before you have to go back to your room," he said. "Daisy doesn't have to go to school today, and Rossie and I closed the office." He stroked her leg through the covers as he spoke. She looked at him with a sadness that seemed to emphasize the shadows beneath her eyes. "Are you feeling ill?" he asked in concern.

She shook her head.

He sat up beside her against the headboard. "Then what is it?"

"Nate, I brought Daisy back here to you. You love her, and you were right all along . . . this would be a better place for her. She'll be happier here than in Pittsburgh with me."

"What . . . what?" he exclaimed. "You're not going back again!"

"Yes, I have to. I can't stay here and . . . and . . . be governess to Daisy." She couldn't bring herself to add that she couldn't stay and be his mistress. She watched him steadily. "Don't you see that?"

He wanted to ask if she had left because she didn't think she could fit into his world. Looking at her now, the very thought of such a thing was like an exquisite pain, sweeter than anything he had ever known. He was afraid of being too blunt, of shattering something fragile and tentative between them, and so he asked with caution, "Is that why you left in the first place?"

"Not entirely," she answered, looking beyond him to the window draped in filmy curtains.

He thought of how she had departed abruptly after the first time they had made love. Yesterday he had vowed to court her respectfully, and then like an insensitive brute he had walked right in on her stepping from the bath and had taken her against the wall. His behavior was reprehensible! No wonder she was again intent upon leaving. He cursed himself in silence. Somehow he had to make sure she stayed and gave him a chance to win her properly. He mused on ways of presenting a decent proposal of marriage to her, one that she would not be able to refuse, but suddenly Eliza pushed back the sheet and swung lithe, sleek legs over the side of the bed. She snatched up his shirt where it lay folded over the chair and was wrapping it around herself before he could get out of bed to stop her. In the next instant she was out the door and running down the shadowed corridor to her room.

Muttering to himself in irritation, he yanked on trousers and a shirt that he left unbuttoned, tails out, as he followed down the hall to her room. She was stepping into a pair of white cotton drawers when he walked into her room and closed the door behind him.

Embarrassed and impatient, she exclaimed, "You can just barge right into my room whenever you feel like it, is that it?"

"After everything . . . Eliza, what's going on?"

She pulled on her camisole and buttoned it, "I'm going home."

"Today?" He tried not to shout.

"The sooner the better."

"*Why?* What is there about that damned place that you like so much? Is there a man in Pittsburgh?" Good grief, he'd never considered such a possibility! The idea made him furious.

"No!" she exclaimed, her face flushing pink with emotion. "I just don't belong here! Daisy does, and so you've won, Nate. I thought you'd have been pleased by that."

He threw himself on the end of the bed next to where she stood dressing. She flung aside her corset in irritation and reached for a petticoat from an opened, bulging valise.

"I'm pleased about Daisy," he said, frowning as he watched her step lithely into the garment and fit it around her narrow waist, then tie the flimsy strings. "But you're being rash! And pigheaded! And I don't think you're being entirely honest. You belong anywhere you want!"

He grasped one of her hands and pulled her down to sit beside him, ignoring the wary resistance in her eyes. "Tell me something," he began, trying to be calm. "Do you really not want to be here?"

Eliza sighed and regarded him patiently. "Nate, these weeks have been wonderful . . . for the most part. But it won't work any longer, and I have to go back now." She started to rise to resume dressing, but he grabbed her arm and pulled her back down again.

He groped for a way to phrase his thoughts. "Because of . . . ? Is it because of what's happened . . . between us?"

"Yes, but it's more than that. Oh, Nate, don't you see? I have no place here. I can't belong here. Your world is entirely different, and it's not mine."

He gave a short, hollow laugh. "Being a bit of a

snob in reverse, aren't you? What the hell difference does it make where anyone lives or how much money they have or what kind of world they live in?"

"It shouldn't make any difference," she said patiently. "But I can't stay here and continue like this. Originally, I stayed only to fight for Daisy. But now . . . now . . . I have to leave." She seemed to shrink a bit in sorrow, but her gaze remained strong and unwavering.

Nate lifted his chin, determined to convince her to stay. He remembered the opera tickets he had ordered last week. They were for tonight's performance and provided him with a perfect opportunity to court her in style before he proposed. He smiled to himself as he pictured how excited Eliza would be at the idea of going to an opera. Suddenly he wanted to give her all the things she'd never had— the finest clothes, the most exciting evenings, opportunities to travel the world with him. He would give her anything and everything she had ever wanted.

Still smiling, Nate reached for her hand. "I have tickets for the opera tonight. Will you go with me?"

Eliza was caught off-guard. The opera. How delightful. How intriguing. She'd never been to an opera. She considered it briefly, but then realized that such an exciting evening with him would only make it all the more difficult to leave. She shook her head sadly. "I can't, Nate," she said.

"Just delay your departure for one day," he insisted, trying to convince her, though he had no intention of letting her leave the following day either.

"I don't know," she said, wavering.

"We could have a late supper at the Palace Hotel afterward." It was the finest hotel in the city . . . and the perfect place to propose, he decided.

Eliza hesitated. What would one day's delay be to her plans? She'd never been to an opera or eaten in a grand hotel. When would she have the chance again? "All right," she agreed, letting her breath out in a swift rush. "I'd like to see an opera."

"Good. It's settled." He was immensely relieved and caressed her hand before releasing it and standing up. "I hope that new evening gown fits properly. Would you wear it tonight? I'd like to see you in it. I had a hell of a time finding that fabric."

She nodded, realizing that if he hadn't invited her to the opera, she would never have had an opportunity to wear that particular gown. There was no place for it in her life back home.

Eliza remained flustered and excited throughout the day. Mrs. Herlihy was pleased as punch to find they'd returned, and she wanted to know all the details. Daisy showed her each and every Christmas present she'd received from Nate. Eliza stood at the kitchen sink, chatting and squeezing white suds through each finger of her pair of ivory gloves while Mrs. Herlihy carefully pressed the evening gown Eliza would wear that night, exclaiming over its beauty.

"I had no idea Mr. Truesdale was planning such a Christmas gift for you. That dear man!" She grinned to herself. "Oh, but he was in a state when he discovered you both gone. Did you see his hand? He took off for the train station and apparently missed you by mere minutes, and smashed his hand into a wall! I'm surprised the authorities didn't summon the police. Wouldn't that have been something!"

Eliza laughed. "He would have been so insulted! I can just picture him—his eyebrows coming down to form a perfectly straight line over his eyes, and his chin jutting out a little, and his voice becoming very clipped and too, too polite, and—"

"That's it! And don't you know, he'd be droppin' brittle barbs about the police and the railroads and, well, just about everything."

Eliza looked at Mrs. Herlihy over her shoulder. "Probably dropping some choice remarks about me in the bargain."

"I don't doubt it." She touched the iron to a fold of satin ribbon on the shoulder strap of the gown. "Such a lovely dress!" Setting aside the iron on the back of the stove, she lifted the garment and shook it, sending waves of reflected light down the yards of ice-green satin. "How does it look? Did I miss any spots?"

Eliza wiped her hands on her faded red apron and walked around the dress to see it from every possible angle. "It looks perfect." She held it to herself and kicked out one leg as she watched the iridescent ripples of satin.

Watching, Mrs. Herlihy clasped her hands together under her bosom and beamed. "Now I just have to stay around this evening and see you off. I can't wait to see you in all your finery. And on Mr. Truesdale's arm, my dear girl, you're going to be the loveliest lady, with the handsomest escort. I have no doubt there are going to be hearts breaking all over that theater tonight, male *and* female!"

Eliza laughed lightly and kissed Mrs. Herlihy's cheek. Still holding the gown to her breast, she danced across the kitchen, unconsciously dipping and gliding to an imagined waltz, her eyes closed. "And do you know, after the opera we're going to have a late supper at the Palace Hotel. Doesn't that sound divine?" She whirled in front of the sink, then paused and looked at Mrs. Herlihy in alarm. "I'm so excited, I hope I don't get sick."

"You'll do no such thing. But you'd better give me that gown before something happens to it. I'll take it upstairs and hang it up to keep it fresh."

"Oh, I forgot about the gloves!" Eliza exclaimed. "I'd better lay them out to dry or I'll be wearing damp gloves tonight." She laughed at the idea.

"Hang them over the stove. They'll dry in a wink."

After a leisurely bath, Eliza carried the bottle of gardenia perfume to her room. Mrs. Herlihy came up to help her get dressed, and they giggled together like girls when they heard Nate march down the hall to Daisy's room and demand to know if she'd been in his room and did she know what had happened to a certain pearl stickpin.

Daisy was playing with Sylvia Hatcher, who had been hired to remain the night to care for Daisy. "I didn't take a stickpin, Nate." Daisy answered. "Just this for my doll's hair."

"*That's* a stickpin," they heard Nate say tightly. "Oh."

Eliza smothered her laughter and whispered to Mrs. Herlihy, "She hasn't lived around a man enough to know such things."

"I think they're both learning a lot, very quickly," the older woman replied with a broad grin.

She helped Eliza lace the corset. "I can't pull this tight, dear girl, or you'll disappear entirely. You don't even need a corset." She fluffed out the petticoat as Eliza sat on the bed and pulled on ivory stockings and clasped them in the garters. When her hair had been piled high in a full soft knot, Mrs. Herlihy gingerly lowered the satin gown over Eliza's head. They adjusted the folds together. The neckline was square, the bodice ribbed and boned, and the dropped waist plunged to a deep point over her abdomen. Around the deep vee seam was a mint-green satin sash that was tied into a loose knot in front at the deepest point, the ends trailing to the hem. Over the thin shoulder straps were ribbons of the same mint-green satin as the sash, and they were starched to stand up in tight loops, lending an overall effect of fashionable height and vertical lines.

Eliza pirouetted in delight. But Mrs. Herlihy, hearing Nate's approaching footsteps, was trying to hurry her. He knocked and called out, "Aren't you ready yet?"

"Soon!" Mrs. Herlihy answered. "You go on downstairs."

"If we're not out of here in ten minutes, we'll be late for the opening."

"Just go on downstairs!" Mrs. Herlihy exclaimed.

"All right. I'll get a cab and meet you there."

In a flurry of activity, Eliza stepped into her ivory satin shoes and dabbed perfume on her throat and shoulders. Earlier in the afternoon, following Mrs. Herlihy's suggestion, she had cut five baby-pink miniature roses from Nate's garden. "Roses are all the fashion," Mrs. Herlihy had remarked. Now with Mrs. Herlihy's help, Eliza tucked the roses into her hair, forming a semicircular crown.

"Beautiful!" Mrs. Herlihy exclaimed.

"They're wet!" Eliza patted the knot of hair. "I can feel water on my scalp—it's cold."

"As long as it doesn't drip down your neck . . ."

Eliza laughed as she fastened the dozens of small buttons on her long gloves. "You're certainly pragmatic! I guess I'm ready now."

Suddenly flustered, Mrs. Herlihy picked at the curls around Eliza's face and wisped them into the fashionable crimped look. Eliza shot nervous glances into the mirror and licked her lips with a tongue that felt as dry as paper. Her heart raced.

She reached for her cape but Mrs. Herlihy took it from her. "I'll carry it. You just go on down and stun that man."

Eliza looked at her in surprise. "I think you're hoping I will."

"Of course I am. Now go on, no more fussing about."

Nate was pacing the foyer when Eliza descended the curving stairs. At first he didn't see her, and she had a chance to admire his elegant attire and the easy, elegant grace of his movements. He wore evening dress, black trousers and a long-tailed coat, and a white satin waistcoat over his shirt. The charcoal and black fleur-de-lis silk tie she had made him was secured with a pearl stickpin. At his stiff cuffs she noticed the gold and pearl cuff links he had worn the day before. His overcoat and top hat were tossed on the rail at the bottom of the banister.

Behind Eliza, Mrs. Herlihy cleared her throat loudly to get his attention. Nate glanced up and broke into a pleased smile. "Well, well, well, Miss *Nol*enberg!" he exclaimed with a laugh of pure pleasure. "You look ravishing . . . Plus gorgeous . . . sumptuous . . . enchanting . . . dazzling . . ."

Eliza smiled as she descended the stairs. "And the same to you, Mr. Truesdale!" She reached the tiled floor and smiled happily, pirouetting for him. "The gown is perfect, Nate."

His eyes were warm, and he said simply, "You look beautiful," as he touched the mint-green sash over her hips and pulled her nearer for a brief kiss.

Daisy raced down the stairs and flung herself at them. "A kiss good bye! A kiss good bye!" she cried. Nate lifted her to his shoulder, and they gave each other quick kisses, then Daisy leaned over from Nate's shoulder to smack Eliza's cheek. "Can I go too?" she asked.

Nate lowered her to her feet again, and said with a smile, "Someday, precious, it will be your turn." He straightened, reached for his overcoat and hat, and said to Eliza, "The cab's waiting at the door. Where's your wrap?"

When Mrs. Herlihy held out Eliza's cape to help her on with it, Nate frowned. The black wool cape had been mended several times and the edges were fraying slightly. "Good God, don't you have anything else?" he exclaimed. "That looks terrible!"

Eliza compressed her lips and lifted the cape to give more room to the starched ribbons on the shoulder straps of the gown. "This is all I have," she said stiffly, her spine rigid, her eyes cool on his. "I could go without, but I'd prefer not to freeze."

Disgruntled, Nate glanced at Mrs. Herlihy. "Isn't there anything else in the house? A shawl or wrap of some kind?"

Mrs. Herlihy frowned back at him. "Not a thing," she said, briskly admonishing.

Nate was immediately ashamed of his outburst. "You look just fine like that," he reassured Eliza, smiling as he donned his overcoat and hat.

The cab was waiting on the flagged drive under the portico. He helped Eliza into the interior and followed, shutting the door firmly behind them and settling beside her on the padded, mohair-covered seat. Eliza leaned into the glare of the porch lamps and waved good bye to Daisy and Mrs. Herlihy at the door, then she sat back as the cab started down the sloping drive.

Nate took her hand. "I'm sorry, Eliza."

With an uncomfortable laugh she explained, "I suppose I'm not entirely prepared for such evenings."

"That's understandable, and I was a beast for reacting as I did." He turned and smiled at her. "It's

just that you look so damned beautiful in that gown,
the contrast—''

''Don't say anything. You don't need to explain.''
Her voice sounded too crisp even to her own ears,
and she tried to put the thoughts of comparison out
of her mind. She squeezed his fingers in what she
hoped was a warm gesture and turned her mind to
the coming evening.

Tomorrow . . .

But she wouldn't think of tomorrow. For now,
there was just tonight.

On Mission Street lines of carriages moved slowly
forward, disgorging passengers in front of the Grand
Opera House. As they waited, Eliza watched ladies
in breathtaking gowns and tiaras, and gentlemen in
evening dress, walk through the glittering light at
the entrance to the opera house, which looked from
the outside rather like a huge barn. She wished she
hadn't worn the cape. She was apprehensive now
as she hadn't been before. But when their cab finally
reached the entrance, and she and Nate stepped
down to the walkway, she held her back straight
and her head high. Nate seemed to take the sight of
so many jeweled ladies for granted and was relaxed,
even casual, as he ushered her into the great, high-
ceilinged foyer. Eliza tried to be equally at ease,
though her heart beat hard with nervous excitement, and she couldn't keep from staring at everything around her as they worked their way through
the crowd toward the coat-check room.

Nate was greeted by several people, and he smiled
and shook hands. Each time she was introduced
Eliza grew more and more aware of the surprised
response with which she was greeted. One older
lady in a diamond-studded necklace whom Nate introduced as Mrs. Sidney Hornett raised glasses to
peer at Eliza with undisguised affront. Mrs. Hornett

lowered the glasses as she looked at Nate and said, "Mr. Truesdale you've always been something of a surprise, but now you've outdone yourself. What would your dear father have said?" She excused herself and left them without a single, polite "How do you do" to Eliza.

Nate whispered to Eliza, "Don't mind her. She's always rude."

Eliza glanced up into his icy eyes and suddenly wished she had never agreed to come with him tonight. He led them to the coat-check room where they left their coats and his hat. Nate then held out his arm for her again and said, "Let's go ahead and find our seats. We don't need to wait around here with the rest of the cattle."

They passed through tall doors, leaving behind the elegant crowd and hum of voices, and walked down a plushly carpeted aisle between rows of maroon velvet-covered seats. Their places were on the aisle halfway to the stage. She entered the row first and Nate helped her adjust her train to the side before she sat down. He took the aisle seat and reached over to hold her hand. He smiled with a warmth that suddenly banished all thoughts of Mrs. Sidney Hornett from her mind.

"Do you know the story of tonight's opera— *Götterdämmerung*?" When she shook her head, he explained, "It's by Wagner, a powerful opera. *Götterdämmerung* means 'The Dusk of the Gods,' and it's about a young man who says good-bye to his love and heads off into the world but is tricked by means of some magic potion in a drink so that he forgets his real love and is smitten by another woman. He is murdered by this trickster, and the woman he really loves learns about the magic potion and forgives him. She arranges the funeral pyre for him and kills herself in the flames."

"How awful!" Eliza exclaimed. "And this is art?"

Nate laughed. "It's all in the music. Wait and see what you think of it. But I warn you, Wagner is deep and dark and full of Germanic melancholia."

Eliza looked around at the rows of seats with dark-wood frames, at the maroon velvet drapes, at the high white-and-gilt scrolled ceiling from which hung immense chandeliers. To her right scalloped box seats protruded high above the audience, and she noticed a familiar face in one of the boxes. Marietta Sharpe stared back at her, gave a brief nod of acknowledgment, and turned to her partner, a young blond man, slender and straight-backed. Marietta said something to him, and the man turned to gaze down at Eliza. He was too far away for her to read his expression, but she felt a blush rise into her face and suspected she knew what Marietta had said to him: *She's a millworker, hired help in Nate Truesdale's home. It's shocking that he would actually bring her here.*

Eliza lifted her head and maintained the crisp dignity that had always served her well in the past.

Leaning closer to Nate, she mentioned Marietta's presence. He glanced up to the box, gave a tight nod, his eyes cool, and muttered, "I can't believe she's here with Putman. She's never liked him."

"Nate? I hope I don't embarrass you in front of all these friends of yours."

He shot a surprised glance at her, then laughed and put his arm around her shoulders. "You come up with the most priceless statements sometimes! Don't ever imagine that you're an embarrassment to me. You're a gem."

"But you were ashamed because of my cape," she pointed out.

"No, no, not ashamed, just taken aback by the look of it over that gown. Like throwing mud over a diamond."

Eliza bristled.

"Look, I'm not explaining it very well. Your cape is perfect with certain gowns. It is not perfect for this gown. Will you let me buy you a nicer wrap? One that will complement an evening gown?"

"It's not necessary, Nate."

"No, but it would be my pleasure. I want to give you beautiful things."

"But, I won't have anywhere to wear such things in Pittsburgh."

"Oh, God." He removed his arm. "Let's not discuss that now."

They had to make room for people entering their row of seats, and more people here and there around them smiled and nodded to Nate.

"You know so many people," Eliza remarked.

"Not many I'd actually call friends. Speak of the devil, I see Rossie and Tess Brody."

"Who's Tess Brody?"

Nate glanced at her with a grin. "Well, aren't you the lucky one, not knowing *her*."

The chandeliers dimmed at that moment, the crowd hushed, and Eliza held her breath in excitement.

But the experience proved to be disappointing for her. She couldn't understand the words, the emotion seemed embarrassingly overwrought and the music thundered through the theater, vibrating in her with heavy and almost discordant resonance. During the quieter moments, the immense silence of the audience and the warm, close air in the theater almost put her to sleep.

When the lights rose for intermission, Nate sat forward in his seat, looking aside at her. "How do you like it?"

"I think I'm dreaming," she answered.

"Come on, let's go walk around a bit and wake you up."

He rose to his feet, and she followed into the aisle. Behind her as they moved with the crowd toward the foyer, Nate fell into conversation with a white-haired man who used a cane as he walked and spoke in a thick Russian accent. She was cut off from Nate by the crowd converging in the aisle and passing through the tall doors into the splendid foyer. Mrs. Herlihy had been right about the roses. She saw American Beauty roses in hair and rose corsages— even elaborate corsages with diamonds and pearls woven around the flowers. Eliza stood uncertainly in the crowded foyer and waited for Nate.

"Is that Eliza?" a masculine voice asked behind her.

She whirled and saw Rossie Watts. He smiled at her, though the smile never touched his gleaming black eyes, and reached for her hand before she had a chance to offer it. Even through her gloves she felt the cool dampness of his fingers. "Yes, I thought it was you. We met at Thanksgiving at Nate's house." He gave a polite nod over her hand before releasing it.

"That's right, Mr. Watts. How are you this evening?"

Rossie, only an inch taller than Eliza, met her almost eye-to-eye. His body was compactly muscled, and he kept restlessly shifting his feet.

"What do you think of Siegfried's predicament?" he asked, grinning. He had very white, evenly spaced teeth, and his nose was small, slightly pug at the end, which gave him a vulnerable, little-boy look—if one didn't notice the eyes, which were hard and flat.

"What . . . ? I'm sorry, I don't quite . . ."

"In the opera. Siegfried had to be tricked with a magic potion to fall in love with Gutrune. No man would need a magic potion to fall in love with you."

"Oh, my . . . Well, thank you, Mr. Watts," Eliza mumbled in confusion.

"Rossie," he insisted, still grinning. His straight black hair was slicked back from a side part. "How is your stay in San Francisco? Are you getting around much to see our wonderful sights?"

"A bit—"

"Are you still staying with Nate?"

"Yes, but I'm leaving soon to return home." She glanced around to see if Nate had emerged yet through the doors. There was no sign of him.

"You don't say! How can I convince you to stay longer?" He stood very near, and Eliza stepped back slightly.

"I'm afraid you can't."

"Are you taking your daughter with you?"

"My daughter? Oh, no, you're mistaken." She wondered how he knew about Daisy, then recalled Nate saying that Marietta had spread the news of his relationship to Daisy.

"But I thought Nate had a daughter?" Rossie's eyes shone black and direct. "My mistake then. I thought you had a daughter by Nate."

"No. I'm sorry, you have the wrong information, Mr. Watts." *Where was Nate?*

As Rossie Watts touched his chin, a gold ring on his little finger caught the light. "You have the most delightful way of speaking," he said. "I can't quite place it. A touch of the East, yet it's something else altogether. Let me see—Baltimore? Do you know Nate's mother? She lives there."

"No, I'm not from Baltimore. It's Pittsburgh."

"Ah! But how did you meet Nate then?"

"It's rather a lengthy story, and much too boring to go into now. It was very nice seeing you—"

Rossie moved nearer, almost brushing against her, and blocked her escape. He picked a wisp of curled hair from the corner of her eye. ''Don't run off,'' he said, disapproving, and gave her a quick wink. ''I wanted to ask if you'd been to the Woodward Gardens yet. If not, I'd be glad to take you there sometime before you leave. You must see it. Tomorrow?''

Before Eliza could answer, the same tall, stunning woman who had been at the Thanksgiving Day dinner wandered up the them. She ignored Rossie, keeping her heavy-lidded amber eyes on Eliza. Her smile was not at all friendly.

''Have we met?'' she asked, her voice deep and rasping. A small diamond tiara on her auburn curls flashed every color of the rainbow. ''You're a friend of Nate's, aren't you? I remember you from the Thanksgiving party.'' She turned to Rossie, her smile lazy. ''Don't you remember, Rossie? She's the one who was so forward with Nate on the dance floor.'' She looked back to Eliza with slitted eyes as she added, ''Looked like she wanted to rape him on the spot.''

Eliza drew herself taut in anger, head high, and put formidable cool briskness in her voice as she said, ''No, we haven't met. And now I'm quite sure I don't care to be introduced.''

There was a jolt of loud laughter, and they all turned to see Nate walk up next to Eliza and place his hand on her back. ''Oh, that was priceless,'' he told Eliza, who was vastly relieved to see him.

Tess' eyes narrowed. ''So she's with you tonight.'' She glanced at Eliza. ''That was fast work, or is she the reason for Marietta's departure?''

''Sheath your claws, sweetheart,'' Nate said, and Eliza was stunned to hear him use an endearment with this woman. She wondered if Nate had ever known her intimately . . .

Rossie, who had appeared disgruntled since the woman's arrival, now said, ''Let's go, Tess.''

"No, this is too amusing." She smiled venom-
ously at Nate. "From the nursery right into the arms
of the lower classes. Is there—"

"Come on, Eliza—"

"—something secretly appealing to you about
common baggage? Some really lewd—"

"Shut up, Tess. Your disappointment is showing." Nate's voice was icy.

"Why you self-inflated—!" Rossie exclaimed.

But Tess ignored them both. "Some lewd and appealing animal behavior in this kind of lowlife?" She
spoke through her teeth. "You like them right out
of the gutter, eh, Nate?"

Nate's hand tightened on Eliza's shoulder. "You'd
know all about it," he said coldly and with preci-
sion. "Why don't you tell us about your adventures
down at the crimps' boardinghouses? Or is Rossie
already in on all that?"

Tess caught her breath in fury. "You filthy—"

"What is this!" Rossie advanced on Nate. "You
had the gall to call me a bastard, and then you—"

"Be quiet, you little chump," Tess hissed in rage.

Eliza was paralyzed with shock, but Nate went
on. "Sure, Rossie. We wouldn't need to worry about
the damned crimps anymore. We'd just open up our
own house for Tess and have all the sailors we'd
need and then some. Now you listen to me," he
added, biting out his words. "You leave me alone
and you leave Eliza alone!"

Nate almost pushed Eliza ahead of him as he
walked away, but she could still hear Rossie and
Tess.

"Just what in the hell did he mean?" Rossie exclaimed, his voice harsh.

Tess sneered. "I don't have to answer to you."

Eliza felt sick. Though she'd seen fights at the mill,
never before had she been witness to a scene that

left her feeling so sordid. That Nate was involved in it and had possibly been intimate with such a woman appalled her. Her heart shriveled.

"Please, Nate," she said weakly, stopping before they reached the door at the head of their aisle. "Please take me home."

"But what about the opera?" he said, his face still tight with anger.

"I don't really care for it," she answered. "Please, can't we just go now?"

"Eliza, listen," he protested tensely, "I'm sorry about what happened. Try to forget it. We don't have to let them spoil our evening."

She frowned vaguely. "Do you know that woman well, Nate? Did you ever court her?"

"For a bit," he replied after a pause.

At this admission Eliza felt even more wretched. How could he have ever been interested in such a woman? She thought again of him with Estelle—a relationship she had pushed out of her mind for weeks now. What manner of man was he? How could she have ever hoped he would be different— honorable—with her?

"I want to leave," she said miserably.

"Eliza—" he started to protest.

"Please!"

"All right," he finally agreed. He was still furious with Tess and wished heartily that Eliza hadn't witnessed that scene. The romantic evening he had planned as the setting for his marriage proposal to her was disintegrating. "We'll go straight to the hotel then," he suggested, hoping to salvage something of his plans.

"I'd rather go home" she insisted, her spirits too dampened to be cheered by the thought of dinner at a hotel.

"Eliza, I lost my temper, and I'm sorry. Let's have

our supper as we planned. You'll forget about Tess and Rossie, and we'll have a wonderful time."

"No," she said adamantly. "Please, just take me home."

Nate scowled in frustration. "All right. If that's what you wish . . . " He didn't want to argue with her and destroy the evening entirely. Maybe at home she would calm down again, and he could talk to her then.

After fetching their wraps, he escorted her outside to the street and signaled to the group of drivers, who were standing about talking in front of a line of black carriages. One stepped forward from the group and held open the door of the first conveyance for them. Just as they were walking toward it, Eliza caught sight of Rossie Watts and Tess Brody arguing in the shadows beside the opera house entrance. Rossie was holding Tess by the arm, but she wrenched it viciously to free herself.

"You don't have any rights to me," she exclaimed, her voice both menacing and chillingly unemotional.

Seeing Nate, Rossie let go of Tess and stalked toward him. Rossie's tie was askew, his starched wing collar unfastened at one side and bobbing with his movements. "You!" he spat, jabbing his finger at Nate. "You've done it this time. All those things you said—!" He paused, then continued hoarsely, "You had no business lying about Tess, and I'm not forgetting it!"

Nate ignored him as he helped Eliza into the carriage, then climbed in himself. As the driver slammed the door and clambered to his seat, Rossie stalked back to Tess. Nate peered through the window, watching the two people hasten stiffly away, Rossie gripping Tess' elbow. He felt deeply disturbed, but he tried to put the incident out of his mind.

Nate sat back against the seat as the carriage started away. Slipping his arm around Eliza's shoulders, he was dismayed by the sudden stiffness in her.

"Eliza," he begged, "don't let Tess and Rossie ruin this evening for us. Please try to put it behind you. We can still go to the Palace Hotel. There's plenty of time."

But she remained silent.

"Don't be angry with me," he said, leaning near and brushing his lips over the fringe of crimped curls on her forehead. "Talk to me. Tell me why you're so upset. Please, sweetheart."

She turned and gazed up at him. "That's what you called her . . . 'sweetheart.' Is that what you call every woman who crosses your path?"

"Of course not." He frowned. "That's what's bothering you?"

"I don't understand you," she said. "How could you have been interested—even intimate, probably—with such a woman?"

"Now, wait just a minute. That was a long time ago. She's still trying to hang on. There's no reason—"

"Where is your sense of decency?" she cried suddenly, miserably. "Tess, Marietta, Estelle, and now . . . me! Lord knows how many women you've known, and you have the arrogance to try to keep me from leaving?"

"That's right," he insisted intently. "Call it arrogance if you want, but I call it love. I love you, Eliza, and I don't want you ever to leave. You're everything I ever wished for in a woman and lifetime mate, but I never knew that until I met you. I struggled with it, was drawn to you and yet resisted all the while. I had never really experienced love. In fact, I think I probably somehow made sure that the only women I knew were those I could never truly love." Nate paused. Eliza's eyes were growing wider and more gentle, and he drew her close, his voice softening. "But you made such a difference to me, Eliza. You and Daisy burst into my life and changed everything. You both saw in me a man I didn't even know existed—a man I'm proud to be. How could I live without you now?"

Nate cupped Eliza's cheeks. Her eyes were shimmering, her gaze tender on his, and he kissed her with almost crushing hunger. Eliza's heart swelled with love. How could she live without him? Passion leaped high and warm in her. The social barriers between them dissolved, giving way to desire, fierce and demanding, in a kiss that seemed both never-ending and over all too soon.

"I've been wanting to do that all night," Nate said, half-whispering, his hand moving between the edges of her cape to find a firm breast.

Eliza reached to kiss him again, her breathing quickening with the delight of his hand at her breast. His smallest touch brought out needs in her, shameless and relentless. How could she think of returning to Pittsburgh now? It seemed impossible to imagine not having the deep, shared luxury of this passion with him.

Holding her close, he murmured near her ear, "Marry me, Eliza. Say you will."

She was caught by surprise. She didn't know whether to laugh or weep with the overwhelming happiness she felt. She reached to kiss him.

The carriage came to a halt on the street in front of the brick stairs, and with an audible grunt the driver jumped onto the curb. Nate hastily released Eliza from his embrace. She dabbed at her moist eyes. He climbed down, assisted her out, paid the driver, and they hurried up the stairs.

In the foyer, Nate pulled off his hat and turned down the lights. Eliza's heart pounded in anticipation as she ascended the stairs ahead of him. She went to his room while he turned down the lamps in the hall.

Darkness, soft and secure, followed him as he made his way to the bedroom.

Eliza stood next to the dresser in his room, her white arms raised as she picked pins from her hair. From the back he observed the delicate curve of her waist and hips in the ice-green satin gown, and saw in the mirror the reflection of high, firm breasts, the beauty in her deep brown eyes and moistly pink rosebud lips.

He watched and closed the door slowly behind him. "Eliza," he said, resisting the urge to go to her immediately. He had to know . . . before . . .

She shifted her glance to meet his eyes in the mirror. Her hair slipped loose with the last few pins, fell around her shoulders with dark richness that increased the ache in him. She reached behind and rapidly unhooked the bodice of her gown. The straps slid off her shoulders, white and sloping and begging to be stroked and kissed. He imagined the rest of her body . . .

"No, don't do that yet," he exclaimed, crossing the room to her. Eliza turned to meet him, holding the front of the gown up with one hand, a confused look in her eyes. "If you take it off now," he said, a wry smile on his face. "I'll lose whatever bit of patience I still have." Unable to stop himself, he was touching her hair, stroking her bare, warm arms as he said, "I have to know—do you love me, Eliza? Will you marry me?"

Looking into the shining intensity of the blue eyes

she loved, Eliza nodded. "Yes," she answered, breathlessly. "I do love you very much, and there's nothing I want more than to marry you."

She let the gown drop from her hand. The petticoat and corset and stockings followed, and Nate didn't bother with hanging up his evening clothes but tossed them aside over the chair. Eliza thought she would never get enough of looking at him or touching him—the dark glow of his skin, the crisp black hair of his chest, the iron contours of chest and arms and loins, the beautiful bursting heaviness of his erection. She lay back on the bed and welcomed him, crying out with a small involuntary sound of pleasure when he entered her.

"Dear God, Eliza," he muttered, burying his fingers in the scented masses of hair spread on the pillow. "I never would have let you get away from me."

"I didn't want to go," she said. She pressed ardent kisses on his warm, hard neck. "I never really wanted to leave, but I was never sure of you. There were so many barriers, so many conventions of social—"

"Hush," he told her gently, smiling. "That makes no difference." He rolled her above him. She gasped in surprise and gazed with wonder at his passion-tightened dark face on the bed beneath her. Perspiration shone on his forehead and the sides of his face.

"Sit up," he coaxed. "I want to watch you."

Eliza did so, and he grasped her waist, lifting and guiding her. She felt his hands on her, felt soft warm thrills of increasing passion as he brushed her hair away from her breasts, and when she looked at his face he was smiling, eyes tender.

Within minutes their thoughts had given way to

the luxurious excitement tightening urgently between them.

Nate grasped her when she slumped over him in languid satiation. His breath escaped in shallow pants. Strands of satiny, fragrant hair were flung across his face, and he reached up to push them aside. She was lying on her chest, her legs alongside his. He let his elbows drop down to the bed, his hands on her back. In the contentment and peace of the moment, there was no need to move or speak or think.

Eliza slept most of the night on his chest.

Early in the morning she returned to her own room before Nate awoke. She was attired in her new yellow silk day dress and sipping coffee in the large dining room when he entered. Her heart beat more rapidly at the sight of him. As always, he was dressed impeccably, his pearl pin anchoring the folds of the tie she had given him for Christmas. In her eyes he was more handsome than ever before, and she smiled tremulously at him as he approached her chair, his expression tender. He kissed her lingeringly.

"Good morning," he said meaningfully, dropping tiny kisses on her upturned mouth. He nibbled at her lower lip. "When do you want to make plans, my love? We have to consider a formal announcement. Would a party so soon after Christmas be agreeable to you?"

"Anything," she replied with a happy sigh.

"Shall we discuss it this evening then?" he asked. "Over dinner at the Palace Hotel?"

"I'd love to." Eliza returned his light kisses until they heard Daisy's footsteps on the tiled foyer.

With a cheerful wave, she saw Nate and Daisy off at seven, then went in search of Mrs. Herlihy. Entering the kitchen, she found the housekeeper in a state of agitation as she worked a mound of bread dough. Clouds of flour rose from the worktable.

"Ah, Eliza!" she exclaimed. "I'm in a pickle for sure today. That young Sylvia took off early before I arrived and she's not due back to work again until tomorrow." The woman kneaded the dough with a hard hand and continued, vexed. "It's my Bob. Had a bad night last night, and he needs more of his medicine. I'd wanted to have Sylvia stay and get this bread started while I fetched his pills from Dr. Culbert. Could you help me out?"

Eliza smiled, feeling too wonderful to refuse anyone anything. She debated telling the woman about Nate's proposal but decided to wait until he returned and they could announce the news together. "Just tell me where the doctor's office is located, and I'll get the pills you need," she promised.

Mrs. Herlihy looked up with a grateful smile and wiped her hands on the skirt of her apron. "You're a dear soul, Eliza. Here, let me get you some money."

Dr. Culbert's office was located in Clay Street near the Bay, a drab section of town, and Eliza stepped over sturdy green weeds and bits of debris in the road. The structure was immaculately cared for on the outside: fresh whitewash covered the clapboard exterior; the two wooden steps leading to the door were spanking new; windows, one on either side of the front door, were as clean as mountain air. In the narrow alley alongside the building milkweed grew in spindly profusion amidst broken glass and bits of disintegrating paper.

As Eliza entered, she found herself in a high-ceilinged room. The walls had been whitewashed to eye-level, where a strip of dark molding circled the room, and then painted an airy sky-blue above the molding and over the ceiling. A heavy old oak desk near the door was littered with papers, but the receptionist was absent. Three worn and empty chairs lined the wall on her right, opposite the desk. Straight ahead was another room, well-lit and crowded with people. Eliza saw a man in a white smock—Dr. Culbert, she assumed—two policemen in tall hats; another slovenly figure, unshaven and wearing faded and creased cotton pants and a long dark coat. And between their forms she noticed another figure, a man in elegant evening dress, lying on a tall table. His breath was punctuated with long, harsh grunts of pain, and he was grinding out slow words that Eliza could not understand.

Dr. Culbert was leaning over the man and at the same time waving back the two policeman. And then she noticed the blood. The man on the table was bleeding heavily from his chest; dark red blood had spilled onto the table, dripped onto the floor. She followed the trail and discovered she was standing in it. Tightening her lips, she stepped aside and sat down in one of the empty chairs to wait. The man must have only just been brought in.

She kept her eyes averted, but the voices reached her ears. "—our duty. It's imperative, Doctor—"

"Just don't stand in my way. Get the hell over there against the wall." It was a rumbling deep voice, not so much impatient as naturally commanding. Dr. Culbert? she wondered.

The injured man grunted harshly. "Tried—to—kill—"

Scissors snipped and sliced into fabric.

Eliza glanced at the receptionist's desk, at the small unlit oil lamp, dark brown envelopes, an empty ink jar, another full one. Gas jets for the lights over the walls hissed quietly, and the wavering flames sent threads of black smoke into the air.

"Do you have any idea as to the identity of your assailant?" The voice was brisk and impersonal—one of the policemen, she thought.

"Tess—" the man gasped, followed by a low growling as if the man tried not to scream aloud. "Brody."

Eliza looked toward the room in shock. As Dr. Culbert, a trim elderly man with white hair and a scowl, moved away to reach into a glass-fronted cupboard, Eliza clearly saw the injured man. It was Rossie Watts! Her eyes popped wide in recognition. His face was ghastly gray, spasms contorting the features, his body writhing.

One of the policemen was talking quietly in a corner with the slovenly man, whose dull brass-colored hair hung in greasy strands over his collar and into his eyes. The man stared back at Eliza, his whitish-blue eyes protruding from reddened lids. She looked away.

Dr. Culbert said testily, "You've got a name now, I want to get him under." He came around the table with a hypodermic needle and a brown glass bottle.

As the policeman backed away from the table, Rossie's labored voice grunted and hissed between his teeth again. "Truesdale. Two of 'em. Together."

Eliza started involuntarily in her chair. Had Rossie just accused Nate of attacking him?

The policeman stepped nearer and bent down to Rossie as he questioned. "You mean there were two assailants? Tess Brody and someone—"

Rossie writhed all the harder, his mouth working. "Nate Truesdale—my partner—"

Dr. Culbert had been waiting. Now he said, "You want anything else, you'll damned well have to wait for it! Clear the room now."

The two policemen and the slouching, brass-haired man left, and Dr. Culbert slammed shut the door behind them. The three men were now standing in the reception area, the policemen talking together, the other man staring at Eliza with the glassy look of a constant inebriate.

She dropped her gaze to the purse clutched in her hands. Had Rossie actually accused Nate of trying to kill him?

Then she became aware that the two policemen were discussing their reports and warrants for the arrest of Tess and Nate. Eliza stood up and stepped out of the small building.

Out on the street, she walked briskly over the thick stalks of weeds, over the bits of debris and hardened mud. After two blocks she was running, her feet flying under the yellow silk gown. She had to warn Nate! Her breathing grew strained, but she ran on, remembering the previous evening and the sight of Rossie disheveled and irate as he shouted at Nate. Why had Rossie accused him? What would happen to Nate?

Chapter 15

Eliza was clutching her side in pain but still running when she reached the broad brick building with the raised gilt lettering above the double doors: Truesdale & Watts Shipping Company, International. She paused to catch her breath in the shadows at the top of the five steps, then pulled open the door and entered the hushed foyer. Ginger-haired Maggie, the receptionist, glanced up with a smile.

"Is Mr. Truesdale in now?" Eliza asked in a breathless rush of words.

"Yes, he is. Do you have an appointment?"

Eliza ignored the question and plucked up her skirt as she raced up the stairs to the second floor. Along the narrow aisle between the wooden balusters, she marched briskly, her purse swinging. Another woman tried to halt her as she approached the door with the frosted glass window, but Eliza ignored her as well and, after a quick knock, thrust open the door.

Nate was alone. Behind his desk the three windows poured sunshine into the office, and the half-lowered green shades glowed. He glanced up from a two-inch stack of papers and began to smile until he noticed her grim expression. "Good Lord, what's happened? Eliza? What's wrong?"

She pushed the door closed behind her and crossed to his desk. "Nate, it's awful," she exclaimed, aware that she might suddenly cry now that she'd at last reached him. "Awful! Somebody tried to kill Rossie, and he accused you and Tess Brody!"

Nate stared at her, stood up, and came around the desk. "Sit down. You look as if you're about done in. Were you running? Sit down, sit down." He took her arm, guided her to the chair in front of his desk, and urged her into it. "All right, now, explain. What do you mean someone tried to kill Rossie?"

Nate propped himself on the edge of his desk next to her, and Eliza told him the details of her visit to Dr. Culbert's office. He frowned. The frown deepened.

He stood up from the desk and took a slow turn around the room. "I can't believe it," he murmured, his voice toneless with shock. "Good Lord, Rossie . . . How is he? Is he going to be all right?"

"I don't know." Eliza watched him in concern. "He was bleeding a lot, and in a lot of pain . . . I don't know. Dr. Culbert was in a hurry to get the policemen out . . . Nate, he *accused* you of trying to kill him. I mean, right there to the policemen, he accused you!"

Nate stared vacantly out the windows. "I wonder what happened after that scene last night at the opera . . . I shouldn't have lost my temper and said that stuff about Tess and the crimps' boardinghouses. I guess Rossie didn't know . . ."

"There was another man there too. The one with the policemen."

"Sounds to me like one of the sailors. Dr. Culbert's office is near the waterfront. If Rossie was brought in to Dr. Culbert, then the stabbing probably occurred in that area. I can just imagine Rossie forcing a confrontation with Tess over what I said at the opera. Goddamn it, I should have kept my mouth shut!''

"Do you think Tess really tried to kill him?''

"I have no idea.'' He heaved a sigh and sat again on the edge of the desk, hands clasped. "I wouldn't have thought she'd ever do something like that, though Lord knows she's probably volatile enough . . . especially if Rossie pushed her too far or forced her to go down to the waterfront to the crimps' boardinghouses.'' He paused, then exclaimed in disgust, "Oh, hell, I don't know.''

Eliza was beginning to shake from the shock. "Nate, they're going to arrest you!''

She saw his face change as he stared at her, the black eyebrows drawing into a line over his eyes, which hardened to iron. He reached for his hat off the stand beside the desk and took her arm. "Come on, let's get home,'' he said.

To the woman at the desk outside his office he said, "Peg, I'll be out for a while.'' Behind the spectacles the woman gave Eliza a wide-eyed glance.

Outside on the street, Nate whistled down a cab, and they rode back to the house in silence. Once, Eliza started to question him, but he shook his head. "Let me think,'' he said.

When they entered the house, Nate led Eliza upstairs. "Eliza, listen carefully to me,'' he said. "You and Daisy have to leave. You've got to go home to Pittsburgh. If we hurry, you can still catch the nine-ten train.''

"What do you mean? We can't leave now!''

But his fingers were like steel on her arm. "Don't be an idiot,'' he said calmly, "of course you have to leave.''

"Don't ever call me an idiot!'' She wrenched her

arm from his grip. "I'm not going to run away now when all this is happening. I'm not leaving!"

"Haven't you been around here long enough yet to realize what a mess, what an absolute carnival this whole situation could turn into? You and Daisy have to get out before the publicity breaks." On the upper landing he headed for the stairs leading to the third floor. When Eliza started to protest again, he cut her off sharply. "Eliza, please do as I say. There's no time to discuss the matter. Start getting your belongings ready. I'll be right back." He disappeared up the narrow stairway, and Eliza flung her purse across her bed in agitation.

Leave? Now? When he was facing arrest, jail. And if Rossie died . . . ?

She hadn't given much thought to Rossie yet, and now she slumped down on the edge of the bed. What if Rossie died? Her own personal distaste for the man waned in the light of what had happened to him. Again she could see the blood and his writhing limbs, could hear again the harsh pain-filled breathing and low growl of words he tried to utter. Shock and fear clutched at her chest.

Nate burst into the room with the two valises belonging to her and Daisy, plus a third, a battered black case. "You'll probably need this too." He regarded her in annoyance. "Haven't you started getting your things together? Please, Eliza, there's so little time."

He flung two cases on her bed and carried the other with him to Daisy's room.

Eliza marched after him. "Why, Nate? Why should we leave now? You must tell me!" She stood in the room, arms folded over her breast, as he flipped the valise onto the end of Daisy's bed and tossed back the lid.

Nate didn't look at her as he yanked open a

dresser drawer and snatched out the contents in one armload. The sleeve of one pink nightshirt dangled over his arm as he carried the stack of clothes back to the bed and stuffed them into the valise.

He spoke without anger. "Imagine how the newspapers are going to describe the incident. Especially if Rossie doesn't make it . . . Goddamn! I'd never wish this on him no matter what differences we had."

As Nate gathered another drawerful of clothes, Eliza protested, "But Nate, you didn't do it. You're innocent, so why should Daisy and I run away?"

"My innocence is the least of the problem! Eliza, you don't understand what my position in this city means. The Truesdale name is a prominent one—my father is considered a damned *saint* here! Can you picture what this situation with Rossie is going to turn into? A three-ring circus, my dear. Society scandal with capital letters. Partner kills partner. Love triangle. They're going to claim that we were fighting over Tess. Sex, murder, high society. Every element to titilate a morbid, bored public."

Nate crossed to the wardrobe and flung back the door, letting it crash hard against the wall. "Use your imagination, Eliza. What the press is going to make of it all will be even wilder than whatever you could possibly dream up. Consider this: you've been living here. The press will call this house a sordid love nest. And what about Daisy? She's an illegitimate child. Every last bit of juicy scandal is going to hit the papers from here to New York. Think about it! Everything to do with Estelle, Daisy, you. Your name will be smeared across the headlines too. Have you thought about that?"

He looked at her as he returned to the valise and thrust more clothes into it. "And they won't stick to the truth. Every angle is going to be blown into the most sizzling, disgusting banquet of sin and degradation. Arnold Truesdale's son, the bad seed. There's another angle. And they'll resurrect and embellish my father's illustrious, saintly past as a point of contrast.''

Eliza stared at him. Words wouldn't come to her mind, so stunning and shocking and horrible were the pictures he painted for her. ''They wouldn't . . . do all that . . . would they?''

Nate straightened from forcing a doll and clattering tea set into the suitcase. He uttered a short laugh. ''Oh, God, you're too ignorant for this mess. They'll do all that and more. That's why you and Daisy have to get out of here now.''

''No, no. I can't leave you here all alone with all that—''

He scowled at her, his eyes icy and hard. ''Do you imagine it's going to help me, your being here?'' He sighed, dropped the lid over the valise, and leaned his hands on top. ''Listen, I love you and I love Daisy and I want to protect you both from what's about to explode around us. You'll make me very happy if you'll take Daisy and go back to Pittsburgh as quickly as you can. Now, get back to your room and pack!''

With angry jerks he pulled the straps on the valise and buckled them, then carried it out to the hall.

Following, Eliza entered her bedroom behind him. She moved numbly, goaded by fear and Nate's relentless insistence. He was right in that Daisy had to be protected. Together they moved back and forth between the dresser, the wardrobe, and the open cases on her bed, packing her possessions. The new gowns, the ivory stockings and ivory satin shoes, the hairbrushes and ribbons and petticoats. Eliza paused with the ice-green satin evening gown in her arms, almost weeping over it.

From Daisy's room Nate brought an armload of toys and a forgotten black stocking, bits of white lint from under the bed clinging to it. He shoved these into Eliza's case, grabbed up the book she'd been reading, a red satin ribbon marking her place, and tossed it in as well.

"But that's yours," Eliza commented.

"Take it," he said and stood back, staring at the pile of belongings in the valise, then shoved his hands into his pockets. Now that they had completed packing, his expression was blank, stunned, as if the full realization of it all had only now hit him.

Eliza folded the evening gown into one of the valises. "I think this is everything," she said tonelessly.

Nate turned around slowly, staring numbly at the emptied room, drawers, wardrobe. He reached for the bottle of gardenia perfume on the dresser, lifted the stopper, sniffed the fragrance. "Don't you want this?"

"It will only spill. Besides, it's not mine." *Besides, it will remind me of you.*

"I don't have a hell of a lot of use for it. Except that it reminds me of you." He put the perfume back on the dresser. "I suppose you're right—it would spill."

Eliza stood aside as Nate strapped the two valises and hefted them off the bed. He carried them out to the hall. "Come here a minute," he said, and Eliza followed him down the hall into his room.

She heard the clink of metal drawer pulls, felt the thick moss carpet under her feet. From a wooden box in his top drawer he pulled out a stack of green bills. He closed the drawer and returned to stand in front of her. "Take this for now." He put the money in her hand. "I'll send more when I can, or my lawyer will send more, or whatever."

For a long moment they stood gazing at each other.

"It'll be all right, Eliza," he said. He tried to smile. "Everything will be all right."

She moved into his arms and he held her close, touching her hair, her back, sliding his hands across her shoulders. "It's not going to be easy," he added. "Even if Rossie recovers, it will be better that you're gone. Hopefully any scandal won't reach you—"

"I'm not afraid of scandal, Nate." Eliza leaned back to look into his eyes.

"Aren't you? I am."

"But I can prove where you were last night."

"Let me worry about that. You just take Daisy and get out. It's not just you and me involved—we have to think of Daisy too. I'll get in touch with you when I can."

He glanced at the clock on his dresser. Eight thirty-five. "It's time. I'll go catch a cab for you. Pick up Daisy from school and then you two hurry and get on that train." He kissed her briefly. "This isn't a good-bye forever, Eliza, you know that."

"I know." She smiled, though it was tentative and shaky.

Nate caught her face between his hands and kissed her again, hard and purposefully. Then he walked out into the hall and gathered two of the cases and descended the stairs, saying over his shoulder, "Just leave that last one. I'll get it in a minute."

As Nate pulled open the front door to fetch a cab, Mrs. Herlihy approached along the downstairs hall.

"Mr. Truesdale!" She was surprised to see him home at this hour. "Are you sick today?"

"Almost," he answered and left the house.

Worried, Mrs. Herlihy turned to Eliza in the foyer. "Is something wrong? Mr. Truesdale looked so . . ." She glanced again out the door in confusion.

"Oh, Mrs. Herlihy," Eliza exclaimed suddenly, "I didn't get the medicine. Dr. Culbert had . . . had an emergency."

The woman heaved a sigh. "I'll go over later when I do the shopping." She reached into her apron pocket, pulling out a white envelope, which she handed to Eliza. "There was a letter for you today. Think it's from that Mr. McPherson."

Eliza accepted it, stunned. The custody fight. How petty and long-ago and insignificant it seemed now. She tucked the letter in her purse and reached for the woman's hand. "Mrs. Herlihy, I have to say good-bye," she explained tremulously. "Daisy and I are leaving—"

"Good Lord, why?" the housekeeper interrupted in surprise.

"It's just that . . ." Eliza's voice trailed off, and she shook her head, unable to finish the sentence. She gave the woman a swift hug. At Mrs. Herlihy's continued astonished questions, she said, "Mr. Truesdale can explain it better."

Within minutes Nate reappeared coming up the steps, and a heavy black carriage pulled by a single horse drew up to the door. Nate entered the house, lifted two valises, and handed them out to the driver. When the third bag was in the carriage, the driver returned to his seat to wait.

"Nate, I can't leave—" Eliza started to protest in fresh agitation, but he shook his head and put his arms around her. Mrs. Herlihy retreated down the hall, dumbstruck and pursing her lips.

"I'll be fine," Nate insisted. "You'll be fine too, I know it. You're the girl who went to work to support a mother and sister. The one who picked up the pieces when everyone else dropped them. You'll do fine, and I'm glad of it. Now you've got to go."

He gave her a quick embrace, released her, and held the door for her. "Give Daisy a kiss for me?" he added.

Minutes later, Eliza leaned her head out the carriage window as it rolled away from the steps. She looked back at Nate standing in the shade of the portico as he watched her departure. His face was tight with barely suppressed emotion, mouth compressed, eyes fixed on hers with such bright intensity and yearning that she almost cried aloud in her anguish.

When a vivid orange blooming bird of paradise plant beside the pillar obscured him from her sight, she sagged back against the seat. She sobbed uncontrollably, pressing her fingers over her mouth to stifle the grief that felt as if it would wrench her apart.

Daisy was not pleased to be fetched from her classroom. When she learned they were heading for the train station again, she uttered a shriek of indignation and stood bolt upright in the carriage. "No!" she wailed.

Her small mouth was open in protest, hazel eyes squeezed shut, fingers clasped tightly into fists. Eliza drew her rigid little body back down to sit and put her arm around the girl's shoulders, but Daisy pushed her away. "Aunt Lizzie, we can't go! I want to show Nate my reading award! I don't wanta go back. I wanta stay here!" She kicked the heels of her shoes against the floor.

"It's not forever, my dear," Eliza said as calmly as she could manage. "We'll save your award. Nate will want to see it."

"Why do we hafta go! I don't wanta ride on a train again." She lifted one foot and slammed it down on the carriage floor.

"Listen to me, Daisy," Eliza announced, wiping back a fresh tear as she leaned close to the girl's face. "Nate is in trouble, and he wants us to leave for a short while."

Daisy screwed up her face and peered at Eliza dubiously. "He's in trouble? Did Mrs. Herlihy get mad at him?"

"Oh, no. There are some . . . bad people." Eliza cast about for a way to explain it. "Some bad people want to get Nate in trouble. And they could make trouble for you and me too, so Nate wanted us to go home to Pittsburgh for a while until he can make things better again. Do you see? And then we'll come back."

Daisy frowned as she tried to understand. "Why do they want to get Nate in trouble?"

"I don't think they like him."

"Why not?"

"I don't know, my dear. Some people are like that. But let's keep this a secret—just for the two of us. Our secret."

Daisy sat up on the edge of the seat and leaned her arms on Eliza's lap. "But we can't leave Nate now. He needs us!"

Eliza stroked Daisy's hair and pushed a stray wisp from her forehead. "That's what I think too, but he wants us to go for a while." Inside, she wanted to protest as much as Daisy. Every instinct told her to turn around. She attempted a smile of reassurance.

Daisy threw herself back against the seat. She slouched down until her head and shoulders were bent against the seat back. "It's not right!" she said with a pout.

Turning, Eliza stared morosely out the window. She gave a sharp, quivering sigh. "I agree." Then she sat up straighter and turned her head to follow something as the carriage went by. It was a hotel. The sight of it gave her an idea so stunning and plausible that she gasped audibly. She and Daisy didn't have to actually leave San Francisco in order to escape the possible publicity—they only had to remain out of sight. A hotel provided a perfect alternative to returning all the way to Pittsburgh. No one would recognize them, and she and Daisy could use different names. She could remain near Nate, even if she couldn't see him or go to him, until the whole mistake of Rossie's accusation was cleared away. Excitedly she ordered the driver to stop the carriage and let them out.

When the carriage had gone on, Eliza grasped the handles of two of the valises and indicated the other for Daisy to manage. "Drag it if you have to. We're not going far."

Daisy was ecstatic about not leaving on the train, and she agreeably pulled and hefted the heavy suitcase. "Where are we going, Aunt Lizzie?"

"I saw a hotel back this way. Now we're going to have to pretend. You pretend I'm your mother and you're my daughter. And we'll use pretend names too. What name do you want?"

Daisy smiled in excitement. "It's like a game then?" When Eliza nodded, she puckered her brow in thought. She yanked on the suitcase and huffed and thought hard. "I want my name to be Angelique."

"All right, and I'll be . . . Anne. We'll be Anne and Angelique Wells. Remember, Daisy, we can't let anyone know who we really are."

"Angelique! You called me Daisy!"

They laughed and continued on in silence. The hotel hadn't seemed this far back when she saw it from the carriage window, but by the time they reached the Lick House Eliza felt as if the heavy valises were pulling her arms from their sockets.

In relief they entered a small, overly warm lobby

cluttered with chairs, spittoons, standing ashtrays, and potted palms. Through a doorway on the right of the lobby a pub emitted the scent of cherry pipe tobacco and the sound of desultory male voices.

Eliza registered at the small scarred desk, requesting a room for a week. When she opened her purse to fetch out money for the requested two-day's advance, she looked curiously at the supply Nate had given her. Holding her purse below the level of the desk so that the middle-aged man across from her could not see, she counted the bundle quickly.

One hundred and forty dollars. Eliza's hands trembled. She had never possessed such wealth.

A lanky, red-faced bellboy helped them get their cases up the stairs to the third floor. Their room was at the front of the building, and contained two iron-framed beds covered with red-and-green-plaid spreads, a washstand, and a handsome dresser of mellow mahogany. When the bellboy had gone, Eliza pushed aside the gauzy white curtains at the single window and gazed down into the front street. The cobbles were dull and swept clean of dirt by the frequent winds. To the right she saw dark brick buildings rising upward on the slope of the hill. To the left she looked down over similar buildings and weathered clapboard structures crowding toward the piers and, in the distance, the brilliant, silvery-blue water of the Bay. Nuzzling each of the many piers within her sight were the moored clippers. Bare of sail, they appeared denuded in the sun, emasculated and powerless.

"What do we do now, Aunt Lizzie?" Daisy bounced on one of the beds, intrigued by this new adventure.

Eliza let the curtain fall back into place and turned around. "Nothing but wait," she answered.

When their valises were unpacked and the gowns

hung up in the small musty closet, the clothing folded away in the drawers of the old mahogany dresser, the hairbrushes and ribbons set neatly on top, Eliza picked up her purse and pulled out Mr. McPherson's letter. She sat down to read it.

Bored, Daisy came to sit beside Eliza. "What is it?" she asked as Eliza sliced open the envelope with her fingernail.

"A letter from Mr. McPherson . . ."

Eliza scanned the brief note. "He's coming here, Daisy. At the end of next week."

Daisy's eyes brightened. "Will he bring me peppermints again? I love peppermints." She rolled back on the bed, hugging her knees to her chest.

Eliza smiled and patted Daisy's leg. "It's a good thing we didn't go on the train. We would have passed him on the way here."

The news of Mr. McPherson's imminent arrival cheered Eliza. Surely he would know what to do for Nate.

"S'ciety murder! S'ciety murder!"

The small newsboy on the corner of the street caught Eliza's attention. After a small, early supper at a nearby restaurant, Eliza and Daisy were walking back to the Lick House in the crowd of pedestrians heading home after work. The newsboy's stack of papers, held down by a chipped cobblestone, flapped noisily in the wind.

Eliza purchased a copy of the *Chronicle*, a copy of the *Call* from another boy on the opposite side of the street, and a copy of the *Examiner* from yet another newsboy. Tucking them under her arm, she shooed Daisy back toward the hotel and, when they reached their room, spread out the newspapers on the bed.

Her heart sank.

The *Chronicle* bore the headline SOCIETY MURDER,

and the subhead *"Partner Kills Partner in What Police Suspect Is Love Triangle."* Across the top were detailed drawings of Nate, Rossie, and Tess. The artist had caught Nate scowling, his eyebrows drawn together in a harsh black line, his mouth tight. Tess appeared aloof but demure, her picture drawn from a three-quarter view, with her face uplifted, eyes half-closed in what looked like pain-filled supplication. Rossie was smiling in his picture; the artist had drawn it from an old photograph. The implications of the three pictures were stunning. Nate appeared the villain, Tess the pure and blameless woman bearing up devoutly under the tragedy, and Rossie the happy, carefree young man struck down at the threshold of his life and career.

Appalled, Eliza began to read.

John Russell "Rossie" Watts, co-owner of the prosperous, San Francisco–based Truesdale & Watts Shipping Company, International, died this morning as a result of knife wounds inflicted in the late hours of the night. Before his death, Mr. Watts told police that his partner, Nate Truesdale, and lady friend, Miss Tess Brody, were responsible for the gruesome attack, which occurred in the disreputable waterfront area of the Market Street Pier. Both Mr. Truesdale and Mr. Watts were amorously involved with the lovely Miss Brody, and police speculate that an argument over the woman in question resulted in the tragedy.

Nate Truesdale, son of the late Arnold Truesdale who has long been revered as one of the City's most generous philanthropists, was arrested this morning at his home on California Street in the exclusive Nob Hill section. Also arrested was Miss Brody, who was at that time making plans for a trip to the Continent. Both were taken to the

Hall of Justice and charged with the murder of Mr.
Watts.

Mr. Truesdale denied any knowledge of the incident, telling police he was asleep at the time the
attack on Mr. Watts allegedly occurred. This claim
is unsubstantiated as Mr. Truesdale's only servant, Mrs. Edna Herlihy, is employed by day and
does not make her home in the Truesdale resi-
dence.

Eliza frowned. Sylvia Hatcher had spent the night,
seeing to Daisy while she and Nate were at the
opera. Had Sylvia heard them return last night?
Should she talk to her?

She scanned the remainder of the story, which described Nate and Rossie's company, their partner-
ship, and sketchy highlights of Rossie's life. The
reporter waxed creative in his description of Tess,
right down to "her stylish auburn coiffure" and
"lovely day dress of green watered silk with insets
of white lace across the bodice," adding, "Miss Brody's remarkable beauty is such as to capture any
number of male hearts."

With an exclamation of disgust, Eliza swept the
paper off the bed. The flimsy sheets separated and
slid apart and fluttered to the floor in a wide puddle.
She grabbed up the edition of the *Call* and read its
account. The headline, demurely placed in smaller
letters than the first paper's, announced: MURDER IN
SOCIETY SET, and below that: "*Love Triangle Ends in
Tragedy.*"

The story was more factual, without the creative
touches thrown in by the first paper's dazzled reporter, but said essentially the same thing. As did
the copy of the *Examiner*. Eliza's shoulders slumped.
Just as Nate had predicted, everyone automatically
assumed Nate and Rossie were fighting over Tess.

Surely the truth would come out eventually, after the first big splash of emotion and sensationalism. So thinking, Eliza tucked Daisy into bed and tried to fill the hours with other pursuits that could take her mind off the situation. She tried to read. She tried to mend Daisy's many ripped stockings. She tried to plan out their days until Mr. McPherson arrived.

The news stories grew gradually worse. From the window Eliza watched for the newsboys for hours before they took up their posts on the street corners, then she rushed out to purchase the latest editions. Despite her hopes, the situation grew more dismal. Nate and Tess were both indicted by a grand jury for the murder of Rossie. In spite of one paper's slanted coverage of Tess' involvement, its continual portrayal of her as a blameless and tragic victim of the incident, the grand jury brought in an indictment of her based on Rossie's dying statement that she had been responsible. The *Call* pointed out the fact that Rossie had accused her first, before mentioning Nate.

It was the one point that Eliza was glad about.

Because the small cells in the Hall of Justice were deemed too public and dirty for a woman, Tess was released on bail, but Nate was retained to await trial. They were to be tried separately, with Nate's trial set first, on February tenth.

San Francisco's Midwinter Exposition opened on January first, but not even the long-awaited international fair could successfully compete with the sensationalism of a society murder. Front-page coverage was still almost entirely given over to lurid details of the scandal that was beginning to catch attention across the continent. The papers delved further into Nate's life and relationship with Tess. Eliza read the accounts with avid horror.

Tess was quoted as saying Nate had courted her for five years and was mad with jealousy when she began favoring Rossie Watts with her attention. The *Chronicle* wrote, " 'He frightened me,' explained Miss Brody. 'I never knew when he might become violent. He threatened often enough to punish me for what he called my unfaithfulness. He just didn't want to accept the fact that I didn't care to see him any longer. Sometimes he would sob and pace about and exclaim over and over that he couldn't take it.' "

The following evening in the *Call*, Nate was quoted as saying, " 'Anyone who knows Tess Brody with even a passing acquaintance could tell you her account of our relationship—if one could even use such a term—is entirely false. I was the one who ended our friendship—and that's a questionable term as well—and she refused to let go. Her relationship with Rossie was simply a means of revenge against me.' "

But Tess' attacks increased. One day she announced, "Nate Truesdale asked me repeatedly to marry him, and when I refused, he grew violent and once shattered a crystal lamp of mine." Another day she said, "He was furious with Rossie for escorting me to several parties and argued repeatedly with him about it."

Nate's denial of each allegation was dutifully printed in the following day's papers.

The *Examiner*: "According to Mr. Harve Dunlocke, warehouse foreman for the Truesdale & Watts Shipping Company, International, 'They—Mr. Truesdale and Mr. Watts—had a fight for sure at Mr. Truesdale's Thanksgiving Day dinner. We were all afraid it would come to out-and-out blows, it was so loud and vehement.' When this reporter questioned

Mr. Dunlocke as to the nature of the argument between the two men, he answered, 'Oh, it was Miss
Brody, without doubt. And I can't really repeat what
was said. Not a proper thing to repeat, you understand.' "

The *Call:* "Mrs. Peg Walters, secretary to Nate
Truesdale, insisted today that any disagreements that
Mr. Truesdale and Mr. Watts may have had in no
way could have resulted in such a tragedy. 'Mr.
Truesdale is a fine man and could never hurt someone,' Mrs. Walters reports. 'I've worked for him for
nine years now, and I know he would never attack
anyone. He just isn't like that. But I can't honestly
say the same about Mr. Watts. He's the kind to start
arguments and be generally offensive. I wouldn't
believe him for a minute.' "

Gradually the line was drawn: the *Chronicle* supported Tess; the *Call* backed Nate; the *Examiner* was
equally acid toward both.

Eliza had difficulty sleeping. After reading each
evening's edition of the papers, she balled them up
and with vicious delight stuffed them into the incin-
erator hatch on the stairwell landing. After perform-
ing this ritual she walked slowly back to the room,
which was becoming enough like a prison cell to de-
press her constantly, and tried to be cheerful for
Daisy's sake.

Though Mrs. Herlihy was hounded by the reporters, she was quoted as saying she had nothing to
tell them beyond the fact that Nate was innocent.
"Mr. Truesdale would never have done such a thing,
and that's the truth—if you want the truth, which I
doubt." Eliza smiled to herself when she read this,
and she found herself missing Mrs. Herlihy terribly.

As Nate had predicted, his father's contributions
to the City were mentioned daily, in large double-
page spreads that included pictures of a hospital and

a school he had helped build, and quotes from old papers that had carried his speeches, quotes from government leaders who had known him, and pictures of him in benevolent poses. Eliza saw little resemblance between Nate and the erect, pious, monocled Arnold Truesdale.

The murder of Rossie was called a "tragedy" in the earliest accounts, but as the days passed, the terms grew more emotional. One day it was "an ugly tragedy," the next day it was "a sordid, unconscionable act," and later "a bestial, revolting, disgusting display of vileness."

Eliza kept the papers away from Daisy's attention and attempted to see that the girl was amused during the long days. They went for walks, saw the Woodward Gardens one day, rode the cable cars and horse-drawn trolleys another, and sat idly silent over cherry ices on warm afternoons or read aloud together in their hotel room on rainy afternoons. Eliza needed the diversion as much as Daisy; each day grew more nightmarish than the one previous.

While awaiting a trolley one afternoon, Eliza overheard an elderly man and woman talking. The man peeled an orange with a small pocketknife and tossed the peels into the street, where they lay like bright bits of paper. Eliza stared at them as the overheard conversation stabbed into her. The woman said, "And who wouldn't belive such a sweet young woman as that Miss Brody. I tell you, Nate Truesdale stabbed his own partner."

The man sucked loudly on an orange segment. "Then why did Watts accuse her, eh? He said it exactly that way . . . that she done it."

"Aaah, you're a fool! She was trying to stop it, don't you see? If they're wrestling around and she tries to get in there to stop 'em, it 'ud look like she's part of it, don't you think?"

The trolley arrived then, and Eliza climbed onto it, grateful to escape hearing the conversation. Her face was flushed red and she was afraid that at any moment she might have blurted everything out to them in anger. Daisy hung onto her arm as the trolley started with a jerk and a ringing of the bell.

But it seemed everywhere she went she heard the same kind of conversation. San Francisco, from one end to the other, appeared to have nothing more in its collective mind than the murder case.

At the Woodward Gardens: "Truesdale's as guilty as they come."

From behind on the sidewalk: "She's a looker, ain't she?—that Miss Brody. Who wouldn't fight to have a go at her!"

Overheard at a nearby table at a restaurant: "It's the most scandalous thing I've ever heard! All of them deserve everything that's happened. I hope they learn to repent, that's all I can say! And Mr. Truesdale with such a father as he had—it's positively sinful."

Though Eliza longed to contact Mrs. Herlihy, she decided to do nothing until she could discuss it with Mr. McPherson. One afternoon she and Daisy strolled toward Nate's house, drawn there out of loneliness, but at the sight of five reporters sitting on the brick steps and waiting for whatever might happen, she turned around and retreated to the hotel.

On the day before Mr. McPherson's arrival, the evening headlines announced: MYSTERY WOMAN AND CHILD SOUGHT.

When Eliza saw it, her hands shook and her heart hit painfully against her ribs. Laying the paper out on the red-and-green-plaid bedspread, Eliza leaned over it anxiously and read:

Sources today disclosed that an unnamed woman and young girl were living at Nate Truesdale's home for some weeks prior to the murder of Mr. Watts. Information is being sought as to the identity and whereabouts of the woman in hopes that she may shed additional light on the events of the night of last December 26. Anyone with such information is asked to contact the *Examiner* office.

Chapter 16

Nate was escorted by a guard into the small meeting room. When the guard left and shut the door, Nate took a seat across the small table from his lawyer, Edward McIvey, a tall, balding, white-haired man. McIvey specialized in criminal law, was highly regarded, and John Ryckman, Nate's general counsel, had recommended him.

McIvey said, "Glad to see you're still dressing well."

"My housekeeper brings clean shirts," Nate answered without interest.

He observed the pink bald curve of McIvey's head as the lawyer rooted through papers in his carrying case. The case was an open-topped box made of varnished pine, much dented from use, and with an oval cutout in the side for a handle. With a grunt of satisfaction, McIvey found what he needed and pulled out a sheaf of papers. The two men sat at a table in a dismal meeting room in the Hall of Justice. At almost six in the evening, the two high windows in the room gave onto a darkening aqua-blue sky, and an overhead, four-globed gaslight glared, shining on McIvey's smooth balding forehead. These kinds of meetings with his lawyer provided Nate with the only opportunity to escape his tiny, single-windowed cell. He looked forward to them.

McIvey looked up from the papers and said, "I spoke with Sylvia Hatcher, but it doesn't look good. She never heard you return from the opera house that night. Heavy sleeper, apparently." His voice was professionally calm, his dark eyes keen yet benevolent. The black and white hairs on his eyebrows were spiky.

"What about the cab driver who took us home?" Nate asked.

"What do you think, Nate?" McIvey said with exaggerated patience. He lifted one hand, palm out, a pencil tucked in his fingers. "So he said he drove you home at nine o'clock—how is he supposed to know you didn't leave again? But . . . I'll look into it. Everything will help, considering that you won't contact this 'mystery woman' I keep hearing about." Edward McIvey lifted his eyebrows and exhaled noisily. "Why is that, Nate? She's your only alibi."

Nate slouched back in his chair and stuck one leg out under the table. By his reckoning Eliza and Daisy should be safely back in Pittsburgh by now, but there was still the possibility that someone could contact the Pittsburgh police by telegraph. Which he didn't want to happen. "I told you—I don't want her caught up in this circus. Just forget about her, all right?"

"You really tie my hands, you know that? How am I supposed to clear you of a murder charge? You could get the death penalty! You could go to jail for the rest of your life. Is it worth it to keep her secret?"

"What if she lived around here and I had simply driven her home and returned to my house? How could she prove anything in that case? The truth was, I was asleep at the time Rossie was stabbed!"

McIvey put his palms together as if in prayer. "Worst alibi you could have, my friend." He separated his hands and tossed the pencil onto the papers on the table. "But we'll take the hard road, if that's what you want. We'll have to prove why Rossie had such a hatred of you as to wrongfully accuse you of his murder. And it can't be over Tess Brody—that would be like pouring oil on the flames."

"But it *was* over Tess, though not in the way you think. Oh, hell, he and I never got along—about anything."

"It *was* over Tess?" McIvey scowled at him. "Why haven't you been honest with me and told me everything? How am I supposed to help you if you keep withholding information?" McIvey fished a clean sheet of foolscap from his case and set it on the stack of pages in front of him on the table. He took up the pencil again, studied the point, licked it, and said, "Will you tell me everything now? Trust your own lawyer, Truesdale—it's a good idea."

For three-quarters of an hour, McIvey listened and scratched out brief notes, stopping Nate once or twice to get correct spellings of names or accurate dates. At last he said, "We've got the details of your problems with Rossie and that disaster at your house at Thanksgiving. But what about this 'mystery woman and child'?"

Nate frowned and stared at McIvey's papers. "I'll tell you on the condition that she not be used in the trial."

"The newspapers are already pulling her into it! Her identity is going to come out sooner or later, and there's nothing you can do about it. Better that I know and possibly contact her quietly than have Miss Brody's lawyers or the D.A. find her first. Is there something here that could be used against you, Nate?"

"You can't contact her very easily—she's gone back to Pittsburgh, where she lives."

"Is that so? That's not something that will sit well for your case, but at least it'll be difficult for anyone else to get to her. So tell me about it."

When Nate had finally done so, McIvey fingered his stiff edges of his collar and stared at his client. "So it's all secret to protect her reputation, is that it? She was in bed with you for the night, and that's it! Her reputation!" McIvey was red in the face, and the redness crept up over the bald curve of his forehead. "You're facing death or life imprisonment without her testimony—you do realize that?"

"Is anyone going to believe her? And what about my *daughter*?" Nate shot to his feet and leaned forward, resting his weight on his hands on the table. "You think I want the world peering into her life and dissecting her and judging her when she's so goddamned innocent of everything! They're both of them innocent of all this mess, and I'll keep it that way if I have to go to jail! It's my fault for ever getting involved with Tess or hating Rossie! And the truth, McIvey, is that I was asleep when Tess stabbed Rossie. Pretend there is no Eliza and Daisy Nolenberg. Pretend they never came to San Francisco in the first place! They don't have a goddamned thing to do with this case!"

McIvey chuckled, a deep whispery coughing chuckle. "You're too noble for your own good." He shook his massive white head. "It won't work. They did come to San Francisco, and she was with you that night, and the press is already on her tail. But trust me, Nate—I'll do whatever I can to work around this, as you want. Actually . . ." He paused again and uttered another whisper of a laugh. "You may just save yourself in spite of yourself."

"What in the hell do you mean by that?"

"Nothing, my friend," he answered with a self-congratulatory smile. "Nothing."

McIvey gathered together his papers, rapped the ends against the table to straighten the stack, and pushed them into the wooden case.

Nate lay awake in the dark cell. His head was propped on one arm tucked behind his head, and he stared at the barred window high above the foot of the cot. Whatever stars or moon might have been present were concealed behind a ceiling of ocean fog, but with the glow of lights from the city, the window was brighter than the interior of the cell.

He pushed back the unease and the fear and the anger that seemed ready to consume him if he gave them half a chance, and he thought of Eliza. He pictured the cleanly swept apartment in that soft-brick Pittsburgh building, with its greasy halls and odor of factory smoke. They should be there by now, walking among those rooms he dimly remembered from the day he had met Estelle.

Each evening he had imagined the train and the soft sway of the cars and the click of steel wheels on the rails. He had followed Eliza and Daisy in his imagination and known escape of a kind.

Sometimes he wished Eliza had not gone as he had insisted. Sometimes he was angry that she had gone. But the anger never lasted. In love he had asked her to leave, and in love she had agreed. She hadn't wanted to go. The thought comforted him.

And in reasonable moments he knew it was better that she had taken Daisy away.

He thought of Eliza as he stared at the iron-gray light of fog beyond the bars of the window. He thought of gardenias and gardens and woman-flesh, soft and warm as sunlight. And he longed for her.

What would Eliza be thinking now? Before their

evening at the opera, she wanted to return home, but he had tried in every way he knew to stop her and keep her with him. Was she happy now to be back? Would she decide against returning to him eventually? He clenched his teeth in frustration. What if a jury found him guilty of Rossie's murder? How long might it be before he was free once more? He might never see Eliza again. And what would she think of him in prison? Now that she was back in her own world and he was an accused and jailed man, maybe she had already changed her mind about him. Maybe she would never come back and marry him.

Driven by a deep physical ache, he pushed back the scratchy wool blanket and stood up from the cot to go to the window. Ridges of mortar on the window ledge felt as cold and grainy as sand under his fingertips. He stared into luminous gray night. "Eliza," he whispered aloud, and the sound was a prayer brushing the windowpane and returning to his ears.

Rain thrummed on the top of Eliza's umbrella. She kept her arm around Daisy's shoulder to hold the girl close under the protection of the wide black umbrella as they walked quickly, dodging the bigger puddles, toward the crude wooden landing where the Southern Pacific ferry from Oakland would dock. They could see the boat already, churning across the pewter surface of the Bay. Mr. McPherson was due to be on it, having elected to take the shorter route directly across the Bay to San Francisco rather than continue by train south to San Jose and then up the peninsula, as Eliza and Daisy had done.

As the big wooden side-wheeler coasted toward the wharf, Eliza and Daisy watched for Mr. Mc-Pherson among the crowd of passengers gathering to disembark. Daisy spotted him first and waved eagerly. A tall, thin man in a fur-lined dark overcoat stood at the upper rail and lifted his hand in reply. He was oblivious of the rain soaking his bowler hat, and he cupped his hands around his mouth to shout, "Ahoy there, Daisy!"

Daisy bounced up and down in excitement as the passengers moved down the gangplank. Around them hotel runners approached the arriving people, calling out: "International Hotel!" "Lick House!" "Palace!"

Mr. McPherson yanked his valise back from a runner who tried to get hold of it and continued toward Eliza and Daisy, grinning broadly. "Well, and here's my darling!" he exclaimed when Daisy rushed for him.

She hugged him. "Did you bring me peppermints? Did you, did you?"

"Let me see . . ." he said, as if confused, and patted his pockets. "Now where could I have put . . ."

Daisy stuck her hand in his overcoat pocket. "Here! Here!"

"How smart you are! But just one at a time."

Grinning, Daisy popped a candy in her mouth.

Eliza smiled in happiness and relief. "Mr. McPherson, I can't tell you how glad I am to see you."

He turned to her. Smiling, squinting in the rain, he said, "You know we're almost family, and I keep telling you—call me Harry, please." Wet blond hair clung to the back and sides of his neck, and his eyes were widely spaced, greenish-gray in color. One upper front tooth slightly overlapped the other. He grasped Eliza's hand and leaned under the umbrella to kiss her cheek. "How are you bearing up? Well, I hope," he said.

"Well enough," she answered. "But there's quite a story to tell. Let's hurry and get out of this rain."

They started at a brisk walk toward the line of carriages waiting along the street. "Did you have a good journey?" Eliza asked.

"I don't mind travel—it was as good a trip as any. Must say, I'm looking forward to seeing as much of San Francisco as I can while I'm here. You'll be an old hand at knowing what sights to see, eh? You've been here long enough! And the Midwinter Exposition is open now, isn't it?"

Daisy patted his overcoat pocket again, and he obliged by fishing out another peppermint. His hand was thin, with prominent knuckles, the fingers narrow and long.

Eliza agreed. "I'll be glad to show you around. I suppose we'll have the time for it."

"How about starting by suggesting a good hotel for me."

"The Lick House. Daisy and I are staying there now."

He peered at her in satisfaction. "Decided to get away from Mr. Truesdale's influence? I don't blame you, what with everything I've been hearing."

"Have I got a lot to tell you," Eliza answered.

At the hotel Harry McPherson registered and was given a room adjacent to Eliza and Daisy's. Still begging peppermints, Daisy trailed the adults to his room, which was identical to theirs except for the blue-and-yellow-plaid bedspreads. When Harry dropped his heavy valise onto one of the beds, the mattress sagged heavily. He unbuckled the straps of the valise and lifted the lid.

"Here, Daisy, come see what I have for you," he said as he lifted out a package wrapped in brown paper.

Daisy rushed to stand beside him, her eyes wide, and held out her hands. "What is it? Can I open

it?'' He put it into her hands. "It's so heavy!" She
set the package on the bed and ripped open the paper. Inside was an eight-inch-long replica of a covered wagon pulled by one horse.

Harry McPherson patted the top of Daisy's head.
"Why don't you play with it while your Aunt Lizzie
and I talk in the next room?"

Delighted with the toy, Daisy nodded and didn't
look back at the two adults as they left the room.

Harry sat down on the end of one of the twin beds
in Eliza's room and held his arms away from his
body. "I feel as if I'm still on a train and moving.
How long will this go on?"

"Oh, a couple of days, at least." Eliza smiled,
sighed, and then took a seat on the opposite bed.
"There's so much to tell you, I don't know where
to begin."

"Well, your custody claim is taken care of. Truesdale doesn't stand a chance of winning Daisy now
that he's in jail for murder."

"How do you know about that?" she asked,
alarmed.

"Picked up a paper in Rapid City, South Dakota,
and there was a write-up of it on the first page. I've
been following the story for the last six days at
least."

Eliza was horrified. "He said it would hit papers
all the way to New York, but I thought he was ex-
aggerating."

"This is big stuff, Eliza. Rich men murdering each
other is headline material anytime. But throw in a
beautiful rich woman and you've got a guaranteed
sensation. But it's nothing for you to worry about.
You and Daisy are in the clear."

"Oh, no, you don't understand at all!" Eliza said
earnestly, clasping her hands in her lap. "I'm . . .

Well, to be very honest, and to start at the end instead of the beginning . . . I'm in love with him."

Harry McPherson said nothing. He regarded her closely.

"It's true," Eliza said, almost laughing. "And he loves me."

"That's what it is," Harry said, grinning. "You looked so different, and it's not just the dress, but . . . Something else. The Eliza I'm seeing now is not the Eliza I put on the train last October in Pittsburgh. What about the murder charge? What's the real story?" But Harry held up his hand before Eliza could answer. "No, wait. Better tell me everything from the very beginning."

The evening papers focused again on the "mystery woman and child." Anyone with information was asked to contact the newspaper.

Harry paced the room with a copy of the *Call* and pursed his mouth as he read. "It can't be long before they locate you," he said. "Did you see in the lobby tonight? A couple of men from New York and Chicago were checking in. Reporters, I'll bet anything. With the trial only three weeks away, San Francisco is going to start filling up to the gills with reporters from all over. And with the Midwinter Exposition just opened, why, there won't be a room to let anywhere." He tossed the newspaper onto the bedspread.

They were in Eliza and Daisy's room; rain streamed down the windows. Eliza rubbed her palms together in agitation. "I'm not afraid of being found. In fact, Harry, if anything, I'll be glad of it. Waiting around here these last ten days has been almost beyond bearing. And seeing the newspapers every day! He's innocent! And I know it! I can prove it, Harry. I was there with him."

Harry had taken a seat on the foot of Daisy's bed and pulled a cigar from his shirt pocket. He snipped the end with a clipper from his pocket as he asked, "What do you mean you were there with him? At the waterfront?"

"No." Eliza closed her eyes, her fingers smoothing her eyelids. She felt uncomfortable and embarrassed about admitting her intimacy with Nate. But then she lifted her head. "He was never at the waterfront that night; he was with me. The entire night." She watched as Harry's glance moved slowly to meet hers.

He started to laugh. "I almost want to congratulate you!" he said. "You surprise me, Eliza! Though"—he paused to light his cigar, letting little cloud puffs escape his mouth, then blew out the match—"this does change things where Truesdale's concerned. He wasn't at the wharf at all then? Could he have planned something with this Tess Brody?"

"*Please*, Harry. I'm not such a fool. He had nothing to do with her for as long as I was living there."

"You couldn't have followed him everywhere he went to know who he was seeing." He pulled on the cigar and his cheeks puffed out. Releasing smoke in a plume from his mouth, he added, "Whole affairs are carried on without even a wife catching onto them."

Eliza paced the floor. "Then listen to this," she said quietly. "It happened the night of Rossie's murder—when we were all four at the opera." As clearly as she could remember the exchange of words from that evening, Eliza related the confrontations between Nate, Tess, and Rossie.

Harry smoked his cigar in silence, his green-gray eyes watchful. He remained silent after Eliza had finished. She waited. At last he said, "I'm glad you didn't go back to Pittsburgh like he wanted you to.

You know, the more I hear about this fellow, the more I want to meet him." Harry rubbed one knee with a large, knuckly hand. "You have to testify for him, you know that."

"Yes!" she exclaimed, acknowledging that fact with relief. "But what should I do, Harry? Should I go to the police?"

"No, not that. Let me talk to his lawyer first. You just sit tight in the meantime and keep out of sight. Hopefully your identity will stay a mystery for a few more days, at least. And pray no one finds out you're here in the hotel, or all hell will break loose."

The next morning Harry went out to locate Nate's lawyer, Edward McIvey, who had been interviewed at length in the newspapers. Eliza waited with Daisy, sitting on the floor playing dolls for what seemed like forever.

Harry arrived back shortly after lunch, swept off his fur-lined overcoat, dumped it onto the bed in a heap, and ran his long fingers through his hair. "Hello, darling Daisy," he said, smiling broadly. "Why don't you play in my room for a while? And here, take some of these with you." He held out a handful of peppermints.

It was enough for Daisy. She took the sweets, gathered her dolls, and started toward the door. Pausing, she turned around and said, "Is Nate going to be all right?"

"Absolutely, so don't you worry about a thing," Harry answered.

"Can I see him?"

"Not yet, but you will soon. I promise."

With the toe of one black shoe, Daisy picked at a scuff mark on the floor, then sighed and left the room. Harry stood at the door and watched until she had disappeared safely into his room, then he closed the door and returned to Eliza.

"Tell me," she said anxiously. "What happened? Did you find Mr. McIvey?"

He hooked his thumbs in the sleeves of his waistcoat and cocked his head to one side. "Another exemplary Scotsman, though his family's not from the Carolinas. More's the pity."

"Oh, you're so pompous about that," Eliza protested with a laugh. "But tell me what happened. How is Nate?"

"He is an absolute fool about you. Do you know he didn't even tell his own lawyer about you until a couple of days ago? Glad he's not my client."

"But what did Mr. McIvey say?"

"Well, he's overjoyed, to put it mildly, to know you're still here and willing to testify for Truesdale. He and I agreed that it's absolutely imperative for you to stay hidden until the trial. Since this hotel is, unfortunately, getting overrun with reporters, there's too big a risk of you being discovered. So here's the plan: the three of us are going to move into McIvey's home until the trial. You'll still have to stay low, but there will be better protection from discovery."

Eliza stared at him intently, in silent agreement. The threat of exposure at the hotel had already occurred to her. In her innocence, Daisy might give them away by a simple slip of the tongue, anywhere or anytime. Also in her mind was the thought that in McIvey's home she would be more likely to hear news of Nate. "When should we go?"

"We'll check out tomorrow morning. In the mean—"

Harry was interrupted by a knock on the door. When he opened it, Daisy and a middle-aged gentleman stood on the threshold. The man was holding Daisy's hand, and he smiled at Harry and tipped his dusty black bowler hat when he saw Eliza. Daisy let go of his hand and ran past Harry to Eliza.

"The little lady here was lost," the man explained. "I found her wandering in the hall."

"I went to the 'cinerator, Aunt Lizzie. Y'know, where you throw the newspapers?" Daisy said, beginning to cry, "and I couldn't find Harry's room again, but I remembered the number."

Eliza put her arm around Daisy's shoulders and said to the man, "Thank you for bringing her here."

"Oh, no trouble, ma'am," the gentleman said, smiling. "I have a granddaughter just about her age. She's back in Denver though. Are you folks in town because of the trial?"

"No, for a vacation," Harry said quickly. "For the Midwinter Exposition. What with the trial and the fair crowds, it's getting a bit crowded. Wasn't the time for a vacation in San Francisco, was it?"

The man chuckled deep in his throat. "I'm glad I came early and got a room. They'll be hard to come by in another few days. I'm from the Denver *Post*, by the way." He touched the brim of his hat and winked at Daisy. To Harry he said, "Well, I'll get along here. Was on my way out for a late lunch." He nodded again and walked away down the hall.

When Harry closed the door, Eliza said anxiously, "Do you think he suspected anything?"

"Probably not." He looked between Eliza and Daisy and said, "But I think it might be wise to get to McIvey's as soon as possible. Anything might happen now, and it'll be better to be safely out of here. We'll go this evening. I can always return tomorrow to officially check us all out."

Eliza set to packing; Daisy solemnly brought out her clothes and placed them in stacks on the bed. The rain continued in a steady drizzle beneath a dull silver sky as they waited out the remainder of the afternoon. Daisy grew silent and listless. She sat on the bed beside Eliza and lay her head on the folds of cranberry fabric on Eliza's lap. Together they listened to the monotonous patter of rain on the windows. And waited.

Harry brought his valise to their room at five o'clock, his expression grim. "I ran out for a paper," he said, and tossed the evening edition of the *Chronicle* into Eliza's lap.

The headline read: MYSTERY WOMAN IDENTIFIED. She caught her breath against the hard pounding of her heart. In horror she took up the paper and read the subhead: *"Truesdale Paramour Revealed to be a Millworker."* The account began,

The mystery woman who had been living at the home of Nate Truesdale has been identified as Miss Eliza Nolenberg of Pittsburgh, Pennsylvania. Though authorities speculate that the child, tentatively identified by the name Daisy who was also living with Mr. Truesdale may be her daughter, no positive information is as yet available. Miss Nolenberg's identity was provided by Mr. George Putman, who observed her with Mr. Truesdale at the opera the night of the murder. According to Mr. Putman, his companion, whose name he would not divulge, was formerly acquainted with Mr. Truesdale and Miss Nolenberg and claims that Miss Nolenberg is a millworker who has been living with Mr. Truesdale since early last November.

When she had finished reading, Eliza looked up. Harry met her eyes. "They're getting too close to the whole story. Are you ready, Daisy? We're going right now."

With Eliza in her cape and Daisy attired in her

new blue coat and old crushed straw hat, they followed Harry down the stairs. He and Eliza each carried two valises. The lobby was crowded with men moving in and out of the pub room, or standing about talking as they smoked cigars. The far doors stood open to allow fresh air into the smoky interior, and the dismal sound of rain pelting the sidewalk was counterpointed by heavy voices debating the points of the murder case. Eliza, Daisy, and Harry had almost reached the doors when the man who had found Daisy in the hall approached them.

"Checking out now?" he asked with a smile.

Harry nodded amiably. "San Francisco wasn't quite the place for vacationing now, Exposition or not."

"More's the pity. It's a grand place," the man said in commiseration. He bent to smile at Daisy. "Hello, sweetheart. Remember me?" She nodded and Eliza held her breath. "And your name is Daisy, right? Well, Daisy, you get your mother and father to bring you back again after the trial."

Exchanging anxious glances, Harry and Eliza both urged Daisy toward the doors. As she walked with them, Daisy smiled and waved good-bye to the man. He winked, then turned back to speak to his companion, but Eliza knew it wouldn't be long before he put the details together and arrived at the truth of their identity.

Chapter 17

McIvey's home was small but comfortable, cluttered with books, periodicals, newspapers, and several Bibles, all scattered about and left open at various pages, as if he or his wife had only set them down momentarily and would return at any time. This was obviously not the case, as Eliza discovered thin veneers of dust on some pages.

Mrs. McIvey was a tall woman, her personality stable and solid and reassuring. Her graying, lustrous hair was wound into a coronet, and she moved calmly and with dignity as she carried sheets, towels, and pillows for the guests and prepared two upstairs rooms for them. Eliza and Daisy had the spare bedroom, a tiny room filled with sewing paraphernalia, more books and magazines, and tiny figurines and fans and delicate vases. They shared a bed. Harry was given McIvey's office, which held only a small couch arranged into a makeshift bed.

Mrs. McIvey laughed quietly in apology to Harry as he helped her stretch a crisp white sheet over the couch. "By the looks of you, Mr. McPherson, this won't be a bed but only a pillow. But I haven't anything long enough to accommodate you."

At dinner, with the five of them squeezed together around a table designed for two, Eliza couldn't hold back her questions any longer. She asked Mr. McIvey how Nate was faring.

McIvey answered between bites of baked chicken and sips of watered whiskey. "He's fine. But why don't you and I discuss it after dinner."

"Would you take him a message for me, or perhaps a letter?" Eliza asked.

McIvey shook his head. "He thinks you're in Pittsburgh, Miss Nolenberg, and I'd rather he kept thinking that. At least for now."

"But why?"

"We'll talk about it later."

After a lengthy dinner during which Harry and Mr. McIvey discussed ancestors and shared anecdotes of their profession, much to Daisy's boredom and Eliza's impatience, McIvey swiped his napkin over the front of his sweat-damp, balding head, tossed it onto the table, and gazed at Eliza. "Why don't you and I have a little chat now, Miss Nolenberg," he said.

He pushed back his chair, raised his heavy frame out of it, and motioned her to follow him. They entered the small, cluttered parlor together, and Eliza sat erect on the edge of the green velvet couch, smoothing the folds of her blue-and-white muslin gown over her knees.

As McIvey settled in the chair directly across from her, she said briskly, "Why should Nate not know I'm still here in San Francisco? He'll find out sooner or later anyway, and especially since I'll be testifying at his trial."

"Miss Nolenberg, you must have some idea of the magnitude of evidence against Nate at this point. He's got one thing in his favor. It's a big thing, and it's what will win or lose this case for him. It involves the fact that he sent you to Pittsburgh . . . or tried to. I don't want to discuss it further until I've thought it all through. So for now, let's just say it's my professional secret, and leave it at that." The black and white spiky eyebrows rose high over generous blue eyes, and he smiled cajolingly.

"All right, Mr. McIvey," she said at last, formally. "I bow to your higher wisdom in this situation. And I trust you."

"Thank you. It is a pleasure to hear that," he said with exaggerated humility. "Now tell me about Nate, about these last few months, about Miss Brody, Mr. Watts, and anything else that might occur to you. Bear in mind, Miss Nolenberg, that Nate faces the death penalty or life imprisonment if he's found guilty. Your complete cooperation is essential." He smiled, again cajolingly. "But let me get some paper first."

He sat back and plowed through the pile of neglected reading material and papers on the table beside his chair. Finding nothing of immediate use, he slid a ladies' dress catalog from the bottom of the pile, pushing aside the other books so they wouldn't topple into his lap. From a sewing basket beside the chair, he pulled a pencil. Folding open the catalog, he wrote notes on the margins of the pages as Eliza talked.

She told him everything.

She told him why she had come to San Francisco, about Marietta Sharpe's relationship with Nate, about the Thanksgiving Day party, the evening at the opera, the night following that, and the morning when she'd heard Rossie accuse Nate. McIvey asked endless questions, which she answered as well as she could. She was exhausted when she'd finished. In the telling she felt as if she had relived the events.

McIvey chucked the pencil onto the table, behind the stack of books, and ripped a section of pages from the catalog. "I talked to Daisy earlier. Quite a charming child. Candid too. I'd like permission to put her on the witness stand," he said.

"Daisy?" Eliza shot him a glance of both surprise and alarm. "I'm not sure I want her to go through such a thing."

McIvey scratched his chin and shrugged. "I can appreciate your concern, but we've got a man's life on the line here, and I think Daisy's testimony is necessary. Think about it. You don't have to decide this minute."

Despite the overt kindnesses extended by Mrs. McIvey over the next few days, and the woman's quiet calmness, Eliza felt more trapped than she ever had before. The days alone with Daisy at the Lick House Hotel now seemed like a lark in comparison. And the days with Nate before that became a dream, golden and seamless and filled with radiance, not quite real.

Newspapers poured into the house through McIvey, who purchased every edition. Eliza read them with mounting horror. The *Chronicle* reported: TRUESDALE SORDID LOVE NEST WAS SCENE OF CUSTODY BATTLE, and below that: "*Child Was Product of Affair Truesdale Carried on with Miss Nolenberg's Sister.*" The stories were filled with grossly exaggerated accounts of Nate's activities in Pittsburgh. How they had acquired any information at all was a mystery to Eliza, but obviously reporters were communicating with the East Coast or had access to the Pittsburgh papers. At this last thought, Eliza caught her breath in deep dismay as it occurred to her what must be appearing in her home newspapers: interviews with coworkers, neighbors, relatives. She felt suddenly exposed, with no way to defend herself.

Various charity and church groups denounced both Nate and Eliza, and said they would take steps to remove "the innocent child" from their "immoral and indecent" influence. Eliza was incensed by such stories, until she remembered her own words spoken in what seemed like another life. She had said the very same thing about Nate, and was now ashamed.

Very little attention was paid to Tess Brody and her part in the death of Rossie. Even the *Call*, which had previously been more honest in its reporting and more in support of Nate, began to deride him. Estelle was portrayed as the virtuous young girl seduced by the jaded passions of a wealthy ne'er-do-well. Eliza herself was described as being without morals or scruples; the kiss during a waltz at Nate's Thanksgiving Day party was blown into a scene of sordid proportions. One evening, filled with disgust, Eliza shredded the newspapers and burst into tears that not even Harry's affectionate coaxing or Mrs. McIvey's sympathy could stem.

Did Nate see the papers? How could he hold up, alone as he was? Eliza thought of him during every waking moment. She ached to be with him.

Daisy's full identity was revealed in the papers within a week of Eliza's. Pittsburgh authorities were quoted, the apartment in which they had lived was reported as still vacant. The *Examiner* ran a story originally run in the Denver *Post*, that the mystery woman and child had been discovered living at the Lick House Hotel in San Francisco in the company of an unidentified man. Eliza knew then that the reporter who had befriended Daisy had finally guessed their identity. Speculation ran high as to the nature of the relationship between Eliza and Harry, and a good deal of space was spent on the opinion that Eliza had abandoned Nate when the publicity broke, and had now taken up with a new lover.

Eliza found sleep difficult; she turned again and again in the darkness, seeking comfort, listening to Daisy's soft breathing. Did Nate see these stories about her in the papers?

But Eliza couldn't consider even stepping out of the McIvey house. Reporters kept a constant vigil on the sidewalk and could be seen at any hour of the day, loitering under the trees on the lawn, sitting along the curb, lying down in the grass and propping their hats over their faces to shield them from the sun. Whenever McIvey appeared, they rushed him, jostling each other and clamoring for information about Nate and the case.

Harry's presence was a boon to her on any number of occasions as he took it upon himself to keep both Eliza and Daisy occupied. Patiently, he played dolls with Daisy, read her stories, invented games, and pranced about during marathon attempts at charades. To Eliza he was an ever-present listener and a source of solid good sense when she needed to talk. Theirs was a friendship she treasured. And when, in rare moments of sadness, he spoke of Estelle, she understood his sense of loss.

"I could have made her happy," he would say. "She was so beautiful but sad. I made her laugh again, and she needed someone like me to take care of her."

"Estelle loved you very much, Harry," Eliza would reassure him gently. "And you did make her happier than I'd ever seen her."

January passed into February.

Mr. McIvey brought in the newspaper one evening and was smiling with amusement as he casually set it on the table in front of Eliza. She was sitting at the dining room table looking idly at the articles in the latest issue of *The Cosmopolitan*. Daisy sat at the other side of the table as she painted pictures with Mrs. McIvey. Harry was upstairs, seeking a few moments of quiet.

Briefly and without interest, Eliza glanced at the paper. Then she looked at it again, and her eyes snapped wide. The headline flashed at her: TRUESDALE PROPOSES MARRIAGE FROM JAIL CELL. She snatched up the paper.

Nate Truesdale today announced to reporters that he hopes to marry mystery woman Miss Eliza Nolenberg "when circumstances permit." According to Truesdale, "I've been in love with her for some time and wanted to formally propose." When asked whether he thought Miss Nolenberg would accept his proposal, Truesdale replied, "I have no idea. I can only hope." Truesdale appeared in rare good humor and joked with reporters briefly. Following this announcement he refused to answer further questions about the nature of his relationship with Miss Nolenberg and indicated to the guards that he wished to return to his cell.

The remainder of the article carried on in the same vein as the previous articles: speculation about her whereabouts, her relationships with both Nate and Harry, the unidentified man. Eliza didn't bother reading the rest of it. She read and reread the quotes from Nate, until she couldn't see the words for the tears in her eyes.

Lifting her head, she smiled shakily at Mr. McIvey, who was watching her quizzically. "I never in all my life imagined I'd received a proposal from a man in jail," she said, shaking her head, laughing weakly in surprise and emotion. "Or through a . . . a newspaper. Of all the—"

But she didn't finish the sentence.

Rising hastily, she left the room and hurried up the stairs. In the room she shared with Daisy, Eliza fell across the bed and scooped a pillow into her arms. She hugged it and rocked herself, weeping with the terrible and yet piercingly sweet ache of longing. If only he were free. Free and with her. She wanted to be with him. She wept and hugged the crisp pillow slip that smelled of lilac sachet and soap.

The trial opened on a Monday morning. Nate shaved and dressed in his cell; Mrs. Herlihy had provided an immaculate shirt, and a collar and cuffs starched to impeccable perfection. As always, she had been sensible and reassuring when she had visited him the day before. He had needed reassurance more than he'd thought. He'd taken to pacing nervously and was irritated about every small thing— McIvey's smile, a crack in the plaster ceiling over his cot, a guard whistling.

He thought of Eliza as he stepped into the gray chalk-striped flannel trousers. Though he had read in the paper stories that Eliza and Daisy had been seen at the Lick House Hotel, he pushed aside his hopes. With so much distortion in each of the stories, he had come to doubt everything. And he couldn't let himself hope.

He pulled on his shirt, noting the scrape of crisp starched fabric against his skin; it was a touch of reality, of his past, of his sense of identity. The waistcoat was also chalk-striped gray flannel. He put on his collar, his cuffs, his gold-and-pearl cuff links. Each item used to act as a piece of protection, but they no longer offered the same sensation. Without the aid of a mirror, he knotted a black silk tie and pinched it between his fingers to position it. His black polished shoes reflected soft flashes of light from the window as he moved.

After slipping into his solid charcoal-gray frock coat, he shoved his hands in his trouser pockets and stood at the window, looking down onto the street. What else was there to do?

He gazed at the crowd gathering outside the Hall of Justice. Reporters, spectators, all waiting and noisy in their waiting. Heavy black carriages pulled up, one after another, to let out passengers. Geoffrey Helmms, Tess' lawyer, was mobbed by reporters as he arrived. He waited, smiled, answered questions. The district attorney, J. T. Landorf, alighted from his carriage with great dignity, sure of himself and his success. Nate watched as McIvey arrived shortly thereafter. McIvey was surrounded as the other lawyers had been, but he barreled through the midst of the reporters and did not speak.

Nate leaned one shoulder on the wall beside the window as he watched the street activity below. He waited . . . until he realized he was unconsciously watching for a small brisk woman with her head held high and her shoulders back. With that thought he straightened from the wall. No, she was in Pittsburgh where she belonged, where he had sent her.

He turned his back on the raucous street below as footsteps approached along the corridor. A key clanked and rasped in the lock, and then McIvey was being ushered into the cell.

"Good morning, Nate," he said cheerfully. His pale eyes were bright, his eyebrows sprouting in all directions. His clothing was as immaculate as Nate's, and he looked every inch the capable lawyer in his flawlessly tailored black frock coat and black trousers. His pine-box briefcase with loose papers sticking out was carried in one hand. He held several books under his other arm. "Today's the day we're going to start breaking all the jackasses around here."

Nate couldn't help grinning as he commented, "Professional reassurance brilliantly articulated."

"Move your tie a little to the left. Didn't they give you a mirror?"

Nate slid his tie, feeling with the finger of both hands to make sure it was centered between the folds of his wing collar. "I didn't want to see a reflection of despair."

"I see courage and calmness. Exactly as it should be. Trust me and remember what I've said. The tie's perfect now. Are you ready?"

"I've been ready forever. Let's go."

The courtroom, the largest in the Hall of Justice, was filled to capacity. The hall outside was crowded with would-be spectators; policemen were attempting to keep order and force back the crowd. Nate and McIvey were moved along by four guards who formed a barrier between them and the mass of reporters rushing forward. Even so, Nate was jostled and pushed.

Faces pressed toward him.

"Where is the mystery woman?"

"Mr. Truesdale!"

"Have you had any contact with her?"

"Is it true that you threatened to murder the man she's been with?"

After weeks of such questions, Nate was still appalled by them. He stared around him, trapped in the amorphous mass of humanity pressing toward him. They looked for the worst in him, hoped for it, lusted for it. He felt sick.

Beside him McIvey had to shout to be heard: "Don't say anything, just keep moving."

Inside the courtroom four banners of sunlight from

the windows along the right wall slanted over the
rows of spectators, the windows had been opened
slightly to allow fresh air to circulate through the
densely packed room, which was already overheat-
ing.

Nate avoided meeting anyone's eyes as he and
McIvey, escorted by the bailiff, crossed the white-
and-black ceramic-tiled floor toward their table. With
a two-story high ceiling, the long room gave the impression of oppressive magnitude.

McIvey sipped watered whiskey and rolled his
shoulders to ease cramped muscles. He, Harry, and
Eliza were sitting in the cluttered parlor while Mrs.
McIvey and Daisy prepared supper.

"After the opening speeches today, we heard testimony from Nate's warehouse foreman, Harve
Dunlocke, and the doctor—what's his name?" Mc-
Ivey snapped his fingers and looked questioningly
to Eliza.

"Dr. Culbert?" She was hanging onto McIvey's
every word.

"That's it."

"Well? What happened? What did they say?"
Eliza clenched her fingers together.

"Dr. Culbert described the stab wounds and reit-
erated the accusations you heard Rossie express.
Nothing new in that. Dunlocke repeated everything
he'd heard concerning the argument during the
Thanksgiving Day party—essentially that Nate and
Rossie were fighting about Tess, that Nate threatened to kill Rossie and then ordered both Rossie and
Tess out of his house." With a small shake of his
head, McIvey added, "It's of no use now to try to
predict anything, Miss Nolenberg."

"But the facts are so against him," she exclaimed.

"Exactly right. So we can't argue those facts."

"How was Nate? How was he doing?"

"Remarkably well, actually." McIvey sipped his drink. "I didn't need to restrain him once."

Harry laughed and put one big-knuckled hand over Eliza's in reassurance. "I'm anxious to meet him."

McIvey gave a whispery laugh. "Someplace where he's not behind bars! You'll probably like him better then."

"When am I going to testify?" Eliza asked.

"Patience, Miss Nolenberg. It won't be for a while yet. I'm saving you and Daisy till last."

In the following days McIvey duly reported the events of the trial to Eliza. "Today we heard from one of the ship captains from his company, a Mr. Pointer. He said there was some trouble with one of the captains causing the death of two seamen on his ship. Nate fired the captain, and Rossie rehired him."

And on another day: "A waiter from Manning's Oyster Grotto testified to seeing Nate and Tess having lunch there together recently."

"But where are the people on Nate's side, like Mrs. Herlihy?" Eliza protested. "Everything so far has been so negative!"

"Oh, she'll be testifying, don't worry."

Then McIvey stopped bringing home the newspapers. When Eliza asked him about it, he remarked, "Do you want lies or the truth? I bring you the truth. Believe what I say and you don't need to look at the papers. All right, Miss Nolenberg? The trial is going just fine. Exactly the way I hoped it would."

Eliza suspected it was going against Nate and that was why Mr. McIvey kept the newspapers from her, but she was willing to trust him. He seemed calm every evening. If he wasn't worried, then neither would she.

It was easy enough to say that during the daylight hours, but at night her fears returned. There was nothing to do about it, though, except to be patient, as Mr. McIvey advised her repeatedly.

It was a morning like every other morning in the courtroom, so why did he feel so beaten? As he approached the witness stand, Nate focused on the drooping California flag—the brown flanks of a bear just visible among its white folds. The golden fringe looked dull with dust.

The judge, a crisp elderly man with not a hint of gray in his thinning jet-black hair, wore spectacles snugly against round pale-blue eyes, and his eyebrows, as black as his hair, rose in high arches. Nate had never seen him evince any degree of humor, but even so, he was not unkind. He sat with his hands clasped on the papers in front of him, his expression alert, his thoughts unreadable.

Morning sunlight fell through the high, narrow windows over the jurors' heads, and their faces were obscured slightly in the haze of dusty sunlit air. Nate avoided looking too closely at them anyway. The densely packed room hummed with voices, coughs, the shifting of feet, the creak of wooden seats.

Nate took a seat in the hard chair, spoke the oath with a firm voice, and resisted the urge to straighten his tie.

McIvey walked toward him, calm, solemn, benevolent. "Now, Mr. Truesdale, we've all heard various accounts of the events of the evening of December twenty-sixth. Would you tell us where you were, who you were with, and what you did on the night in question."

Nate answered clearly. He gave all the details of

his experience at the opera with Eliza as calmly as he could. Then McIvey questioned him as to all the pertinent facts. They went into the relationship between Nate and Rossie, the relationship between Nate and Tess. The silence in the courtroom was palpable. Why feel so beaten? Nate asked himself. Among the spectators he could see Peg Walters, Mrs. Herlihy and her husband, the Ruggles, and others from the office. He saw Marietta near the wall on the right side of the room. Her forehead was creased sharply; a line between her brows looked as distinct as if it had been cut into her skin with a knife. Nate found himself staring at it, unable to look away. She watched him, the frown line slowly softening. Then she was reaching for a handkerchief from the bag on her lap and rising, squeezing past the many people in that row who had to shift to let her by. She left the courtroom. Nate was relieved; he hadn't wanted to see her sympathy, or worse, her pity. After that he kept his eyes on McIvey.

"Tell me now, Mr. Truesdale," McIvey said. "What is the nature of your relationship with Miss Eliza Nolenberg? Is it true you've proposed marriage to her?" McIvey smiled broadly and clasped his hands behind his back.

"It's true that I proposed to her through the newspapers, but so far I haven't had a chance to ask her in person. Formally."

"Do you intend to when you next see her?"

"Of course."

"All right. Describe your relationship with her."

The top of the seat was digging into Nate's back. He shifted his position. "Miss Nolenberg is my daughter's aunt. She came to San Francisco to get my signature for authority to assume complete legal guardianship of Daisy . . . my daughter. I refused, deciding that I had more to offer Daisy. In the course of waiting for the custody hearing, I fell in love with Miss Nolenberg. Thank goodness for the sluggish legal system.''

Laughter rippled across the courtroom. McIvey walked slowly back and forth in front of him. He glanced up. ''Where is Miss Nolenberg now?''

Nate spread his hands. ''I have no idea.''

''When did you last see her?''

''On the morning I was arrested.''

''On the morning after the attack on Mr. Watts?''

''That's right.''

''Tell us what happened that morning.''

Nate described Eliza's visit to his office, what she had told him, and his decision to send Eliza and Daisy back to Pittsburgh.

''So the last time you saw Miss Nolenberg was when you put her into the carriage to go to the train station.''

''Yes.'' Nate watched McIvey closely, wondering where the man was heading now. He disliked having to talk about Eliza to the world at large. Everything he said was material for the reporters. As he had feared, McIvey stabbed right into the heart of the matter.

''Mr. Truesdale, this is a delicate question, and perhaps I can phrase it gently. Was Miss Nolenberg with you in your bedroom during the night of the attack on Mr. Watts?''

Nate's expression turned to ice. ''Yes,'' he bit out.

''The *entire* night? From the time you returned from the opera house until the next morning?''

''Yes.''

Low murmurs like the sound of a soft waterfall filled the room. McIvey glanced at the jurors, across the courtroom, then back at Nate. ''Mr. Truesdale, for a man who has been accused of attempted murder to send his only alibi out of town is a rather unusual—some might even be inclined to say foolish—thing to do. Do you agree?''

"No, I do not!''

"Why is that?''

"I knew what was going to happen. I knew what kind of carnival this was going to turn into, that everything about her and my daughter would be printed in the papers. They were entirely innocent, and I saw no reason to subject them to all the press and publicity. My daughter is only seven years old. And we can already see what kind of stuff is being printed for mass consumption.'' Nate paused, and his jaw tensed. "Eliza and Daisy didn't deserve that.''

McIvey stood directly before him. "Would you say you were protecting them from publicity?''

"This kind of publicity, yes!''

"Do you love your daughter?''

Nate's mouth tightened even more. "Yes,'' he said, then his voice grew louder. "Yes, I do very much.''

McIvey retired to the defense table, moving calmly. In the interval, as J. T. Landorf, the district attorney, rose from his seat, Nate glanced at the high windows. Branches swayed against a dull yellow sky; leaves swirled on their slender stems. Through the opened tops of the windows he heard the clop of horses and squeak of wagon wheels and the footsteps of someone running past on the sidewalk.

J. T. Landorf was of medium height, his brown hair combed back from his face in deep waves, his nose disproportionately large in an otherwise delicate face. His small mouth puckered in thought as he approached the witness stand. Eyeing Nate through narrowed dark eyes, he grasped the lapels of his black frock coat and began, "Mr. Truesdale, it's already been established that you had known

Mr. Watts since you were fourteen." His voice was light and piercing, his wide-legged stance a motionless swagger. "It's also been established that your relationship of late had been marked with arguments. Specifically, we have learned that there were any number of incidents in which your employees heard raised voices between you and Mr. Watts. Also there was a confrontation of some magnitude at your home at Thanksgiving, and several people have testified to having witnessed another confrontation between you at the opera house the night of the murder. What was the nature of your argument with him at the Thanksgiving Day party?"

Nate kept his gaze direct and unflinching. "He was making improper suggestions about Miss Nolenberg."

"Describe the 'improper suggestions.' "

"He wanted to know if Miss Nolenberg and I were involved with each other and asked as to what her . . . responses were."

"Responses in regard to what?"

Nate wiped the palms of his hands on the knees of his trousers. McIvey had warned him what to expect, and he knew he had to remain calm. "Responses to . . . making love."

"Did you threaten to kill him 'with your bare hands'?"

"That's merely a figure of "

"Yes or no, Mr. Truesdale."

"Well, yes, but—"

"And you ordered him out of your house?"

"Yes, that's true."

"All because he merely inquired as to Miss Nolenberg's responses to you?"

"No, that's not it."

"Enlighten us."

Nate shifted his back against the sharp edge of the

seat. "His suggestions about Miss Nolenberg were of a very crude nature."

"And he angered you to the point of threatening to kill him—yes or no?"

"I didn't mean it."

"Yet you used those exact words. Do you often threaten to kill people?"

"No, I don't make it a habit."

"Have you ever threatened to kill anyone besides Mr. Watts?"

"No."

"So, in other words, he angered you to the point of actually threatening such a thing?"

Nate tried not to clench his teeth. "Yes."

By the time J. T. Landorf finished his cross-examination, the day had waned to dusk. Every detail of each argument had been explored, and in such a way that Nate felt sick and trapped. Shaken, he left the witness chair and walked back to the table where McIvey was sitting. He sat down in the chair beside McIvey.

"Don't worry, Nate, you handled it superbly," McIvey whispered.

Nate glanced at him in silence. He had never felt so empty and exhausted. He remembered the clear sound of footsteps running past the building, wished he could be out on that sidewalk, running, running. Running toward a crystal-blue lake where, on a sunlit hillside, a beautiful drowsy woman lay on a blanket amongst wildflowers and smiled at him.

At last the evening came when McIvey told Eliza to be ready to go with him the following morning. The trial had been in progress for three weeks.

"Tomorrow!" Eliza was aghast now that the moment had arrived. For weeks she had been on edge, anxiously awaiting this day. And now, faced by it, she sat down abruptly on the couch and buried her face in her hands. "Oh, no, what if I can't do it? What if I say the wrong thing? What if I'm so nervous the jury doesn't believe me?"

"Do you believe your testimony?" McIvey countered.

"Of course."

"That's all you need."

Lifting her head, she looked at him closely and nodded. "All right."

"Fine. And you'll get a chance to see Nate for yourself. You won't have to pester me with questions about him."

Eliza uttered a brief, nervous laugh. "I'll probably cry."

"That's fine too. Don't worry about it if it happens."

"Oh, I'm so nervous." She pressed her hand to her breast. "I feel as if my heart's going to burst."

"You'll do just fine."

Eliza wished she could believe that.

Chapter 18

Following Mr. McIvey's directions, Eliza, Daisy, and Harry arrived early and found seats near the back right corner of the courtroom. Eliza had wanted to see and hear the proceedings. "Just don't draw attention to yourselves," McIvey had said.

Around them ladies in whispering silk and rustling taffeta gowns took their seats; men in tall hats or bowler hats and black frock coats hailed one another. Daisy sat wide-eyed and silent on the edge of her seat. Her hair was pulled off her forehead with a shiny white satin bow secured at the crown. Beneath the hem of a black-and-red-plaid dress her tall black shoes swung energetically, brushing the floor in rhythm, and she kept one hand on Eliza's arm at all times.

Eliza sat stiffly in apprehension, eyes forward. From this distance the raised dais on which the judge's bench stood appeared as magnificent as a throne. She clutched the strings of her purse and absently patted Daisy's hand gripping her forearm. Tucked in her left glove was a folded slip of paper, a note for Nate. If she had the opportunity to give it to him . . .

They waited for almost three-quarters of an hour before they saw Nate. The bailiff escorted him into the courtroom, and as Eliza watched his familiar elegant strides, saw his gray flannel trousers and black frock coat, her heart tugged fiercely. She saw him in profile and admired the crisp black curls of his hair, his lean and tensed jaw, the flash of his blue eyes between thick black lashes. She had never loved him so much.

He sat at a table with his back to the courtroom, his black hair a vivid contrast to McIvey's white head. Eliza couldn't take her eyes off him. As if he could sense her presence, Nate turned his head twice and scanned the group of spectators, frowning. But he never saw her.

So engrossed was she in watching Nate, Eliza's pulse jolted when she heard her name spoken aloud. Mr. McIvey stood in the front beneath the judge's bench and announced, "The defense calls to the witness stand Miss Eliza Nolenberg."

An immediate tumult arose in the courtroom. Voices exclaimed, heads turned, eager glances swept the assembled spectators. All awaited sight of the woman who had been the mystery sensation. Nate turned completely around in his seat, his face tight with shock, his eyes wide and bright and seeking.

Eliza's heart beat violently. She patted Daisy's hand and met Harry's reassuring wink before rising to her feet and squeezing past the knees of the people between her and the central aisle. She looked at no one. She kept her head up. But she felt hundreds of eyes digging into her from all sides, heard murmurs and exclamations echoing around her as she approached the front of the room. Her cranberry taffeta gown rustled with each step. She avoided looking at Nate but felt his bright, radiant stare touching her, and was so filled with gladness to be near him again that she was afraid she would be unable to speak.

Passing Mr. McIvey, with his calm reassuring smile, Eliza stepped into the witness stand and took the oath. She sat tensely on the edge of the hard oak chair.

"Miss Nolenberg, we're all very glad to see you." Mr. McIvey spoke with laughter in his voice, and the audience chuckled in appreciation. Eliza relaxed, unable to resist a smile in return. She chanced a look at Nate and met open warmth in his eyes. He sat forward at the table, his frock coat hunched up on his shoulders, his hands clenched into fists. McIvey continued, "Why don't you tell us where you've been all this time."

"Do you mean since leaving Mr. Truesdale's home?" Her voice sounded distant to her own ears, but after Mr. McIvey's nod, she spoke more loudly. Her brown eyes were direct and unflinching. "Mr. Truesdale wanted me to return to my home in Pittsburgh, but on the way to the train station I had great reservations about that course of action. So my niece and I sought rooms at the Lick House Hotel. After staying for almost two weeks at the Lick House, we moved into your . . . Mr. McIvey's home and have been there ever since."

"Pittsburgh has always been your home, is that right? Tell us about your occupation."

"I'm employed as a weaver at the Geddes Cotton Mill. I've worked there since I was twelve years old. . ."

As Eliza briefly related her history, Nate watched her with growing warmth and love. He couldn't get enough of looking at her—the way her hair shone in the peaks and crests of soft waves around her face, the velvet fawn eyes so unafraid, the rosebud mouth mobile as she formed words that didn't quite penetrate his preoccupied concentration. She was beautiful beyond his memories in these last many weeks apart. He recognized the firm bearing and dignity and had never been so thankful for them. Would she accept his proposal? Tensely, he listened to the questions, hoping McIvey would spare Eliza any embarrassment and protect her reputation.

"Did Mr. Truesdale tell you why he wanted you to return to Pittsburgh?" McIvey asked.

"Yes, he didn't want Daisy and me to get mixed up in the trial and publicity. He knew it would be very unpleasant, and he preferred that we not have to endure such a thing." Eliza chanced another glance at Nate, who was staring intently at the tabletop between his hands.

McIvey stood his ground before the witness stand as he asked, "Why didn't you leave as he requested?"

"I just knew it wasn't right. I knew he was innocent, and it felt cowardly to leave. Daisy and I both felt it was not right for us to leave."

"How do you know Mr. Truesdale is innocent of the murder of Mr. Watts?"

Nate abruptly shot to his feet and exclaimed, "Leave her alone! Don't make her answer that!" His eyes blazed at McIvey.

The judge's gavel struck with a sound like the crack of a pistol. Eliza jumped in surprise. Judge Newton peered solemnly through his spectacles. "You're out of line, Mr. Truesdale. Take your seat."

Nate waited momentarily, staring at McIvey, before dropping into his seat and leaning back angrily.

The judge's expression was courteous. "Answer the counselor's question, Miss Nolenberg."

She nodded and faced Mr. McIvey again. This was the question she had known would come, the question she had dreaded having to answer in front of the world. A blush suffused her cheeks, but she said clearly, "Mr. Truesdale could not have had

anything to do with the attack on Mr. Watts because
. . . he was with me at that time."

"What do you mean 'at that time'? What time was
that?"

"Well, all that night. We were together, you see."
She felt her face burn under the eager stares of the
spectators. She gripped the strings of her purse and
sat straight and kept her eyes on McIvey's face.

"Mr. Truesdale was with you from the time you
returned from the opera house until the following
morning?"

"That's correct."

"What time did you return from the opera
house?"

"Sometime around nine or shortly thereafter."

"So you can vouch for Mr. Truesdale's whereabouts from that time until what time in the morning?"

"Till about seven in the morning, when I left
to go to Dr. Culbert's office. I was going to fetch
medicine for Mr. Truesdale's housekeeper—for her
husband."

"According to your testimony, then, Mr. Truesdale was at his home throughout the entire night
and could have had nothing to do with the murder
of Mr. Watts."

Eliza nodded. "That's correct."

"Thank you, Miss Nolenberg." Mr. McIvey gave
her a slight bow and said, "No more questions, your
honor."

J. T. Landorf rose to his feet. Nate scowled at
McIvey as the lawyer returned to his seat beside him,
but he said nothing, and both men turned their full
attention on Landorf.

"Miss Nolenberg," Landorf began with a disarm-
ing smile, "you say you can vouch for Mr. Truesdale's whereabouts for the entire night?"

"Yes." Irritated by the man's patronizing tone, Eliza answered briskly.

"If you were asleep, how can you be sure of that? It's entirely possible for someone to leave a room undetected by the sleeper."

"I didn't sleep much. Mr. Truesdale kept me awake most of the night." Snickers and hoots of laughter filtered across the room. Eliza wanted to smile but kept her head up and resisted the temptation to glance at Nate's expression. Now that the initial embarrassment had passed, she was ready to say whatever was necessary to prove Nate's innocence.

Landorf pressed with another question. "Mr. Watts accused Mr. Truesdale of being responsible for the attack on him. You yourself heard this at Dr. Culbert's office?"

"Rossie Watts was not the sort—"

"Just answer the question, Miss Nolenberg. Yes or no?"

Taken aback by the interruption, Eliza paused momentarily before answering, "Yes."

"Mr. Truesdale didn't necessarily have to be present at the waterfront in order to be held responsible for the murder of Mr. Watts. It could have been prearranged with Miss Brody."

"That's out of the question!" Eliza insisted, incensed. "Nate would never do such a thing. And he and Miss Brody were not friendly in the least."

Landorf exclaimed sarcastically, "Oh, you think he'd let you know what was going on with another woman, a woman he admits to having been involved with for several years already? I hardly think a man would talk about his mistresses in front of each of them! Do you, Miss Nolenberg?"

Eliza said nothing; her mouth tightened. Landorf

continued. "Regardless of your blind infatuation with Mr. Truesdale, the fact—"

Mr. McIvey rose to object. The judge glanced at him, waiting, but McIvey changed his mind and sat down again.

Landorf went on. "The fact remains that Mr. Watts *did* accuse Mr. Truesdale of his murder. The old saying goes that love is blind, does it not, Miss Nolenberg?" He smiled sympathetically and strolled across the front of the courtroom.

Eliza drew herself up briskly, spine as straight as a broom handle, as she said, "You've obviously never loved anyone with any greater depth than merely surface emotions, Mr. Landorf, and then only because it momentarily pleased you to do so. Love clarifies; it does not blind."

With a grand sweep of his arm, Mr. Landorf announced, "You stand to gain much through Mr. Truesdale. Out of the mill and into wealth. Rags to riches. I suggest, Miss Nolenberg, that your interest in Mr. Truesdale's fate could be motivated by some less than noble reasons."

Eliza held her anger in check. "I was happy enough in my life. I was not seeking more. And, in fact, at one point before Christmas—"

"Happy enough making seven dollars a week in a cotton mill? I'm sure such happiness would pale in comparison to the possibility of Mr. Truesdale's money and way of life. Are you so different from the rest of us?"

"If you see money as your primary motivation, Mr. Landorf, I suggest you don't have much more than a passing acquaintance with happiness. Mr. Truesdale has nothing whatsoever to do with the murder of Mr. Watts. I testify to that, under oath."

Mr. Landorf turned, facing the jury, and leaned his hand on the witness stand as he addressed Eliza and the courtroom at large. "You're making statements based entirely on emotion. Women are ruled by feelings, and thank heaven we do not have women making decisions in our society!" A scattering of applause greeted his exclamation. "You have no proof to back up your statements concerning the nature of Mr. Truesdale's involvement with Miss Brody, or Mr. Watts, for that matter. Such devotion is, of course, delightful, but only in the home, where it belongs. This is a court of law! And in order to make valid decisions in the area of justice, we require more substance than the whims and whimsies of feminine feeling."

With a mock bow, Mr. Landorf announced, "No more questions."

Eliza was livid, her face deep pink, but she held her tongue, and when the judge excused her, she stepped briskly down from the witness stand. Nate was watching her with a soft sparkle of admiration in his eyes that melted her anger and brought an involuntary smile to her lips. Unhesitatingly, she walked toward him, slid the folded note from her glove, and before the bailiff could halt her, pushed the note onto the table in front of him. Redirected to her seat by the bailiff, Eliza walked quickly back down the central aisle, conscious of the stares and murmurs that followed her.

The judge motioned for McIvey to bring the note to him, and when he had done so, the two men conferred quietly over the top of the judge's bench. At last, McIvey returned the note to Nate, but J. T. Landorf rose to his feet. "Your Honor—"

"Yes, Counselor," Judge Newton interrupted. "The note Miss Nolenberg passed to Mr. Truesdale has no bearing on this case, but for the sake of your curiosity I'll let it be known—Miss Nolenberg accepted Mr. Truesdale's proposal of marriage."

From among the spectators could be heard appreciative laughter and a few enthusiastic hand claps. Harry applauded the loudest and winked at a confused Daisy. Nate met Eliza's eyes in the crowded seats and smiled warmly.

McIvey announced, "The defense calls Miss Daisy Nolenberg to the witness stand," and Nate's smile froze. He shot to his feet, the chair scraping harshly against the floor. "I refuse to allow this," he exclaimed. "She is my daughter and I will not permit it."

Judge Newton ordered him to sit down, then glanced questioningly at Mr. McIvey. "Miss Nolenberg has the proper authority," the lawyer explained, "given her by the child's mother, and she has granted permission for Daisy to testify."

"Go ahead, Counselor."

Prompted by Eliza, Daisy edged her way from the row of seats, took one glance back at her aunt, then walked to the front of the room. McIvey had explained the procedure to her the previous evening, but she glanced nervously from side to side. As she approached the front of the room, Daisy paused and waved to Nate, then she skipped across to where Mr. McIvey stood motioning to her.

"Hello, sweetheart," he said with a smile. "That chair's going to be too big for you, so why don't you stand right in there." McIvey helped her step up into the witness stand.

When it was time to take the oath, she put her hand on the Bible as Mr. McIvey had explained to her, but the judge interrupted. "Do you know what you're promising, young lady?"

Daisy nodded at the judge. "I have to tell the truth, and not tell any lies."

When the Bible was removed, Daisy stared solemnly at Mr. McIvey, her hands side by side on the front railing of the witness stand.

"Now, sweetheart, we all want to know some things about your daddy, so I'm going to ask you some questions, and you have to answer the truth." Daisy nodded. "Can you point out your daddy to me? Which one is he?"

Daisy pointed to Nate, then she smiled at him and gave a tiny wave. Nate smiled softly.

"Tell us about your daddy. Is he nice to you?"

Daisy nodded.

"How is your daddy nice to you?"

"He lets me cook supper with him, and he said I'm a good cook. And I help him in the garden. He said I'm a good gardener. He's going to help me make a rose bush all of my own. And . . ." Daisy bit thoughtfully at the end of her tongue. "He reads me stories, and he helps me with my lessons, and he lets me wear his hat, and he tells funny jokes."

Nate looked down at the tabletop and studied the finish, smoothing it with his fingertips. Listening to Daisy's light voice made him feel as if his heart was overflowing with love.

McIvey remained near the witness stand. "Daisy, has your daddy ever hit anybody?"

"No. It's not right to hit people." Daisy's eyes grew round. "But he hit a *wall* one time. At the train station. I saw his hand and it was all messy." She rubbed her knuckles for emphasis.

"Tell us about when your daddy hit the wall. Why did he do that?"

"Aunt Lizzie and I left on the train to go home, and Nate didn't want us to leave. He got to the train station after we left, and he hit the wall." She waited alertly, watching Mr. McIvey's mouth for the next question.

"Why didn't your Daddy want you to leave?"

"He was sad without us, and he wanted us to be at his house."

"But then, why did he want you and Aunt Lizzie to go back to Pittsburgh later?"

Daisy's eyes widened, and she looked at Nate and then the judge and then back at McIvey. "Should I answer for true?"

"You have to, don't you? You promised to tell the truth."

Daisy frowned. "That's right. Well, you see . . . Some bad people were trying to hurt Nate, and he didn't want us to get hurt too, so he wanted us to leave so we'd be safe."

"Who were the bad people?"

Daisy shrugged elaborately.

"How were they going to hurt your daddy?"

Again she shrugged, her arms flopping like those of a rag doll.

"Does your daddy love you?"

"Yes." She smiled at Nate. He rested his chin in his palm, watching her closely, and matched her smile.

"Do you love your daddy?"

Daisy nodded brightly.

McIvey patted her hand where it rested on the rail of the witness stand. "I don't have any more questions for you, Daisy, but you wait here because another man wants to ask you some."

Daisy nodded again. McIvey walked back to the table and sat down with Nate, then she turned and Mr. Landorf approached.

He grasped his lapels and smiled broadly at her. She smiled hesitantly in return. "Hello, Daisy," he said. "I have some questions to ask you, and you must always tell the truth."

She nodded slightly.

"You said your daddy hit a wall with his fist, huh? That sounds to me like he was pretty angry."

Again she nodded.

"Does he get angry a lot?"

"Sometimes."

"What does he do when he gets angry?"

Daisy tugged nervously at the ends of her hair. "He shouts."

"Did he ever get angry and shout at you?"

She hung her head and nodded, sending little quivers down the thin hair.

"What does he get angry and shout at you about?"

"Well . . ." Daisy let her breath out in a long sigh. "I got purple paint on his shirt once, and he got angry."

As the titters of laughter died out in the room, Landorf leaned closer and said loudly, "He was really angry, and so what did he *do*?"

"He took the paintbrush away from me."

Landorf stepped back, glanced around at the amused spectators, and then asked Daisy, "Is there anybody else he gets mad at? Who's that?"

"Aunt Lizzie. They had fights about me, I think."

"Did your daddy shout at your aunt?"

"Sometimes." Daisy's eyes were large with concern.

"Did he ever do anything else when he was angry besides shout?"

Daisy looked alarmed. She hung her head and stared at the floor.

Landorf pressed in. "Come now, Daisy, you have to tell the truth about everything. What else did your daddy do when he was angry?"

Daisy's eyes filled with tears, and she said tentatively, "I didn't see him do anything. I just heard it."

"Go on. Tell us what you heard."

She picked abstractly at a blemish in the wood of the railing. "Well . . . The night they went out . . . when they went to the opera, I think that's where they went . . . I couldn't sleep. Aunt Lizzie wasn't in her room so I went to Nate's room. The door was closed, and I think I heard—" Agitated, Daisy rubbed her fingers over one eye. "I thought they were fighting, but they weren't shouting."

"What did you hear?"

"I heard Aunt Lizzie making little sounds, like moans, and Nate was breathing real hard, and the bed was moving—" Daisy glanced up in alarm as laughter and shocked gasps erupted in the room.

Eliza wanted to bury her burning face in her hands. Nate sat back abruptly in his seat, scowling in embarrassment, and folded his arms over his chest.

Landorf waited, straight-faced, though his attempt to incriminate the defendant had only produced more proof of innocence. When he could be heard again, he asked Daisy, "Did you go back to sleep then?"

Daisy nodded.

"Did you wake up again for any reason that night?"

She shook her head, and the lawyer stepped back. "No further questions."

Harry, Eliza, and Daisy were mobbed by reporters as they left the courtroom during the lunch recess. Questions were fired from right and left, and Daisy hung back, clutching Eliza's hand. Harry fielded the questions with professional charm. At last they broke free of the crowd and hailed a cab.

Once inside, Eliza sank back against the sun-faded mohair seat and asked dispiritedly, "What happens now, Harry?"

He clasped his bony knees with his hands. "The summing up. Landorf and McIvey will make their final arguments and remarks to the jury, and then—" He let the sentence drop.

"Then the jury makes its decision," Eliza prompted. Idly she stroked Daisy's hair. "How do you think it went, Harry? And be honest."

"It'll be fine. There's nothing to be gained by worrying about it. You and Daisy did just right."

Daisy hunched up her shoulders. "I was so scared."

Harry chuckled. "But what a little lady you were up there in the witness stand!" He winked at her.

"You don't think it looks very good for Nate, do you?" Eliza persisted, her voice intent.

"There are plenty of points in his favor. And if just seeing him and his reactions today influenced me favorably toward him . . ." Harry smiled, his one overlapping tooth prominently displayed. "How could the jury be completely immune?"

"Oh, you're prejudiced because of me." But Eliza laughed, pleased.

J. T. Landorf spoke to the jury. He was alternately thundering and pompous, then quiet and sorrowful as he summarized the case against Nate. "How can any of us rightfully ignore a dying man's testimony? Mr. Truesdale had already, in front of countless witnesses, threatened to kill him! They had argued not only over the fiery problems engendered by their situation as partners in business, but over women— not one but *two* women . . . Motivation on top of motivation!"

Eliza, listening, felt her spirit plunge lower and lower. So many points against Nate! How could the jury *not* find him guilty? And how could any of the meager facts in his favor dispute Rossie's dying condemnation? She glanced over at Harry, who was listening closely, his head tilted back slightly to watch over the heads of the people in front. Daisy twitched and swung her feet and tried to find something of interest in Eliza's string-purse.

At last Landorf was finished, and Mr. McIvey rose and approached the jury box. He walked with a strength that Eliza detected even from this distance. When he spoke, instead of the theatrics of J. T. Landorf, his voice was thoughtful and resonant with calm authority.

"There are a lot of facts to remember, aren't there?" He smiled in commiseration with the jurors. "That can be a big mental chore trying to tote up the facts. Which ones are relevant and which ones aren't . . . how much weight to give to one over another . . . which fact goes in which column, for or against? It's easy to get lost in the labyrinth, and especially when one is trying to be completely impartial and fair, as I know each of you wants to be. Facts are important to remember, but they can obscure the greater picture.

"At the heart of this matter are two men—Mr. Watts and Mr. Truesdale. One says, 'You killed me,' the other says, 'I did not.' As the jury it's your responsibility to choose which man to believe. How to do that, though, that's a big question. Hard to know the right answer unless you're inside the minds of the men themselves. We can't literally do that, but we can do the next best thing. We can look at the mirror-reflection. What's in our hearts, what's in our minds, reveals itself all around us. Every man reveals himself in his words and deeds every day. I'm a parent, as I'm sure many of you are. One of the old sayings in our society is something I frequently wished I could say outright to my children on occasion. That is: Do as I say, not as I do. There's a big truth in that! What we *do* reveals us in greater clarity than what we actually *say*. The indisputable truth of ourselves is in the doing, not just the saying."

McIvey paused and spread his hands, his spiky eyebrows lifting. "So in this situation, we have two men who are each saying something that contradicts the other. Where's the truth? Truth is in the doing, not just in the saying. Every man and woman reveals himself or herself in the acts of everyday life. This is what gives authority to what is said. And *that's* the *light* by which to view the facts of this situation. The facts reveal the truth of each man's character and thus the truth of their words.

"All right, in that light, let's look at the facts." He ticked them off on his fingers as he discussed each one. "We learned that Mr. Truesdale fired one of the company ship captains because he was responsible for the deaths of two seamen. Mr. Watts hired him back. Why? Because the captain was responsible for the highest profits. What do these actions reveal about the characters of the two men? Mr. Truesdale valued human life above profit; Mr. Watts valued profit first. We also heard from several employees at the office to the effect that Mr. Truesdale and Mr. Watts argued over the law as it pertains to their business. We learned that Mr. Watts ignored the law on several occasions; Mr. Truesdale, on the other hand, had regard for the law."

Strolling slowly in front of the jury box, McIvey continued: "We heard also that they had an argument at Thanksgiving and that Mr. Truesdale finally ordered Mr. Watts out of his home. According to Mr. Truesdale's testimony, Mr. Watts was making lewd and indecent remarks about Miss Nolenberg. This aspect of Mr. Watt's personality was verified by the company receptionist, who also testified to

Mr. Truesdale's more gentlemanly behavior. Thus we see more revelation of the characters of the two men. This same test of 'the doing' can be applied to each and every detail that has been presented in these last three weeks. And don't disregard another mirroring of the truth—the reactions of those who knew the two men.

"Now we come to the final testimony we heard, that of Miss Nolenberg and Daisy Nolenberg. Both, in their own ways," McIvey paused and smiled slightly, "verified Mr. Truesdale's own testimony that he was in his house for the entire night in question. He could not, therefore, have been directly responsible for the death of Mr. Watts. But now, the two Miss Nolenbergs pointed out something else also, which is of the greater significance in this case. Though Miss Nolenberg and Daisy were the only ones who could clear him, providing the *only alibi* he had, Mr. Truesdale nevertheless insisted they leave and return to Pittsburgh.

"*Why did he do that?*"

Pausing, McIvey cocked his white head and smiled as he said gently, "The only alibi he had . . . and he sent them away to protect them. Regardless of his personal situation, his first response was one of love and protection. He wanted to save them from the curiosity and publicity and public scrutiny that would occur. Integrity is operating here. Integrity has been attributable to Mr. Truesdale in each of the facts brought out in this trial.

"So how do you know the truth when you have two men who each claims something quite opposite? The truth rests in the actions that reveal the character of the men involved. One man is a man of integrity, the other has proven by his actions his lack of integrity. Whose words then would be the truth? Who should you believe? Would a man of integrity,

*a man who would cast himself at the mercy of the world
to save the only two people who could prove him innocent,*
be capable of committing murder? I say to you:
Where integrity is operating, such a crime is impossible. You know whose words to believe. You know
how to decide in this situation. You know it already.
You know it by the best and clearest proof that can
be offered. By the proof of integrity. And you recognize the proof of integrity because of your own
integrity.''

Harry, Eliza, and Daisy remained in the courtroom to await the jury's decision. Others stood up
and stretched, murmuring quietly together as they
made their way outside into the hall to light up cigars or stroll in the sun. Tablets of paper crackled
softly as the many reporters scribbled notes and
glanced back through what they had already written.

Harry hefted Daisy onto his lap. ''That was quite
a speech,'' he remarked with quiet intensity. ''But
it's the truth, and he hit it right on the nail.''

Eliza twisted the strings of her purse through her
fingers. ''But do you think the jury will believe it?
That's the only thing that counts right now.''

In reply, Harry reached over and squeezed Eliza's
restless fingers in his big hand. She hardly felt the
touch. The testimony was all over; there was nothing more she or Mr. McIvey could do. She tried
to will the closeted jury to believe Nate—they *had* to
believe him. Otherwise . . . She refused even to
think of what might happen if Nate was found
guilty. The impotence of her position drove her to
distraction, and she clenched her hands together.

The afternoon waned. At last Eliza and Harry took
Daisy outside to let her run in the sunshine. But
Eliza stayed near the building, waiting and hoping

the call to return to the courtroom to hear the jury's decision would come soon. It came just before six.

The jury foreman, a bespectacled and sandy-haired young man, rose to announce the verdict. Nate stood beside McIvey, acutely aware of the grit of the black-and-white tiles beneath his feet, the warm wood of the table beneath his fingertips, the haze of dusty and dimming sunlight in his eyes. He saw the young man's mouth moving, but silence enveloped him, as if he were underwater, though he was aware of the movement of people. He saw them rise to their feet throughout the courtroom. It was pandemonium in slow motion. Reporters' notepapers were rippling. Mouths moved in exclamations. People pushed toward him. The doors in the back of the room swung open, and then the nearby doors out to the sidewalk. Cool sweet evening air, mixed with the scent of fragrant cigars, rushed into the room as the crowd forced its way out.

McIvey was shaking his hand and smiling. *Not guilty.*

Nate could feel himself smiling, feel the strength in McIvey's fingers. The lawyer was laughing and rubbing one hand over his broad balding forehead. *Not guilty.*

"Nate!" He heard Eliza's voice and swung around to look for her. There she was, squeezing toward him, squeezing past reporters who were clustering around him and mouthing questions he did not hear. Her eyes were vibrant and wet with tears, that beautiful mouth open in a smile of joy, her abundant hair shimmering in waves. She rushed toward him, and he opened his arms. She had never felt so good there, her delicate body molding to fit his embrace, her happy exclamations tickling his ear. He thought his heart would burst with gladness.

Daisy was hopping around him and tugging on

his arm. He lifted her to his shoulder. She clung to his neck. Nate put his other arm around Eliza's shoulders and bent to kiss a shining curl on her forehead.

The flash exploded with a loud *poof*.

That picture of the three of them appeared on the front page of the San Francisco papers the next day and on the front pages of papers all across the United States in the days that followed.

A week later a wedding photo took its place.

Epilogue

Though the sky had been gray and heavy with coastal fog most of the day, by late afternoon the sun had burned its way through the clouds, bringing colorfully to life the verdant hillsides and rolling fields, and coaxing a silvery-blue blush to the surface of a pewter ocean. Along a crest of the steep cliff skirting the water, a large black carriage moved slowly as it rocked and sank over wheel ruts in the road. Its occupants had made a late start from San Francisco that morning, and now the day was waning as the sun slid ever closer to the far hazy lip of the ocean to their right.

To protect the infant in her arms from the long bright rays slanting in through the carriage window, Eliza held one edge of the blanket over the tiny boy's face as she peered out curiously. She couldn't see the house yet, but she gazed in wonder at the fields of lush green plants in black soil. They were traveling south, and the fields stretched eastwards from the road toward the foothills of the Coastal Range.

"Is all this yours, Nate?" she asked in surprise.

"Ours," he corrected her. Nate sat on the opposite seat, Daisy beside him. He leaned near Eliza to glance out the window at what she was seeing.

"We'll start by planting just a few hundred acres

and see if we can't make a go of it with artichokes,"
he said with unsuppressed excitement. "Keep
watching. The house is coming up soon."

Daisy tugged at his lapel. "Papa?" she asked with
nose-crinkling curiosity. "What about our real
house? Are we moving forever and ever?"

"Oh, no" he assured her. "We'll have two
houses. We'll go back to the city sometimes, for visits and special parties and that sort of thing."

The infant in Eliza's arms woke and tried to work
his eyes open, fretting all the while. One tiny fist
clutched against the side of his cheek. Her attention
on the baby, Eliza sat back against the seat and happily cuddled him nearer. In this last year there had
been miracle after miracle in her life—the exquisite
fullness of loving Nate and knowing his love in return; the legal adoption of Daisy; the birth of Brett,
her own child with Nate. Her heart was overflowing
with the joy of her life now.

Early in the previous spring, to escape the continued curiosity around Nate as a result of the scandal
and trial, they had sailed to Europe for a wedding
trip. Eliza had fallen in love with everything she'd
seen. They'd visited Paris and Marseilles, Florence
and Milan, and made a stop at the island of Sardinia
before returning home to California. When they had
returned, Nate had sold his half of the Truesdale &
Watts Shipping Company and, though he still retained investments in other shipping enterprises,
had bought this land near the coastal town of Pes-
cadero. Working together with an architect from the
city, they had designed the house they would occupy for the greater part of each year. Nate had
overseen the construction, which was still not entirely finished, but Eliza couldn't wait any longer to
see it for herself and move in while she handled the
decorating.

"There it is," Nate exclaimed.

Eliza shot a swift glance out the window. The house he pointed to was a yellow wood-frame structure nestled in a stand of Monterey cypress trees and shaded by towering oaks. She caught her breath in surprise. "It's so big," she murmured. It was three stories high, and four brick chimneys rose tall above the roof. She caught glimpses of balconies, stingingly white columns framing the entrance, a broad veranda off one side, gabled third-floor windows.

"Do you like it? Is it the way you pictured it would be?"

Eliza turned quickly. Nate was watching her with shining blue eyes. Her heart melted. "It's beautiful," she said.

"The master bedroom has a view of the ocean," he added, smiling with lazy suggestion.

"I look forward to seeing it," Eliza said lightly, though she was growing suffused with warmth under his bright and meaningful look.

The carriage, which Nate had purchased to accommodate the needs of his growing family, dipped through a rut as it turned into the drive. Later there would be tall, flowering camellia bushes to line the wide lane, but for now the view across the expanse of lush, sloping fields to the cliff's edge was unobscured. They came to a stop under the tall front portico.

Immediately the front door opened, and Mrs. Herlihy rushed onto the porch, grinning hugely as she smoothed her hands down the front of her apron and tried to see into the carriage. She and her husband had already moved into their third-floor suite of rooms. After their return from Europe the previous summer, Nate had hired additional servants—three maids, a cook, two manservants. More recently he had also secured a competent nurse for Brett and a highly recommended married couple to maintain their home in the city. Mrs. Herlihy supervised the servants ably and with fairness.

"And where's that little boy of mine?" the woman called when Nate stepped out of the carriage. "I haven't seen him in a week, and already I miss him."

Nate took the baby from Eliza's arms, then helped her alight. Daisy jumped out behind Eliza and ran ahead up the stairs, her footsteps thumping hollowly on the wooden boards. She flung herself at Mrs. Herlihy for a hug.

"Did you miss me too?" she asked eagerly.

"You know I did! You're my little lamb, my special helper."

Eliza had plucked up the skirts of her pearl-white silk day dress and was running nimbly up the steps. "Hello, Mrs. Herlihy. Did the furniture I ordered arrive yet?" Until they could get down to the business of decorating, Eliza had purchased a few pieces for their use in the interim—a table and chairs, two couches, beds, and a dresser apiece, among other things.

"They're here. And mighty lovely, I may add."

Eliza was just laughing over her shoulder as she crossed the porch to the open door, impatient to see the interior, but Nate called out, "Stop right there, Mrs. Truesdale!"

He carefully handed the swaddled infant to Mrs. Herlihy and strode toward Eliza. "Do you think you can just rush right in and deprive me of my rights?" he protested. Chuckling, he swung an astonished Eliza into his arms. "I want to carry you across the threshold," he explained.

Eliza grinned and looped her arms playfully, daintily around his neck. She wondered if she would always be surprised by his easy strength. The power in the arms that held her made her head light.

Nate stood still, his expression growing serious as he gazed at her. "Happy first-year anniversary, Eliza," he said, and dropped a quick kiss on her mouth.

Eliza looked back at him with vague astonishment. "I can hardly believe it's been a whole year already since that awful time . . ." The murder of Rossie, Nate's arrest, and his trial were not subjects they mentioned often. Tess had been found guilty and given a sentence of life imprisonment.

"Did you forget it was the anniversary of our wedding?" Nate chided her, teasing.

"No," she assured him with a quick laugh. "Never!"

Nate carried her into the house and didn't set her down as he quickly toured the first-floor rooms, which were as yet neither painted nor carpeted. His footsteps echoed in the empty expanses. "Over here is where I thought we could put those paintings we brought back from Florence, and how do you like—"

"Would you put me down?" Eliza said with mock seriousness, though secretly she enjoyed being carried by him. "I have two perfectly good legs."

"Oh, how well I know," he answered, cocking one eyebrow at her. He continued seriously. "Now, the ballroom for the weekend parties we'll give is upstairs on the second floor. Do you want to see it?"

Eliza had given only a cursory glance around the empty rooms as he strode along the downstairs hall. With the distraction of being in his arms, the greater part of her attention was raptly focused on him. She leisurely twined her finger through a curl of black hair above his ear. "I'd really prefer to see that view of the ocean you mentioned earlier," she said, keeping her face straight with an effort.

"Forgive me, I've been remiss," he acknowledged graciously. "I'll take you up there right now."

And he did, his step light on the darkly polished stairs. He didn't set Eliza on her feet until they stood before one of the four immaculately sparkling windows that looked out over velvety green fields and, beyond the jagged cliff edge, to the endless expanse of water, glittering with salmon-pink light from the setting sun.

Nate laid his hands on her shoulders, feeling thoroughly content. He bent his head, grazing the back of her neck with a light kiss. A faint essence of gardenia and the warm texture of her skin stirred his senses. There was no hurry now. He let his fingers glide down her arms. Every moment was theirs, each complete in their shared living. All through the preceding year he had marveled at the feeling of union he had known with her. Even when Eliza was away or just in another part of the house, he had felt the bond between them almost as tangibly as if they were joined physically in love.

She turned from the window and gazed up into his eyes. "Did you think I only wanted to see the view *out?*" she asked with teasing frankness. "What about that just as exciting view *in?*"

"But you see me all the time," he pointed out innocently.

She reached for the buttons on his waistcoat. "Not entirely," she murmured, grinning wickedly.

"I'm all yours."

Mrs. Herlihy had prepared all the newly delivered beds for their arrival, and it was only a matter of minutes before Nate and Eliza were christening the large four-poster bed in their room. They lay entwined, each stroke of a silken limb against his leg rousing Nate to greater heights of passion, each touch of a warm hand or velvet mouth on her skin kindling a deeper ache of desire in Eliza.

When the last crimson glow of the sunset had faded from the windows, they still lay together, wrapped in the sensual and languid world their intimacy created around them. Protected, invulnerable, they basked in that luxurious exhaustion found in the aftermath of love.

Eliza listened to the faint, distant splash of waves against the base of the rocky cliff. Soon she would have to see to the baby to feed him. She could feel the swelling pressure of the milk in her breasts and knew the infant would be crying before long. But there was time yet. Contentedly, she rolled toward Nate and gazed at his peaceful, handsome face. He was looking at her, his eyes serene. He lingeringly stroked the curve of her face.

"Little did I know the day I met you what would be in store for me," he said with a gentle smile.

"I was terrible to you," Eliza remarked, laying her head on his chest and hearing the soft rhythm of his heart.

He laughed quietly. "Then I must have deserved it."

"No. But you said some pretty nasty things to me."

"I did?"

"Do you remember 'prudish old maid'?" she asked, raising her head to peer at him with an impudent lift of her brows.

"Good Lord!" Nate choked on his laughter. "I never said that, did I?"

"You most certainly did, Mr. Truesdale," she retorted crisply. "And I set out to prove you wrong. Fairly successfully, I might add."

"Oh, most successfully," he agreed, still chuckling.

Eliza nestled closer beside him. She emitted a long, deep sigh of appreciation. "Nate?" she said dreamily. "Remember that night you sang to Daisy when she was frightened of the earthquake?"

"What about it?" He put his arm around her, his hand stroking the voluptuous curve of her waist.

"Would you sing me a love song?"

He leaned up on his elbow beside her, lifting her face with a light finger under her chin. "My entire life is a love song to you," he murmured. The tenderness in his eyes brought a swift rush of happiness to her. He smiled leisurely. "You just haven't heard it all yet."

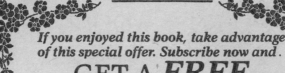